Lucky Dogs

Lucky Dogs

A NOVEL

Helen Schulman

ALFRED A. KNOPF
NEW YORK
2023

LIBRARY OF CONGRESS CATALOGING-IN-PUBLICATION DATA
Names: Schulman, Helen, author.
Title: Lucky dogs : a novel / Helen Schulman.
Description: First Edition. | New York : Alfred A. Knopf, [2023]
Identifiers: LCCN 2022023615 (print) | LCCN 2022023616 (ebook) |
ISBN 9780593536230 (hardcover) |
ISBN 9780593536247 (ebook)
Subjects: LCGFT: Novels.
Classification: LCC PS3569.C5385 L83 2023 (print) |
LCC PS3569.C5385 (ebook) | DDC 813/.54—dc23
LC record available at https://lccn.loc.gov/2022023615
LC ebook record available at https://lccn.loc.gov/2022023616

Front-of-jacket photograph by Christopher Brand
Jacket design by Janet Hansen

Manufactured in the United States of America

First Edition

To the memory of both my brave grandmothers,

Dora Liebling Yevish and

Zelda "Jennie" Gluchowsky Schulman,

who taught me to see the world through the lens of story

Very early in my life it was too late.

—MARGUERITE DURAS, *THE LOVER*

Part One

To say I was lonely the summer I turned twenty-four was like saying Donald Trump's hair was the precise color of Cheetos dust; there was nothing original about it. Almost all kids crowding close to quarter life feel old, used up, and fucking stuck. Childhood dreams die painful deaths, jobs are boring as shit, and finally it dawns: there is no such thing as love, and most sex sucks. In France, where I was staying, the chic postmenopausal grandmamas sitting outside at the cafés on Boulevard Saint-Germain sipping their *coupes de champagne* in their leopard-print jeans and cold-shoulder shirts were exultant with the confidence that comes from being sexy without being prey. They seemed to know more about contentment than anyone I ever hung with (be they derelicts or movie stars), as if the volume of the balloon of happiness one was born with was proportionately inverse to the time left to enjoy it.

    This was true even for lucky dogs like me: a fugitive in Paris, cursed by beauty, no crap nine-to-fiver, no factory or phone bank to head home from; all I'd had to do to get out of California was point a gun to my manager's head, rob my own bank, and run. But I'm not sure that even the most resolutely miserable twentysomething's everyday existential angst was as empty and ceaseless as the black hole I swam in. My isolation was a bright neon-orange warning, like the Trumpster's shellacked awning. It permeated my skeleton.

Still, I did my best to conceal it. When I was not sitting at home in front of my computer, I walked the damp, dark streets at night, the cobblestones perpetually steaming. To preserve my anonymity, I made my face as blank and expressionless as I could, the way an executioner wears a long black hood. To hide his shame. What shame? To hide his identity! Sometimes, in those medieval fantasy epics, in an effort to stir things up, it's the condemned to die who wears the shroud. Audiences love a firing squad. Gallows and kicking feet. Victims and criminals. Draaaama. It's what my limited series on AMC was all about, even though it took place in a present-day overpriced hothouse coastal community, all of us banging some other Barbie's husband. I was the preacher's daughter—except this man of God was the trusted head of an exclusive private day school. Newly separated, I taught art sweetly to spoiled children and blew cute, rich fathers in pool houses during fundraisers, while trying to outrun my checkered past. It was typecasting. The TV critic at the *LA Times* described me as having "an embryonic allure." My eyes are bigger than big and so widely set apart they look like a bug's; their violet color I got legit from my mother. Lashes batting, they have been the subject of far too many close-ups.

On those berserk, blood-soaked shows—not mine, the gothic ones—maybe some sad traitor slips the sack over the wronged woman's head, maybe he's her erstwhile lover, maybe he's already fucked her. He's just following orders. He drops that long black bag over his prisoner's face so he can't see her terror or how well she *knows* him, or her humiliation when the platform drops, when she shits herself and swings. I wore my flat expression in Paris like a lead apron, so no one could see the radioactivity inside.

If I was living in one of the places where I grew up, be it trailer park, or motel room, or the little wooden house with the chipping green paint we had for three and a half years outside of Winthrop, Washington—a western-themed time capsule that the few tourists who bothered to come that far north couldn't resist— there would be Sunday church, or potluck suppers, or a local dive where you could drink beers and dance on the bar, "community" my daddy's gal pal back then called it. But I'm sure even there I'd find some way to get canceled. I've been run out of town, or should I say town*s*, so many times . . . It's almost impossible for me *not* to speak my mind. My craftsman, weed-selling, anarchist father was what you might euphemistically have called "itinerant." We moved around a lot, up into Canada sometimes and then back down into Idaho; for a while we lived out of his pickup, so with zero to lose I usually was too stupid to hold back. All's to say, I have one big fucking mouth.

Paris, France, was not my problem. At twenty-four, I was lonely everywhere I went. I was lonely all the time.

Winthrop was what Daddy called the "most Mayberry" of all our base camps. I rode to school there on a yellow bus like kids do on TV, and skipped two grades because my vocabulary was so damn genius (I read a lot, there never was much else to do), and had numerous, at the time, not-so-sucky semi-siblings, only one of whom got shot at the community college in '15, Tommy, but on FB I saw he made it out alive, just a flesh wound to the shoulder, a post I'd made certain to "like." I also had a pet guinea pig, Carmel, her fur a light, creamy amber, but we couldn't call her that because that was my father's girlfriend's name. Humanoid Amber worked at Mercy Medical. That lady felt certain she could diagnose us all, even though she was only a physician's assistant;

my daddy was "immature with a learning disability," and Tommy was ADHD (his jumpiness saved him: he dived out of one of the second-story classroom windows as the shooter began to fire), and I was manic depressive, up and down, up and down. "You're on the seesaw of life, Meredith," Amber liked to say—sitting at the kitchen table, drinking her evening beer, untying her white shoes and ditching her support hose, rubbing the dirt out from between her toes, making me want to puke—which sounds just about right. Plus, she said I had oppositional defiant disorder, which is definitely true and was one of the reasons she finally asked us to leave. That and Daddy sleeping with her sister, Topaz—Topaz and Amber, my hand to God.

I was sad to go, but Daddy wasn't. He said, "Merry, you've never seen the Rockies; the sun shines three hundred days a year, cliffs get so red at dusk they look like steak cooked rare, everyone is rich as Croesus and wants nothing more than to ski and buy handcrafted tables." We moved to Woody Creek and into a trailer, which we shared with a bartender at the tavern around the corner. My daddy worked in Aspen. I sort of went to high school, got bored, and then started dating high rollers when I slipped into waitressing at the tavern. Talk about your melting pots: oilmen from Texas, Silicon Valley zillionaires, Mexican landscapers, coke-snorting ski bums. We all ate queso together, me behind the bar snarfing down that gooey melted cheese and chips for free. One was a movie producer who got me to Hollywood. The rest you would know if you kept up with your TMZ. I only ever saw my mother when she was getting divorced or was being released from a mental hospital. She was a world-class beauty, always at her most gorgeous upon reemergence, eyes moist and shining, cheeks hollow, hope burning so bright I'd light up alongside her same as a contact high. She'd stayed in LA and then Vegas and LA again; my visits and her comebacks usually dovetailed with those times when Daddy and I fell out. It was inevitable. I swung between my parents like a monkey between two trees. Sometimes it was less lonely being in her shade, sitting on the couch across from her, listening to her make promises.

I thought about this a lot in Paris. Wanting my mommy. Not the real her but the existential mother of my soul. I didn't have much else to do. In the mornings, I roamed the streets and sat at café tables smoking and drinking those itty-bitty little bitter black cups of coffee that cost too much—I was too broken to eat— watching couples (gay, straight, mixed race, old) walk by holding hands until I couldn't stand it anymore. Then I'd go back to my Airbnb on a shit street off Rue de Rivoli, walk up my four flights, and strip down as soon as I triple locked up behind me—with all those fancy public toilets, you'd think not every man in France would take a leak in my doorway; daily, I'd have to broad-jump a stinking puddle.

There was no AC anywhere that boiling summer—half the old people died—except in hotels and the large department stores the French called *grands magasins*. Sometimes I wandered those, too, out of dullness and a desire to survive: Printemps, Le Bon Marché, Go Sport, flipping through the clothing racks as my sweat dried. But mostly I lay on my stomach on my unmade bed, in my underwear, a teenage boy's tighty-whities. I'd dive into cyberspace until my teeth ached from grinding and I was seeing double. The MacBook Air was my very own opioid crisis, except in July, I weaned myself off Twitter and googling my own name— victory! The contestant's scrawny arms shoot up into the empty air! I started writing a book. Sometimes I also played *Words with Friends* with strangers.

For the first time in my entire life—me of the ever-changing do's: the Farrah, the Rachel, the Bo Derek, ironic and sexy, new and improved; me of the dyed purple underarm hair, the hen- naed hands and shoulders, the mile-high over-the-knee boots and platform shoes, look at me, me!—all I'd wanted was not to be seen, because being seen was what had led me to this disaster. To the Rug, with that fake black toupee like a furry Frisbee landed on his egg-shaped pate and the weird way he carried his weight: those twiggy arms and legs and huge, hard, repugnant stomach, like a tick with a belly full of blood. To nobody giving two shits— not my friends, not my costars, not even Marietta, my agent. I'd always wanted to hang out in Paris, and now had seemed as good a time as any. How was I to know, even when I was invisible, it would totally suck living there, too?

I gave myself a crew cut, wore a knit beanie, bound my breasts. I even trimmed back my eyelashes with a pair of embroidery scissors I'd picked up at an outdoor flea market. I wanted to look as androgynous as possible. I was sick to death of people, and yet self-imposed solitary confinement wasn't exactly doing me any favors. As day turned to night, sometimes I'd work on my manuscript for hours and sometimes I wouldn't. Either way, I was at the computer forever, and after a while my skin took on a weird metallic stink, like my mind and the machine were merging, and then I'd take a shower. I'd reemerge from my cave, from the bile of writing, to the sheer boredom of Instagram, crossword puzzles, old *Friday Night Lights* episodes, and my sad attempts at fan fiction. I'd go back outside, sunglasses on, chest flat underneath a sleeveless black hoodie, the hood itself up even in the heat, a Mall of America burka. The last thing I wanted was a run-in with a reporter.

The rats were out now, as I wandered closer to the river, some as long as my forearm, which was also covered with light brown fur, the lanugo that comes from self-starvation—I learned that ten-dollar word from the pro-ana sites I turned to for thinspiration. I subsisted solely on ice cream. Berthillon. Île Saint-Louis is full of their outlets, but I always went to the kiosk at the café at the end of the island, across the street from the bridge, where I gazed on Notre-Dame, that insanely magnificent cathedral. I figured the flavors were better at that particular stand because it was the only one with long lines. I'd go at lunch on days I couldn't bear being inside and then again after regular folks finished their dinners, when the Parisian night sky spilled a wine stain over the dying light, some corners of the firmament more saturated, the black plum of an internal organ. (Not that I'd ever seen one; the only human entrails I've encountered were in the wreckage of car and snowmobile accidents, bar fights—blood made red instantly when hemoglobin meets the air.) *Glace* was the only nourishment I managed to slip through the anxious, narrowing walls of my gullet: crème de menthe, *myrtille, caramel beurre salé*. Sometimes I couldn't even manage the cone; so as not to choke, I'd end up spitting the chewed-up mash out into my napkin.

One particularly fetid night, I waited for my scoops behind a large extended family of North Africans, the women in brightly colored dresses and headscarves, the men in patterned short-sleeved shirts. Each person—the grandparents, parents, cousins, and several tag-playing, shrieking children—had to be served before I could even approach the counter. As I killed time, eyes on the sidewalk, I noticed that I was draped in a lamppost shadow, tall and thin, elongated like a Giacometti. I'd recently visited that sculptor's tiny, reconstructed studio, after an afternoon of refreshing *What's New in Paris* on my browser. Sick of moldy old movie theaters, dark and full of pervs, across the river on the Left Bank, and stumbling alongside the bus tours just to hear other beings breathe—soft people, pudgy retirees, who'd earned their rights to giving up—I decided to take the plunge and look at art. After gazing at the drawings and wire frames and the reconstructed studio's buckets of hardened plaster and notebooks and sketches and dust—How do you reconstruct dust? I thought. Isn't dust itself a reconstruction?—I'd found myself oddly weeping over a bronze sculpture in the more formal exhibition area in the art deco mansion that housed his works; it was called *Woman with Her Throat Cut*. Said female looked far more like a vivisected lobster or an insect seizing in agony than a human, even though she was cast motionless in bronze.

The shadow hanging over me in the ice cream line contained

a suggestion of movement, too, around a peculiarly humped and bony left shoulder, so I turned slowly and saw a thin, tall woman whose straight blond hair was tied back in a glossy knot. She had on a blue Breton striped top—the sailing shirts all the Frenchmen wore with those boatneck collars—and hemmed white linen shorts; I noticed she carried a simple brown leather backpack over her left shoulder, explaining that ghostly bulge. She was a few years older than me and, for all the normcore, somehow managed to look both casual and snotty.

"What flavor are you getting?" Her English was accented. German? Eastern European? Her voice startled me, husky and deep like a man's.

I wondered how she knew I spoke English, but then again, everyone in Paris spoke English, and besides, I was dressed like an agender Midwestern mall rat.

I said, *"Caramel beurre salé."*

"My fave." She smiled. Her teeth were crooked—not bad, kind of cute in fact, the one in front doing a tiny curtsy before the other. She was striking. Her skin stretched tight across her good bones. She had a strong nose and jaw. Cheekbones so sharp they could slice a snacking ham. Thin lips she accentuated with a dark color I'd bet she'd applied to make them look fuller. She gave me a little wave forward, and when I turned back to the counter, I realized the North Africans had disappeared down the block—I could see the kids bouncing along the street like a stream of just blown iridescent bubbles—leaving a line anyone could cut. So, I leaped forward and ordered a cornet, sugar not waffle, with three—count 'em—three scoops. All the same flavor. I thought of those old bank commercials: "Live richly."

Two American cowboys, forties, likely in town on business, big, thick wedding rings on their short, stubby fingers, stood sweaty and red-faced behind the woman standing behind me, in man-tailored shirts with rolled-up sleeves that even untucked still strained over their bellies. Both bros wore khaki shorts, one with tiny blue whales sewn on them. It was as if they'd ditched only the tie and suit pants after work in their hotel rooms in their haste to get outside and soak up some mad, phat Parisian action. They'd probably read about this ice cream stand on Tripadvisor.

"That sure looks good, unh," the redder one said, grinning at the woman behind me. He had matching carroty scruff on his neck and surrounding his shiny dome.

She smiled politely.

"Merci beaucoup," I said, pushing my euros across the glass worktop to the older woman who'd scooped my cone and placed it in a nifty plastic rack. Until I'd come to Paris, I'd never seen one. I thought about fake-stepbrother Tommy, gunshot wound long healed; from his profile pic on FB, I knew he was working at the Salt & Straw in Seattle now, scooping Freckled WoodBlock Chocolate behind the counter. I thought of taking a picture of my cone in its rack and posting it on his wall. Then I thought better of it.

Even in a cute dress, the server here looked too tired and frail to be out this late at night assisting tourists. When she leaned forward to wipe the trickles of sweat from her forehead with her wrist, I could see telltale bands of silver roots in her dark hair's meandering part. I left her a nice tip—yep, I realized that in France gratuities are included, but this old lady was clearly exhausted, and I myself always felt lifted by a small token of appreciation back when I tended bar in Woody Creek. Then I grabbed my cone and scooted to the side so the woman behind me could fall in line. With all my leaping and scooting, I felt like I was part of a musical without the music. It was as if the whole scene in front of the ice cream stand were part of a show, and everyone else knew all the lines. Perhaps this feeling of inauthenticity was a symptom of a rare form of anxiety attack previously unknown to me. I figured I could pop a couple of Xanax when I got back to my apartment, swallow them down with a bottle of cold white wine, and wait for the silken creaminess of on-the-edge-of-OD to glide throughout my bloodstream.

"*La même chose, s'il vous plaît,*" said the woman behind me, that throaty voice.

"What does that mean?" the red-fringed baldy asked.

"The same thing," she said. "As in, I'll have the same."

"Well, I like that," he said. "Would you order one for me?"

The server finished balancing the next three scoops and stood this new cone on the cone rack. The veins in her temples were starting to bulge gray, like worms swollen after a rain. It was too late at night for a person her age to be toiling away, and in this heat! Was she about to have a stroke? I'd heard grumblings about Macron's rising taxes and the cost of living. Is that why she was working so hard? On the other end of the frustrated and angry spectrum, refugees and others who were homeless slept in doorways and on sidewalks, sometimes in cardboard lean-tos; sometimes, they cocooned themselves inside the sweaty safety of a sleeping bag. The heat lightning of desperation was crackling in the air. I'd been reading about France and its socialism shit on Wikipedia in my spare, spare time. You know, all the entitlements? So, I wondered why this old lady was slogging it out so late on a putrid night. It didn't take long to realize that real-life Paris, like real-life Hollywood, wasn't anything like *Paris!* Paris at all.

The bald guy pushed forward a fifty-euro bill like he was scrubbing the counter clean. "This one's on me."

"No, thank you," said Goldilocks. She searched her wallet, counting out her change.

In the meantime, the man waved the bill insistently in the server's face. That old lady looked from one to the other wearily.

Just fucking pay me, I thought for her. She appeared too exhausted to think for herself.

Now it was my new acquaintance who pushed her coins across the glass. Ten euros. Somewhere between thirteen and fifteen American dollars for ice cream, depending on the exchange rate.

"Oh, don't be like that," Baldy's pal admonished her. Whale Boy.

Goldilocks didn't say anything. She just urged the server to take her money with an upward nod of her head and a lowering of her eyes.

Sighing, the server picked up the coins. She untied and removed her apron, wiped her hands on it, and left it on the counter. Then she disappeared inside the café. I guessed she'd had enough.

"Aw, sweetheart. He's just trying to be friendly," Whale Boy said to Goldilocks. "We're new here. Maybe you'd like to show us around?"

"You sure have pretty hair." Baldy reached out a hand to touch it. She flinched.

"Get the fuck away from her," I said.

"Whoa!" Baldy raised his hands in an exaggerated stick-'em-up. He appeared surprised to see that I was still there. I guess he hadn't noticed he'd had an audience.

"I don't think anybody asked you," he said in that neutral, metered way men can get when they're very, very angry. Cold and constrained enough to scare me. Which was the point. Although if he were ever summoned into a court of law and told to repeat word for word what he'd just said, he could spin it to come out politely.

His eyes narrowed, as if he were squinting. "Wait, what are you? Are you a girl?" he said. Then he reached out and grabbed my left breast through the shapeless hoodie—it was 95 degrees; I'd neglected to put on my binder. There was nothing between my skin and the sweatshirt's matted fleece. "He's a girl, dude," he said to his friend, nodding toward the proof in his hand. "The boy's a girl."

He let go and turned back to me. "I thought you were an emo boy, but you're not." His interest suddenly increased; in the artificial glow of the streetlights, it appeared to my mind's eye as if a dark red light bulb went off excitedly above his forehead. "Are you a tranny?"

I was too stunned to move. His hand had been there only a second, but I could still feel it squeezing. I can feel it even now, just thinking about it.

In one smooth move, Goldilocks pulled a switchblade out of her back pocket and snapped it open.

What? I thought. You can do that?

Baldy took two steps rearward, again with his palms up.

"What are you, crazy? It's not the Bronx, lady." Now Whale Boy was playing backup, safely, from behind Baldy's shoulder.

They always call *you* crazy. They always protect their friends.

"Try me," she said.

Just then a waiter came up behind the counter, head down while tying his apron. "Next?" he said in ordinary American English. He was young, but his neck and arms were thick with muscle, sandy with freckles. When no one answered, he looked up, eyes cornflower blue, bushy eyebrows raised.

I guessed he was the cavalry, although he didn't seem to notice as my protector quietly slipped the knife inside her bag. He was too busy picking up the used apron off the counter and dropping it on the floor, gently kicking it aside, as if it were a nosy kitten.

"La même chose?" Goldilocks repeated to Baldy; she made it sound like an invitation. "Any place, any time, you bald fat fuck." She lifted her cone from the stand.

A bunch of middle school–aged boys in matching soccer shirts and shorts had gathered in line behind the Americans. Their skin tones were the same eggplant, ivory, and coffee yogurt as their idols on Paris Saint-Germain FC. The kids must have just come from a match or a practice, as they were sweaty and buzzing; a few of the players were knocking a ball off the curb and onto the cobblestoned street. The others were watching our sidewalk theater unfold, and they whooped delightedly at the cuss words. One covered his mouth with his elbow to keep from cracking up.

I didn't hear the rest, the response of the fratty, fucked-up middle-aged bastards behind her or the preteens joining in the fray, because I was already walking away, slowly, like I didn't give a shit, even though I could feel my heart's keyboard tapping odd-ball messages inside my chest: *Let me die before they hurt me, let me die before they hurt me.* I hadn't even thanked my good Samaritan for coming to my defense. This was because I a) was unused to kindness, b) had lost the ability to speak, or c) didn't want my ice cream to melt. Answer: all and none of the above. I was so wigged out; I was on autopilot.

I crossed the street and walked over to the top of the stone stair-case that led down to the path at the bank of the river, descended a couple of filthy steps, and sat on the scummy limestone. There was trash everywhere in Paris, especially at the end of the day. Cigarette butts, silver foil and the smeary wax paper that once held together gloppy falafel sandwiches, many empty bottles of wine. Newspapers, chip bags, and plastic cups overflowed from the garbage pails. The gutters were clogged with sopping rubbish. Some of the litter was French litter: picnic detritus. Mostly it was tourists': McDonald's fries containers, used condoms. Once I saw a dirty tampon unfurled in the middle of the street, like one of those radish rosettes we used to put in the salad at Thanksgiving to dress it up.

In August, the Parisians skip town if they can and head to the mountains or the sea.

I often thought of throwing myself into the Seine while I ate my ice cream in this very spot, but it had been raining a lot lately and the water, which was usually a steely metallic blue after sun-set, was pure Dijon mustard that night. I took off my sunglasses for a better look. Now it looked like diarrhea. I couldn't bear the thought of drowning in sewer water. So, I just sat and ate my ice cream. In a few minutes, the woman who had come to my defense in the line took a seat next to me. I was surprised, but not. It was that same funny script-like feeling that I'd had earlier—like God was taking a pass at screenwriting.

"Mm," she said, licking her now dripping cone. "You picked right."

"Thanks," I said. "I mean for back there." I noticed her eyes were emerald green. Like, *emerald*. Contacts? Everyone always thought I wore contacts, but I don't. Maybe hers were just naturally luminous, like mine.

She shrugged. "You stood up for me first. Nobody ever stands up for me. Besides, I hate men," she said. "They're all assholes."

I nodded. She wasn't going to get any arguments there. "Do you always carry a knife?" I asked. I'd often thought of carrying a knife.

"I was gang-raped when I was a teenager." She started to chew on the cookie part of her cone.

"That's horrible," I said. Before I could stop myself, I blurted out, "What happened?" Then I covered my mouth with a cupped palm. I hate myself sometimes. "I'm sorry, I shouldn't have said that," I said through the pup tent of my fingers.

"It's okay," she said. She stopped for a sec. Some of her hair had gotten loose and a strand of it was sticking to the half-eaten cone. I thought of that man touching it. As if she could read my thoughts, she fished it out and sucked it clean, then stuck it behind her ear.

"I always put my foot in it," I said. "Soooo totally not my business."

"It's okay," she said again. "For a long time, forever even, I never told anyone. But now I do a bit of public speaking. I'm an activist. That is, I try to be. Really, I just tell this story a lot, at schools, women's groups. I warn girls to be careful. I was so trusting, I just walked right into it." She finished off her cone and licked her pretty fingers one by one, then dried them off with her crumpled napkin.

"I've done that," I said. "Walked into things. I'm never exactly trusting, I just kind of fling myself at stuff."

She smiled as if she knew me already, the me that nobody

knows. "I'd grown up with those kids," she said. "One of the guys was even my boyfriend. We'd been going out for almost two years. I can't tell you how many times he told me that he loved me." She mimed playing a violin. "He even gave me a little ring. You know, the kind with the hands clasped right over the tiny heart?"

"Claddagh rings. They're Irish. My mother used to wear one."

She let that surprise sink in—I actually had a mother and hadn't sprung from the chemical swamp of the Seine—before she continued spilling. "There was this cabin in the woods behind our church where we used to go to be alone, and all his buddies were waiting . . . At first I thought it was kind of a surprise party because my birthday was in a few days."

"Oh my God," I said.

"I know," she said. "And would you believe, a couple of weeks after it was all over, my quote-unquote boyfriend asked me to go with him to a school dance?"

"Oh my God," I said. I was repeating myself.

"Since then, I carry a knife, but I've never used it. Usually, they just step back like that idiot did at the ice cream stand. They're all cowards."

"Who?" I asked dumbly.

"Men," she said. "Cowards with penises. I should have cut it off."

I nodded. I felt the same way. *I should have cut it off.*

That thought made me stand up.

"When that bastard touched my hair, it was like I was sixteen and lying on the floor again. What you did, it means a lot," she said.

Did she want me to sit back down? Continue talking? Maybe, like me, she was kind of hoping we'd hang out.

"Where are you from?" I said. "Prague? Germany?"

She nodded yes, but to what? Now she reached into her bag and took out a cigarette. Gauloises. She offered me one, but I shook my head no. She lit up. "I live in Amsterdam." Blew out her smoke. "I'm here for a weeklong holiday. It's three and a half hours on the TGV."

I didn't know the train between the two storied cities was that fast. A gaffer on one of my sets had said the best hash he'd ever smoked was there at a place called Coffeeshop Club Media. I'd tucked that little tidbit away just in case I'd ever get a chance to use it. Maybe that time was now?

"I work at Gateway: Insights and Visions."

What was Gateway: Insights and Visions?

"We're a team of digital strategists and consultants."

Ah, something to do with tech. I thought, I'm a TV star. Well, more like a "starlet." Or I was one once. Now, nobody recognizes me. I don't want them to. Really. I really, really don't.

"It's more exciting here in Paris: the museums, the fashion, the food," she said. "Plus, it's book country. You can sit all afternoon outdoors in a café reading. You can have company without having company. The restaurants are so much better! In Holland they actually ask you if you want 'old cheese' or 'new cheese,' can you believe that? It's like all Gouda. And I love cheese! Also, I'm a big walker. Everyone says they come to Paris for romance, but that's the last thing I want. I want anything that frees up my mind. That's why I come, to dump stress."

"That's why I came, too," I said. The stress dump, the liberated and untamed psyche.

She stretched and stood up. I could see her hip bones rise above her waistband. She tried to brush off the seat of her pants with her free hand. "Why did I sit down there in white shorts?" she asked herself. "I better be heading back to my hotel; I've got emails to answer." She took a last drag on her cigarette and ground it out with her foot and picked it up. That impressed me. She wrapped the butt in her napkin; she was going to put it in the trash. I never did that. Then she reached into her backpack. She pulled out her card case, and with the same ease with which she'd handled the knife, she snapped it open. "Here," she said. "If you ever want to meet up."

I put the card into the kangaroo pocket of my hoodie. I didn't even bother to check out her name then. I did it later, when I got back to my apartment. After the Xanax and the *vin blanc*. I downed a bottle and a half watching late-night talk show reruns on my double bed in my underwear. Then old Rachel Maddow shows, on Hulu, just for the sound of her voice, since I couldn't stream the news. Rachel read her stories like a high-speed rail train coming at you, fast and intense. That's what I liked about her. All that passion and energy being expended by someone else, well, it slowed me, some. I found it calming. She could surf the waves of anger for me, like I was riding high up on her shoulders. After a while, I was so drunk and stoned and tired and roasting, I no longer needed the reassurance of seeing Rachel's long, authentic forehead crinkling when she came in for the kill. (Was she the only woman on TV who wasn't a Botox junkie?) I was comforted just by the sound of hearing her go off.

I turned away from my laptop and lay sprawled over a pillow, with the fan aimed at the small of my back. It was hot as hell that summer, have I mentioned that? Even at night, sweat beaded up on my body like rain on a windshield. When I moved, the drops joined up and rolled down my spine in rivulets. With my head hanging off the bed, I reached for my hoodie on the floor, wiped my face with it, brow and upper lip, and then used it to towel off. I pulled out the card from the hoodie's pocket, reading her name: NINA WILLIS. There was even a little photo of Nina in the corner wearing a smart blue suit. She smiled at me from the card. Her hair hung loose and wavy around her shoulders, like she'd finished it with a curling iron. I thought I could make out those same crooked teeth, but truth be told, by then I was seeing double. I threw the card back on the floor and let Rachel lecture me to sleep, my bed spinning dizzyingly, a sensation I'd learned to sort of like. It made the world feel to me the way I felt to myself: unsteady and unsafe. A shrink might call this "validating."

I didn't pick up Nina's card again the next day or the day after. Instead, I went back to writing my book. Besides hiding, I'd come to Paris for another purpose. A memoir was the only way I could think of then to get them all to take me seriously. Like Nina, I had a story worth telling. Only, of the two of us, she was the one doing the work of the world. I'd been trying, but now I wondered if I hadn't been trying hard enough. So, I lay on my bed smoking in front of the computer and thought a lot about what I had already written and in what way I could get the rest of my account down; some of what was missing was how all this shit got started. Me and my agent, Marietta, at a film festival in Telluride. I had a small part in a great picture, and people were taking notice. The Rug's company called me in, ostensibly to discuss a role in a movie, an adaptation of a southern book by a southern author about a small-town girl in—where else?—an upscale southern suburb. Marietta had arranged the introduction. It's hard to describe how jazzed we both were. The part reeked of Oscar bait and would be my first ever costarring role. Marietta texted me at eight a.m. to wish me luck and told me to call her when the meeting was over.

After, instead of calling, I stumbled out of the Rug's hotel suite and down the stairs into the lobby, passing the same two attractive female assistants, both young blondes with carefully tousled bedheads, who had set me up earlier that morning. I was supposed to have had breakfast with the Rug in the hotel's restaurant, something I'd been looking forward to—just being seen dining with him in one of the industry's buzziest hangouts alone would totally up my ante—but the prettier one had said, "He's still on a call," when she flagged me down. She checked her clipboard and continued to whisper into her headset. Then, "Why don't you guys just go ahead and meet him upstairs? I'll let him know you're on your way."

At that point, I'd been joined by another producer, the one

who'd brought him the project. "You must be Meredith Montgomery," she said, coming up behind me, in an oh-so-cool
British accent. "Jilly Waters," putting out a hand to shake. Thirtysomething, chic, and low-key in jeans and cowboy boots, a
blond-streaked ponytail. "Pleased to make your acquaintance."

"Me, too," I said.

"It's so fucking stunning here," she said, looking out a giant
window. And then when I didn't say anything, because I didn't
know what to say, she smoothly filled in: "Shall we? He's on three."

The assistant gave us both the thumbs-up and flashed a big
tooth-whitened Chiclet-y grin.

As we climbed the stairs, Jilly set me at ease. "I'd never been
to Colorado before I started attending the festival, and now I'm
a total convert. We have nothing like this in the UK. In fact, this
afternoon I have an appointment to check out a little piece of
land." She smiled. "A girl can dream."

"I grew up here, sort of," I said. "I mean, in the state, a little
town outside of Aspen. Back in high school."

"Oh, that's right," she said. "I remember reading that. Honestly, I'd go anywhere to get away from the squidgies for a couple
days. They're six and three. I told my husband, 'Give me a clicker
and a minibar and a white terry cloth robe, fuck me, and leave,
that's my idea of a perfect birthday.' But Telluride is brilliant."

On the third-floor landing she inspected me closely. "An
American rose. You are absolutely perfect for this picture."

Later, on my way *down*stairs, the Rug's minions were too busy
with their notebooks and phones at the lobby bar to acknowledge me as I raced off the bottom step and ran toward the exit.
Jilly Waters, who, yes, had joined us in the suite for room service
but only had time to nibble on one "rasher" of bacon before her
next meeting, was now ensconced on a fat couch with a few other
actors I knew, picking at breakfast number two. It looked like
bacon again; she was delicately teething another strip. She'd told
me earlier she was on paleo. One of the guys was really famous. He

caught my eye. I felt like the bastard could see right through me down to my filthy, torn, wet panties. I went straight out the door and raced through that mountain town's six streets to find Marietta back at our hotel.

She was streaming a yoga class when I pounded on her door and was clearly surprised by the interruption, opening it while toweling her dewy neck. "That good, that you couldn't wait to tell me?" she said, but then she saw my face. "Uh-oh, what is it, honey?"

Marietta was a perfectly aging hippie chick, in her tie-dyed Bandier top and sweatpants-gray capris, her waist-length brown hair piled fetchingly on top of her head. She must have been in her early fifties, but with all that meditation and I'm sure the help of some Cindy Crawford–approved injectables, she could have passed for forties. When I told her what the Rug had done, she cried, right there in the doorway. Then she hugged me and guided me inside her suite.

"I shouldn't have gone with him into the bathroom when he wanted to keep talking, but he said he needed to take a shower," I said.

"How could you have possibly known what would happen next?" asked Marietta.

"He got naked," I said. "I dunno, I guess I thought it was just a Hollywood thing." I really did. You know, hanging out by the pool, hot tubs and stuff. I figured he'd talk to me through the closed shower door. I even politely averted my eyes when he let his robe fall to the floor. Worse, I reached down and hung it up for him.

Her big brown eyes got even bigger. "Honey pie, that's just awful. You're so cute and darling and so incredibly unsophisticated. He took advantage of your trusting heart." We both sat down on her bed. My hands were continuing to shake, so she clasped them palm to palm, like we were joined in prayer. "Don't worry. I'll help you. I'll speak to his partners," she promised, tears running down her cheeks. "We can't let him get away with this. Baby girl, I'm so, so sorry this ever happened."

I'd cry, too, if I'd set up that meeting.

The next Saturday, after everyone had flown back to town, we met at the outdoor terrace of the Starbucks on Sunset, not far from Marietta's offices, so she could see how I was "faring." She was in a long flowing white linen dress, her chestnut hair loose, sleek as a cape, and her signature mauve lipstick, a Chanel classic, no other discernible makeup on her lasered face. An orange mango smoothie for her and an iced peach green tea for me were resting on the table, our usuals; mine with the straw already thoughtfully poked inside it. There was something über-maternal about Marietta: she had three kids and a chocolate Lab named Coco. You've met her before. I've met her before. On television or in a magazine. In real life, no one else was ever quite as generous and kind, as *tender,* as Marietta was—like Tami Taylor in *Friday Night Lights,* or Shirley MacLaine at the end of *Terms of Endearment.*

When she saw me, she put down her phone and put on that face. You know the one. All sympathy: brows knitted but eyes big as ever and just as liquidy, lips pressed together, shaking her head wordlessly to show me how worried she was.

"I'm sincerely glad to see you," Marietta said, standing up.

Which was weird, that "sincerely." A tip-off? It lived in the same Pandora's word-box as "no offense." She pulled out a chair right next to hers and I sat down.

"They told me that they are going to handle it in-house," she said right away, before I could even speak, one hand resting on my knee. Her palm exuded all the heat of a feather comforter. It warmed me, and it made me weak.

"That's good, right?" I asked. I took a sip of my drink.

She nodded again. "They sounded very sincere." That same word twice. "And contrite. 'It's just horrifying,' Howie said."

I was glad to hear it. "Thank you," I said. "But what does that mean, exactly?"

"I'm not sure yet," she said.

"But what do you think?" Nevertheless, I persisted. "Rehab? Will he be kicked out of the company? Do you think we should go to the police?"

"Unclear at the moment," she said, "but they've been told, and they listened. They really truly listened. And they promised— promised!—that they will take decisive action."

I blew bubbles into my drink.

She took her hand off my knee and brought it to my chin, which she lifted like a kindergarten teacher so I could show her my eyes. "In the meanwhile, you and I have a job to do," she said, "and that is to focus on your career."

"We've got to focus on putting his bony ass in jail, you mean."

Marietta picked up her bag and retrieved a vial of Rescue Remedy, shook out a couple of drops, and stirred them into her drink. She offered me some, but I demurred.

"Meredith," she said, "you're a wonderful actress and a very, very attractive girl. But you've done sex scenes. You've been naked on the screen. That makes it harder. He's a very, very powerful man. Let's let the people close to him do the work. Hopefully he'll get the help he needs." She took a sip of her smoothie. "Fingers crossed you'll get the new film, but I heard that they are a bit wobbly on the financing."

"What about the help I need?" I said.

"I'm steadfastly by your side and forever in your corner," Marietta said. "You're going to be a big star. You'll see."

I loved that, but I wanted more.

"Forget it for now, honey," she said. "It's Hollywood."

I did a spit take of my iced peach green tea. It was all so canned, it made me laugh out loud.

"Chinatown," I said. "The line is 'Forget it, Jake. It's Chinatown.'"

Marietta wiped the lipstick off her mouth with her napkin. She also quickly ran it across her teeth. "I'm trying to help you, Meredith," she said, folding it up in her hand. "I'll bet you Jake Gittes went on with his life, and so will you."

I got her meaning. My career was just taking off. I was what my daddy called "free, white, and twenty-one," which meant it would be my own fault if I didn't make it—I sure wasn't about to lose everything I'd fought so hard for.

Mother Marietta cautioned patience. "I believe in karma," she said. "Yours and his."

But when I told the whole story to my manager, Liz, Manager Liz said, "Fuck that shit," and she got me a lawyer. That jerk said it was too late to go to the police, there was no corroborating evidence, and, besides, it would make for bad publicity. Victims always lose in sex crimes trials, even when they win. Best to just get on with building my career. After several conversations, it was made clear that the concerned party was contrite, and his company had made me an offer they hoped would please us. He had me sign a settlement for $150k—I'd wanted $2 million. Once the paperwork was done, the Rug himself reached out and left me a voicemail:

"Meredith, I'm sorry I scared you the last time we met. I'd like to take you out to make up for it. Just as friends. You know that new place downtown, the Broker? I'm hosting a dinner there next Thursday. A bunch of nice people, people it would be really great for you to meet. Most importantly, there's a part in a new picture you'd be great for. I'm ready to sign if you are. The camera really loves you. The director will be sitting at our table."

What? Wow! What? I didn't know what to do then. Just the sound of his voice made my body shake. Hate and a jittery optimism wrestled inside me. He said he had a part for me. The director was sitting at our table! I felt like I was going to throw up. But I didn't. Instead, I poured myself a glass of wine, and then I called Manager Liz after I'd listened to that message half a dozen times.

She sighed loudly. "Well, if he could keep it in his pants . . . But I'm dubious."

I said, "He said he's ready to sign if I am. He wants to take me to that new resto out on Wilshire. That's in public."

"Most restaurants are," Liz said dryly. "And it's impossible to get a reservation. One of the suits at Netflix took me there last week. Very retro. I had the seafood sausage." She paused. "I was such a shitty mother." She paused again. "I want to do good by you, Meredith. Who was it who said, 'When someone tells you who they are the first time, believe them'?"

"I don't know," I said. "You?"

"I would say that," she said, "if I was smarter."

Which was true, so I didn't tell her that the second we hung up I was going to reach out to Marietta.

"Hello," Marietta said, all breathless. I guess when she saw my name on her cell, she started hyperventilating? "Meredith, are you okay?"

I said, "Guess who asked me out to dinner? I mean, what the hell? Is he fucking kidding? But he said he has a part for me."

"Oh, that's so exciting," she squealed. "You know it's not the Jilly pic, right? I think that one's on ice?"

"Okay," I said, instantly dejected. But then hope sprang eternal! It always does. It's my Achilles' heel, hope. I wanted a movie so badly. I asked, "Do you know what it is? Is it anything good?"

"It's great," she purred. "An ensemble piece, but an A-list ensemble. You'll be catapulted into another category."

"Wow," I said.

"I confess," she said, "I put a tiny little bug in his ear. I'm so, so glad he listened."

Marietta, the queen of the humblebrag.

"Really? It's legit?" I asked. "Marietta?"

"There is a part, and it sounds like it's yours if you want it," she said. "I think he feels very badly about your misunderstanding," she added, lowering her voice as if she was about to relay a confidential piece of information. "He knows how talented you are. This is a win-win for all."

"Misunderstanding, my ass," I said. I was so infuriated, I hung up on her.

But after smoking a doobie in my kitchen, I decided to go out with him anyway.

Can you guess my favorite piece of equipment on the playground?

(The answer for ten points: Seesaw!)

I figured I'd already lost what I had left to lose. And weird guilty revelation #35: there was something I actually liked about the word "misunderstanding," when it wasn't coming out of double agent Marietta's mouth. If that was true, if in some metaverse the Rug and I had gotten our signals hopelessly crossed, then maybe what had happened to me on the floor of that hotel bathroom wasn't so completely, unbearably, *unlivably* awful. If I could hit the backspace key on the whole horrible episode—the top of my skull bouncing against the base of that fancy toilet, the Rug's hand clamped across my mouth—maybe it could be erased? Or sufficiently whitewashed down in my memory to a semi-illegible stone rubbing?

The night of our proposed "date," I took an Uber, wearing my best little red strapless minidress. The restaurant was in a refurbished space in one of those cool old downtown banks—very glam and Hollywoody—they even left in the giant safe. From the maître d's station, I spotted the Rug sitting center stage on a burgundy leather banquette encircling the half-moon of a white-clothed table. There were famous people flanking both sides of him: two male movie stars, one older but still desirable actress, *my* soon-to-be director, and a celebrated composer of film scores. Had I finally made it to the big time?

I stood indecisively at the front of the house, one knee bent, silver platformed hoof off the floor, an on-trend doe frozen in fashion's floodlights.

"Meredith," he called, and waved me over. "Come now, sit next to me!"

I raised my shoulders and gestured *How?* because I was scared and embarrassed and he was surrounded on both sides. All the king's chess pieces were buffering him while eating and drinking on his dime, and enjoying themselves, royally. Even the two rooks at the end were in conversations with diners at nearby tables.

"Come, come." He beckoned me to his banquette, so I went.

Since the table was full, I approached him from behind, perching casually on the seat back. Without warning, he reached out with one surprisingly strong arm and slid me over the edge.

"Whoa!" I said, as I toppled down into his lap.

My cell phone fell out of my mini clutch and skittered across the table. The director caught it with two hands. He winked and flashed me a winning smile.

Now everyone was laughing as the Rug gently guided my body onto the seat cushion next to him, my knees over his knees. I was practically in his lap at that moment, and the director took a photo on my phone of the two of us in hysterics in that pretzeled-up position.

What can I say? It was wild. The director and I gabbed all night, and I got the role, as promised.

I guess after that the Rug thought my selective mutism gave him free rein. He put me in another movie, although that part wasn't starring, either. From time to time, I allowed him to take me to more sparkly dinners. Meanwhile, out of his hands but well within his circle of influence, my show got renewed for another season. I sucked his cock once on his boat in Cannes, before we walked the red carpet. Another time I did it in the outdoor shower of his Bel Air estate.

Scene of the crime, you say. What was that girl thinking?

Well, you know what? Who knows what the fuck I was thinking. I certainly don't, not now, not then. I was keeping a constant buzz going—weed, pills, booze, whatever was around—so I didn't feel much besides high or hungover. I was freestyling the game of survival. Like how sharks need to swim or they'll die? I figured if I was still moving, I was still alive.

At the tail end of winter, I wore a transparent gold jumpsuit to the annual Oscar weekend picnic Diane von Furstenberg and Barry Diller threw for Graydon Carter, the editor of *Vanity Fair*, in the backyard of their estate in Beverly Hills. I accessorized it with a pearl-chained G-string riding up my crack and a blond mink merkin hiding what only a lover was meant to see. It was a dumb move, I realized as soon as I got in line at the buffet station behind this relaxed, barefoot, cool Black girl with a huge natural in torn jeans and a plunging white silk Dolce & Gabbana blazer with nothing underneath it. She was retro and elegant and casual at the same time, as she stepped aside to air-kiss a Eurotrash brown man who looked like money. She let me pass by politely without gawking—far classier than I could ever be. Worse: she didn't seem to notice me at all!

Everybody wears naked shit like my outfit; this chick was covered up. Confident *and* still sexy. My look was as ubiquitous as tattoos. I felt like a total has-been, radiating loserdom and desperation.

Still, I made the tabloids and the gossip sites! I was riding high, but I was sinking low. I mean, I'm an actor, I can deal. But then something began to fissure and goo inside my brain.

Since I was a little girl, I've always pictured my mind sort of like an egg, separate from the gray matter that controlled everything else like swallowing and breathing, running and punching. The shell part was contained and smooth, girded by some supremely thin superpower, while my thoughts flew around inside it like a flock of wild birds. But after the Rug, that clear slime, the albumen of my psyche, started to slither around inside the rest of my cranium, and then the yolk of my being (you could call it my soul, if you're that literal-minded) broke and a yellow liquid viscously followed, dripping, dripping, dripping, and all of a sudden, my stomach hurt real bad—talk about mind-body connection! I'm a performer, I can play the part, but when I'm freaking the fuck out, I'm just not all that good at anything. I couldn't find a way to pull myself back together.

When I heard he finally offered the dough to green-light the Jilly movie, I had a moment of elation, but then when the Rug gave *my* part to another girl—to pay her off, too? I honestly didn't know—I smoked some weed late one night and started to tweet. Nothing concrete. I just "leaned in." I had signed my life rights away, see, when I penned my signature on the Rug's settlement. All I could do on social media now was *imply: the devil is in holly-wood with his bathrobe open, doesn't anybody care? actors are inden-tured sex slaves.* After that little episode, the feral pig put the kibosh on me. He was the criminal! But I couldn't get arrested! The offers stopped coming. Marietta the crying agent disowned me; it was all too much for her.

"I'm a very sensitive person," she said, while sniffling over the phone. "I mean, I love you, Meredith, you're a great actress. If I was a better person, I could handle this," and then six weeks later she took a job at the Rug's company. Manager Liz at least gave me the pleasure of calling ex-agent Marietta a "closet asshole."

"Three kids, three nannies," she said.

She told me to get out of town, take a rest. "Stop fucking tweet-ing! Remember the NDA," she'd said. "Lay low, he'll move on to someone else."

I typed all that shit up in my Parisian apartment, and then, when I closed the lid of my computer after *that* episode of graphomania, I thought, Wow, that Nina girl really got to me! So I decided to go back to the ice cream stand, hoping I'd run into her again. I was stuck in a strange and sticky web of ambivalence—I wanted to see Nina (no one had ever stood up for me before, either), but I was afraid to take the next step. What if I got rejected?? She was older, fiercer, more polished. She had a job that required brains and education; sometimes she even wore a suit. She was too good for me. I wanted to run into her by accident! But there was no Nina at the Berthillon kiosk that evening, even though I hung around patiently for hours. When I returned downcast to the apartment, sick of the sugary film that coated my teeth after my evening feed, I finally broke down and searched for her card again. I found it on the bedroom floor beneath a pair of peeled-off inside-out black skinny jeans and studied it closely. Then I opened my laptop.

Easy-peasy, Nina showed up on her company's website, in a "Who We Are" bio with a canned headshot, her hair tied neatly back, a wavy ponytail gracing her right shoulder. There were some candid photos on the link Gateway: Insights and Visions: Nina in meetings (leaning over a conference table to gather some papers, wearing a black sleeveless turtleneck and matching leather pants, her hair coiled up into a Ballerina Barbie's bun), and Nina in a yellow shift sitting on the edge of her desk in her office, two male clients—one Black, one white—across from her in metal chairs, diversity personified, listening intently. (I pictured her saying, *I should have just cut it off*.) In one sunny pic, Nina was standing shoulder to shoulder with several guys and another woman out in a field; they all seemed happy and at ease in corporate playclothes—she was wearing jeans and a gauzy shirt, and her long blond locks were set loose in the breeze—as if they'd just had a company picnic or something. A retreat. A bonding exercise. I know jack shit about this stuff, having never retreated or bonded over anything. They seemed carefree. They looked the way I've always wished I felt.

The more I searched the more I found. The website and a bare-bones Wikipedia entry suggested that Gateway was a German-based multinational tech consultancy. Per its mission statement, it did digital PR for mostly green companies worldwide and appealed to a do-goody twenty-first-century sensibility. The firm was Berlin groovy and had what that bitch, Amber from Washington State, would have called "pizzazz," meaning it also had offices in Silicon Valley, Austin, Shanghai, Tokyo, Tel Aviv, and, in Nina's case, Amsterdam, all high-class technology hubs.

On her bio page, I learned that Nina's master's degrees were from the London School of Economics, in data science and culture and society, and, before that, Cambridge, where she studied business and management and computer engineering. Tiring of subjects that I had little knowledge of or interest in, I turned to her social media; like almost everyone in her generation, she had an out-of-date Facebook account, and she also wasn't much for tweeting. Further info was to be gleaned on FB when I scrolled some, but her page had been left high and dry for a good three years. I scanned her pictures: here, too, she looked younger, freer than when I met her earlier in the week. Apparently, back in the day she liked to drink Aperol spritzes at sunset in roof bars in London—I guess while she was studying at LSE?—and New York, surrounded by attractive, laughing companions, the photos so curated they could have been booze ads in a slick magazine. A boyfriend took center stage for a while, but then abruptly his name and pictures stopped appearing. A quick search: he was no longer on her "friends" list. So, he had been unfriended or he was dead. I googled him, Joshua Strauss, a handsome curly-haired Jew; he was now living in Jersey City and working for Goldman Sachs. He appeared to be American. He had a newish girlfriend, Tessa, brown hair and eyes, who was a dermatology resident. She also ran marathons. In every photo on her page, when she wasn't wearing an off-the-shoulder figure-hugging minidress, she had just crossed a finish line, a medal around her neck. Her thumbs were perpetually up. She was a winner. Tessa! She had a crazy-big smile. I hated her for Nina.

Interestingly, at least to *moi*, about nine months ago Nina also became vice president/head of communications for an organization called Women's Work, which showed up as an update on her Facebook page. So this was the advocacy activity she'd spoken about that night. A friend named Ilse replied with a link to an article. It was written by an American, Matthew Anastos. Matt was one of the few journos to show an interest in my tweets, and he'd written some items about me on his blog—once he even DM'd me *Sounds rough* and reached out about the possibility of writing a longer story. We'd chatted, and I'd found him sympathetic, but that's when the heat had turned up, and Manager Liz had me pack my bags and ordered me to "just get fucking lost." I'd told him I had decided to write my own book, and instead of laughing out loud, he'd politely wished me good luck. So, seeing his byline piqued my interest. The article was a feature on Jenna Taylor, a civil rights defender who'd founded an organization called Free to Be Me for African American girls who were survivors of sexual assault. Ilse referred to Nina's organization as W2, as in *This kind of profile would work great for W2.*

I was proud that with just a little bit of sleuthing I'd figured a whole lot out about W2, a women's rights group based in Amsterdam—it was almost too easy, but that's internet addiction for you. I toggled back and forth from several sites, instantly forgetting what I'd just gleaned, the blah blah blah of statements of purpose and the psychosocial-wonky speech of case studies. Bottom line, W2 was a watchdog for women's "safety and rights at home, at school, at work," and helped "take action" by finding pro bono lawyers for plaintiffs "of any age" who had been sexually harassed and/or abused. This last tidbit intrigued me for obvious reasons and made sense, since Nina had blurted out that nasty bit of her personal history during our night by the Seine. Sadly, I had never used my own waterfall of hate and fury in the sane, positive, political manner Nina had. Her championing of just causes, *my causes,* made me admire her. It also made me wonder: Was my writing a book even vaguely enough? Would the NDA keep it from being published? And was I kidding myself, who'd really want to read it, anyway? Only people who cared about the subject, aka the already damaged, and therefore a preemptively discredited audience. We don't count.

Internet stalking gave me something to do. A new lease on life, ha! After a day of writing, I spent a couple of evenings on Facebook and Instagram, trying to connect the dots. I even followed Tessa's twin sister for a while; her name was Ella and she looked exactly like Tessa, except her iteration of the same set of DNA preferred shapeless T-shirts and hiking boots, and she kept her hair boy band short. It was amazing to see how the same core ingredients could produce such distinctly different results: one captivating in a straight, cisgender way, calculated to entrance men; the other obviously tailored to go unnoticed by them. Ella was clearly a no-nonsense lesbian, and I liked her a whole lot more than bubbly, braggy Tessa, but you know how all this goes: after the initial thrill of a Facebook find and some funny six-degrees-of-separation connections—Ella was in Nina's long-frozen group of "friends"—it all rapidly grew boring. I checked out their various accounts: all those vacation pics, the girls in tight skirts, boobs out, shoulders back. The guys on sailboats and at soccer games, drinking in British pubs. Joshua seemed mildly uncomfortable amid all this sporty joyousness. Too preppy? Maybe. There were a few early pictures of him and Nina, arm in arm at some beach somewhere or clowning around when he had that how-did-I-get-so-lucky look, the fleeting bloom of young love, but that didn't seem to last very long. These were replaced with shots of him brooding, on his own, studiously avoiding the crowd and presumably the fun. When he showed up as BF on Tessa's feed a couple of years later, he looked relaxed, though his own page remained dormant. At this point, he had only one friend. Tessa.

It hadn't taken long for me to attach attributes to some of these new characters on the screen. In the theater of her own cultivation, Tessa seemed game and fun-loving. Nina's page was sparsely populated even when she was active and somehow felt more somber and poetic: the beach at dusk, Nina gazing pensively out a window. She seemed aloof, maybe moody, hard to reach? Or perhaps she was just a more sluggish curator of her photographs. I wasn't sure. To me, all that polish hid so much desperation, but look at the glasses I was wearing, not rose-colored but those of an injury—yellowy blue and purply green. I saw her as a first cousin once removed, the kind you could marry in the red states that I came from. I'd already bonded with her. She was haunted. Me, too.

In the last season of my nighttime soap, all the characters left breathing had pretty much gotten together and broken up. Pickings were slimmer by the finale. We survivors felt blessed just to find someone else to cling to, which was why my character married the kind, middling owner of the town's taxi fleet in an ending sequence that misread *The Graduate;* I ran out of the church with my train looped over my right shoulder, hand in hand with my whooping suitor, as I joyously left studly Rich Dad #3 at the altar. But that was TV. In the virtual world of social media, it didn't take a psychologist to see through all that careful cultivation of personality and subliminal boasting. (Tessa! I'm talking about you, girl!) I understood the impulse. I'd lived a large part of my life in the public eye, and for a short time all that attention made me feel golden. But once the trolling started, outsourced by you-know-who, and I fried daily in an electrified pool of livid retaliation, I couldn't wait to deactivate. The purging of FB, Twitter, and Instagram felt like ritual purification.

Now, look at me then: the amount of time I was putting into Nina's ex-boyfriend's current girlfriend's twin sister was starting to scare the shit out of me. I reminded myself of my mother, the way she used to watch the soap opera network for hours and days and years it seemed, singeing her fingers on cigarettes and her tongue on caffeinated beverages. Like her, I had become addicted to lackluster lives. Since there was nothing left to glean about Nina and Joshua, this amounted to a growing obsession with minor characters—a spinoff, which we all know leads nowhere. I decided to get some air.

Outside was one of those sticky gray days of summer, lots of heavy cloud cover, like it might spit or pour at any moment; the ground was always wet, afternoon and evening indistinguishable from early morning. I'd lost all sense of time. I wandered for a while, past the shoppers and their shopping bags, the Roma women lying on torn, moldering mattresses on the street breastfeeding their children, into the haute Marais. I liked it up there. The vibe was kind of Venice Beach, where I owned a house: all these vegan restaurants and markets, Moon Juice types selling charcoal lemonade and activated almonds, raw salads that wilted and browned inside their plastic cases. Tattooed skinny French boys and girls of all ages drank turmeric lattes and smoked on the crowded terraces of shotgun cafés, their interiors long and narrow and invariably empty. No one seemed to want to sit inside except for cave dwellers: a stray architect or two and what I assumed were poets, the dudes with their wispy beards and the girls with their messy topknots, pecking away on laptops. Several of these tiny tea shops and coffee bars faced Square du Temple, a three-by-five-block-long patch of green with a playground, a raised pavilion and fenced-off trees, a pond and grass for ducks to waddle on and squirrels to hop along. Hobos and refugees from civil wars often slept there behind the low wrought-iron fencing, quasi-hidden by decorative bushes, until the gendarmes arrived and reliably swept them away. No one seemed to care if migrants set up their makeshift tents on the sidewalks or cooked their coffees on little portable oil burners in the gutters—they were camped

out all over the city center—just not on the thick public lawn in
the cool private shade.

I got why displaced people were drawn to the park; I liked it
there, too. In the mornings, elderly Chinese women would gather
to practice tai chi in groups, their swaying movements like liquid language, composing sentences of abstract calm. While they
flowed their way to a better place, their husbands sat side by
side on benches studiously watching over them. Sometimes they
shared newspapers or played cards together. I liked to think that
they would rise in an instant of old-man unification if anything
or anyone were to threaten their wives, but maybe they just came
for the company. Often, I'd glimpse them speaking to one another
out of the corners of their mouths.

That day I didn't see any Chinese couples, so using my God-
given smarts I deduced that it was not morning after all, but afternoon. I walked up a block, poked my head into this princess café
called Lily of the Valley—yep, the lettering was in English—and
decided it was too sweet for me: flocked wallpaper, painted china
cups, and banana chocolate chip muffins. I preferred a minimal-
ist coffeehouse/concept store nearby called the Broken Arm. It
sold silly but cool designer clothing, like sneakers for nine hundred euros, tracksuits and black trousers, arty T-shirts and rubber skirts, carefully curated down to three or four racks so loosely
packed you could insert your entire body between the items to
have a good look-see. The five or six pairs of shoes it proffered
stood stupidly atop Greek pedestals of varying heights, which
for some reason cracked me up, but it was two streets away and
I needed to pee. Like the other places I'd walked by, the outside
tables at Lily were full, but the inside was completely vacant. I
made my way briskly to the back, so as not to be stopped by the
solitary waitress, sitting at a table, smoking and tapping on her
phone. She didn't even look up. I figured she wanted her alone
time same as anyone. The kitchen was fairly empty, some brown
male cooks prepping vegetables and a chef de cuisine, also *un*

homme, perched on a stool reading a magazine. Across from the place where the magic happened were two doors, one marked PRIVÉ and the other WC. I reached down to open the latter when it unlocked on its own. There was Nina, her hands still damp from the sink; she was rubbing them dry with a paper towel. To this day, I don't know how anyone managed to choreograph this "meet-cute" or if, for once, we were just a part of one of God's holy chess games, our running into each other seemingly completely serendipitous and therefore wholly innocent.

"Nina," I said, startled. "It's me."

"Yes?" she said, playing it cool or not remembering. Which was it?

I pulled down my hood, took off my dark glasses. "The ice cream? The other night? You gave me your card? You pulled out a knife."

I watched her stiffen and then drink in the information, the facts registering hard behind her eyes.

"Yes, of course," she said. "How are you?" She was staring at me searchingly, the way you might study an older person, trying to find a younger face amid the ruins. "I'm not sure I would have recognized you on my own. My apologies."

That hurt. But then again, I'd spent most of the week in a girl crush, gazing at her on social media. What stood before me—a long loose blond braid, a white eyelet summer dress, strappy sandals, that same brown leather backpack—now was completely familiar. Except she'd just freshened her lipstick. A glossy pinky red.

"Do you want to use the toilet?" she asked, still holding open the door.

"Yes, please," I said. I started walking past her into the bathroom.

"When you're ready, would you like to join me and my friend for a coffee? We're sitting outside on the *terrasse.*"

"That would be great," I said.

She started to close the door and then thought better of it: "What's your name?"

"Merry," I said. I don't know why I didn't say Meredith. No one but my father called me Merry anymore. "Like in Christmas. Merry Christmas."

"Merry. That's pretty," she said. "Okay, I'll get out of your way now."

She slid out and I slid into the restroom.

I immediately locked the door behind me. My hands were shaking, and I was so nervous I forgot I needed to pee. Inside was what you could call "untidy," but way short of disgusting. I looked at myself in the oxidized mirror; it had a plaster frame of white roses, even though the café was called Lily, and a dirty white wicker basket was overflowing with used paper towels under the sink. No wonder Nina emerged still holding hers. She was a good person! She didn't want the trash to avalanche. I remembered how she'd picked up her cigarette butt, careful to throw it out. My hair was buzzed; my eyes and the circles beneath them were the same color, "contusion purple," one of the makeup artists once called it. He told me to sleep with Preparation H under my eyes to reduce the puffiness. I was wearing no makeup, and I was clothed in black jean cutoffs fraying at the knee and that same freaking fucking hoodie. Underneath, I'd wrapped my breasts in an ACE bandage. The day before, I think, I'd taken a shower. There was no way to primp, to make me look perkier or more adult and less like a skate rat. Still, I washed my face and bit my lips, pinched my cheeks, hoping to add color. Having avoided the sun for so long, my skin was the color of lukewarm skim milk, the kind served in school cafeterias.

Nina was sitting at one of the poky café tables on the sidewalk when I came outside. They were wrought iron, painted white, and the chairs were matchy-matchy with the tables. Across from her was a handsome guy, thirtysomething, with unruly dark hair, dark eyes, black jeans, and a *Yeezus* T-shirt. He had about three days' growth of beard. He was leaning forward, entertaining her it seemed, because she was inclined toward him, too, looking somewhat rapt as she demolished a fancy dessert, a Paris-Brest, a circle of choux pastry filled with praline crème.

"Jean-Pierre," she said, tilting back in her chair to acknowledge me as I approached, while forcing the remaining bite into her mouth with her fingers; the skirt of her white dress swooped down to the ground like a sail. "This is my new friend, Merry."

He looked up and extended a hand. "You're famous," he said, staring. The sentence made me instantly swell up and recoil, both. Since my hand was already outstretched, he took it, and I dead-fished him. "You're on TV."

"TV?" said Nina. She cocked her head and widened her eyes, looking at him and then at me and then back again to him, questioningly, some of that crème still sticking to her ruby lips. "I am so impressed!"

Was I wrong to think a look of excited jealousy flashed behind her eyes?

My whole life other girls had gazed at me that hungrily.

Now, thinking back, I understand that Nina was finally up close and personal with something she'd long wanted. So tantalizingly near, she could have hit me over the head with a brick and mugged me for it. Too bad celebrity doesn't work like that. You can covet it, but you can't steal it.

Jean-Pierre motioned his napkin to his face, and she caught on and laughed delightfully. "My manners," she said, dabbing her serviette to her mouth.

"She's an actress. She's famous. A sex symbol! I mean that politely," he said. "Please understand." Then back to Nina: "The character she plays is waaay gorgeous and hot. They write about her in the magazines."

"They write about Merry or the character?" said Nina, green-eyed—or still trying to wrap her head around this hard-to-fathom information?

"Both," said Jean-Pierre.

"No way. Those assholes thought she was a fourteen-year-old boy!" Nina said.

"What assholes?" he said. He pointed at me. "That's no boy. She's famous, I tell you, I've seen her. A celebrity. In America."

"In America." Nina nodded, the information clearly news-worthy.

"On television," he repeated himself. I must have looked anxious, because he pulled out a chair for me. "Sit, sit," he said. "Don't worry. I won't call the paparazzi."

I sat.

"Are you really famous? A celebrity?" Nina said, playfully suspicious. "Prove it. What show are you on?"

"It's hilarious," said Jean-Pierre. "All these evil, witchy women living in mansions in California." He turned to me. "You are by far the best one. When I was visiting my friends in New York, we streamed the whole season. You were our favorite! Such meanness. Such treachery." He turned back to Nina. "You have got to see it for yourself. This girl can act!"

"Maybe I already did," said Nina, something clicking in. "Merry, when you came to my rescue—she came to my rescue, JP—were you acting the other night?" She was joking, teasing, but also, I felt, wow, she really wanted to know.

"No," I said. "I was scared shitless."

"Rescue? What are you talking about? What happened?" Jean-Pierre said. But before either of us could speak, he asked, "Merry, do you want something to drink?"

I looked at the table. Nina's treat was gone, but she still had a coffee; he was sipping wine. "It's five o'clock somewhere," I said. My daddy's old breakfast routine. He loved him a morning beer.

"Yes?" he said. "What does that mean?"

"It means I'll have a glass of wine," I said.

"Good," he said with a smile, then leaned back in his chair and waved inside for the waitress. She saw the gesture and pointedly looked away. So he stood up. "What kind?"

I glanced at his glass. He was drinking red. *"La même chose,"* I said.

Nina laughed.

I felt the pride some guys feel when they finally make you orgasm. I smiled back. Not performative, but a genuine, human grin.

"Hold that thought," said Jean-Pierre. "About the 'rescue,' I mean. I'll just be gone a second."

"Okay," I said as he walked into the café. "Thanks."

"So, you are a *thespian*," she said with a teasing grin. "Is that why you hide?" She pointed to my getup.

"Yes," I said. "And no. Really, what I want is not to call attention to myself."

"I understand that feeling," said Nina. "I'm the same way sometimes, but no matter how I dress, I can't escape things like the other night. I wonder, will they still torment me later, when I'm old and ugly?"

"They were awful," I said. "But you were dynamite."

" 'Dynamite'?"

"My daddy's word," I said. "He's almost fifty. It was his daddy's word. It means you're cool. You were brave."

"I was angry. I am almost always angry," said Nina, as Jean-Pierre came back with two more glasses and an opened bottle of *vin rouge*.

"Voilà," he said. "A lovely Bordeaux. A celebration. You see, it is not every day I get to drink with someone famous." He poured a glass for me and one for Nina, and then he topped himself off. He took his seat and inched in closer to the table. "What makes you so angry, Nina?"

"These guys, these Americans, they were trying to flirt, and then Merry stepped in to help me."

"Ah, the rescue," he said. "Merry, that is good."

"They were both so creepy." Nina shuddered. "One of them touched my hair and then grabbed her breast." She pointed at me. "Merry looked so scared, I pulled out my little knife."

"Oouf," said Jean-Pierre. "Where was this? Were you clubbing?"

"Are you kidding?" said Nina. "Me? We were at that Berthillon by the river on the Île de la Cité. Just two kids out buying ice cream."

"*Je suis désolé,* Merry. *Je suis désolé,* dear Nina. That this should happen to you in Paris." Only he said it the way they all do, *Par-ee.*

Rhymes with "crime spree."

"Don't be sorry," I said. "They were ugly Americans. My country's fault."

"She has a point," said Jean-Pierre. "Still, it is terrible. A terrible thing to have happen to you." He sipped his wine. He brought out a packet of loose tobacco and some papers and began to roll a cigarette.

I reached into my kangaroo pocket and pulled out my pack of Marlboros. I offered him one: "Pre-rolled," I said.

"You are most kind," said Jean-Pierre. "But I smoke less this way." He took a silver lighter out of his pocket and offered it to me, flame up.

I tapped a cig out of the packet and leaned in.

Then he finished rolling his. "Please do not feel offended, but I see an opportunity." He lit his own cigarette and sat back in his chair, blowing smoke into the sky.

"You always do," said Nina.

"You asked for my help, but then you mock," said Jean-Pierre.

"Help in what?" I said, feeling left out. I took a sip of my wine. It tasted like licorice and jam and smoke, or maybe the smoke was from the cigarettes. Both were plush and satisfying.

Jean-Pierre said, "Merry, there is money in it."

I was listening.

He went on: "Nina and I are friends, we like to have fun, but what brought us together is not so funny. Have you ever heard of the advocacy group Women's Work? They are headquartered in Amsterdam."

Of course I knew about W2, but that was only because of my cyberstalking. I decided to play dumb. "Uh-uh," I said dumbly.

"How could she possibly know, JP?" said Nina.

"She is famous," he said, waving away his smoke. He leaned toward me. "We are looking for a speaker—more, a face."

What was I, if not a face?

"It's for a good cause and we have a real budget." He turned to Nina. "I know a little about her story."

"Her story?" said Nina. She reached for my pack. "Merry, do you mind?"

"Not at all," I said. "Have at it."

Nina tapped out a cigarette. "What about my Merry's story?"

"Different from yours," said Jean-Pierre. "But unfortunately, a lot like Soroya's."

Nina got very quiet. Jean-Pierre misted over. He was a better actor than I was. On my series, whenever I had to cry, the makeup artist used Vaseline and fake tear drops. Jean-Pierre's didn't fall through his thick lashes, they just pooled in his big brown melty eyes, like two Hershey's Kisses that had been sitting in your pocket, waiting for math class to be over. It was masterful, now when I think about it.

I opened my mouth to ask, but Nina mind-read my question. "His sister," she said. "She was an editor here in Paris for a fashion magazine. *Envieux*."

"I love *Envieux*," I said. You could get it in French or in English.

"She was raped at work by her boss," said Nina.

"That is a lot like me," I said. When I drink, I tend to leak.

Jean-Pierre nodded. Apparently, he did know about me already.

"Oh, Merry. You, too?" said Nina. She reached out and patted my right hand, which was inching its way back to my wineglass. "I can't stand it!" she said. "Has this happened to absolutely everyone?"

Jean-Pierre looked at us both, soulfully, sorrowfully.

"I felt so bad for you the other night, Nina," I said. I felt the need to confirm that I was legitimately interested, even if I was also sniffing down a paycheck. She'd shown me hers; I would show her mine. "When you told me what you told me, I should have said something, then. I should have let you know how mad it made me feel and also that I truly understood."

She was buying into me, or so I thought. "You owe no one an apology. Especially me. We are alike, us two. Sisters of the soul. You owe nobody nothing." She took a breath. Then, like a little explosion: "I hate your boss. If he were here now, I would kill him with my knife!"

She was so intense, she made me laugh. "Would you cut it off?" I said.

"You bet I would," said Nina, and now she was laughing, too.

We already had inside jokes. Fast, quick, we had a secret language.

I started to cry, which I never do. There was something so warm and relieving about having someone to talk to. Even as I was gaming her when it came to W2. And she, me, apparently, for she gave me a little hug.

I almost spilled my wine. I hadn't been touched by anyone in so long, except for the pervert at the ice cream stand. "It was the second time," I said, pulling back, wiping the tears from my eyes. "I was raped before, when I was a teenager in Colorado." I couldn't believe what I was saying—*that* was a story I never told—but also, suddenly I could. The shame at the time had been overwhelming— when you're a kid you think it's all your fault, you did something wrong, you asked for it. But this felt like a safe space, with these two, and I had written about it in my pages, so why couldn't I say it out loud? The first thing I learned from all those cheesy scripts is that opening up helps win people over. And these nice people, Nina and Jean-Pierre, were already on my side. I really believed they were into me.

Nina's eyebrows arched. "You were raped before? You poor thing." She sat back in her chair, arms cradling her stomach, like it hurt, as if it were she who had been wounded. "You'd think somehow once would be way more than enough; I mean, you already had yours."

"'Had yours'?" Jean-Pierre asked.

"Why her? Why twice?" she said to him. "Merry's had enough for a lifetime. It's criminal. It's unbearable." Nina was still shaking her head in anger as she poured me some more wine. "Was it a boyfriend? Someone you knew?"

"Thank you," I said, taking another sip. "Not a boyfriend. Older. A director. He owned a house on the Roaring Fork River near the Woody Creek tavern where I tended bar. I was so scared that time, I didn't tell anybody, except my girlfriend . . ."

Nina nodded me along encouragingly.

She passed the girlfriend test. Giving me strength.

She put her cigarette in her mouth, and Jean-Pierre lit it for her.

"Yeah, I was seeing this girl, she stayed in the trailer park that I was living in outside of Aspen—I mean, at the same time I was seeing another bartender, a guy. Sometimes the three of us . . ." Was I going too far? "I guess," I said, "I've always been a bit wild."

"We've all been a bit wild," said Nina, blowing smoke out her nostrils and waving it and my disgrace away with her hand.

"When I told her, she said just forget about it. 'Face it,' she said, 'eventually this happens to all of us.'"

Jean-Pierre spoke up. "In a way, that's what Nina just said."

"She'd had kind of a hard time herself," I said. "My girlfriend Lulu."

"Lulu," Jean-Pierre echoed.

"Louisa," I said. "Her grandma was also named Louisa, and

since Granny ended up being the one who raised her . . . Well, everyone called her Lulu. It was Lulu's idea to put sugar in my rapist's gas tank and leave prank calls for his wife. Telling her what he'd done, I mean. Describing his dick, which was shaped funny. You know, one of those where the hole is on the bottom."

"Eeeow," said Nina. "Is it someone that we've heard of?" She shivered. "That dick thing makes me feel sick. Sounds like a faucet. Why didn't you go to the police?"

"I was too scared," I said for the second time.

"Me, too," said Nina. "It took me years and years to tell anyone."

She was right. We were alike! The same! But still, I was neurotically trying to explain myself. "It was all over for me in Woody Creek by then anyway. I mean, I moved out about three months later when I got 'discovered.'"

Suddenly, I felt shy, like I was talking too much. Like I was talking to a shrink or an interviewer, God forbid.

"Am I talking too much?" I said. "I'm told I do that sometimes. That sometimes I'm not fit for human consumption."

"Then you've come to the right place," Nina said. She gestured her wineglass at Jean-Pierre. "It's something the three of us have in common."

She took another sip and so did I, just to continue twinning; plus, that French shit tasted so amazingly good.

"For years, I didn't say a word to anyone. But these days it's hard for me to stop talking about it."

Jean-Pierre patted her on her arm. "It takes strength to hold it in and bravery to let it out. But eventually, we all must confide in someone." Now that drivel sounds to me like a saying on a T-shirt you buy at an exercise studio, but then, when I was naive, I lapped it up.

"So, the director," Nina asked again. "Is he someone we might have heard of?"

I nodded. "Remember that doc? All he ate was Taco Bell?"

The waitress passed by us, still focusing on her phone but

walking and texting at the same time. Jean-Pierre reached out and tugged on her apron string. *"Madame, une autre bouteille, si'l vous plaît."* He held up the bottle so she could read the label.

"Oui, monsieur," she said, and disappeared back into the bowels of the café.

I turned to Nina. "It's weird, but I still don't want to say his name."

"Of course, sweetie. Never. Never say something you don't want to say. I always tell that to myself before I make a speech."

"Women's Work would not ever ask you to do anything you didn't want to do. That is, if you agreed to join forces with us," said Jean-Pierre. "No pressure."

"But you already have Nina," I said.

There's a big part of me that likes to be pursued.

"Nina is great, the best, I love her like a sister. But we need someone who will create real enthusiasm."

She gave him a little studied side-eye, and we all laughed.

"You, my dear, you have star power. I was impressed with you even before I met you," said Jean-Pierre, talking directly to me. "For this time, lately, last winter and spring. You were so much, how do you say, courage?"

"Courageous?" said Nina.

"Yes, so much courageous to speak out on Twitter that way, even if you were being coy." It was the only time his English stuttered. It felt purposefully phony, like a fly landing its creepy little feet in my mind. I brushed it aside.

"It took me a while. But I was so angry. It pretty much put my career on hold."

"Same thing happened to Soroya," said Nina.

A "long beat," as the screenwriters write.

"Soroya is dead," said Jean-Pierre, sort of interrupting—that is, if you can interrupt someone else's silence. His declaration shot through the air like a bullet, shattering Nina's resonant cloud of calm.

I wonder now if Nina was kicking him under the table. Wasn't it all a bit too much? But at the time, I was riveted by his face, a perfect map of anger and sorrow and gorgeousness. Why were they both so sexy? And thus, so seemingly appealing? Again and again, I fall for the same old scam, as if outer beauty ever safeguarded against inner rot. I, of all people, should have known better.

"It was Soroya's choice," he said. He said it like a resolution. "Maybe it was the only choice she thought she had left to make, I don't know. But after, when a friend told me about W2—you know, Women's Work, WW, W2, that's what we call it in the office—I took the train to Amsterdam . . ."

"The TGV," I filled in for him.

"Yes, of course," he said. "I am an adman. I volunteered my services. My friendship with the brilliant, knife-wielding genius over here"—his chin jutted toward Nina—"was a surprising and cherished bonus."

"I don't understand," I said, although of course I knew full well where this was heading.

"How could you possibly?" said Nina, sympathy coating her voice like cough syrup on a spoon. And then to Jean-Pierre, "She won't want to, she doesn't want to be recognized. She's safely underground now. Let's change the subject."

The waitress finally came over with the new bottle. She opened it by holding it beneath her armpit and twisting out the cork, which she handed to Jean-Pierre to sniff. Then she decanted a little *vin rouge* in his empty glass, which he tasted, nodding his approval. After that, she gave him a nice pour, set the bottle down, and walked away.

Nina pouted. She lifted her empty glass and gestured toward mine. "What about us, ladies-in-waiting? How about our *verres de vin*?"

"But of course," said Jean-Pierre, as he leaned over, generously filling both glasses. "I have forgotten my manners."

"I'm sorry, Jean-Pierre," I said. "I mean about your sister." I took a long sip. I was being sincere. I *was* sorry. Then like clockwork, someone else's suffering made me think about myself.

"I, I, I," my mother used to say when she was sick of me. (She hardly ever saw me—how could she get sick of me?) All those times, I thought she was speaking Spanish: *"Ai, ai, ai."* But apparently not. She was in fact mimicking me, her only kid. After her sixth session of ECT, she said, "I, I, I, that's all you ever talk about—yourself. It's so boring, Meredith." When Mom began to speak again, after the initial blank and hollow hours that followed the bolts of lightning through her head, it was always a bit of a shock, like if your cockapoo spoke English, or your throw pillow, Japanese. But this time, her words gutted me.

I'd flown to Nevada to be by her side for this latest hospitalization when the show was on hiatus, and as she'd been struggling to unscramble her brain, I'd been taking a crack at entertaining her with stories from on set. Apparently, there had been way too much of me, me, me, and not enough of *her* in my ultra-"boring" narration.

So far, living in Paris, I'd kept myself from leaping into the Seine, flying off the rooftop, jumping in front of a subway train, doing a forward roll off a balcony at a theater, more than haphazardly mixing pills and alcohol at a club, but still, I continued to drink until I passed out, passed out a lot, while thinking, I don't care if I die or not. But this Soroya, she'd made a choice. She'd made a statement. I wanted to ask how she'd done it, but I was afraid that I just might make use of that information, if I ever got the guts.

Nina lifted her now full glass to her lips, and her eyes met my eyes. At that moment, I stopped thinking about Soroya as anything less than a tool for staying close to Nina.

"I want to be of help," I said to Jean-Pierre, but my eyes were still on hers.

"Merry," she said, "you don't have to. No one understands more about what you've been through than JP and me."

"I want to be of help," I repeated, and now I turned my gaze toward him. "I want to stand up for Soroya," I said.

And then didn't Nina, for the second time that evening, sweetly reach out and squeeze my hand?

"I want to stand up for Nina," I added, empowered, pressing her palm back now, pumping it for blood, her blood, my blood, my fortification. I was playing for my audience. I turned to that gloriously handsome faux Frenchman and said, "I want to stand up for myself."

I suppose everyone, from a world-class crime lord to a professional con artist, has her moments of honesty. Even me. This was one of them.

By then we were all emotionally exhausted. Happy, too. We drank some more at that café, and then Nina burst out: "I'm starving."

Jean-Pierre suggested we head to Chez Omar on Rue de Bretagne to revive ourselves. "My God, it's been so intense!" he said. "We need to celebrate our fortuitous meeting. We need sustenance."

"I've never been there before," I said.

"Then I insist," said Jean-Pierre. "It will be on me! I'm so glad that you are willing to help us."

I hoped they remembered that they'd promised to pay me. I thought, This will be great publicity for my autobiography! Then I remembered signing the Rug's papers.

"I'm writing a book," I blurted out.

They stared at me and then at each other.

"I wish I could write," Nina said.

"A book is good," said Jean-Pierre slowly, as if thinking aloud. "We can help you sell it and promote it. We have lots of ties in the publishing industry. At least here in Europe."

"We always need writers at W2," Nina said. "Good writers. I bet Merry is great at this!"

"I signed an NDA," I said.

Again, Nina and Jean-Pierre exchanged a look, Jean-Pierre noticing me noticing them. Was this the inevitable deal-breaker that I should have seen coming?

"No worries, Merry. We can help you with that, too. Now let's go to Omar's. The food is okay, but there's plenty of it, and I, too, am starving. The atmosphere"—he kissed his fingers to the air like a cartoon character—"there is nothing like it in all of Paris. I bet there is nothing like it anywhere. It is very close by, only two or three blocks away. We can stagger over and fill our bellies. We've had so much to drink. You'll love it. It's full of long wooden tables and old funny waiters always in a bad mood."

Which all proved to be true. The tables and the curmudgeonly staff. Somehow, we stumbled through the Marais, and you'll laugh, but when we got to Chez Omar and sat down, the restaurant felt instantly familiar, like déjà vu. It reminded me of those classic Jewish delis in LA, Canter's on Fairfax or Greenblatt's on Sunset, the kind with pickles and coleslaw sitting out all day on the table catching flies, overstuffed menus, and sandwiches so tall you had to partially dismantle them before you could open your mouth wide enough to bite.

Of course, there was nothing Jewish about Chez Omar, it was Arab and French, but how good did that *couscous royal aux sept légumes* taste, the vegetables still firm in a rich, aromatic sauce—I could detect paprika, turmeric, ginger, black pepper, saffron, cinnamon, and cardamom—the tiny balls of semolina light and fluffy, like rice if it were on a diet. I ate and ate, I couldn't stop. Nina, either.

"I love food," she said. "I'm always hungry."

I felt like I hadn't eaten a real meal in years, probably because I hadn't. All the while, Nina passed me bread and Jean-Pierre poured me wine. Bread and wine! What could be better? I dipped the former into the latter after watching a middle-aged man do the same at another table—heaven! As for Nina and Jean-Pierre, we talked and talked about what I could do for them and vice versa. Was I willing to go public? They'd love for me to speak at their next board meeting in Amsterdam! Also, they had a production team offering to work pro bono on some PSAs. Was that kind of work of interest? (Hell yeah, I thought, if W2 was willing to pay me!) What else? They were certain they could help find a publisher for my book. I was a sympathetic public figure, see, and I had a story to tell, which was exactly what they needed. It all sounded pretty great to me, but I tried to play it cool and said I'd think stuff over. I had that pesky NDA to deal with . . . Voilà! They had a crew of top-notch volunteer lawyers. If anyone could outmaneuver it, these guys could, Jean-Pierre insisted. Could I get him a copy?

Sure, I said. You betcha!

Worse comes to worst, there was a wealthy donor he wagered would pay back the $150 grand for me—she'd done it before, several times, for other girls in my position. This lady didn't believe in "muzzling" anyone and was a former model married to a very famous basketball star with deep pockets. If I had to return the money, it would still be a drop in the bucket against my future sales, and this new kind of respectable publicity would do a great deal to get the Rug's fatwa rescinded. It even might revitalize my career. I'd be buying my own freedom.

"Tell us, what's in the book?" Nina asked. Her expression was so greedy she couldn't seem to contain herself; gleefully, she leaned over and snatched a cookie off a giant platter left unattended on another table—it was piled high with multicolored Middle Eastern sweets—and crammed it in her mouth. There were sugary sparkles on her lips and golden crumbs blowing out when she breathed. We all burst out laughing.

Jean-Pierre said, "*Chou,* you could have waited until dessert was served." He looked over where the drinks were being made—maybe he wanted another round? "Omar!" he called out.

An older man with a head of thick gray-and-black curls looked up from his proprietary seat at the bar.

"*Alo,* Omar." Jean-Pierre's voice carried, buoyed by the frantic wave of his hands. Reluctantly, holding tight to his cocktail, said "Omar" came over, and in French Jean-Pierre regaled him with the story of our cookie thief. Did that man laugh! His belly shook beneath his white collared short-sleeved shirt. Was the story all that funny? Or was "Omar" already so many sheets to the wind? Jean-Pierre asked him what he was drinking. *"Un Maghreb mule,"* "Omar" said. This time we all laughed along with him.

Or perhaps "Omar" was that mirthful because he wasn't the real Omar of Chez Omar, who at that point in time was quite dead. Although it was of course possible that our "Omar's" name was also Omar, or Oscar, or something that made him think Jean-Pierre was calling out to him specifically. I mean, his name also could have been Roger, pronounced the French way, *Roe-jay,* or Arthur, pronounced *Ar-tur,* and he was responding only because of Jean-Pierre's friendly hand gestures. Who knows? Maybe "Omar" was terminally polite or terribly lonely or just game. What I do know is that the real Omar had already kissed the stony face of God some years before. I learned this much from a Where's Waldo? hunt of the involved players in the months that followed, a tortured twisting-in-the-whirlwind time that could only be cured by a psychotropic straitjacket. It robbed me of any capacities I might have had left, and all I could do was google. I'd traced real Omar to an article about his daughter, who had opened a Bar Omar in Brooklyn in her father's honor. The restaurant itself didn't last long.

Whatever, whoever, this secret agent man actually 'was, he played the part of Omar goofily and, I must admit, kindly. He

promised Nina as many cookies as she wanted for dessert, before
toddling back over to the bar.

We were all pretty giddy that night, the three of us getting
exactly what we wanted. Nina had a train back home to catch in
the morning, but she said she would return to Paris the following
Friday. We made a date then for dinner so that I could hand over
my pages—I'd told them no way I'd pass any along until they were
sufficiently tidied up. Secretly I knew I had a megaton of work
to do! Plus, I didn't want anything confidential flying across the
porous bands of the internet. It was far too dangerous. No email,
encrypted or not. Nothing that could wing those hard-fought-
for chapters into enemy hands. Ha, ha. Now you are laughing. I
would, too, if I were you.

I said, "I want to use the week to fix it. I really want you guys to
like it."

Jean-Pierre offered the use of his apartment for our next
meeting. He lived in the sixth arrondissement, not far from Les
Deux Magots—"Hemingway's favorite. Hemingway was an American writer just like our Merry!"—he stressed this to make me
feel good, I suppose. It worked! He also promised us a *grand aioli:*
cold poached fish and vegetables with a delicious garlicky dipping sauce. When he described it, again he kissed his own fingers
to the air. Oy. This Israeli with a French Canadian mother who
taught him English, which accounted for the accent. (I was such a
dupe.) I learned that much from *The Daily Beast* after many moons
had passed, when the docs cut me back on my meds enough to be
able to read and interest in the Rug was at an all-time peak. But at
the time, that summer, I was feeling good. "We three will go over
the pages together," Jean-Pierre said, weaving his web, coaxing
me to land pads-first on its sticky, silky threads. "I'll have plenty
of rosé to drink and beautiful white peaches. A perfect summer
meal."

We parted sliding around on his sappiness. Comrades in arms, me already counting the seconds until I saw them both again. My friends! I had friends! Friends with access to money! Jean-Pierre, that gentleman, took the check. He held open the door to the restaurant, and Nina and I stumbled through it out into the hot summer air. He offered to walk me home, but I declined. I was flying so high. I wanted to be able to skip down the street if I was so inclined, I wanted to leap and leap! He then offered to escort Nina back to her hotel and gallantly held out his arm, which she took. For all I know he walked her back and then he went upstairs with her that night. Maybe they spent the whole next week fucking in that leased room, while I was up, day and night, clicking away at my laptop, and in between fucks they were merrily planning my demise. It's possible there wasn't even a hotel. It's possible Nina had her own little flat in Paris. Maybe the powers that be rented it for her. Maybe the people who were paying them both to virtually assassinate me had them staying together to save a dime. Or, conversely, they hated each other. He was gay, and so was she. One of them was married? (She wasn't! She is! I know that much now.) At the time, I knew absolutely nothing.

That next Friday night, after a week of typing, typing, typing, smoking, not eating, whittling my fingers down to a new definition of bony, I found Jean-Pierre's classic Parisian limestone building, tucked away on a short street, Rue de l'Odéon, off Boulevard Saint-Germain, and pressed the door code that I had memorized, that Jean-Pierre had entrusted to me, and then I walked through the pretty little courtyard full of potted plants to the entrance of a back building. There, as instructed, I used the intercom, and he buzzed me in. The hallway was dark—I'd forgotten to press the oblong *lumière* switch, the timed *minuterie* that was there to turn on the light in the doorway when a guest or resident first entered—so I made my way down the long corridor through shadowy dimness. There was a little closet-like elevator with a vintage metal scissor gate at the end near the garbage nook—which smelled of summer fun: beer, wine, and cheese rinds—

and when I opened the lift's door and folded myself inside, it lit up. I pressed the button for French floor five. As I watched each story come and go, I felt like I was growing taller, older, wiser; that I was climbing the staircase of my spine to become a real live adult. Jean-Pierre's door was already open when the elevator finally stopped. Music was playing—Debussy nocturnes, he said later.

When I entered the apartment, Nina was wearing a silvery slip dress, Jean-Pierre his trademark black T-shirt and jeans, making me feel so glad that I was freshly showered and had put on lipstick and mascara. I'd gone back to the Broken Arm during the week and purchased a little black rubber minidress and a pair of very cool high-top sneakers—I was confident in the moment that I looked really good. Already the two of them were laughing. Jean-Pierre led me into the living room, where the atelier windows were wide open and long lace curtains were being gently blown by some charmed cooling breeze. There was a bottle of pink Veuve Clicquot on ice. Nina and Jean-Pierre were already imbibing *coupes de champagnes*.

"Madame Merry," said Jean-Pierre, as he graciously poured one for me.

"Merry, like Christmas." Nina beckoned, and then she and I sunk into the fat pillows of his overstuffed white sofa and clinked our glasses. The champagne was perfectly chilled, and the bubbles were soft, the liquid rose pink, and for a moment I thought, This is what heroin would taste like if it effervesced into a drink. We sipped, as Nina ate the warm nuts Jean-Pierre had laid out in a small porcelain bowl on his low, black-lacquered coffee table, her long, beautiful fingers constantly reaching. "My, my," she said, somewhat surprised, staring at me. "You are simply dazzling." Then, as if brought down to earth by some internal force of gravity: "Oh dear, I'm eating them all again," and passed the bowl over to me.

I tasted one, a salted roasted hazelnut, and between the earthiness like bone and the salinity of the sea, I was as overcome by its inherent nuttiness as if I were tripping on LSD.

"Try the *gougères*," said Nina. "You'll see God," she promised.

Instinctively she knew that my senses had been altered and that for once my own chemistry, plus some of that fancy bubbly and her seemingly earnest flattery, was taking me exactly where I wanted to be. Said *gougères* were also laid out attractively on the coffee table; Nina picked up the plate and offered the cheesy puffs to me. I took one, a soufflé-like cloud of a warm cookie, and bit in, just as Jean-Pierre retreated through a pair of glass French doors into the dining area and then headed back into the kitchen. As it melted, the pastry, light as air, filled my mouth with what felt like a scented breeze. Never in my life had I tasted anything as delicious.

"I see him, I see him," I said.

Jean-Pierre called out to us: "Who do you see? Me?"

"No," I whispered, "God." And then some of my saliva spilled a little out of my mouth, which pitched Nina into hysterics as she handed me a napkin.

"Not you," Nina hollered back, laughing, curled up on the couch. "God, she's seeing God."

I threw a pillow at her.

"She's having a mystical experi—"

Since that didn't shut her up, I picked up another pillow, and giggling, she put up her hands as I pressed it gently toward her face. We were sort of wrestling by then, laughing and throwing pillows and squealing like a pair of preteens at a sleepover party, when Jean-Pierre came back into the room.

"Tsk, tsk," he said. "I can't leave you two alone for even a minute."

I sat up then and straightened my dress. "It's just that it all tastes so good," I said.

"Mm-hmm," said Nina, as she picked up another *gougère* and popped it in her mouth.

"If you eat all that you won't have room for my splendid feast."

Jean-Pierre was pretending to scold, but I sensed that he was pissed. At the moment, I wondered if he was feeling competitive. It was hard to tell what he might want from Nina or from me. When I'd mentioned my long-ago threesomes in Woody Creek, he hadn't registered a beat. Most straight men would. Maybe he was just cool or gay. Or European.

"Don't be mad," said Nina.

"Well, I've finished setting the table," he said. "Come, come, chop-chop, dinner is served, it's time to eat."

Nina got up and clutched the champagne bucket proprietarily to her chest, and still laughing, she danced it like a partner to the table. She refilled his glass, and when he sat down, she ran her fingers through his blue-black curly hair and kissed him on the cheek.

"The table is beautiful, *mon cher,*" said Nina. "Stop pouting."

As soon as he took a sip, he seemed revivified. "Who's pouting?" he said, as her hand caressed his stubbled cheek.

It had been a long time since I'd had sex with anybody or had even felt like it, probably the longest it had been since before the very beginning. I realized with a start that I was up for anything. So, I joined them by sitting down at the long table, which was dressed in white linen. Nina sat across from me and tried to pour more champagne into her own glass, but the bottle was empty. She made such a silly sad face, all three of us had to laugh again. The ambiance once again turning to joyful esprit.

"No worries," said Jean-Pierre, "I am ready for you."

It was then that I saw the chilled wine in a standing silver bucket, wrapped in a matching linen napkin. He leaned over, and as I watched him pour that beautiful rosé from Provence into our waiting wineglasses, just as he had promised—the bottle was wet and phallic and glistening, the napkin soaking up its tears of condensation—I wondered if there was anything I could do to bring back that sexy feeling that had rapidly arisen and then even more rapidly escaped me. I was definitely not in the mood to be entered.

"I love that song," I said out loud.

Sometimes my neural synapses make the strangest connections.

"Pardon?" said Jean-Pierre. "What song?"

"You can penetrate any place you go," I sang.

Jean-Pierre still seemed confused.

Nina looked at me mischievously. "You mean the Beatles song?" she said.

Then we both broke out into the chorus: *"All I want is you."*

Laughing and shaking his head, Jean-Pierre said, "The onion galette will get cold, girls. Come on. *Bon appétit!*"

And like that, the crosscurrents of confusing impulses and uncertainty that often disordered and perplexed me passed.

I was hungry.

Boy, did we eat. First that warm little tartlet, then the *grand aioli,* followed by a light, luscious green salad and some wonderful cheese—Camembert aged in calvados, an intense Roquefort, and a Comté surrounded by more of those toasted hazelnuts and slices of tamarind gelée. For dessert, as promised, he served perfect white peaches, their flesh so juicy and pearly, they reminded me of the aril in lychees, food for a fairy princess ballerina, dissolving weightlessly in my mouth.

When the coffee came out, Jean-Pierre gave me a stern look. "Now, Merry, I never took you for a tease."

I must have registered uncertainty, because Nina broke in: "The book, the excerpt, the two of us are very excited to read."

So, I got up and walked back to the couch, conscious of their eyes following me, and reached into my bag and pulled out a single copy of all of my now seventy-five precious pages.

From the dining room, I heard Nina gasp at the sight of it.

It was the story of me, of me and the Rug.

And me!

And what he'd done to me!

Plus, what every other fucking piece-of-shit man had done to me, too. And all the rumors I'd heard about the Rug and other women. Suffice it to say, I didn't hold back.

She called out, "Do you have a picture of him? So I can send hate vibes his way while I'm reading?"

"I have a picture of us together on my phone," I said. I reached back into my bag and pulled that out, too.

I hugged both to my chest and, copying her little dance with the champagne, brought them back to the table. With a flourish and a bow, I placed the manuscript squarely between them on the dining room table.

They gave me a round of applause.

They had studied me, see. They knew exactly what I needed.

"Me first," said Jean-Pierre.

"No," said Nina. "Me."

Meanwhile, I was scrolling through my photos.

"I made dinner," said Jean-Pierre.

"I discovered her," said Nina. "You know me, I have to go first, or I'll die of jealousy."

"How about a coin toss, then," said Jean-Pierre. "No one wants you dying."

He reached into his pocket and pulled out a two-euro piece.

"Heads," Nina called.

Jean-Pierre tossed the coin and caught it in the same hand. He looked at it and declared, "It's heads. Of course it is. What else would it be?" He hung his own pretty one in mock defeat.

She held my pages to her heart, just as I had minutes before. From mine to hers, we were communicating through our bodies.

I showed them the photograph: the Rug was sitting at a banquette in that hoity resto out on Wilshire, with me in my strapless red dress, my knees draped over his knees, practically sitting in his lap, laughing into his shoulder. His arms were protectively looped around me, his mouth open in what appeared to be a giant guffaw.

"That's the nastiest-looking animal I've ever seen," Nina said.

"I keep it to remind me of how gullible I was," I said.

"We'll make mincemeat of him, I promise," she said. She held out her hand, and we pinkie-sweared. "I have to go straight home and begin." She stood up with my book in her arms.

Jean-Pierre said, "Only if you vow to get it to me over the weekend."

"I give you my word," said Nina.

This was music to my fledgling writer's ears. I stood up as well. I was following her lead.

"Okay, okay," said Jean-Pierre, "but, Merry, must you go, too?"

"Yes," said Nina. "She must go, too. I'd be too envious of the time you got to spend with her without me." She tugged on my arm, sending a shower of sparks down my spine. "Come on, we'll split a car home."

When the dark sedan Jean-Pierre had ordered for us arrived in front of his building, it was kind of like Nina and I were at a series premiere; it felt that fancy. Jean-Pierre gallantly opened the car door for us, and we ladies slid in. We held hands as the Uber driver ferried us along the charismatic black river, silver that night, like mercury where the lights dribbled down to the water. He was to drop me off first, as my apartment was en route to Nina's hotel. The whole city was sparkling. People were drinking and partying on their balconies, on the footbridges that crossed the Seine, and on the concrete and stone banks below that hemmed the water. There was live music playing everywhere, and as we passed by, I could see flashes of fire near Notre-Dame and Saint-Michel from the jugglers who made their livings busking. When the driver finally pulled over on my street, by my doorway, I spontaneously leaned in and gave Nina a full kiss on the lips. A real one.

It lasted only a moment, but I was sure she kissed me back.

Then she looked up at me like a lover, eyes misted, lips parted, tongue faintly touching her top two teeth, and her hand found its way to my cheek. "You are absolutely adorable," she said, holding it there.

I almost died then, living through that moment. I mean, I wish I had. It would have guaranteed me a perfect ending.

"Thank you, dearest Merry," said Nina. "You and your book are going to help women everywhere."

I nodded. I wanted more but was still grateful for her gratitude.

"And thank you for your 'so much courageousness,'" she said, making fun of Jean-Pierre with a wicked little grin and a wink, as if to say, Everything is copacetic between us.

So we weren't lovers, yet, but coconspirators. I'd take that. As long as he was the odd man out.

She went on. "Thank you so much for entertaining the idea of being the face of W2, the beautiful face. We would just adore it if you would be our heroic and valiant spokeswoman."

Then Nina kissed my hand. It left an alchemical shadow. Sometimes in the dark I can still see her lips' dusty-rose imprint glowing against my skin.

"Get a good night's sleep, dearest," she said. "I'll send you a text when we've both read and know exactly how to proceed. I'll be back next week. Same time, same place. JP's for dinner!"

"Okay," I said.

Famous last words. "Okay." Then I got out of the car. By the time I leaped over the piss puddle in front of my door, punched in the door code, and turned to wave goodbye, the Uber and Nina had disappeared.

I'd spent the week before I was to meet Nina and Jean-Pierre shopping for a new dress. Monday night, I received some breathy texts from Jean-Pierre: *these pages are ONLY genius* and the sassier *you literary vixen you!* Around the same time, Nina sent me some longer, poignant emails excerpted here for your reading plea-sure: *As I study your work I now know for the first time in my life what it means to find a true soul mate, someone who feels the way I feel, someone who understands what it's been like to be used and thrown away. You've touched me so profoundly, Merry! I am in awe of your honesty, your talent, your artistry!*

My heart was beating so fast I had to pound my fist to my chest to slow it down.

I wrote back to her right away: *Nina, you can't begin to know how much these kind words mean to me, especially coming from you!*

She typed, *I'm not kind, I'm thankful. This book makes me feel seen!*

You make me feel seen! I said.

I love the person who wrote this book!

(Nina actually put that in an email. I have it in my saved folder. *"I love."*)

Tears in my eyes, I wrote back to her, *I love you too!*

And then I wisely deleted that last line.

I replaced it with *I love this reader*.

Then I made the sign of the cross, forehead to chest, and pressed send.

When a couple of days went by without receiving another response from her, I totally freaked the fuck out. Had I gone too far? Confused the signals? Driven her away? I tried to push my insecurities out of my mind. Yes, *I'd* kissed *her,* but *she'd* kissed *me* back! That line of thinking worked for about fifteen seconds out of every tortured minute—I'm no self-soother. I must have writ-ten around thirty unsent emails, fishing for compliments, beg-ging for forgiveness, when on Thursday midday, while wrapped naked around a bottle of wine in my filthy bed, I finally received a response: *crunch time at work, have just this moment finished these brilliant glorious pages, the book is awesome, sweetie, can't wait for friday night!!!*

I wept with exhaustion and relief. She used the words "brilliant" and "sweetie" about *moi,* you see. If she wasn't into me, no way she'd write "can't wait," with three exclamation marks!!!

With just one measly day left to clean up my act, I decided to use my time readying for our next date. Since I met Nina I'd been letting my hair grow, so now it was the length of an unmown lawn. I bought pretty new underwear—a black bra and panty set—and more makeup of the girly persuasion. That afternoon, I took a bath. I shaved and exfoliated. I powdered and I creamed. I put on a new dress, a simple electric-orange sheath. I donned my fancy sneaks. I painted my face and walked slowly from my apartment over to Jean-Pierre's, stopping to buy flowers and natural wine along the way. A host and hostess gift. When I got to the building, my fingers tap-danced through the first door code, muscle memory, and I practically skipped through the courtyard. I was on cloud nine at the prospect of seeing them both! I tried next to ring their intercom and get buzzed inside the interior building. There was no answer. So, I rang and waited. And then I rang again. I took out my phone. I texted: *hey guys, i'm downstairs!* No response. I started to sweat a little, under my arms and between the tops of my inner thighs. I don't know why I always perspire there, but I could feel the moisture slipping down my legs. At one point, I leaned my head back and called up: "JP, it's me! It's Merry!" Apparently, he couldn't hear me, because there was no answer.

Finally, a pretty little French girl, around fifteen or sixteen, came out the back building's front door in bell-bottom jeans and a flowy tank top, her curly white poodle in her arms. *"Bonsoir,"* I said, as I slipped inside the building behind her, before the door could slam itself shut. I walked down that long hallway once again and took the tiny elevator up to Jean-Pierre's apartment. There was no music this time, no guiding path of light, but just like the week before, the door to his place was open. I walked toward it.

"Hey, guys!" I called out, but when I stepped in the apartment, I saw that most of the furniture was gone, and what was left lived as shapes under sheets, like kids playing ghost. The walls were being painted. No more rose gold, but crisp paper white. There was a ladder standing free form in the foyer and some brushes soaking in plastic buckets. A tarp had been laid down to protect those shimmering wooden floors. It looked like the painters had left for the day and had simply forgotten to lock up.

I took that bottle of *vin blanc* and smashed it against the glass French doors that divided the living room from the dining room. One of the panes shattered along with it. I took my flowers, and I threw them across the tarp. With tears in my eyes, the broken glass looked like diamonds, and the flowers, like wild things growing in a glade; the wine was a shiny precipitation, evening dewdrops.

I left the same way I'd come in, the door still ajar, only this time I took the stairs, no way was I getting back into that little coffin of an elevator. Outside was still a summer night in Paris, although I noted that in one brief week it had begun getting darker earlier. I walked down to the river and then along its banks and across its bridges back to my neighborhood and my apartment. Where else was I going to go? What else was I going to do?

In the frantic days that followed, I rolled around and around on my bed, suicidal, sending and refreshing my email, checking for texts, escaping only to haunt the establishments I had frequented with both of them—Berthillon, Lily of the Valley, Chez Omar—picking up bread at the nearest boulangerie, wine at the wine shop, and drinking the *vin rouge* from the bottle and force-feeding myself the bread in my underwear, layering the sheets with crumbs that stuck to my skin when I spread out on them, in an effort to stave off the inevitable hangovers that kept on coming. In daylight, I took out my clippers, and I buzzed off the sides of soft meadow on my head, leaving the top floppy, like a lesbian's faux-hawk. Why, oh why, had I kissed her? Is that the reason she blew me off? I was so rusty and fucked up when it came to love, maybe I'd misread her.

Finally, I received an email the following Sunday from Nina, saying that there had been a family emergency for her and a pipe leak in the apartment above Jean-Pierre's, which explained the paint job and lack of furniture. They'd gotten their signals crossed—each thought the other had already contacted me. *Merry, how's my favorite genius?* she wrote. *I can't wait to discuss the pages!!!* (Those three exclamation points again. She liked me! She really liked me!) They would be in touch, she said, when things calmed down for them both. This note pacified me for a little while. Like half an hour.

But of course, I never heard from either of them. I'd written and written, sweetly at first, then cajolingly, then angrily, then beggingly, but my texts were eventually blocked, and all my emails bounced back. It sucked so bad in Paris. The pain was intense enough that in due course it entered each and every one of my teeth. The marrow in my bones had melted into liquid fire; my skin itched all over and I scratched it raw wherever my fingernails could reach. I'd look in the mirror and I missed myself. It was as if I'd had plastic surgery. I was unrecognizable; when I slapped my own face, I shouted, "Ugly, ugly!" and "Stupid, stupid cunt! Why did you fucking kiss her? Why didn't you just fuck the other one instead?" I was surprised when my hand left a palm-shaped red welt on the cheek, I'd felt so disembodied then, as if my hand were not my hand, as if I were invisible and weightless and not present physically on any planet—no less Earth, the planet that is our home, the one that you and I live on together. I was completely untethered from myself, a balloon flying higher and farther away, and yet the dreadfulness of the world was all visceral and immediate, utterly unendurable and horrifically consuming. I began to think about going back to Venice Beach. Maybe entering a mental hospital. I could call my mother, ask her which one she'd liked best.

I'd entered hell and I was burning.

It was at that point that I got an email from Matt Anastos, the reporter who wrote the story on Jenna Taylor that had shown up on Nina's FB. He'd written, *Does this woman look familiar?* Embedded in the note was a picture of Nina, wearing a car coat and hat and sunglasses, dashing through the rain in London. She was camouflaged, of course, but I'd know my girl anywhere.

I wrote back, *That's Nina Willis.*

At which point he wrote, *Can you call me?*

As I said, Matt and I were on good terms. During the time the online rags and Page Six were comparing me with a nutjob former Disney star, he'd reached out. We'd talked some on the phone before, but always off the record. I called him at the office, and he immediately picked up. "Meredith, I have reason to believe Nina Willis is really a Bosnian woman living in Israel named Samara Marjanovic, who goes by Smadar Marantz, her Hebrew name."

"Hebrew?" I said. "There's nothing Hebrew about Nina. She's a total 'shiksa goddess.' I mean, take it from one who knows."

"Shiksa goddess." That's what the Rug called me, over breakfast in his hotel suite in Telluride, *before,* when he was pretending to discuss the role. "It's perfect for you," he'd said. "They want to give it to Natalie Portman. I love her. Everyone loves Natalie, but she's a little old now and too Jewy for this picture."

"There's nothing Nina about Nina," said Matt. "I mean, yes, it's a name she uses, Nina Willis, but it's an alias. I know because she contacted me. I did some background on her. She is trying to get information on you. She's read my blog posts."

"On me?" I said. "Why?" She had all the information she needed. "We're friends. I mean ex-friends. I mean we were friends once until she stood me up."

"She stood you up. When?"

"About two weeks ago. I'd given her the manuscript pages of this book I'm writing. Her and this guy." I laughed what I hoped was a sarcastic little laugh. "Ha! I guess they didn't like them as much as they said they did." The "Ha!" was because their rejection really, really hurt. I mean, I'd have bet money they would have loved it! The book was perfect for W2, perfect for all our purposes.

"Jean-Pierre Desjardins?"

"Yeah," I said. "Do you know him?"

Matt sighed a long-distance sigh, far away, across the Atlantic. "Not personally, no, but neither do you. His real name is Martin Klein."

"Martin?"

"Marty. It doesn't matter. You gave them your book?"

"Yes, I gave them my book," I said. "I mean, the parts that are already written. What are you telling me, Matt? You're beginning to scare me."

"She's looking for ways to discredit you. She's trying to prevent the publication. How much did you disclose?"

Disclose? Me? Ms. Discretion? Only the Woody Creek rape, my old girlfriend, the threesomes, my meth preference, the days I dabbled in heroin, the petty crimes and the not-so-petty ones.

And then I thought about what else was in there. Notes for the final scene, me and the Rug. His fleshy tongue between my legs, while he pushed his hand down hard over my mouth to stop my screams, my head banging between the bases of that fancy Telluride toilet and bidet. I remembered my nails skidding on the loose skin on his neck as I tried to reach up to his eyes to scratch them out, but he was so oily and flabby I couldn't seem to find them.

I forgot to keep breathing.

"Meredith, you there?"

I coughed some, trying to catch my wind.

That's when Matt told me about the piece he was working on. It was about a spy agency made up of ex-Mossad. Spooks who'd already served their country, retired or were fired, and now wanted to make real money. Some, I found out later, just couldn't quit the business for whatever reasons . . . Lifestyle? A penchant for diving out of airplanes brandishing an automatic weapon? I could totally relate to that. A team of these guns for hire had been "engaged" by the Rug, Matt said, and his swanky lawyers. Their job: to dig up dirt on me.

"I don't understand. The Mossad? Me? What would the Mossad want with me? I'm not a terrorist."

"Ex-Mossad. This is their second act, and they charge a pretty penny for their expertise. They call themselves Dark Star."

"Dark Star?"

"You know, like the Grateful Dead song. Although I'm sure that's my association, not theirs."

I almost laughed, but I still didn't have the air space inside my lungs. So, I coughed some more. "If they are ex-Mossad"—*cough, cough*—"don't they have to be Jewish? Nina's not Jewish." *Cough.* "She doesn't look Jewish. Her accent sounds German or Dutch or something."

"A lot of Mossad are foreign-born. That Hebrew accent is a dead giveaway."

"Oh," I said. "I see." And at that moment, I did see.

"So, she stood you up?"

"Yes," I said. "They both did. We were supposed to have dinner, but . . ."

"But?" said Matt.

"When I arrived, no one was there."

I had felt like shit that night, but now on the phone with Matt, I felt like an oyster: all belly, no skeleton. Not warm, not cold, structureless and colorless, like something you coughed up. A puddle of pathetic pulp. Like the blubbery blubber balls in the movie *Wall-E;* like one of them on steroids.

"Do you know where I can find them? Are they still in Paris?"

Matt said, "She told me she was in New York. She wants to meet me Tuesday night for drinks. She said she had information on you becoming more and more unglued. She wants me to write an article. She knows I've written about you before."

"Me?" I said. "Unglued? Why would she say that?"

"So your top Google hit will destroy what's left of your reputation and the publisher will cancel your book."

"I don't have a publisher," I said.

"My guess is she wants to stop that step from happening. Stop you from writing it. Stop people from reading it. She didn't tell me that, but she did say she has ideas on how to control the search engines so that whatever I write comes up first. She's still pretending she's a woman's rights advocate. She thinks your unreliability or whatever 'hurts the cause.' I'm quoting her."

"Oh," I said.

"I have to talk to my editor, but I think I'll go," Matt said.

"You mean they're definitely not here in Paris?"

"Meredith, she says she's in New York. More than that, I can't honestly tell you."

This conversation was a lot like the ones I used to have with my mother's doctors. "We hope your mother will improve over time." And: "People with depression often have setbacks." Matt was trying to soften the blow. But I couldn't have taken the whole truth that day. I don't think I can take the whole truth ever, any day. Can you?

Now I let the internet do the talking. The asshole Americans at the ice cream stand, the waitress at Lily of the Valley, Nina and Jean-Pierre, most probably "Omar," even the Uber driver—all of them were Dark Star operatives, none of them ever who they purported to be. Now I knew W2 and its website were all a ruse, and the Facebook entanglements, too; they came down around the time that Nina blocked my texts and emails, except for Joshua's page, still up, still populated by one friend, Tessa, and Tessa still had a sister, Ella, but Ella no longer had Nina on her "friends" list. What the hell was that about? Was Joshua and Nina's relationship ever real, perhaps for a time? Young love? IDK the extent of it even to this day.

When I hung up the phone after speaking with Matt, I called

my manager, Liz. Told her half of my story while hiccuping and making revolting sounds, gulping and crying my eyes out; and eventually she promised to help me out, find me a book agent. Manager Liz was an old softy, hard as nails with a sweet spot for me; I think I reminded her of her late daughter who'd OD'd when she was a sophomore in college back east. Manager Liz also booked me a flight home to LA the next morning and arranged for a car from the airport to deliver me to my house. When I got there, the cleaning lady was just leaving and all the rooms smelled safe, like ammonia and bleach, like a crime had been committed and the guys in the hazmat suits had come and done their thing. Manager Liz had thought of it all. She even stocked the fridge with local juice flights, fruits, and veggies (celery, pickled green beans, cucumbers, carrots, and prewashed lettuce leaves), so I'd have something healthy on hand to eat, and sucked the money for all these expenses out of my accounts. She had power of attorney.

I've been back for almost a year now, and a lot more shit has gone down, but whatever, you know? I may not have clocked that many hours with Nina in Paris, but from the first moment I saw her, I felt this effortless coupling, some core quality in our DNA, our beaten hearts, our rotten souls. I'd basked in the golden glow of her attentions. Even her rivalrous nature made me feel that I was worthy.

But then she dumped me.

My destruction was simply the précis of her job description.

O callous bitch. You were my sister. My sister!

How could my sister do this to me?

Naturally, I've got some ideas. But I'm a very private person and I'm not quite ready to talk yet.

Part
Two

D o you live in a beautiful city?

Does a river run through it?

At night, do its pretty bridges light up like brace-lets encircling the emerald waters' long, sinuous arm?

Is it possible that these crossways are low-slung? Some made of stone and gypsum? In case of snowmelt, were a few built with "relieving open-ings" set between their pillars to stave off cyclical flash floods? Do these holes in the walls look out upon you and a couple of desultory fishermen like a centuries-old witness with a pair of panoptical eyes?

Is your city surrounded by five thickly forested green mountains? Are they perfect for alpine sports? If a competitive skier took a chairlift up one of those Olympian cloud-capped ranges, would the roofs of the buildings below undulate in waves of red clay tile? Is it likely that the people left behind in the valley might seem to scurry like insects and

drive around in minuscule toy cars? After landing in the bil-
lowy heaven of a snowy peak, could it occur to this athlete, What
a perfect sniper's lair—perversely for her, as it would be for any
of us, of course!—and out of the sky blue, because aside from her
enormous physical gifts, she thinks of herself as "decent" and "a
good person"? Imagining and doing are two separate things. We
all know that's true. So, it's natural that her frightening thoughts
instantly turn to one deity or another, a quick prayer, perhaps a
form of genuflection, to cleanse the soul and psyche, to beg for
forgiveness and also for luck, as she readies herself for what she
has long been building toward: a medal-earning, free-flying,
breakneck plunge.

In this city, maybe your city, are some of the streets dark and
narrow? Like Odessa's, perhaps, or Via dei Cappellari off Campo
de' Fiori in Rome, or the long, dank alleys of Ankara, smelling
of frankincense, mint, coffee, and the ubiquitous cologne that
passes from hand to hand as hygiene, water and soap? Is the
municipal map so complex and rich and crazy making, reflect-
ing epochs of exotic and opposing architectural approaches,
disputatious city planners, the powerless and the powerful, that
there are also wide boulevards that used to be filled with open-
air markets selling vast arrays of sturdy fruit—oranges, apples,
grapes, and pomegranates—fish, smoked meats, jellied sweets,
layered pastries soaked in syrup and honey, the best sticky with
nuts? Plus, dry goods and trinkets! Badges and medals, ski shoes
and refrigerator magnets, premade wedding bouquets of reliably
wilting roses. Are there myriad cafés and beer halls and hookah
bars in your city? Shitty modular housing? Is it "Soviet style"?
Also, magnificent municipal buildings that would make anyone
seduced by Belgrade or Vienna or Zagreb feel instantly weak-
kneed and delightfully at home?

Is the sky full of minarets, like ballerinas frozen mid-spin on
point, church spires yearning to reach closer to God, and cocktail
ring bauble-like oxidized green domes? Are there cathedrals?

Mosques? Does a single resilient synagogue still sit stubbornly on the horizon like an eternal flame marking the massacre of a once fertile and vibrant society? On the High Holy Days, if and only if there is a full male minyan, which is rare these days, might the rabbi recite the liturgy not in Hebrew but in Ladino?

Could your city be Jerusalem?

Nope. Plenty of Hebrew-speaking rabbis still in Jerusalem.

Could it be like Jerusalem, as there is only one Jerusalem, let's face it—why else would so many die fighting over it, the Temple Mount, the Dome of the Rock, the Church of the Holy Sepulchre?—no matter how many declare it as their own? Although the city of your heart has its own claims to sacredness and epiphany. Bragging rights. Don't they all.

In your hometown, do the faithful of different faiths dwell cheek by jowl? Living together, in such close quarters, do they bubble and froth? Could your city be New York, the famous melting pot that's inherently too cool to melt anything, where the residents cram together thigh to thigh on the subway and the buses, residing sometimes even in the same buildings on the same blocks, inhabiting identical apartments but still functionally apart? Could it be Singapore? São Paulo? Dubai?

Do you love your city? Or do you just not know better? Do you love it "in spite of"? Do you love it spitefully? It's your home. It's only natural to feel spiteful sometimes.

Do you take it for granted? Roil at its costs, the schools, the police, the transportation, garbage collection, taxes? Do the hospitals suck? Do your children play in the park? Do they drink the water? Bathe? Use toilet paper? Turn on the lights? Do they eat? If your children eat, then it's your essential job to feed them. Not only daily but ideally at least three times.

Plus, treats.

Once, at the end of a long summer weekend, did your dearest friends bring you some of the overflowing harvest of homegrown tomatoes they carefully tended at their dacha in the hills, the fruit sweet from the sun, skin splitting from swelling flesh, bubbling juices, and leave them in a basket with fresh bakery bread on your doorstep? Did this simple act of kindness warm your heart? Because for ten years the two families who resided next door to each other lived like one.

What pointless questions! Like a test. Boring maybe. A total waste of time. Except, true story: even if you only once took out your psychic #2 pencil and checked off a single imaginary box, then you, too, can lose your beautiful life.

Sometimes it happens overnight. Like the Greek city of Helike that simply sunk, *blerp,* into the earth. In Berlin, first the barbed wire was laid down and then the wall went up, two walls, if you want to be exact, separated by the "death strip." You, however, are brave and intrepid, the type to build a tunnel underneath this ribbon of expiry, with its booby traps and sharpshooters and trip-wire machine guns, to rescue your family and friends, carry your wife on your back through the muck and darkness safely to the other side. Hiroshima. (You were busy fighting in the Pacific.) Nagasaki. (Your uncle lives in Fukushima. You are a good relative; surely, you'd have been visiting with him at the time.) Most likely you wouldn't have been in that nuclear theater anyway. You've never lived in Nagasaki. You're not even Japanese. My God, man. You weren't even born yet!

But when it is not only combatants against citizens that destroy a city but God against the world—Lisbon, San Francisco, Pompeii, Sodom and Gomorrah—that's some scary shit. You, however, can run faster than God. If you look hard enough, you can distance yourself from almost anything that might threaten someone else.

So, it was a shock when the streets of your city became assassins' alleys overnight, the limestone of the public offices pockmarked by bullets, housing projects crumbled under mortar fire, centuries-old red-roofed homes turned to rubble and dust. The library, crown jewel of all civilizations, a blazing lantern of burning books. You'd watched with your neighbor of ten years, the one with the dacha in the country, in the last moments of what you had believed would be a lifetime friendship, sickened by what you'd thought of then as the ultimate desecration.

Before all this craziness began, his children played soccer on the street in front of your building. Often you, your wife, and your young daughter sat on the curb alongside the parents and watched them. Their oldest, Teodor, was the kindest kid you ever knew. He'd gently punt the ball toward your little girl, who would try mightily to kick it back to him. His two sisters would sigh and squeal when her tiny foot missed it completely, and once in a while she fell backward on her bottom.

"It's okay, try again," Teodor would say.

Every time her foot connected to that ball, all of you, grown-ups and children, would rise to your feet and cheer so loud, it was as if your country beat France or Brazil at the Olympics. Now that same neighbor, these dear children's father, was suddenly your enemy, even as once he had been your brother. His family is Orthodox like yours, but not your wife, who is Muslim. Before, you were all so close. Sometimes his children slept at your house so the parents could go out to dinner. "Indulge in a little alone time," your wife would say; she was hungry for so long for babies of her own. The kids called the sleepovers "camping." Your wife was curvy and soft. When you made love her breasts spilled into your hands. It was almost unbearably pleasurable to put your palm on the delicate skin underneath them, where it was warm. She'd tuck all three of the neighbor's kids in at night, in the living room, under quilts passed down in her family, and give them your polyester pillows, the floor too unyielding, she said, for their little heads; "Yours," she'd say, laughing, "is hard as rock."

When the giggling got too loud, she'd leave your arms and reenter the living room, her long, dark hair brushed one hundred strokes each night, her nightgown hand-embroidered by her dead mother at the neckline and at the hem. It was worn thin, close to diaphanous; she looked like an angel.

"Shush, children, if you don't go to sleep, you'll have to go home to your own apartment," she pretended to scold. "And there won't be anything to eat there. Your mama planned that you would be breakfasting here with me."

That was the threat. Next came the wheedling.

"I was going to bake breakfast *kifle* and serve it with honey and Nutella. I also have a little chicken pâté, if any of you don't like sweets." (Here a big smile. What children don't like sweets?) "I was saving it for a special occasion. And what's more special than having all of you here with me?"

The kids settled down then. They squeezed their eyes shut tight. One of the girls pretended to snore.

"Good," your wife said, trying to ease sternness into her voice. "Now. Go. To. Sleep." She said it like that almost every time. A cheerful, staccato proclamation.

You were on the quiet side. Your wife was a little chatty by nature, a blessing, although when you were irritable, not so much. But always she was a creature of kindness. The neighbor, your buddy, he used to stare at her too long. He was not alone in that, but you were proud of your wife's appeal, natural and unadorned; her loveliness radiated from the inside out. When she was happy, she was lit from within. It wasn't that her features were so fine—perhaps her nose a little big, her sweet chin a little small—but when she laughed, wow. Who could blame that guy for appreciating a light like that? He came one day, near the beginning of the fighting, only a few months in, with guns and a backup crew of other neighbors, now thugs, and kicked you out, respectfully of course. The city at this point was divided in two, not only by the river but by ethnicity, the Orthodox like you in the east where all of you had been living together, and the Muslims being forced into a civilian pen in the west, you realized, for target practice. The whole city was under siege. It was hard to tell an enemy from a friend. So why was it a surprise when your neighbor and his gang of criminals knocked on your door before entering your apartment?

"So sorry," he said, shrugging, "but the light's always been better in your place, there's an extra bathroom and closets." As if it were a natural cause of events, as if it were rational. He sent you and your precious family out of your shattered snow globe, but not before he raped her.

"For God's sake," your wife screamed at you, "shut your fucking eyes!" It took two men to hold her down on your marital bed. You kicked and screamed, of course, your face a gluey mask of tears and snot, but others held you back, laughing. Was it an insult or a courtesy that he put on a condom? One had a gun to your head, one to hers, while *his* boy, Teodor the footballer, held your baby; the children watched for a while, saucer-eyed, until he took your little girl into the living room to comfort her as she cried.

After, neither one of you, husband or wife, could look at the other's face. You talked sideways. You didn't hold hands and you didn't touch. She clasped your daughter tightly in her arms, her eyes stunned, although from time to time her lips met the child's forehead, not in a kiss but in an act of reassurance, you supposed, that she could still feel something, the heat of the child's body, the smoothness of her skin. You were kicked to the curb, without resources, but with suitcases. He let you pack suitcases.

"Go ahead," he said, zipping up. "Take your stuff."

You could tear him apart with your bare hands, shred him with your teeth, gouge his eyeballs out with your fingers, gut him with a knife, stuff his balls down his throat. His son gave your daughter a short, sad wave goodbye after she dove out of his arms and into her mother's. Teodor and his father then left your apartment; but the scum that had accompanied them, with their guns and their cigarettes, stayed on. Those animals kept watch as you crammed your belongings into whatever containers you could find, to make sure you didn't go after him.

Later, you and your family crossed over the river to the other side, not knowing where to go, who to turn to. You juggled four bags and a huge backpack, while your wife carried two rapidly stuffed laundry sacks, their cords twisting across her left arm and shoulder as she walked. The rope burn alone should have stopped her, even though in all that heat she was wearing three sweaters and her good winter jacket; at the very least it must have cut off her circulation. But at that point, terror, that soporific, was a numbing anesthetic. What did she throw in those cloth sacks? Toys for the child, photo albums. Sentimental stuff and tampons and toilet paper. Toothpaste and brushes. Whatever she'd found, she'd grabbed with hands that trembled like aspen leaves in the wind. She balanced the baby on her right hip. It was hard not to stagger under the weight of all you two bore. The going was slow. You hopscotched from doorway to doorway, where you huddled, away from the random gunfire, as if attempting to evade a sudden shower. They were aiming for your heads, so you ran like turtles. You needed to think; you were trying to strategize. By luck an old office mate from your first law firm saw you all stumbling between the bullets on the street. His name was Bilal.

"Come quick," he called, gesturing while pushing a wheelbarrow full of water jugs toward the entrance of his building.

In one fell swoop your city had been pulled back into the Middle Ages. Electricity, gone. Transportation hubs, shuttered. Gas, intermittent. Who even knew about the phones? Without energy, most places had no water. The first thing they did was blow out the utilities. Assholes. They thought that would quickly bring the people to their knees.

"Think again," Bilal said with spite—it was your country's native fuel. Spite and cigarettes and coffee.

He ushered your family inside.

"Fuck you," he said to nobody, holding his middle finger up to the noxious, violent air.

After he helped you onload your baggage, you helped him maneuver his cart over the front steps into a scuffed-up hallway. Already, team effort. There was an elevator, out of order now, and a staircase. Once inside, the two of you men unloaded the filled containers; they were heavy, maybe because your arms felt like rubber, and you were already sweating like a pig. You'd been carrying all those bags dressed in two coats—it was your wife's idea. "Wear them like a hanger," she spat at you when she'd flung them at your feet. Your back was burning. Exhausted, your wife sunk down to the floor; it was as if she melted onto the scratched and filthy granite, her legs giving up and folding underneath her. She frantically wriggled out of her own weighty outerwear. Your daughter was asleep in the puddle of your wife's skirt, curled like a kitten in her lap.

Bilal had been returning from a cousin's house—they used diesel fuel to pump their well—when you ran into him.

"It's good to see you, man," said Bilal, when you all collapsed inside the lobby.

You nodded your head in agreement, your hands resting on your bent knees, panting like a dog.

"The guy has brains," Bilal said, pointing toward his head. "My cousin and his wife, they've also been collecting rain in a bathtub in their yard."

He reached into his pocket and pulled out a pack of cigarettes. He offered one to you, but you were still catching your breath. He lit up, smoke pouring out of his nostrils.

"I'm going to run some gutters into buckets in the shelled-out apartments," he said, motioning with his elbow up the stairs.

He talked a lot like that. Like you already knew what he was saying, as if you'd been hanging out daily instead of not for years. A presumed intimacy. Other times he spoke as if you were not even there. When he looked up and noticed you, he seemed to find it unremarkable that you'd ended up homeless on his doorstep, the shreds of your life and family scattered like a car crash on the ground. He didn't ask questions but ranted. Was that sensitivity or cluelessness? It occurred to you he might be lonely. Or maybe it was trauma that made him go on and on that way. There was something resolutely boyish about him, unserious, uninvolved, although the skin was starting to hammock under his jawline, and his unshaven black beard was dusted with silver, as if it were winter and, even at forty, he'd turned his face up ecstatically to greet the snow. His cousin was lucky, according to Bilal: his home was next to a brick factory, so they had some physical protection from mortar fire; also, they faced away from the mountains where so many of your former neighbors now took their target practice.

"There's this rumor floating around," Bilal said, and took another long, slow drag. "Have you heard it?"

Wordlessly, you shook your head. You had no fucking idea what he was talking about. You guessed this was his coffee break—why else were you hanging out in the entrance hall? It was as if Bilal had all the time in the world. You didn't. You were afraid of outside. You had to piss; your bladder was full to bursting. Your wife! You hadn't yet even had the chance to try to comfort her. Your daughter was lying spread out like a rag doll on a filthy floor, fast asleep, and you were grateful not to have to deal with her. Bilal had locked the front door with its glass panels behind him. The quaintness and pointlessness of the gesture struck you as absurd, but you had no resources left for even an internal sardonic smile.

He exhaled. "The snipers are charging two convertible marks per bullet to war tourists looking to break the boredom."

"You mean they are now shooting at us for sport?"

Even after this day of days, you could not believe your ears.

Your wife put her head in her hands. She was sobbing. You reached out to touch her shoulder, but she pulled away.

"Don't worry," Bilal said. "You guys can stay here. There are two families living in our basement, but we've got space for more. This place is huge." He flung out his arms. "It used to be a nice building. You can have your own room. It's not much, but at least it will be yours."

"Thank you," you said, from the bottom of your heart. "And, sorry, but I really need to take a leak."

"After me." Bilal picked up one of your bags and a water jug, then led you down the stairs to a small room that your family could hide in.

You offered to take the baby, but your wife wouldn't have it, so you grabbed a couple of sacks instead, trying not to broadcast your worthlessness and incompetence, and followed them.

"Congratulations!" Bilal said, opening the door. It looked like it had once been a storage area; there were still some empty metal cages, places where tenants might have once put boxes of old paperwork and bicycles, but maybe now you could use as closets? Luckily, there was a sliver of grimy eyebrow windows, street level, so there was air. Also, boxes of their new neighbors' stuff— Bilal kicked one toward a corner. "We can pile their shit out in the hallway for them, don't worry, they won't care."

At first you looked at him in surprise—"Congratulations," he'd said. Behind door number one? What was he, a game show host? Then you saw he was smiling broadly at your daughter, blinking sleepily in her mother's arms.

"Wishes come true," said Bilal.

"Thank you," you said. "They do."

"The bathroom's down the hall. Near the staircase. You can use it." He handed you a jug of water.

You must have been sleepwalking, because there you stood, holding it dumbly with two hands.

"So you can flush," Bilal said gently.

Bilal was a good guy, a little weird, maybe, but there was still decency left in his skeleton. Back in the day, you two would go out for beers after work, when neither of you wanted to go home just yet. There was no alcohol allowed in your place, and sometimes you wanted a little distance from your wife, to have fun, get wasted. One night you and Bilal went to a restaurant near the river, drank and smoked outside on the deck.

"It's the baby stuff," you complained. "That's all she can talk about." Why weren't you enough for her? She was far too much for you. Just that morning, you'd found her crying on the couch, and by the time you'd pulled her together, you were late for work.

" 'I can't imagine a happy life without being a mother,' she said. 'If I were you, I would divorce me and marry someone else.'

" 'I don't want to marry someone else,' I said. I said, 'I want to be married to you.' "

"Good move," said Bilal. He kicked back in his chair. "You handled that perfectly."

"She said, 'Why should you live such a barren existence?' And I said, 'I like my life. It isn't barren, we have each other. Besides, it will all be fine, I promise you.' "

"That was the exact right thing to do," Bilal said. He drained his beer. "You want another?"

"Yeah, sure," you said. Why not?

He motioned to the waiter: *Two more.*

"I bet that kept her from squawking," said Bilal.

Yes, you'd told your wife it would all work out to stop the endless anxious chatter, Bilal was right on the money. But also, you believed yourself. You were both healthy and young. A family would come in time. Honestly, you didn't care so much about having kids then anyway. You cared about her. You liked being able to do what you wanted to do when you wanted to do it. Your friends with children were living under house arrest.

Bilal chortled in agreement. "House arrest," he said. "You've got that right."

He had two boys, they played ball inside and broke shit, expensive shit, "like only the expensive shit," he said. "Family heirlooms. Wedding presents."

The beers arrived, carried in by an older man. Bilal lit up.

"See this guy, he's the owner. My friend," he said, pointing to you.

The man put the beers down on your wooden table and the two of you shook hands.

"I love this place," Bilal said.

"Good to see you, B," the guy said. Then he frowned at their table. "Nobody gave you glasses?" He started to walk back across the terrace. "I'll find some nice clean ones inside."

Bilal called after him: "No worries, we're happy to keep drinking out of the bottle."

You put yours against your forehead. It was so cold. The glass felt great. You rolled it across your neck.

"The crap that she likes and I hate"—he took a swig, wiped his mouth with the back of his hand—"they never, ever run into and break."

It took you a second to follow. Again, he was talking about the kids.

"She's got this collection of snails—china, plastic, ceramic. Snails. I mean, why? Why can't the little fuckers just smash them up?"

When the boys were quiet, he and his wife knew it was time to worry. Maybe one had the other in a headlock, or the other one was holding his brother upside down outside the window, and Bilal had to run into their room and smack the hell out of both of them.

"I bet you still have sex," he said. He was lighting up another cigarette.

You nodded. You had sex all the time. She wanted to get pregnant. It was a benefit.

"When the babies come, that's the end of that," said Bilal. He blew smoke rings in the air. "They're the ones she wants to cuddle."

You were free; he was captive. You were jealous of each other, in a friendly way. There should be a word for that, when people are happy for a buddy's good fortune, even when they think they want what the other one's got. But you didn't go out together much after that, even though you were still friends at work. It's hard to watch people eat when you yourself are hungry.

. . .

There were two other families living now in the basement of Bilal's building. They were somehow interrelated and shared the big room, which they subdivided with old sheets slung across a clothesline. There were mattresses made up with real bedding on the floor. A rug. A sofa. A kitchen table. It was almost homey. They were not far from the boiler, which they seemed to use to dry their clothing. There was a bathroom for all of you to share and a huge industrial sink for washing, but that day, no water. One arm of the family used to live in an apartment upstairs on the west side of the building, but it had been hollowed out by a shell. They were always scurrying up to search through the rubble and bring supplies back down. It was their own private junk shop. A pressure cooker turned into an oven. A baby's washtub made a good dish rack. A bicycle up on cinder blocks worked as a half-decent bit of exercise equipment. They were polite but kept to themselves. "Good neighbors," said Bilal.

Like you, they were smokers. A gray cloud contributed to the grottiness of the cement walls.

"Look now." Bilal was bathed in happiness. He chucked your daughter under her chin, making her cry, which made him laugh. "Pretty girl," he said to her. And to you and your wife: "You guys have the family you always wanted," as if you hadn't noticed.

Then you both went upstairs so he could lug his water jugs four flights up and gather some bedding and an old mattress to bring back down, and you could haul the rest of your possessions into the basement. He'd left you another jug of water. So, again you went back up for that, and you crossed paths on the basement stairs, him still cheerfully carrying charity your way. When you joined him once more downstairs, he was already helping to set up a semblance of an apartment, so your wife took your daughter to the bathroom to wash up. She'd even packed soap and towels. As they walked away, that little hand in hers, a puffy ball of dough,

the fingers still dimpled, you remembered the years of empti-
ness and longing. Eventually, like a virus, it infected you as well.
Your wife was so unhappy. She could not conceive, and when she
did, her womb could not keep hold. Again and again the blood
would come, sometimes in clots that whirled around the toilet
trailing membranes as delicate and thin as butterfly wings, your
wife doubled over in agony, her neck sweaty to your touch. Your
brother once suggested it might be nature's way of protesting a
mixed marriage, and you'd slapped him.

Until finally you convinced her to go with you to the Old Church
of Saint Michael the Archangel, even though you were secular. It
was a pretty little sanctuary, hidden behind a stone wall, along the
electric bus line surrounded by flower gardens and a tiny café—
a lovely place for coffee. Upstairs there was a shrine—a local boy
was drowned in the Miljacka river by a resentful stepmother.
He was buried on the land behind the church, and when the body
was exhumed two hundred years later it was miraculously intact.
That's when the congregation brought his remains inside. Once
a week for forty weeks, you and your wife walked hand in hand
around the child's tomb three times, as was the custom; it was
laid out on a raised platform. Then you both crawled underneath
it. When you came out on the other side, there was a shrine. Still
on your knees, you lit a candle and said your silent prayers. It was
a practice that many infertile couples swore by, and you figured
what the hell, it was worth a try. This was several years before
the raid upon your home. This is how you and Lejla created your
daughter, Samara.

While you were in the basement, Bilal lived upstairs on the fourth
floor with his parents and his brother, their apartment facing
east away from the shelling and the snipers, but he still stacked
sandbags up against the outer walls to be safe. His wife and the
boys were in Toronto visiting her parents when the fighting broke

out. Their house was one of the first to be destroyed, so he moved back in with his family. Now he was planning on joining her; he'd just applied for documentation from the government, saying he had business in Slovenia. With papers, he would be able to get through the checkpoints and cross Croatia to Zagreb and then to Ljubljana, where he could fly to Canada. He liked to joke. He called the politicians "the kids." Like, "I can't believe I need the kids' permission to get the fuck out." He called being separated from his family a "vacation." But it was clear that he missed them. Often tears stood in his eyes.

From the beginning he knew something was wrong with your wife. She was so quiet. "You said she couldn't shut up," Bilal remembered. "She's quiet like a little mouse."

You shrugged. "The war," you said.

It was the right answer for anything. No matter what anyone said: "I can't pay my bills." "The war." "My cousin lost his left eye." "The war." "This chocolate tastes like shit." "The war." There had been plenty of problems before the war, but now there was an excuse for everything, for your wife's lack of love.

Bilal's parents still had a piano, and on good weekend days, he'd invite you up to play. As a boy, for a while you had hoped to be a musician, first classical and then rock and roll. You'd switched to guitar and played in a band all through university. The piano upstairs was out of tune, but still, you could bang out whatever hit he'd asked for.

"You're like a human jukebox," Bilal said. " 'Smoke on the Water,' " he called out. He loved that song. "Deep fucking Purple," he shouted, while pouring a glass of rakija for you and a glass of rakija for him. "A fire in the sky!"

You swallowed your shot, clear and blazing, pure alcohol. It warmed your bones even though it wasn't quite yet winter. Thus lubricated, your fingers coaxed that hackneyed hit out of those sagging piano strings. The song was basically four notes, G minor, bluesy, and you turned it into elevator music. That was your special gift: Guns N' Roses, AC/DC, even Metallica—you made heavy metal sound like something out of a doctor's office—while Bilal laughed. When it was time for you to go downstairs, he threw you a bottle of Pipi orange soda.

"For the kid," he said. "It looks like her."

It wasn't exactly true, the hair on the child on the trademark was carroty, while your daughter's was Nordic white, but Pipi wore her mop in pigtails like Samara.

When you brought it downstairs, you were greeted by big smiles. "See, cutie," you said, "your picture is on the bottle."

Samara hugged the plastic in delight.

Your wife told you the illustration was inspired by Pippi Longstocking, a character in a Swedish book for girls.

"I loved that book," she said, her face lighting up. "Pippi was so strong she could lift her horse. She lived with him and a monkey."

It was that smile that broke you. You hadn't seen it in a long time. It was like the ghost of a friend who died.

"I'm so sorry," you said, tears running down your face.

"It was not your fault," she said. "There was nothing you could do. Both of us were helpless."

You took her hand and squeezed it, and she squeezed back. For a while that day you were like normal people.

As time went by, and the shelling continued, below the ground in the cellar you and your family huddled among the rats and the bugs and the pools of dirty water—it was as if the walls themselves were weeping—and because isolation is eventually not good for anyone, often you kept the door to your little room open, your daughter eager to play with the other children. They were all older than she was, so of course she worshipped them.

"Teodor," she said, when she saw any of these new young neighbors running or screaming about. You supposed that was her word for "friend."

The extended family who lived next to you periodically sent their two fastest kids, a nine-year-old boy and a seven-year-old girl, out to the winding breadlines. They were little and quick, so they could scoot in and out of the shadows—smaller targets. The husband spent all day on his ham radio, talking to friends, relatives, trying to get the news.

"You should have seen him before the war," his wife said, when they were first introduced.

"Why?" Lejla had asked.

"Because exactly nothing's changed." The wife laughed. "The rest of us, it's like we were shot out of a rocket into a different life. He was all day at that damn thing anyway. Now he has an excuse."

The wife still sometimes worked. She was a hairstylist—during cease-fires she went out, occasionally customers came to her. "I do everyone's hair here for free," she said, "friends and family special." Lejla had been grateful for the warm welcome.

The other family, holding tight to their ideals about a civil society and the importance of education, risked their lives each day to take their preteen daughters to school. The parents dressed up to go to work: the wife, a departmental secretary, wore makeup, sometimes a skirt; her husband, a professor, donned a jacket and tie. Even though it was hit or miss, day to day, if the students could even show up, his classes went on. One night, the couple attended the war theater underneath the Olympic stadium to see a play performed by candlelight. That wasn't for you. But neither could you stay at home with the wife you could no longer look at, the wife who could no longer look at you. She slept on the mattress with your daughter; you, on top of a tarp and some carpet on the moist ground in the corner, or sometimes on a faux-leather recliner you found abandoned on a cobblestoned street, inviting anyone at all, hunter or hunted, to sit down and kick up his heels. So, when the shelling paused, you'd go to work. Resistance! You believed in reclaiming your life. You needed your salary. You didn't know what else to do. Your great-grandfather was a peasant. He worked at a flour mill. Every day four white horses were harnessed to individual wooden shafts attached to a central major axle. As the animals walked in circles, the spindle ground the wheat. On Sundays they were allowed to play, run free, kick up their heels, take a break; your great-grandfather, too, was allowed on Sundays to rest. "But what did those horses do, smart boy?" he asked. "They just walked around that mill all day anyway, grinding nothing."

Now, you were your great-grandfather's white horse.

Time swam. There were no edges to the days. You'd wait at street corners, kneeling behind cars, an abandoned ambulance, if you were lucky the armor of an UNPROFOR van or truck, with other diligent, distressed office workers, strategizing the right time for a gallop across the pavement. During those suspended-in-air moments of cease-fire, it felt as if you leaped through the intersection, your heart flying behind you, like wings, outside your chest. In your office there were rumors, gossip, shared misery, but often not much to do. Your firm specialized in real estate law—who in their right mind would be buying or selling in a time like this? Even the speculators realized your golden city was a war-torn slum. The Serbs kept up the blockade. They hid in the surrounding hills, continuing to pummel civilians—men, women, children, little old ladies, someone's grandmother—with shells and gunfire. Relief packages came and went. For months, you did not hear the crack of an egg. You made your calls to your brother in Austria with your neighbor's ham radio. Most of your coworkers who stayed on were Muslim like your wife, but there were a few Christians, same as you, including your boss; also, Jews. There were two Jews. Like you, both guys had intermarried.

"I always thought I was Yugoslavian," Adam said, shrugging. He was older, handsome but balding. "The Muslims let us settle here five hundred years ago, without being forced into a ghetto. Where else in Europe can you say that? We owe them our lives. I'm going to run away now?" He paused, as if arguing with himself out loud. "Finally, we've got a genocide that's *not* focused on the people of the Book. A good time to become Jewish!"

It took you a moment to realize he was being funny. Jewish or Balkan humor? You could see no difference. You laughed: "Ha, ha, ha." It was a sour joke.

While everyone else was busy killing each other, the Jews, an afterthought, were initially allowed to exit the city. Some left. Some stayed. Nowhere to go. Or maybe just too stubborn and too angry. During World War II, many Muslims had tried to save their Jewish neighbors from Nazi puppets. Now some of those survivors' children, like Adam, wanted to return the favor. They shared what they had, including medical supplies and food brought in by foreign relief agencies. "Never again," they said. The Jewish adage. "Don't forget us," the local cri de coeur. But the West couldn't forget people it had never thought about in the first place, now could it?

Fifty years before, Lejla's grandparents had hidden a Jewish family in their basement. The mothers of both households had been friends since childhood, and the couples felt like family. In Jerusalem, Lejla's grandfather was one of the first Muslims to have his name engraved on the Wall of the Righteous and a tree planted in his honor in the garden at Yad Vashem. That's what Lejla's mother told her. None of Lejla's relatives had yet to view it in person.

"How did they manage to escape?" you asked.

"Are you looking for ideas?" asked Lejla. Her voice took a bite out of the dank, dark air. "Somehow they made their way to Jerusalem. My mom only told me that story about a million times. A million times, but now I can't even remember." She sighed an old person's sigh. "I guess I took it for granted that she'd keep on telling me."

Lejla's grandfather paid for his heroism with his life. After the other family had found their way to safety, he was arrested and taken to Jasenovac.

"Where he died for his sins," Lejla said. "He was murdered as a young man, before I was born . . . Now we're the ones in the basement."

She shook her head in disbelief.

So, it was good to get away from the house. Every so often, you and your boss would gather together for lunch in his office, share the thin gruel pancakes your wife made out of flour and oil. She rolled them around a piece of rubbery feta wrapped in the nettles you picked in a vacant lot, and if you were lucky and there was power that day, she'd brush the tops with more oil, coil the stuffed dough into snail shapes, and press down on them with an iron you'd found in the storage space, so the cheese would melt. It was a wartime facsimile of your favorite, spinach pie, which was why she made it. She prided herself on how close to the original it looked. It would have broken her heart for you to tell her how awful it tasted. When the UN was giving out rations, or you dared to brave the breadlines, you'd bring a half a loaf and a tin of fish or meat. Your boss, a Serb, always had something on hand to share. He was a big fan of potatoes. You wondered if he had his own garden, but you let him do the talking. He used to live with his twin, but when the fighting broke out his brother went up to the hills to fire down on the city. Still, sometimes they talked on the phone. "We were always the most important person in each other's life," your boss said. Sometimes they still whispered tender mercies, expressions of their undying love and support. "We miss each other," he said with a shrug. Other times their screams overlapped like madmen's, one voice louder than the last. Constantly they fought to show each other the light.

"Don't be a fool," said his look-alike. "They wanted to secede. So, they should go! This is our time. Come join me!"

"What has happened to you?" your boss shouted. "Where is my brother? When did you become an animal?!"

"What happened to you?" his brother retorted. "When did you become a pussy?"

Your boss was preparing a copper pot of coffee for you two to split as he spoke. That was generous of him. It had been a while since anyone besides your wife had presented you with something warm to drink. He had a hot plate on a table in an inner room away from all the windows, and when there was electricity, he boiled the water with ground beans. Before the war he used to present the copper pot and small cups on saucers with a piece of Turkish delight served on a toothpick. Sometimes he simmered milk in a little saucepan to dollop on top, the way it was served in cafés, with a tiny matching bowl for sugar cubes. In your former life, Lejla used to dip one in the coffee and put it in her mouth to sweeten it before each bitter sip. You thought it was so erotic. The red lipstick, her pearly teeth, the white cube, her pink tongue. That day your boss's brew was black and thick, muddy, how you liked it. You both waited for the grounds to settle.

"Once the JNA attacked Slovenia and Croatia, it was clear that they could no longer be trusted. My brother does not care who or what he kills. Hard to believe that under Tito, I was a commander in that same army." He stopped to take a swallow. "Ah," he said. "Not bad."

You brought your cup to your mouth; the thick scalding liquid felt good burning down your throat. Took out your cigarettes and offered one to him. Lit his first, and then you inhaled. The pleasure shuddered throughout your body. It was like a little sexual climax. All of it tasted good.

"Now my brother calls me a traitor. The same man who is shooting from the hills at his own city. His own family.

"Do you think I'm a fool?" your boss asked you.

"I would never call my boss a fool," you said, the intimacy of the moment allowing you to risk speaking your thoughts out loud. "That would be foolish." You could feel yourself smirk. "I'm too smart for that."

Were you trying to be funny? Or bragging? To your boss? You were friendly although not friends. But aside from Bilal, these days you hardly spoke to anyone. Your loneliness leaked from your lips in inappropriate shapes and forms.

"No offense, but your brother sounds like a sociopath!" That sentence came out in a tiny explosion.

For an instance, your boss hauled back like he might hit you. Instead, when your eyes met, the two of you cracked up. You both laughed until you were gasping.

Oh, the curdled comedy of the wounded!

At home in your basement, your daughter never saw the light of day, like a mole rat; you wondered if the darkness affected her eyesight. When a restaurant near your office was blown to bits, you joined the feral crowd, looking for bottles in the back to pilfer. For the first time in your life you stole. Others did, too! You ran away with a case, miraculously intact, and bartered some fine red wine for a kerosene lamp you found at a pop-up market. Under that purloined light, your wife played with your daughter with the doll she'd managed to rescue from your apartment. She read the same book to Samara over and over again, making up new endings and beginnings, eventually new middles, each time as if the slim volume were a magic library of endless stories perfectly suited for a preschooler. Lejla had purposefully saved *Hedgehog's Home* from when she was a child for *her* child; you called that "thinking ahead!" She'd loved it so. Sometimes you listened in as your wife "read" to Samara, but always from afar. As far away as the close basement room would let you go. Inches were miles. At the sound of mortar fire, in the beginning, before she got used to bangs and screams and the thunder of footsteps thudding, Samara would burrow her face between your wife's breasts as if she wanted to crawl back inside her. Even after Samara no longer seemed to flinch at these heart-stopping crashes and reverberations, the two of them were forever entwined; you could not have peeled mother and daughter apart if you wanted to. And you didn't want to. Because then they would look at you.

In the past, you two fought. About money. Lejla liked clothes.

Shoes. Especially shoes. She prayed five times a day, which you found cumbersome and sometimes irritating. What if you were taking a walk together? Having a fine old time. Or you were in a hurry? Still, those pretty shoes came off. Her little stocking feet, too small for her curvy body. As part of the ritual she washed her hands. Her palm was always so cool when she slipped it back into yours. You were lucky that in your beautiful city, mosques were a dime a dozen. At home, she had a small prayer rug by a window angling toward Mecca. Somehow, she'd forgotten it in your mad dash to this basement. These days she and Samara prayed on a towel on top of the tarp.

You irritated her. Once she yelled, "You are the most infuriating man alive! Why, oh why, did I marry you? I could have married anybody I wanted!" You hummed and cracked your knuckles. You smoked like a fiend; your fingers were yellow up to the joint. You did not read poetry, you spent far too much time with your friends, your music. Your socks were always on the floor.

"Throw them in the hamper," she said. "I wash them, I fold them, I place them in your drawer. For God's sakes, just throw them in the hamper!"

Once she'd gotten so fed up she stuffed a pair into your briefcase, and you carried those loose smelly socks back and forth from the office for a whole week. Back and forth, and you didn't realize what you were doing. That's when she'd said, "They stink to high heaven and you didn't even notice?" She shook her head and laughed at the same time. You fought, sure. Like married couples do.

But now you weren't fighting. You weren't accomplishing much of anything. Except some days you put on your jacket, ran between the bullets, and went to work. Other days you braved the artillery to find food, water, to be a man. There were still streams in the woods at the edge of town. Although you risked your life hiking through them, you hardly cared anymore, anything to get away from that wretched basement. On good days there was snow. You could run outside and scoop it up in buckets before some sniper popped you off. Sometimes you had to dig away from the gore and body parts on the drifts, the aftermath of an earlier attack. It was hard to keep children inside when outside was a snowy fairyland. You could always tell when the crust was stained by kids' blood, it had a distinctive consistency. It hurt to look at, but it didn't deter you from your mission.

Back at home, too often it was so cold inside you needed to light a fire in your neighbors' makeshift stove, just so the frozen slush would melt. Your family wore hilarious arrays of your combined wardrobes—the baby waddled when she walked, her layers were so thick; even in your misery, she evoked laughter. "Like the Michelin Man," your wife said. Mostly they huddled together beneath Bilal's old moth-eaten blankets.

Six months it took. Six months for shock and disbelief and numbness to be worn down to a sharp spike striking again and again at the pulp of your last surviving nerve. Only then did you realize that there was no going back to a world you knew how to stride through, no returning to the habitual progression of recognizable days. Streetcars and cafés. Movies and markets. Summer drives up to medieval Lukomir Village. The mindless meditation of hiking and staring at herds of sheep with tails. Those tiny chimerical A-frame stone houses. Posing for pictures on top of shaggy cliffs, gazing at the pristine gorges at the bottom. The joyous cries of outdoorsy nuts canyoning, swimming, and rappelling below. Picnicking with friends and toasting your own good sense for choosing terra firma. What a blockhead! All that squandered quotidian pleasure was already wiped clean from planet Earth.

It was a shame it took you so long to wise up to the knowledge we should all be raised on from birth: the fact that your good name and education, your profession and your paper money, your singular talent for turning rock-and-roll anthems into elevator music, "like wine into water," Bilal chortled—none of it mattered. Cats liked you. So what? The ladies, too. Before Lejla, you'd been a bit of a rogue. Your mother loved you with all her heart. After she passed, you still used to be able to summon that sensation when you needed it most. Her devotion was death defying. When you had a clan of your own, you were surprised to feel the same way about them as she had felt about you. You'd thought you were unique and deserving—your mother nurtured you on that hokum; long after she'd weaned you, it dribbled out of her breasts and into your mouth. You entitled, spoiled, pathetic bastard.

When you'd proposed to Lejla—near the Latin Bridge, in front of the Gräf & Stift convertible Archduke Ferdinand was riding in when he was assassinated—you'd bent her backward in a Hollywood kiss your brother caught on camera. (It was one of the pictures Lejla "forgot" to grab during the forced exodus from your apartment.) Still, in your mind's eye, when you gazed at that lost reflection, it was obvious you were crazy about her and that you expected to dote on your future family; it was a kind of societal given. Marriage plus children equals unconditional love, or something like that, although most of your previous life all of your relationships had only been *full* of conditions—that's what made them work. A woman had to be smart and sexy, or remarkably pretty; it was a plus if she came from money, made you laugh, sucked your dick without you asking, kept your interest piqued in conversation, knew when to be quiet and when not to. But never had you anticipated the crippling factor of this rapture! The accompanying emotions engulfed and enslaved you. Yet for all that overwhelming attachment, the bottomless barrel of your passions and affinities, your sense of loyalty and duty, there was nothing you could do to defend your wife and child. These conflicting truths, like venomous snakes, writhed mercilessly in your belly, making you hate your family for loving them so painfully and utterly despise yourself.

After all, who but useless you, in the splintered sanctity of your own bedroom, watched toothless and immobilized as your wife was assaulted by the filthy swine that once had been your most honored guest—a man you fed the finest dinners and poured your very best wine—bearing witness, doing nothing. At night, that brutal scene was so vividly etched into your inner lids that you could not rest. You were afraid to sleep and afraid to waken. For a while you'd hoped that your marriage could heal, that you would be able to redeem yourself as a husband and father. Before all of this, you'd taken your family's respect and trust as given, just like the water in your pipes, the paycheck in your pocket, the good food on your table. What a fucking idiot.

After the torment she suffered, your wife was crushed, very thin now, but still bizarrely pretty. That trampled-flower fragility so achingly new to her was oddly alluring; she seemed perpetually frightened, you could scatter her seeds by simply blowing on her. Surely a better man than you would come along, one who actually was capable of taking care of her. You feared you would lose her, and who could blame her? And what if there was no end to this ceaseless violence? Your wife and daughter might get injured, they could starve, or even worse. The unthinkable happened every day in this new world.

So, you went to battle, joining a scruffy crew of untrained volunteers, in their Converse and their black concert tees and logo sweatshirts, a ragtag army made up of your desperate, pissed-off fellow citizens, to fight off the aggressors, your nationalistic former sidekicks. Who was who? Sometimes you weren't so sure. It was hard to tell when the jeans and jackets of warring civilian squads seemed the same and everyone looked familiar. Like escapees from a mental asylum. For a while, your AK-47 had no bullets in it; apparently, you were carrying it around for appearance's sake or for comfort, a grotesque stuffed animal for adults. As for the professionals, even their camo was similar. Sometimes the only way to tell one team from the other, in the cities, in the mountains, was if they shot at you. And even then, it could end up a coin toss. Whoever fired at you, you fired at back. Law of nature. It was chaos, a total fucking shit show. You tried to get word to your family. You were cold. You were hungry. You missed them more than they could fathom. They loved you, too, your wife said over the neighbors' ham, her words garbled by radio static and gulped tears. They prayed for your safety. "Come home," she said. "Darling, come home."

But then your letters and notes stopped arriving. The other soldiers, those returning for a visit or the smart ones who'd gone AWOL, used to slip them under your building's locked front door for your wife. Before Bilal left for Canada, he'd bring these scraps of mail downstairs to your family, and lonely guy, he'd sit down too long for a chat—he was cheering but wearing. Soon, even Bilal was gone. And no matter how many times a day Lejla checked the lobby, there was nothing.

What happened to you?

Where did you go?

The Jewish cemetery was an ideal battlefield. All those fallen and desecrated tombstones, perfect shields for hand-to-hand combat, like a video game on steroids. Were you shot slipping across its blood-slicked weeds? Or were you nearing the airport when you were struck by enemy or friendly fire? Who knows? Does it matter who pulled the trigger? The landing field was under UN control by then, but a fat lot of good that did you. Some guys were planning on digging a tunnel underneath the runway: egress for the frantic and the suffering, an avenue for supplies. When you were young, you took a summer session surveyor's course while you were still in school—you'd already shown an interest in real estate, so wouldn't it be ironic if in the end you were mown down on all sides while trying to volunteer some of your crappy, meager know-how?

Or perhaps you'd had enough. You decided to cut your losses and walk to Vienna, Prague, or Rome. It was hard to decide. You loved Vienna. People said Prague was pretty like Paris, but wasn't your hometown once gorgeous, too? Before its inmates chose self-obliteration. To get to Rome it might make sense to try to swim, but you didn't like to swim, and the water, in winter, is icy cold. If there was a time to embrace your delusions, this was it. So, you made a choice to part the curtains of the actual and step through the glass doors of your daydreams. There were other European municipalities with elegant eggshell charms remarkably not in the midst of battle. Go there. A sympathetic comrade introduced you to a little heroin up your nose, and then over time, when you'd become addicted to the memory of honeyed blankness you'd first felt, your arms ultimately failed you, so you shot up through a lively vein in your right big toe. Smack floated you over the borders and under the crosscurrents of your imagination. Vodka warmed your bones.

Leaving town for the foothills, maybe you got hit by a shell as you crossed the highway. If so, it was more than likely that your blood filled the impressions the metal left in the asphalt, staining those ruts crimson in a pattern of large petals, a gigantic gruesome rose.

Or instead of dying by that now rather commonplace atrocity, while hiking up those same daunting and glorious mountains, did you step on a mine and, in the instant when legs turned to pink mist, think, Oh shit, oh God, oh fuck?

Maybe you survived long enough for the concentration camps to form. Were you tortured? Beaten to death? Buried alive or torched?

Finally, to save what was left of yourself, did you shoot your own head off your neck? Or did someone take pity and cut your throat?

The human body is nothing. So instantly you, my friend, are nothing.

Speak now, ghost!

For ten points, the name of your beautiful city?

Sarajevo. My beautiful city was, is, will always be Sarajevo. Sarajevo, mon amour!

W hen Sammi was forced to think about the war, the memories came in sections. Some were sensorial: the gag-inducing stench of the hall toilet, too many people using it and not enough supplies, no matter how hard all three families tried to keep it tidy. She'd hold her nose and lean forward, burying her face into her mother's knees while Mama reached behind her bottom and wiped her with a dampened cloth. There was that nasty grout-like mold that mysteriously collected beneath her fingernails in the moist basement when there was no spare water for bathing; it was so gross, Sammi shuddered even now when she thought about it.

"Eewy, eewy," she'd say, waving her hands at her mother in disgust. Mama knew what to do to calm her. She used an old hairpin to scrape the gunk free from the nail bed, piling the little crumbs into anthills on a piece of paper that she then shook out over a bag for garbage.

"All gone," said Mama. And like magic, it was.

One memory that was not all gone, but invaded Sammi's dreams throughout the years that followed the siege, was the rude surprise of sunshine on the rare days when mother and daughter emerged from underground out onto the sidewalk, dazzling the little girl to the point of blindness. After so much time spent below street level, even with the kerosene lamp on high, Sammi's pupils were perpetually dilated; lazy from lack of use, they couldn't constrict fast enough to take in the brightness. The first time it happened, she'd been terrified. "Mama," she cried, "I can't open my eyes." Her hands shot straight up into the air, confident her mother would then lift her into her arms, which of course she did. Mama was always by Sammi's side, kissing her eyelids open, shading her daughter's small brow with the visor of her palm. Some mornings even now, Sammi roused to that searing light—"lucid dreaming," a doctor called it. Nightmares were more like it. She often found herself crying out, fighting her way past sleep and into wakeful solvency. If she was loud enough, big girl that she was, her mother would still come rushing to her side to comfort her.

These shards of memory infiltrated Sammi's thoughts. But she had no recollection whatsoever of her father.

Her mother pestered her with pictures. One Sunday over lunch, when Sammi was innocently working on a jigsaw puzzle instead of paying attention to her mother's nattering, Mama got up from the table and walked over to the sideboard to retrieve some family portraits. "See his green eyes," she said, "two emeralds, like yours."

"What's with the funny mustache?" Sammi asked. She'd moved her plate away from the puzzle pieces—it was vintage Spice Girls; a neighbor had given it to her when cleaning closets, and Victoria Beckham still looked human instead of like a Siamese cat—Sammi was trying to avoid dripping tahini on it. She filled the pillowy fresh pita Mama had lightly toasted directly on the burner with a composed salad of humus, falafel, chopped tomatoes and dill from their terrace, and onions from the store, and when some of the food fell out of its warm casing, she caught it in her hand and shoved it in her mouth.

Mama glanced at Sammi's napkin still sitting by her plate, as she held the picture out to her. That glance was like a silent command. Sammi wiped her fingers before taking the framed photo from her mother. She gave it a cursory scan.

Sammi didn't like to look at photos, and she didn't care about the color of her father's eyes. "It's like an eyebrow under his nose." She handed it back over. "The mustache."

Her mother smiled. "You loved it when you were little. He'd give you 'face lace' kisses. He used it to tickle your tummy." She stroked Sammi's father's image, her forefinger against the glass.

Sammi shrugged. "Tickles and face-lace kisses? That doesn't sound like me at all."

"You were just a tiny baby girl. You liked dress-up and make-believe."

"I liked soccer."

"That, too," said her mother, sitting down. She reached out to her own colorful plate, but her fork danced away from the vegetables to the pastes and back to the golden fried fava balls, like a bee at a picnic who could not make up its buzzing mind. "That's what you said you wanted to do when you grew up. Play for the men's football team. We called them the Blues, when we were all still Yugoslavia."

Sammi picked up the remains of her sandwich and squished down for another bite. "How come I wanted to be a soccer player if we never went outside? How did I even know what the game was?" She spoke as she chewed. She quoted her mother in the silly accented voice she used whenever she was making fun of her: " 'It's not like we had television.' I could barely talk then, anyway."

"You had words," Sammi's mother said. "Sweetie, wipe your mouth."

"I had words? I was retarded." Sammi used the back of her hand.

"You were not retarded, Samara. You were quiet. Now use the napkin." Mama sighed. "You were never allowed to be a child."

"If I was 'quiet,' how did you know what I wanted, anyways?" Sammi dabbed theatrically at her face with the cloth.

"Believe me, you've always been capable of making your wishes known."

Sammi glared-smiled at her mother.

Mama smiled back. Then laughed.

"What?" said Sammi. She wiped at her face again. Was there still food on it?

"You'd say, 'Samarala Footballer.' " Mama laughed harder. "You thought it was your last name."

" 'Footballer'?"

"Yes," Mama said.

" 'Samarala'?"

"That's what we called you. You also called yourself 'You,' if you must know. Whenever you saw your own reflection you'd point and say, 'You.' Your father always held you up to shiny surfaces and said, 'Look how pretty *you* are.' You thought 'You' was your name. You'd point to your own face in the glass and say, 'You!' " Mama was really laughing now. She had her hand on her belly. "Once you even said 'You Footballer' when you saw yourself."

Sammi smiled, too. "I told you I was retarded," she said.

Her mother waved her off. "What can I say? You loved soccer. You children played in the basement. We made two nets out of clotheslines and kitchen chairs." Her mother's hands knitted the air. "I sort of weaved them together."

"Hmm," Sammi said. The smile turned into a mouth twist.

"Don't *hmm* me," her mother said, dipping her pita into the humus.

Sammi guessed she was finally ready to eat, but Mama just held it in her hand.

"It worked fine. You loved it. You also loved when you and the older girls put on runway shows."

A flashbulb backlit Sammi's memory bank, a surprisingly pleasant form of detonation, like a string of paparazzi shooting her favorite supermodels. Claudia Schiffer. Linda Evangelista. Kate Moss. She remembered huddling with the bigger girls over fashion magazines in the basement.

"You girls would wrap yourselves up in all the mamas' clothing. The eldest one, she'd borrow my eyebrow pencil and draw a big mole by your nose so you could pretend to be Cindy Crawford. Her mother still had that popular shade, what was it called? The name was so long . . . Almost Lipstick in Black Honey. Ha, ha. Clinique, I think. She wore that one herself."

"Almost Lipstick?"

"You know, not like rouge and not like gloss. Creamy, not slidey."

A glimmer of something red shimmered across the mirror in Samara's mind. "She put some of yours on me, too, right?"

"You begged for it. I had a tube I still kept in my pocketbook. It's not like I went out often, but sometimes I put it on just to cheer myself up. Then I'd kiss you and leave little lip prints on your sweet cheeks."

"I'd smear it all over my face to be more beautiful."

Her mother put down the pita and clapped her hands in delight. "That's right, you remember."

"The big girl was the one who wore the bathing suit and the high heels? With a sash across her chest. Like in a beauty pageant? Miss Sarajevo?" Wraithlike mannequins catwalked through a gauzy haze on the stage of her mind.

Her mother shook her head. "No, that was the little one. Nina. Her mother was from Slovenia. She was killed in the first Markale massacre the very day we left. It was so sad. Those poor people. They got the news while we were saying goodbye to everyone in front of the building. The family had helped us carry our bags upstairs. She was so fast, that one; they were always sending her out to get something. Bread. The rumor of coffee beans, and she'd dash over to the market. We always joked that she would represent us in the next Olympics when the war was over." Sammi's mother dabbed at her eyes with her wrist. "I meant Dalila," she said, trying to recover. "The smart one from the professor's family? A brilliant student, almost a young lady, but she still loved to play with costumes, like a little girl . . ."

Sammi had already stopped listening.

Her mother's voice began to speed up, becoming more animated, trying to reel her daughter back in. "If the radio was working, you'd all march out to some music, swinging your bottoms, you know, the way the models do." Mama stood up and swayed her ample hips. "It was so funny; you girls were so cute. One of the mamas was a hairstylist. She did your hair the best she could, in an updo, you know? You held your head stiff like a queen, although the curls still tumbled out. It almost didn't matter what was on. Pop, Bach, some jingle. You just wanted a working station. And no news, of course. No one wanted news. If not the radio, one of the dads would sing, and the rest of us would join in, we were your backup band! We'd croon that Whitney Houston song—you know, *'And I-yi-yi-yi-yi will always love youuuuuu'*—we were a good audience. You girls would sashay around the apartment, and we would ooh and aah. Dalila talked into a candlestick pretending it was a microphone. She described your outfits like a professional announcer. 'Samara Marjanovic is draped in a sumptuous red leopard-print wraparound frock created by the world-famous fashion designer Dalila Ibrahimović, blah blah blah,' when it was really just her mother's old nightie tied around you Greek-toga style."

Sammi remembered that little girl. The one who'd been blown up. Nina. She was faster than anyone in the house. When she came home with bread it was always so triumphant, like she was carrying the Olympic torch. Who wanted to be reminded of that? The shiny red face, flushed and proud. Sammi had been so jealous of her.

"It's important, Samara, to know where you come from. We lived in a beautiful city. We were a loving, happy family. Your father and I adored you."

If you say so, thought Sammi. But fathers who adore their children don't abandon them for the world's most moronic war. Fathers who adored their children moved them to Germany or Switzerland. They saved them from that shit.

"You are keeping me from my puzzle," Sammi said.

"You are so right, sweetheart. Mama will leave you alone."

"Are you going to eat your lunch?"

Mama had not touched her plate. "Take what you want if you are still hungry."

Other times a fount of memories came bubbling up out of nowhere, or almost nowhere, first one and then another. Sometimes there was a little trigger, like when a stray cat spots a bird in a bush in the park, stalks it, and then a dozen explode up into the sky. During Hanukkah, when Sammi ate *sufganiyot,* greasy jelly-filled doughnuts, after school with her girlfriends, buying more from the bakery to take home to her mother, her thoughts flooded back to the cake Mama made for her birthdays in the basement apartment—with what? Flour, oil, cooled brewed coffee, some-times ground lentils soaked in water in place of real beans if there were none to be had, she remembered that part from the morn-ings. Maybe her mother would sprinkle in some treasured sugar, a little water, and a splash of vinegar. In place of citrus? Sammi didn't know. What else? Why had it tasted so good? Even now, she could feel Mama's velvety sponge on her tongue while her real mouth was filled with eggy, yeasty cake and raspberry preserves. Her arms were linked with three other girls, powdered sugar dusting their sweatshirts and baby breasts, as they walked home from school singing Avril Lavigne—*"That's where she lies / Broken inside"* —at the top of their lungs. She wondered how her mother had done it, no eggs, no milk, no butter, no salt. No chocolate. She could ask what had made it so very delicious when she got home, but that would thrill Mama. It would make her want to talk, about the pleasure she took in baking, about how hard she'd tried to please her dearest daughter. Sammi wanted her mother to be happy, but she couldn't stand hearing about her lost childhood, her stolen father. She couldn't remember either one of them, so what was the difference if any of it happened or not? She was fine.

"You were never allowed to be a little kid," her mother said often, sighing, but this time it was later that night, after home-work, as they lit the candles, her graying dark hair now tied up in a loose and sloppy bun. Sammi was reaching the shammash, the caretaker candle, toward the last taper. She liked the way the tiny wick stood up straighter when it tasted the fire. "I wish I could have given you then what I can give you now."

"Then, now," said Sammi. "You were always the best mama."

Her mother's eyes filled with tears. "I gave up my food so you could eat, but still, you were always hungry." She pointed at their little table for two. It was laden with dishes: latkes, sour cream, baked fish and rice. A big challah stood as a centerpiece. (It was also Shabbat, so there had to be a challah on Mama's table.) And eggplant salad. Sliced tomatoes, cabbage, and feta like in Sarajevo. Spinach pie. Why spinach pie? Because Sammi liked it and it reminded Mama of home.

"It looks yummy," said Sammi, as she took her seat and her mother took hers.

"Thank you, sweetheart," said her mother. "I tried my best; we had some fun."

"It was fine, Mama," said Sammi. "I can't remember any of it anyway."

"You're lucky you're so slender," said her mother. "The way you eat. If I just look at food, it goes straight to my thighs."

Sammi reached for the challah and tore off a hunk. She used her knife to slice a pad of butter and she spread it thickly over the bread.

"You get that part from your father."

What part? The not-fat part? Or the ravenousness, howling void, a famishment that could never be sated? Was he born, too, with a black hole for a stomach?

Remember this? Remember that? Air pie?

" 'Air pie'?"

"Exactly as it sounds. There was no filling. But I made a great crust. Top and bottom. I put dried beans between the layers while it baked so it would keep its shape. We pretended we were eating clouds." Mama was forking some of the fish and rice into her mouth.

Sammi rolled her eyes. "That sounds like you." She plopped some sour cream on her potato pancake. "No apple sauce?"

"Tomorrow."

Her mother was silent for a moment. The lights of the menorah flickered in the wet breeze. The door to the terrace was cracked open. With so much cooking, it had become quite warm in the apartment, even though it was pouring outside. It was the rainy season. It was the seventh night.

"I know," her mother cried out. "Bread in the shape of schnitzel? Seriously, you loved it. I'd pound down stale rolls and then fry them in their own crumbs and serve it with mashed potatoes, like the real thing."

Her mother was trying to stuff Sammi's head full the same way she might stuff a chicken, her hands forcing the gooey dressing inside its rubbery, slick, raw pink gut. Sammi resented this, she preferred her head empty, but her mother had spent all evening defrosting and cooking after a long day of work, so just to satisfy her, Sammi nodded along. "I don't remember that, but I remember the Pipi orange soda." That was a lie. She remembered nothing of that stupid drink, but her mother had told the story so often when she was younger, the loop Mama had implanted in her brain felt like remembering, the same way that real memories recalled over and over again often felt like something she'd made up. What truly happened was almost always hard to know.

Her mother brightened. "You do?"

Sammi the liar nodded yes in response. Someday I will be a world-famous actress, she thought. I can convince anyone of anything.

"You remember Tata brought it down from his friend's apartment? How much the little girl on the bottle looked just like his little girl? That was you. His little girl."

Her mother reached her hand across the table to cup Sammi's cheek in a way that made her think of her father's dead gray hand reaching out, detached from his long-lost grave, but she kept still. She could smell onion on her mother's fingers, from the latkes, the fish, the onions also fried soft for the rice. It was Hanukkah. Everything was oil. She'd bought her mother a present.

"It was like gold, that soda. Such a rare find during the war. You loved it so. You weren't used to sugar then, so it made you dance around with joy. You called it 'happy juice.'"

"No way. You mean I got high from it?" Sammi asked.

"Sugar makes little kids act nuts," Mama said. "You wouldn't let go of the bottle. It was so sticky, and we had to save the water for drinking, but you took it to bed with you anyway. Your curls stuck to it. With that little face on it, plus your hair, it was like a toy doll."

What is it about old people and their bullshit? Sammi stared at her mother. It was so easy to cheer her up. Just play the everything-was-rosy game and pretend and fib and smile a fakey smile. Why couldn't she do this for Mama all the time? But Sammi didn't care for fabricated accounts of a time and place and people she could not remember. She cared only about now and, of course, her future. She wanted to be famous, a celebrity, a model or a movie star, but she'd have to get her teeth fixed first. She wanted to live on Shabazi Street in the fashionable Neve Tzedek neighborhood in a penthouse apartment all her own. People would turn their heads when she walked down the street and say, *That's her! Sammi M! Can I have your autograph?* It was preferable to dismiss all thoughts of when she was little and how much she'd loved the sweet, fizzy soda her mustachioed *"tata"* brought downstairs before he left them. How lucky they all were then to be together! Seriously? What planet did her mother live on? With that stinking sewer down the hall? That sickening moss growing underneath their nails? These days, Sammi's were perfect. Her mother's were, too. Sammi saw to it; she was practiced at manis and pedis from inhaling all the teen magazines, and she performed both weekly for the two of them on lazy Sunday mornings. Recently Mama had been wearing Nuditude, and Sammi liked Sassy Shelly. When Sammi drank orange soda, it was Fanta. Like the other kids, she used it as a mixer with vodka, rum at sleepovers, gin at the bar mitzvah parties. She and her girlfriends were naughty. They'd always go up to the youngest bartender and ask him to spike their drinks. She'd never sip it straight. It left a syrupy coating on her teeth, and after breathing hard through her mouth during all the dancing, at the end of the event sometimes they felt furry.

Her mother's hands flew as she talked, and talk she did, Mama loved to go on and on, she was driving Sammi crazy, but out of the corner of her eye, Sammi could see the candles were burning low, so in not too much time her ordeal would thankfully be over. She wouldn't scream at Mama now, *Shut up,* no matter how much she wanted to, because shortly they would have dessert. Sammi's whole life, it had just been the two of them, Mama and Sammi. "More like sisters," Mama liked to say. It wasn't as if Sammi didn't believe the things Mama told her; it was just that her fairy tales of woe felt like what teachers in school called "propaganda." They were about what happened to another daughter, one who died in the war, running to get bread. But this night was a holiday. Her mother was a good mother. The best! The sooner they finished the dinner, the sooner they could get to the doughnuts.

"Mama," she said, "I remember the birthday cake you used to make me in the basement."

The sentence just popped out of her. Sometimes it was easier to be nice when she wasn't trying.

"What made it taste so good?" Sammi asked. "You barely had anything to make it with. And don't tell me the secret ingredient was love."

Her mother thought for a while. "Maybe one year we had sour cream?" She said it with a question mark, like she didn't know.

"Sour cream? How?" asked Sammi.

"We went to the market," Mama said. "There was enough for the cake, and also for grass soup. Do you remember my famous grass soup?"

Sammi remembered her mother's famous grass soup. Water and grass. They'd venture outside to the lot across the street and sort through the weeds and the rubble. Dandelion greens made a nice peppery salad.

"Your father loved it," said Mama. "Before the war, I made it with chicken and okra and sour cream. Bey's soup, we called it. When he first left to defend the city, you would look for him behind the chair, the door, out in the hall, hoping he would come home. When he didn't, I made the soup to cheer you up."

"Mama, there was only water and grass in that soup," said Sammi. "It wasn't Bey's soup."

"No, not only. Sometimes I put in other things, like corn."

"Corn?" said Sammi. "I don't remember corn."

"From the cans, the rations," said Mama. "Tata loved to nibble on your toes, he called them 'corn niblets.' He'd listen to your little ear because he said it was as pink and pearly as a conch shell. I know you've never been to the beaches in Croatia, but your father loved to dive straight into the cold wet waves after running on the fresh hot sand. Just like you do."

"I do. I do do that," said Sammi. When the beach was hot, she ran so fast her feet barely skimmed the searing surface until she leaped headfirst into the sea. That's why they lived outside of Tel Aviv, so far from Mama's work, but near the water. Also, they were not Orthodox. Sammi liked it better. Less Middle Eastern and more Mediterranean. Tel Aviv was where the cool people lived. It was *her* beautiful city.

"Mama, what did we do for money?" Sammi asked. It just occurred to her. For as long as she could remember, her mother had a good job at an institute for Israeli studies. It was a long commute, but she loved it. She took the bus.

"You know I trained to be a teacher," said Mama. "So, I taught the kids in the basement. Sometimes children from a neighboring building came, too. We used rock to write on the walls instead of chalk when we ran out of paper. Tata's family wired us money. I had some jewelry that I sold. The neighbors shared.

When things got quiet, we would go to the outdoor market. Potatoes, cabbage, to make a stew. Every once and a while there was a cheesemonger—the kind you liked best was called *skorup,* they stuffed the curds into animal-skin sacks to ferment, and the seller would scoop it out directly from the carcass into a glass jar. She also sold sour cream, which she would make the day before, so it was only sometimes available. For your birthday, we got up early in the morning to be one of the first in line. Once we waited all day at the brewery for water, when a grenade exploded."

Sammi remembered that day. They fell to the ground, Mama covered her with her body. There was a little boy behind them with his older brother. "Mommy?" he called out. "Daddy?" He was looking at their mangled corpses. "Are they taking a nap?" The bigger boy said, "Are you kidding? You moron. Mommy's got no face, and Daddy's been cut in half!"

Mama said, "It took me a moment to realize we'd better get out of there. I put my hands over your ears, there was so much screaming, but you were already used to that. You just sat quietly on my hip, your mouth a little O."

Mama stood up and began clearing the plates. Soon Sammi could hear them clattering in the sink. She came back out to the table.

Sammi wondered, What happened to him, that little boy? She sat at the table like an android as Mama carried the serving dishes into the galley kitchen that faced the table, back and forth three times. It was amazing what came out of a workplace so small, what tricks Mama could conjure in that space. Sammi knew she should get up and help her, but she didn't want to.

"I just held you close and ran. Even though we needed them, we left the water jugs behind us." Mama shuddered. "A dog ran by with what looked like part of a man's calf in its mouth."

Mama talked as she leaned over the sink to open a cabinet and bring out the Tupperware. She started to scoop the salads into individual containers.

"I don't know if you remember," she said, but it was difficult for Sammi to hear her in the other room, and it was raining harder then, so that the noise of the downpour snapping on
the air conditioner, especially with the terrace door open, was
drowning Mama out. It sounded like hail, not that Sammi was
listening. She wasn't, she was singing Alanis Morissette in her
head: "Hand in My Pocket." This one was her favorite. She and
her friend Yael sang it earlier in the day as loud as they could,
they just let fly, when they were strolling the streets eating their
doughnuts. Michal was too cool for school and walked ahead of
them. Yael was an easy girl to bully. She wanted other people to be
happy more than she wanted to be happy herself.

Mama didn't seem to notice if Sammi heard her or not, she just
kept at it. "They used to hang colored sheets across the streets so
the snipers couldn't see us and take aim."

I care, but I'm restless / I'm here, but I'm really gone.

Sammi sang her girl Alanis in her head.

Mama put the leftover food away in the fridge. "You were
so little, you thought we were playing. We ran through this big
dark brown sheet with thick swirling white lines on it, and you
grabbed on. I think the white lines made you think it was a game.
You wanted to wear it like a cape." She turned the water on in the
sink. "I called you 'Super Samara,' like in the comic books. I said,
'Next time, Super Samara!' But you wouldn't let go, you were a
baby still, so I tied my scarf around your shoulders and with your
arms like that"—she held her arms out straight in front of her—
"we ran all the way home."

Mama came out with a glass of water. She looked so tired. She
leaned against the doorframe. It was painted white, as was the
door made of slatted white wood always vented open. They never
closed the door to the kitchen because there was no window to the
room; it was like a walk-in closet. Sometimes it was Sammi's job
to take a dry cloth to the narrow planks, where dust collected, but
her mother usually took care of the cleaning by herself.

"Luckily we still had the cheese and the sour cream in my bag. When we got home, I baked that cake for your birthday and made the soup. I'm so glad you remember it, sweetheart."

Finally, her mother drank. She seemed so thirsty. It was like she was sucking the whole salty Dead Sea down her throat, plus the Kinneret.

"Happy Hanukkah, Mama," said Sammi. "I got you a present."

"Really?" said Mama. "For me?"

"Yes, for you," said Sammi. "Silly. Who else is there? It's behind you on the counter. I hid it behind the coffeemaker."

Mama turned around and looked at the counter. From where Sammi was sitting she could see that Mama's hips were really wide and her ass was fat. She hardly ate anything. Maybe at night when Sammi was sleeping, Mama stole some of Sammi's food. No one who was that heavy ate like a tiny bird. Mama put down her glass and picked up the bag of doughnuts, the paper translucent in patches now from the grease, some red jelly smeared across the top from the doughnuts Sammi snarfed with her girlfriends; it looked scabby, like a bloody nose.

"*Uštipci*," said her mother. She said it like it was the greatest gift in the world, that crappy little bag of old fried dough.

"*Sufganiyot*," said Sammi.

"*Sufganiyot*," said Mama. "Perfect, sweetheart." Her eyes were shining. "Perfectly perfect, just like you."

———

Before Lejla was born, there was another war. Always, wars and wars and wars. World War I started in Sarajevo, and during World War II the Nazis occupied the city and placed it under the control of Croatian fascists. The Ustaše rounded up Serbs and Roma and Jews and transported them to concentration camps, where they were systematically slaughtered. Lejla's grandparents had hidden a Jewish family in their basement. The SS had a headquarters located near their local market.

"We could hear those poor people screaming as the Nazis tortured them," Lejla's mother had said, when she was alive and still talking. "We were all scared to death. But there was a long, loving history between both our families, so there was no question that we would take them in."

Lejla's mother's friend had broken her arm while they were jumping rope at school, and Lejla's grandmother had insisted Lejla's mother carry her injured friend's books to and from school until it healed. By the time that one could play tag again, the two were like sisters. (Here in conversation, Lejla's mother would always hold up two fingers, tight, "like that.")

Five hundred years before, during the Inquisition, many Spanish Jews fled to Sarajevo, where it was safe for them to live freely, without being forced into ghettoes, unlike the rest of Europe. Some carried their house keys along with them, in the misbegotten belief that they would soon return to Spain and simply go home. Lejla's grandmother's friends still had their forbears' set; they had been handed down from generation to generation. Once in hiding, their plan was that after the war they would build a lock to fit the keys in a different place.

Lejla's mother said that she remembered as a child their guests had let her hold the original keys once. "We will have a home someday where all of us can live peacefully, God willing, and you all will be our guests," the mother said. As things became more dangerous, the family fled to friends in Vihovići, because it was under Italian rule, but of course that didn't last long, and they all had to flee again, this time hiding in the mountains, the father joining up with the partisans, never to be heard from again. It was all terribly tragic for Lejla's mother, because her own father was arrested after the family had already left—a neighbor had tattled—and he died in the camps. She and her mother took some solace in the news that their dear friends had finally made it to

Israel, although the war had robbed both women of their beloved husbands.

What a long, awful story! Often, Lejla hadn't paid much attention—she was a sensitive girl, it upset her to listen—and whenever she tuned in, she got lost in the names and the places anyway. But what had stuck with her all these many years was that the Israelis had termed her grandfather "righteous among nations," for his bravery in saving this family. It was a big deal for a Muslim. Lejla and her mother had always said they would go to Israel together someday to see in person the tree planted in his name, but they never did: Who had time or money for such a trip? Her mother died far too young anyway, of ovarian cancer, when Lejla was still a teenager. It was all very sad and kind of confusing, when she thought about the Palestinian situation, with the Nakba and keys and its dreadful asymmetries, neighbors robbing neighbors of their homes, as had happened so ruthlessly for Lejla and her own husband. So she was surprised and yet not surprised when, at the prolonged height of this civil war, she was contacted by La Benevolencija, the local Jewish organization, who had made it its business to support Sarajevo's endangered citizens throughout the siege. The call came during the depths of winter, and yet somehow, the group had managed to find her and Samara via their neighbor's ham radio. In the coming days, La Benevolencija was evacuating not only Jews but also Serbs, Muslims, Catholics, Croats, so profound was the Jews' gratitude to the city that had done its best to protect them; although the Nazis had murdered at least ten thousand Jewish citizens—out of the twelve thousand or so who had lived in Sarajevo before that genocide—they were now eager to help anyone escape this fresh hell.

No one could fly in and out of the city, that freedom was long gone, but there had been several bus caravans, and six of those buses were scheduled to leave the following Tuesday from in front of the Old Synagogue. There was space set aside for the Marjanovics on one of them. The Avivi family of Tel Aviv and Haifa—a sister and a brother, now older people, with children and grandchildren of their own—hearing about the atrocities in their native city, had petitioned for Lejla's family's safe passage, and the Israeli government had agreed to press for it. This news brought tears to Lejla's eyes. The idea that someone far away, not family, worried about her and her loved ones brought her to her knees. Avivi. She had not even remembered their last name. She'd thought it was Amoros or maybe Amoras; her mother had said their last name had meant "loved one" in Spanish. The daughter was now Weintraub, Esther Avivi Weintraub, and the son was Jacob. Avivi, she learned later, was a Hebrew translation, although not exactly; it meant "springlike" or "fresh." The new name did not completely make sense, but nothing made sense, so Lejla didn't suffer over it. What she knew was that these Avivis, all strangers to her, had thoroughly embraced their new homeland, and they wanted her family to join them so badly that they'd hounded the Israeli government into action.

"We are only two now," Lejla said. Her neighbor had put the headphones on her ears and had given her his seat, which she could feel through her jeans was still warm. As always, he stayed put at his ham radio day and night, transcribing messages between families and officials on a thick pad he kept on the table next to all that American-made equipment.

Today was only the ninety-nine thousandth time that Lejla was grateful for this man's hobby, although the staticky noise sometimes put her teeth on edge. "How can you hear it through all the shelling?" asked his wife, whenever Lejla had put her fingers in her ears to drown it out.

"Yes, two seats, although it is possible my husband is alive somewhere. We have not heard of him for almost a year."

The man on the radio, the head of security at the Jewish community center, perhaps responding to the tremble in her voice, or just because he was a human being, said, "No worries. Later, you'll sponsor him."

UNPROFOR vehicles would escort the buses to the suburb of Lukavica, and then the convoy would continue on to Makarska, near Split. Normally, this kind of trip took about four hours, but there would be many checkpoints, he said, which would slow them down. "Make sure you bring enough food and water. If you have whiskey or cigarettes, bring those, too. Money. We have to bribe our way through."

"Oh," said Lejla. "Okay."

"Don't worry," he said. "The bus drivers know what they are doing."

When he hung up, her teeth were chattering.

It didn't take long to pack up their stuff—there wasn't much—and they were allowed only a pair of bags, one for each person. Lejla tried not to think about her last hurried move as she began to pack. This time, she left her husband's clothes and shoes, the bedding and towels for him to use upon his return neatly stacked and wrapped in tarp in the old storage cages. She gave the cookware and the rest of the wine in the case he had confessed to having stolen to their neighbors as farewell gifts—she did not drink. She packed clothing for her and Samara, the warm stuff in case it took them a long time to leave the refugee camps in Croatia, and summer things, too, because she'd heard Israel was temperate. Also photographs! A book for her baby that she herself had read as a girl and loved to this day.

The morning of their departure, both couples helped her carry the bags to the sidewalk. Dalila, the eldest child, came as well. She was fond of Samara and took her for a final piggyback ride up the stairs. The plan was for all of them to walk to the synagogue together.

"It's just a few blocks," Lejla had protested.

"We want to wish you a real bon voyage," Dalila's mother had said, the day before when she'd suggested it. It was so kind of them to see Lejla and her little girl off this way. As she exited the building's front door, Lejla wondered, Would she ever set eyes upon them again? Strangers at the start, they'd lived together in that basement now for several years. They'd seen it all and heard it all and pretended politely not to know all the ins and outs of each other's lives, although most of it was hard to miss: the fights, the sex, the breaking of wind, the dysentery, the despair. Lejla had always been careful to close the door to their room at appropriate times, to give the others some privacy. She had often resorted to screaming into a rolled-up blanket while Samara slept.

Now there was promise of an end to all that. The sun was high as the cohabiters stood awkwardly in front of their building. If Lejla was still down in her room angling her gaze up through the grimy windows, she might have been able to see their footwear and their pants legs. She had dressed carefully that morning for the journey in boots and tights and a sweater dress—if they made it out of Bosnia alive, they were to be guests of a foreign country, and she wanted to make a good impression along the way. She'd tied Samara's hair up into a little curly topknot and let her wear her favorite hand-me-down pink sneakers. Samara was still on Dalila's back, swinging her feet in front and cocking her head so she could admire them. Both Lejla and her daughter were wearing their heavy winter jackets even though it was surprisingly warm outside. Lejla had twirled her own hair into a bun downstairs, but in that noonday sun she checked it to make sure it came out okay—she could see her reflection in one of the broken panes on the front door windows—and carefully reapplied her red lipstick. When she turned around, Dalila clapped, Lejla surprised herself by performing a little curtsy, and everyone laughed. Surrounded by friends that way, she felt like she was being seen off to a party or her wedding. She'd worried they might be a bit jealous, but in truth both couples looked happy for her, a single mother with somewhere now to go. And with the Marjanovics gone, there would again be access to that extra room. Already, she'd over-heard Dalila's father calling the fake-leather lounger on her way back from the bathroom the other night.

Now everyone was looking at her expectantly. Lejla was scared but excited, butterfly wings in her belly, firefly sparks in her teeth.

"Thank you all so much!" she said. "I don't know what we would have done without you. Literally, I just don't know." That's when the tears started to flow. "From the moment Bilal took us down to the basement you have all been so kind and generous. And when my husband left . . ."

Here, she broke down. How could she have gone on without them? She had been scared of her own shadow. How had she gone on without him at all?

Dalila's mother hugged her. "Don't cry, Lejlachka, today is a good day. This is good news for you and the baby."

"You are like my sister," Lejla said to the woman, now in tears herself, even though they both knew this was not true, and she handed Lejla her cloth handkerchief. Lejla used it to wipe her eyes and blow her nose, and when she was done, she didn't know what to do with it, so she gave it back to her, and Dalila's mother blew her nose in it, too, and then everybody laughed.

"Oh my God, what time is it?" Lejla asked.

Dalila's father looked at his watch. "A little after noon. I hear there are buses leaving all the time. You want a later one?" He was teasing. Everyone knew it. He picked up Lejla's bags. "Come. We go."

"Yes," said Lejla. She hugged his wife again. "I will miss you."

She hugged Dalila, and when she dipped forward, Samara reached out her arms and Lejla caught her and sat her on her hip and said, "And you, I will not miss, because I will never let you go." She kissed Samara on the nose and smiled at Dalila. "Thank you for always being so patient and kind to her." Impulsively, she reached into her handbag. She pulled out the lipstick tube. "Here, my dear, for you."

The girl was so pleased and surprised.

"Take it. Take it," said Lejla. "Come on, we must go now. It's the perfect color for you."

A woman screamed. There was shouting. Some people started running down their block toward the river.

"What?" shouted the other husband, the one with the ham radio. "What happened?"

"It's the Pijaca Markale," a man shouted. "There's been a shelling! Many dead and injured. Bodies everywhere!"

"Nina," said his wife.

"You don't know," said the husband. "She's so little and quick."

"Nina, my Nina," said the wife. And she was off against the tide, running toward the open-air market. Just like that he was running, too, quickly overtaking her.

"Go," screamed Dalila's father. He was screaming at Lejla. "Go to your bus. Dalila, get inside." He took his wife by the arm. "We must go downstairs, now." He started to usher his family back inside the building. "Safe travels, Lejla," he said over his shoulder. "Call me on the ham when you get where you are going."

The open-air market had been hit by mortar fire. Lejla knew what that looked like. She picked up both bags, with Samara hanging on now across her back, and headed away from the bloodied and the dead toward the synagogue. It was slow going. Fortunately, after about a block, a man carrying his own bag offered to take one of hers, and they hurried on anxiously together.

Lejla's heart was still pounding as they approached the buses. Even as a little girl, she'd always loved to walk by the Ashkenazi synagogue; it was painted a dusty pink, and the building next door was bright green, and the colors had delighted her then and soothed her now. Just blocks away, there was a massacre at the market, and a child she knew and had lived with might or might not have been grievously hurt, but she couldn't think about that at this moment. She needed to find her bus. The streets were lined with well-wishers, families and friends sending their loved ones off. So many tears, so many handkerchiefs. Her companion spotted a buddy in the crowd and waved.

"Good luck," he said. He put down her bag and was gone.

The crowds moved in to fill his space. Some people were standing on the roofs of the low-slung buildings across the way—they were boarded up with metal. What were they used for, Lejla thought, now and before? Her whole life she had walked these streets and had never noticed them. Today was not the day for pondering storefronts; they were completely camouflaged by people in hats and puffer jackets, a long-haired teenage boy sitting on a suitcase in a coat and tie, smoking with some friends. Many of the passengers looked like they were going off to work as they left one building and boarded a bus out front, men with tweed caps on and carrying briefcases, women like her in skirts or slacks; others wore camouflage and jean jackets. Some stood in clusters, some stood in line. Should she and Samara go inside? Who knew what to do? It was a busy scene, but not unpleasant. Did they not know what had just happened at the market? Children weaved between their mothers' legs, chasing each other like kittens, or grabbed on to their waists and held on for dear life. A woman her own age was smoking a cigarette, careful not to drop ash on the toddler in her arms. Lejla saw an old man wave across the street to a younger man standing on a roof as he was helped up the steps of the bus by a nurse in a white coat. She wondered if this woman was an official accompanying him, or perhaps she was his daughter? A moment later, the nurse disembarked and vanished into the crowd. There was an UNPROFOR vehicle in front of the bus that looked like a small tank. The nose of the bus was wrapped in a light blue bunting with white letters on it: AMERICAN JEWISH JOINT DISTRIBUTION COMMITTEE. Of course. The Americans. Always taking credit for something. Where had they been all this time?

"Lejla, now you, too, are turning Jewish?" a man grabbed her elbow. It was Adam, her husband's old friend from the office. He had a checklist in his hand and a duffel bag at his feet. "Turning Jewish" was a wartime expression. The Jews were the only neutral populace left in the city—everyone else had forgotten about them, too busy with killing each other. The Serbs still allowed them to get their mail. She had benefited from this when some Jewish friends smuggled medicine to her for Samara's ear infections.

"We have a place," she said nervously. "We are allowed. On one of the buses. My grandparents hid a family, now they want us to join them in Israel."

"Shh, shh, you don't need to explain, it doesn't matter," Adam said. "I am only joking. I'll help you find your bus." He looked at the checklist in his hand. "I'm sorry about Peter," he added.

"He will join us when he returns from the war," said Lejla. "You will tell him if you see him?"

"Of course," said Adam.

"You work here now?" Lejla said.

"I help Josip out. What can I do? No one can say no to Josip. Now let me see, I can get you and your daughter right on that bus." He indicated to the one that was loading.

"Really? Oh my God," said Lejla. "Thank you."

"Those are your bags?" He pointed at her feet.

"Yes, yes," she said. "But you, too, have things to carry."

"No worries," said Adam. He put the checklist under his arm and picked up her two bags and his duffel. He nodded in the direction of the bus and said, "Follow me."

So Lejla followed. By now Samara was asleep in her arms, which was good news but always made her heavier to hold. Adam weaved his way through the crowd to the driver's side of the bus.

"First things first," he said. He pulled two folders of paper from the duffel and then hoisted them up to the driver through the open window. "Champagne for the generals," he said. He handed the driver the papers. "Documentation for each group. Keep it in different pockets for the different checkpoints, so you don't forget."

The driver nodded. "I know the deal," he said.

"Take good care of this lady," Adam said, showing him Lejla's name on the checklist.

"My pleasure," said the bus driver, nodding at her courteously.

Adam turned to Lejla. "Forty-four checkpoints from here to Split, four armies, warlords, militias—in Bosnia everyone is thirsty." He picked up the bags again and took her to the passenger side of the bus. He climbed the stairs with her stuff while Lejla waited. She guessed it took a moment or two for him to find their seats. When he reemerged, his thinning hair was standing up on end; it appeared that he'd been running his fingers through it. It looked so crazy.

"Want me to carry her?" Adam held out his arms for Samara.

"No, she'll wake up," said Lejla. "When she is a little tired, I am afraid of her."

"Okay," he said. "You are four rows from the rear on the right. The bags are above on the rack." He held her elbow as she climbed onto the bus. "Good luck."

"Thank you," she said. Then when she reached the top stair, she said thank you again over her shoulder, but by that time Adam was gone. "Thank you, too," she said again, nodding to the driver, but he was hanging out the window talking to someone else.

Now there were people in line behind her, so with the toddler in her arms, Lejla walked to the back of the bus. It was only when they sat down and she'd moved Samara into her own seat by the window like a snoozing floppy puppy dog that Lejla realized she still held the lipstick in the fist of her left hand. Poor Dalila! All this time, it had been supporting her daughter's bottom. The hand was so cramped now, she needed to use her other fingers to pry it open. That poor girl! What would become of her now?

Part
Three

I'll admit it, I can be an asshole sometimes.

In flight from Paris to LA, I stashed my red leather billfold—where I kept my euros and various other foreign IDs and bank cards—in a side pocket of my backpack next to my lip balm, tweezers, and magnifying mirror. My plan had been to spend the next twelve hours revitalizing my career by plucking out each and every one of my eyebrow hairs, a blissfully labor-intensive succession of satisfaction-inducing pain. Trichotillomania, the docs call it. Most trichsters pull the hair right out of their scalps, aiming to yank that little white pith with the black ball of root attached. I can still picture my mom's open-mouthed stare whenever she tugged up the whole package in one shot—she had bald patches and bloody scabs all over her head— was it proof her luck was changing? Personally, I find the nerve endings on my face extra zingy, a more gratifying ping of pain. Plus, I'd thought I'd like the look, my forehead as clean and smooth as a baby's butt, signifying my inner purity. Instead, I ended up wasting the entire twelve-hour intercontinental time-hammock in the fetal position on my ultra-classy sky-bed. I only stood, ninja-like, in a black tracksuit, beanie, and matching sunglasses, to go to the loo. For exercise and to prevent blood clots, occasionally I'd prop up on an elbow to flag down a flight attendant so I could order additional mini-bottles of whiskey—waving an arm in the air burns more calories than not waving an arm in the air—and when I actually stood, I swayed (that does, too). Whether the oscillation was from an inborn sense of rhythm, turbulence, or a history of drug abuse, it's hard to tell—time is running out now, and I have more existential problems than the fact that maybe I shouldn't have done so much ayahuasca. Let's just say I was never not in enough control to break my own fall, which I did by bouncing from headrest to headrest.

During my initial trip down the aisle, I aimed for the curtains that separated business from the riffraff in steerage, until a nice, short gay steward turned me around and pointed me toward the fancy bathroom at the front of the cabin, one with upmarket products (Malin + Goetz) and real hand towels (the kind that get laundered and folded), located next to the flight deck. Of course, the airlines lock that shit up, but a hottie pilot was coming out of the cabin just as I approached, to stretch his long, long legs maybe or to urinate in a silver bowl and get a free squirt of expensive hand lotion. From the double take that starstruck boy gave me—damn, didn't I think he'd whip it out—as his antenna went up, his shoulders swelled to fill out his epaulets—it felt like his eyes were commanding me to fall to my knees in front of him. Why do so many guys respond to yours truly that way? This pilot recognized me, I'm sure of it; it might also be that he was a natural-born rapist and smelled vulnerability. My natural scent could be called "eau du easy mark," an odor only vermin can detect, a spicy mélange of paralysis perfume with prior-history-of-abuse essence.

That nice flight attendant had followed behind me the way parents do when a toddler is learning to walk. He and the pilot met eyes over my shoulder, and the latter turned around and went into the cockpit to his captain's seat, locking his door behind him. I had a protector on board! I nodded to thank said short knight before entering the restroom. Suffice it to say, I didn't think twice about leaving my backpack and all my other crap under my airplane-issued duvet. The cabin was a small, well-guarded place, my guy was on duty, and I could see my private lump while entering and exiting the lavatory. Besides, I was lit. All I cared about was making sure my in-flight Dewar's on the rocks kept coming, continually reigniting the Ativan in my bloodstream. I was aiming for a heavy and steady thrum of numbness, near drool, but I didn't want to satisfy anyone—Nina, JP, the Rug—by going out the way so many messed-up rockers and starlets had gone before me. At least not while we were pinned up in the air and Earth spun like a motherfucker beneath us. The tabloids would have a field day. Too undignified an exit.

It wasn't until the plane landed, and I stumbled through customs and into the car Manager Liz had ordered for me, that I turned on my phone—she'd wisely arranged to FedEx all my stuff to the States so that I could avoid the scrum at baggage claim. The LA air was cinder block hot. Somewhere nearby were fires and horses—probably people, too—being hosed down or, worse, being burned to death. The AC was on in the limo, but still I asked the driver, my regular guy, Branimir (a middle-aged one-armed Croat), to open my window, so I could feel the heat sandblasting against my face, hoping it would slap some sense into me after that drunken flight. This was my town, all those low-slung mini-malls, karate-class storefronts, and sushi restaurants. Mile after mile, we passed auto repair shops and taco stands; some joined at the hip by the same ambitious owners. At various crosswalks, sign spinners danced their sweat-soaked ballets, boys and girls in crop tops and short shorts, adept as pizza makers: CONDOS FOR RENT, twirl twirl, CAR WASH, a behind-the-back flip, GIRLS GIRLS GIRLS, foam finger pointing the way to someone's daughter's degradation. Sporadic palm trees lined the streets, the majority tall and giraffish, others bent and dying of thirst, the short ones scaly and thick-middled as old men with spare-tire psoriasis. I had Branimir drive real slow to my house because I wanted to take in all of it. I was home, see. LA was refreshingly fly-by-night, a hodgepodge of ostentation and poverty, temporary structures, most of the buildings inspired solely by the size of the owner's wallet or someone's lack of taste. I'd left a city with a grand plan for one that had held no plans period. Ad-libbed and extemporaneous. More my style.

But as soon as my cell phone powered up, I realized my Twitter account had been locked down tight.

My crime? I'd done a wee bit of tweeting on my way to Charles de Gaulle and in the business-class lounge at the airport. *all little red riding hood wanted was to write her story about how she was __ by the big bad wolf, so he hired foreign spies to stop her   oh what a tiny thing you have she said when he pushed that wizened mushroom in her face   when the woodcutter cut that skinny f—k open how many of his victims fell out of his rotund belly? half of female Hollywood!   end the systematic abuse of women and boycott all his pictures!* Then I posted a photo of the Rug's former offices up on Sunset not far from the Viper Room and Whiskey a Go Go, captioned: *where Satan spent his early years*. If you squinted real hard through your bifocals or blew it up, the address of the building appeared in the corner, and that apparently was against Twitter law. I don't know who snuck that address in there. A fellow traveler, I bet; not me, I swear on a stack of Bibles. I hadn't even noticed it. I'd just been doing my daily friendly neighborhood cyberstalk of the Rug, and it was one of the images that popped up when I googled him so I'd tweeted it.

I pivoted to Instagram.

I kicked away one of my sneakers, yanked off my sock, and tied it around my mouth as if I were being gagged, before taking a selfie in the back seat of the limo. Branimir's eyebrows shot up in the rearview, but smart dude, he said nothing. He was impervious. He'd survived a war and lost two brothers. "Hollywood is for amateurs," he once told me, when we blew a joint together in a parking lot after a particularly bad screening of one of my movies. "Wait until your schoolteacher decapitates your grandmother." Plus, he was used to me. Nothing I could do would faze him one bit. My caption read: *Twitter has locked down my account! Not the idiot-in-chief's! He tweeted about the Kahn family. He advertised Lady G's phone number. But who gets canceled? Just little old me from bumf—k USA. LADIES SCREAM THE TRUTH FOR ME! GIRLFRIENDS BE MY AMPLIFIER!*

One of last year's best supporting actress nominees tweeted: *We've got your back, Meredith!* God bless her knobby clavicle. That old stalwart, Rosanna Arquette, came out for me, too: *Imagine if every woman in this town opened their doors and called the names of their abusers?* And then: *How many of us would shout the same name? #thisisnotawitchhunt*

I DM'd her: *Thank you for your strength! I fucking loved Searching for Debra Winger!*

Even Busy Philipps, who I always thought effing hated me, acted like an ally. I guess because she, too, was raped by a boyfriend at fourteen? It was Nina who told me that horrifying detail, while she was pretending to dream up a new board list for the bogus W2, reeling me in with those fluttering woke angel wings of hers and the shiny goodness of an activist's halo. She'd been emailing me names to see who I could help her "get to": Mira Sorvino, Annabella Sciorra, Salma Hayek, Sarah Polley, and Busy. Thinking about Nina then, I wished with all my might that I could travel the wrong way in time to when I'd first drunk the Kool-Aid, before I knew anything about who she and Jean-Pierre really were or why they were seemingly so into me. I know it sounds counterintuitive and completely cringey, but I would have been happy to embrace my lost innocence.

Now I was guessing she'd just been sussing out whether I was in cahoots with any one of these famous former friends of the Rug. Not lowly me, not then; all I had in common with those girls three weeks before was *him* and his various communicable diseases.

By this point I was typing and scrolling like a maniac. I'd received about a zillion texts and emails since my nighttime *rat-a-tat-tat,* and I was aiming to answer every single one of them. That's when I saw that a stan I didn't know had insta'd me a private message. The image was iconic: a small pyramid of white powder sitting on a shiny black countertop next to a rolled-up hundred-dollar bill. It was captioned: *Meredith you rock (heh heh) but on the plane they found your wallet and your coke.* I looked in my backpack: wallet, check. A Hello Kitty pink plastic one I'd picked up at one of the Paris fleas. Since I have never in my whole drug-addict derelict life done coke—my daddy perforated his septum and it was fucking disgusting—I thought this was just another scare tactic set up by the Rug to convince me I was going crazy, but still it effing bugged me. When we pulled into the driveway in the rear of the house, Mercedes, the cleaning lady, was just pulling out. The dude who'd sold me the place had set up an orange canvas awning that matched the orange roof and casements to make it seem more distinctive. The rest of the building was painted white. I suddenly realized my house looked like a Creamsicle. Sweet! Made me glad to be coming home. I climbed up out of my window to see over the top of the limo and blew Mercy a couple of kisses. Then I slid down into the car seat again, opened the door, got out, and sent Branimir on his way.

"Don't drive wasted," he said. "Call me if you're drinking."

"You got it, Brani," I said, slamming the door behind me and giving him the finger.

No one tells me what to do, even when they're being nice.

My house sits directly on one of the canals, so the back is at the front and vice versa. Almost everyone, from the cannabis delivery guy to a potential producing partner, enters through the rear, on Strongs Drive, which is two-way and narrow. The Grand Canal, man-made, which I face, has no room for cars, just a pretty paved footpath. Different forms of greenery and fencing border the house on one side, and thick, short, bristly bushes keep folks from falling in the drink on the other. On the far shore of the canal is another row of cottages, bungalows, and a bunch of modular monstrosities. Like I said, LA architecture, no rules. I love no rules. There are flowers and cacti and palm trees lining the skinny paths along the estuary, sometimes egrets, herons, multiple streams of ducks. A totally artificial ecosystem. Magical little white bridges link the serene walkways, perfect for harnessing up a Maltipoo or your pet Goldendoodle and going for a stars-are-just-like-us stroll.

From where Branimir dumped me on Strongs, my place looks pretty much like anybody's house, Anywhere, USA, any fucking time, save the orange highlights. The house is blind to the street, and I have curtains. Short ones. Orange. To match. When the ocean wind blows just right, they tease up like a flouncy miniskirt. There's a two-car garage with an automatic door, so it's easy to disappear through the mudroom without being seen, in case of paparazzi. But the real formal entrance faces the Grand Canal and it's out of a storybook, which is why I bought the place. The facade is covered in ivy, a fence surrounds the postage-stamp-sized property, and tall, wild hedges and flowering bushes keep the inner courtyard private. Damn, I waste a lot of water. The only possible way to peek inside would be through the second-story deck, and even that would prove difficult: you'd have to be a cat burglar or Philippe Petit to get up there. I've got the whole place wired anyway. SimpliSafe. I've also got a nice hand-knotted macramé hammock for smoking dope and drinking tea, so it's like my spot. Works for me. I like my solitude.

Near the garbage and recycling bins on Strongs—which Mercedes thoughtfully put out for collection the next morning—there is a narrow alley between my house and the one on the left, which I can walk through to get to the water. I'd neglected to bring my keys with me to Europe, so I needed to enter from the front yard, where there is always an extra set stashed beneath a potted cactus, on a cracked Delft plate I'd brought back whole from Holland. Dirtbag tourists drop their fast-food wrappers in that passageway on their trek to the canals and sometimes there are mice, so I was sweating in that tracksuit and kind of holding my breath as I trotted along the cement—that alley makes me run just about every time, out of fear and often the need to pee, but it spits out into Shangri-La.

Now, as I exploded out on the canal side, on that fraught, hot September afternoon, I saw that my red canoe was still waiting for me, moored as I left her in front of my property, behind a freestanding three-foot-wide white picket fence surrounded by short green bushes. That fence was hilarious. It came with the house, but it looked like I'd stolen it straight from a stage set and plopped it there. I mean anyone can step over it or even just walk around it and climb into the canoe, but there was pure fun silliness in unlatching it—it even came with a little key. When I saw that bright carmine slash, like a lipsticked smile, I smiled back. It was all I could do not to crawl across the pavement and the grass and embrace that dumb, inanimate boat. It looked like a mirage.

All this, and just three blocks from the boardwalk, which God designed with me in mind. There are guys by the beach who for a dollar will inscribe your name on a grain of rice! Between the temporary tattoo artists and the muscle builders, the T-shirt hawkers and the nipple piercers, it's got the low-rent feel of a town fair or rodeo full of con men. I love that shit, the bikers and the vapers, the hustlers and the skaters, the boarders and the runners, the ever-evolving thirst trap of volleyball players, out-of-work actors, and models filling the void of their days with exercise and preening, leather vets selling each other dope from their wheelchairs with their braided beards and their piss bags swinging beneath them golden in the light like packaged auras.

Everything in Venice is so stratified, even the air has its own ROYGBIV; it smells like weed, ass, cotton candy, BO, and coconut oil. I acronymed it WACCBOCO.

It had been thirteen weeks since I'd left for Paris, but from the outside my house looked simply amazing without me there to screw things up. When I bought it, Manager Liz installed a state-of-the-art alarm system, as a few of the houses in the nabe had been burglarized, and I guess she'd wanted to safeguard her investment. That afternoon, I turned it off. Inside, the house smelled mental hospital clean, all bleach and disinfectant. Mercedes had left on the AC, so I kicked off my sneakers and slipped out of my sweats, leaving on my underwear, and pulled off my various tops: a hoodie, wife beater, and a stanky straitjacket of binder. I couldn't wait to shake them loose.

I let the cool air dry my sweaty skin tight as paint as I surveyed my surroundings. Mercedes had left a stick of sage wrapped in red ribbon in a bowl on the kitchen counter, I guess as a present for my homecoming—she and I both believe in evil spirits—so I turned on the gas on my stovetop and lit it like the world's largest spliff. Then I danced around the place to get any last bad juju out. There were magazines spread across the coffee table next to a gigantic fresh fruit basket with a welcome home note from Manager Liz. It said: *Call me when you read this!*

I went into the kitchen and opened the fridge and saw the food Manager Liz had ordered in for me, salads and shakes; the kale bowls layered in mason jars with earth-colored rice and beans looked like sand paintings. I took out two wellness shots (ginger, lemon, and cayenne pepper) and hit them hard, like they were booze, one after the other while sitting at my breakfast bar in my soggy tighty-whities.

"Alexa," I said, "play me some Beyoncé 'Run the World (Girls)'" Alexa did as she was told, and I sang along: *"Girls, we run this mutha (yeah!)"* Then I listened to my phone messages, hopelessly hoping that Nina would be one of them. How totally pathetic! I crossed my fingers and my toes, which meant that it was hard to balance, and I had to hold the phone with my shoulder pressed up into my ear. Manager Liz, asking me again to call her when I got in. Marietta the ex-agent, going on and on. She was like guilt on roller skates! "Meredith, it's me, Marietta. I'm, um, really, really hoping you're okay, no need to return the call, just thinking of you. I hope you're taking good, good care of yourself, baby girl . . . Was Paris amazingly great? Miss you so much! [*sniffle, sniffle*] I understand you just got home, so we can talk another time. It's Marietta. Don't call me."

She handed *me* over to the enemy. Now she was crying crocodile tears? When did she morph into a crazy ex-boyfriend?

Then there was Jilly Waters—still no Nina, no Jean-Pierre—just the Rug's producing partner from Telluride: "Meredith, I have Jilly Waters on the phone." So not exactly Jilly herself, but one of her minions placing the call for her. Hearing from her kind of freaked me out and was a little scary; to tell the truth, my hands began to shake, but mostly I was pissed. I mean, after setting me up at the breakfast meeting ("Eat a scone for me, Meredith, I'm on keto and you're so scrawny") and then leaving me alone with the Rug so that he could fucking rape me, that bitch could not even pick up her own phone? Besides, they'd cast another girl, when Jilly did all but promise me the part! Remember, "You are absolutely perfect for this picture"? I stuck my finger down my throat and pretended I was gagging.

Next: "Meredith, it's Matt Anastos, I'd like to talk to you." This one made the corners of my lips turn up in a smile. Was my journo pal, please God, worried about me? Hope, hope. Pray, pray. Supplication and petition. Then there was a whole bunch of those weird calls from different sotto voce women whispering in Chinese. Also, one from a Roger Norman at the *National Enquirer*. I love the *Enquirer*! And one from a detective at the airport saying that they'd found my wallet, and could I please come by to pick it up at my earliest convenience?

I deleted them all. That bitch Nina hadn't called. My heart sank.

"I have my wallet, people!" I screamed at no one in particular.

I opened the fridge and took out another juice, this one called Goddess of Green, which was the color of moss, consisting of wheatgrass, cucumber, green apple, fennel, pineapple, thyme, and spirulina—mulch that honestly looked like something you scrape from the sides of a fish tank. It was labeled a "boost" and cost an extra three dollars a shot and came in its own little accompanying test tube. I took a gigantic sip from the big bottle and left the mulchy sidecar in the butter compartment to become a future science project. In the freezer, there was a nice cold handle of vodka. I poured about a quarter of it into the remaining juice, shook it up like I was still tending bar, and headed upstairs to drink until I passed out.

Miraculously, I slept through the whole night and even woke up the next morning. Dreamless! I detest dreams. Nightmares were more like it. They have plagued me all my days and nights since I was a teeny-tiny baby. My daddy said that's what drove my mother loony—all my screaming; if I couldn't sleep, no one else for miles around was allowed an ounce of shut-eye. He said, "The thing about you, Merry, is you're miserable and you share." Well, I'll bet you my tummy hurt, and no one bothered to burp me properly. I'll bet you I was lactose intolerant, or I had thrush, or they weren't feeding me enough, or they were feeding me only garbage. I'll bet you my mom was too zoned out on meds to take care of me and that she counted on my not-so-quietly starving to death, while my daddy was out carousing or partying; neither one of them would've mourned my absence. But I do not go quietly! However, that night, the first one home, went just fine, thanks for asking. My head hurt when I woke up, but I was used to that.

I put on my shades and looked around. Mercedes had left a bottle of mineral water and a clean glass by my bedside, like I was staying in a nice hotel, which is what it felt like after that endless flight and all those months in my cruddy Paris apartment. The sheets were freshly laundered, soft, dove gray, made in Brooklyn, and the pill case next to the bed was turquoise and silver, a gift from Marietta during more hopeful days, outfitted with Advil, like a candy dish of mini orange M&M'S. I took a handful, sipped, and swallowed. Then I stepped out of my underwear, which were so loose by then they basically fell like brisket off the bone, and I slipped on my flips and walked into the bathroom and shower. There was a skylight in there, so I kept my shades on. I turned the water on extra hard and extra hot and then let the spray pummel the shit out of the rest of me. "Not food, not sex, not books, not nothing, is better than the pounding of hot water on an alky's neck." My daddy taught me that. I stayed in there as long as I could, and when I got out, I looked at my naked wet body in the mirror and my ribs showed, my hip bones stuck out like handlebars. I still had boobs, but they were smaller. I hid them with my hands and crossed my legs. I could pass for a boy tucking. This was good news. I needed work. It had been months and months since my last paycheck.

When I finally called Manager Liz, she took an audible breath. Relieved? Angry? Terrified? "Meredith, you're alive," she said, and sighed out. "Don't leave the house, I'll come to you."

She arrived around noon on the Strongs side with two smoothies, more green juice in large clear plastic go-cups, nestled in a brown cardboard drink container. I let her in through the back door. "You need to eat," she said, handing one to me. "I'm on another diet."

I looked at it, took a sip, and made a face. "You already stocked me up full of this shit," I said, as we entered my living room.

"Thank you, Manager Liz," said Liz.

"Thank you, Manager Lizzard," I said, with the emphasis on the last syllable. I put the newest vegetal concoction down on the coffee table, where it instantly began to separate. "Do you want to sit outside?" I was back in my Paris uniform: black jean shorts and my binder, a black T-shirt, and my sleeveless black hoodie.

"Why did you do that to your hair?" Liz asked. I'd forgotten what I looked like. I took off my shades for a second and admired myself in the glass reflection of a framed photograph of who else but me, blown up, from a magazine shoot. In that picture I had hair halfway down my back in ringlets and I was wearing a sundress. Your prototypical make-believe virginal high school sweetheart. Freckles on my nose. Red highlights in my curls. But staring me back in my reflection, the sides were growing in and the top was beginning to puff.

"I think I look good," I said, and put my sunglasses back on again.

"Nothing could ruin you," said Liz.

I leaned forward, loaning her my head. "You can pet it if you want, it feels nice. Like an animal pelt."

She didn't make a move but stared at her polished fingernails: Cinnabar, to match her lipstick and her rouge.

"Okay," I said, "be that way. So, don't. So, let's go sit on the patio. It's a beautiful day in sunny California. What is it, like 106 degrees out?"

"My face will melt off," said Liz. She was a profound believer in contouring and foundation.

"You in a bad mood? You're not firing me, too, are you?" I said.

"I should, but I won't," said Liz, "but I think we're better off talking inside with the AC on and both doors shut."

So, I closed the doors, while she walked over to my couch. Manager Liz was too old for her blond hair, but I'd seen her wedding pictures and she'd earned it honestly. When she was young, she'd looked a little like the wife on *Mad Men*, an icy champagne blonde, only with a horsier face. Now she was more Martha Stewart, heavier, but put together, in a suburban bougie way. She was wearing a white silk shell with a featherweight beige sweater tied around her shoulders and beige slacks and a shit ton of gold jewelry, long thin chains around her neck, fat rings on her fat fingers, thick Bulgari loops that looked like clip-ons hanging from her earlobes. When she sat on my couch it was all in one motion, a little like falling, her knees couldn't hold her and then . . . she just sank, as if she were in a rocking chair, because my couch was big and plush and downy. You could see her cankles swell over her sockless Gucci loafers.

She sipped her green drink. "I don't know how you can keep this crap down," Liz said. "I should have gone to Eggslut and bought us two breakfast sandwiches."

She sighed loudly. I'd forgotten that she did that. Sigh loudly. She also rubbed her thighs with her hands. I think because she was old and lonely, and no one ever touched her anymore. So, she had to touch herself. She'd been divorced for years and years, even before her daughter bought it. I couldn't remember if she blamed the husband for the kid or the kid for the marriage, but it was all awful enough that I tried not to notice her hands going up and down the fronts of her legs, from knees to hips on the fabric of her slacks, because the action itself for some strange reason made me want to roll on the ground and scream. She didn't deserve any of it.

Liz gave me the once-over from top to bottom. "You do look good," she said begrudgingly. "Too skinny. I think I hate you."

I wiggled my rib cage back and forth, then pointed one toe and jutted my hip out. "I thought I could do some modeling."

"Hmm, maybe Tom Ford," she said appraisingly. "Men's wear. He loves that androgynous look." She took another sip. "Sit down, Meredith."

"Eat, shut the doors, sit down? Who are you, my mother?" I asked. "Are there spies everywhere? Is that why you want the doors locked up? Or did you join Greenpeace while I was away and you're just doing your bit for global warming? You know there were spies following me all over Paris, right, Mommy Lizzard? You believe me, don't you, right?"

"That's what you said," said Liz. "And yes, Meredith, I believe you. Now can you sit down, please?"

I sat down on the floor, crisscross applesauce, in front of her.

"Did you get me a new lawyer?" I asked. "I'm not going back to that asswipe chump-change motherfucker."

"Yep," said Liz. "We're going to meet with her this afternoon."

"This time, I'm going to sue the living shit out of him," I said.

"Not so fast," said Liz.

"*And* I'm going to publish my book. I don't care what Israeli spook agency tries to get in my way. Matt Anastos told me he thought it was a great idea. That reminds me, he called me, too. Also, Jilly Waters. Maybe Marietta could help with that?"

"Marietta?" Liz said snarkily. "Since when are we talking to Marietta? I'm already working on it. I think I may have found you literary representation. But first we need a legal read on the subject. Like exactly what can you and can't you say?"

I clapped my hands; I was so excited!

"I said 'I think,'" said Liz. "So, let's stay away from Marietta."

"She called me."

"Really?" said Liz. She looked and sounded doubtful.

"She said she was just checking in or something. She told me not to call her, but she hoped that I was good. She referred to me as 'baby girl,' just like she always used to. I think she wants me back."

If Manager Liz's eyebrows could have gone skyward, then they would have. Instead, I saw that little bit of skin fold up above the Botoxed territory near her hairline, as if skepticism chased her wrinkles all the way to the top of her head.

"Honestly, I half expected her to show up with you today, so you could broker a reconciliation."

"Meredith, don't be crazy."

"What's crazy?"

"You and Marietta. It's magical thinking. She works for him now. I don't know, she's so wacky, maybe she thinks she can help, but she can't. It doesn't matter, let's forget her. I never liked her anyway. All that hair, she's too old for all that hair. She's always flipping it around like a shampoo commercial. Once, when I was sitting next to her at a client lunch, she kept flipping it in my face, even when I asked her politely several times and then point-blank to stop. You know what she said then? She said, 'I experience you as violence.' 'Violence'? Just because I didn't want to eat her dye job. Forget her, Meredith." Liz sighed again and sipped her juice. "I think the best thing we can do now is keep quiet and try to find you an assignment. He's all riled up because of your latest tweetstorm, and now he knows about your book."

"So what if Nina told him? What can he do about it? It's a free country, isn't it?"

"Meredith? Do you read the newspapers? We're already divided in half and are rapidly becoming a totalitarian state."

I ignored that one. Hollywood was full of lefties.

"Anyway, who's Nina?"

"The spy who loved me," I said. "Matt outed her over the phone. Now I know who she really is and she's been defanged in my eyes. Neutralized. It's not a good look for someone in espionage to have their cover blown, right? Remember that CIA agent . . . She moved to Santa Fe."

"Valerie Plame?"

"Valerie Plame. Being exposed sank her ship. What does she do now?"

"I think she writes thrillers," Liz said.

My heart skipped a beat. Nina wouldn't dare do that to me . . . would she? I'd noticed that she was a little, um, competitive. But she couldn't write, she said that the very first night at the café. She said they *needed* a good writer at W2. A good writer, like me! Although at that point, Nina hadn't read a word I'd written. And W2 didn't exactly exist, to put a finer point on things. Was everything about her deep cover? Or was there some tiny piece of her, a human part, maybe a little bit drawn to me? I remembered that back-of-the-Uber kiss that glorious night in Paris. Sex may lie. Shit, sex lies all the time. But kisses? There's a reason hookers don't deal in them. Did the real Nina and her undercover persona get all mixed up in her blender, like my hash does when I am acting?

"I wonder what that nasty gal will do next," I asked Liz, hoping she would say something to ease my angst, like *I'm sure she feels guilty as sin* and *Mark my words, she'll soon be begging for forgiveness.*

"I don't know," said Liz. "Maybe she'll keep tailing you. Follow you home? El Al flies to LAX, you know."

I gave her a teenage eyeroll. I knew that already. "But I haven't heard from her in weeks and weeks now."

"I'm not clear on the protocol: Do spies call you, or do you call them?" Liz said.

"Ha, ha," I said.

"Or maybe she already got what she wanted," Liz said really slowly, like something new was occurring to her, "and now she's working on someone else? I know!" she exclaimed like a newsflash. "She took an in-house position at a multinational corporation! She's opening a falafel stand! Settling on the West Bank! She's a gun for hire, Meredith. An employee. It's *him* I worry about. He's a vengeful tyrant. He's going to do his best to discredit you. On a good day, he's a barracuda. Now that he's a wounded animal"—she paused theatrically—"he's Kim Jong Un." Then she sighed that Manager Liz sigh. "Plus, you signed an NDA."

"I don't care about that," I said.

"You will when he sues you for all you've got. You don't even have a high school diploma. You've seen what happened to the other girls. How many are now trying their hand at interior decorating? You've heard all the rumors. I bet every single one of them is true."

I gulped a bit there. I mean, some of those gals hadn't worked in centuries. "They're not me. And I don't care. None of them have my guts."

"You won't win, Meredith. He will. He always does. He's allergic to failure. He's lawyered up—the big guns. *Bush v. Gore. The*

People v. O. J. Simpson. And the whole town is scared to death of him. The whole world, really. People all over the world are scared of him. France. London. China. Listen to me, please. People in China are scared of this guy."

"You said he was Kim Jong Un," I said.

"LOL," said Liz dryly. "Oh, what's the point? You're just a child." Liz stood. "I'll send a car to pick you up around four. The meeting is in Brentwood. Please wear something more conservative. A dress, even a skirt. Put on a hat. No. Maybe not. Maybe that dopey haircut makes you look even younger and more pathetic. What big violet eyes you have!" She shook her head. "I'll call Jilly Waters. We can't assume she's *not* on your side, she always struck me as a straight shooter. Maybe she's got a new producing partner or something. You call no one, okay? Not even one of your crazy friends."

That part was easy. I nodded yes. Then, as she started toward the door, I said, "Whoops, I forgot to tell you, Roger Norman left me a message, you know, from the *Enquirer*? I guess that's a hard no, too, right?"

Manager Liz stopped for a moment. "It's a mushy maybe," she said.

"A maybe?" I said. "Great."

"They pay real money, and everyone knows they speak the truth."

"Whaaat?" I said. "That hottie on the *Star Trek* redo is having an affair with a male alien from another galaxy?"

"It's true," said Liz. "He's having an affair with a male somebody. And he's from another galaxy. All those Scientologists are. I'm surprised you haven't already joined them." She sighed again. "Call no one."

As soon as I heard her car door slam, I was on the phone.

. . .

Blah blah blah and blah, stuff happened. I called Matt back. He said, "So, I met with your pal Nina since we last spoke," and my heart stopped beating. My pal *Nina*. I'd just been talking about her rather calmly in the abstract with Manager Liz, but that wasn't the same. He'd seen her. He'd said her name. A single word can do that to a person—I'm serious—stop your fucking heart.

Get your mitts off my Nina! I thought, but I didn't say it out loud to Matt.

I'm still effing proud of the self-control I exercised with that.

"That voice!" he said. "She sounds like a man!"

For a minute or two, or maybe just thirty or forty seconds, or longer, maybe longer, the major muscle in my chest froze, my blood standing at attention in all four chambers, and I swear I was on the threshold of being dead, because instead of viewing the inside of my living room from my squooshy, comfy couch, I found myself in a kind of sensory kaleidoscope, like a Russian discotheque in the Fairfax: strobe lights, smoked fish, vodka shots, mayonnaise salads, and glitter balls. *Nina, Knee-nah, Nein-nahhhh*. I was back in LA all of thirty-six hours, and she was already here in the States!

I've heard some people (my mother) say, when they've heard scary news (my daddy was leaving us), it was like they were in a rising elevator that out of nowhere began to fall, their bodies went down but their guts stayed up, which made them feel like they'd throw up (which she did do, I was there and it was disgusting, all over the kitchen floor; we'd just finished eating our Honey Nut Cheerios, it was 2:30 in the morning, and it was our *supper*!—he did it over the phone). I always thought that was a clichéd, stupid thing to say—an excuse!—but that's exactly what happened to me when Matt Anastos said *her* name. "Nina." It was like I'd drunk Mr. Clean and Hula-Hooped, that's how bad it felt, except also it was exciting, like I had hummingbirds in my chest, and I couldn't feel my palms.

"Only now she calls herself Andrea, *Ahn-dray-a*, to match her British accent," Matt told me.

"Wait," I said. "She's still playing espionage games? You're kidding, right?"

"Nope, not kidding. And she wanted to talk about you."

"Uh-oh," I said, even though I found the thought of it sort of thrilling.

"We met at the Polo Bar, Ralph Lauren's watering hole on East Fifty-Fifth Street. Her choice. It cost me a fucking fortune. But at least I could walk over there and didn't have to take a cab." He paused. "She's even more attractive in person. Except her hair is red now, auburn, reddish brown like yours."

"Don't tell me you watched my stupid show. My hair was dyed then."

"You look like a redhead in all your pictures. What color is it really?"

"I change it so often I don't really know. Maybe it is red, a little. It's coming in brownish, but kind of bleaching out from the sun. Yeah, but there's red in there for sure." Then I said, "Can't you just expense it?"

"What?" he said.

"Your Nina lunch."

"I'm not at Condé Nast," Matt said. "I work for Hearst. It doesn't matter. Her burger cost me twenty-eight bucks, and she started with twenty-dollar pigs in a blanket. Plus, she drinks like a fish and their martinis are twenty-three a pop."

That's my girl.

"I thought you said it didn't matter?" I said, and he laughed.

"You ever been to that place?" he went on. "Everything is wood-paneled, paintings of horses, and leather. I bet the urinal looks like a saddle, but I never got a chance to check it out. Anyway, she's obsessed. She wants me to write an article about you."

"You said that already."

"But now she's changed her tune. Like I wouldn't have taken notes or remembered from the last time?"

"They must be lowering the standards at ex-Mossad-agent school," I said.

"Ha," said Matt. "She's still posing as a women's rights advocate. And she's much more sympathetic to you. She said, 'Meredith has been the victim of some truly traumatic incidents.'"

She had a heart after all!

The line got a little buzzy then, his voice kind of staccato, like the connection was unstable. "'Current science suggests that'—um, let me see, oh yeah—'the kind of . . . ord can . . . dam . . . brain. Poor . . . she . . . unhinged . . . days.'"

"You're hard to hear, Matt. It sounds like you're burping."

"Sor . . . Mer, can't read . . . own writ . . . Let's see, 'If you . . . story . . . her, you help thousands of oth . . . ust li . . . her,' you know, 'other injur . . . part . . .'"

"Ugh, you're breathing so loud!"

"I . . . not breathing. I hold . . . phone way from my mou . . ."

It was every other word. "Hit your phone!" I said.

"I . . . call ba—" he said, and hung up. Then the phone rang again. "This better?" he asked. "I'm using my landline."

"Yep," I said.

"Then she asked me if I'd read your book, and of course I hadn't. So, it was an easy no, but while she was talking, she pressed her thigh against mine. Maybe she was wearing a wire . . ."

"So, *are* you going to write about me, Matt?" I asked.

There was a pause. "Only if you agree to go on the record."

"I told you before I was writing my *own* book."

"I know. But one thing doesn't preclude the other. My piece is on Dark Star, your book is about you. In fact, it might be good publicity. Eventually someone will talk on the record. You've already tweeted that you've been spied on. Things are rapidly changing."

I thought for a moment. What a stupid fucking thing to say.

When in the world had it been otherwise? Things are always changing rapidly. He'd been on my side before.

"How much will those cheapskates at Hearst cough up?" I asked.

"Meredith, I'm a journalist, I don't remunerate my sources."

"The *Enquirer* wants me, I'll bet they pay a pretty penny."

"Sure, they want to interview you. They're in his pocket," said Matt. "And they'll pay you with his money, but then they'll own your story."

"Are you saying I shouldn't talk to the *Enquirer*? Why should I listen to you? They're your competitor!"

"Well, they're not exactly my competitor," Matt said. "But I'm certainly not telling you what to do. Eventually her story is going to blow. I think you want to be ready for it."

Then I heard the call waiting beep. "I gotta take this call," I said, and hung up.

I pressed accept call. "Nina?" I said.

Wouldn't you know it? It was another Chinese lady. I wondered if she was telling me they found my wallet that wasn't lost.

When we got to the new lawyer's office later that same day, selling my story to the *Enquirer* was one of the last things that I asked about. First, she shot me down when I said I wanted to bring charges against the Rug for attacking me in Telluride.

"Way too late for that. His word against yours, you lose. Forget about it."

A haiku! It came after we agreed to a $50k retainer fee. I dunno how we managed that, I think it was equity in my house or Liz's, maybe I had money in stocks or in the bank, I don't know, and I don't care, and I don't even remember. We had an oral agreement and then there were papers and I signed them.

"He fucking raped me."

"I'm sorry," she said.

"You're sorry?" I said.

"No witnesses, no physical evidence, you continued to associate with him, he can say it was consensual."

"You mean if I had come out of the room screaming with his jizz in my ripped underpants I could have called the cops?"

"Yes."

"Then why the hell didn't I do that?"

I was hyperventilating.

Manager Liz put her hand on my leg. "You were scared and intimidated." She sighed. "He's a monster. No one else has done that, either."

"I told Marietta; I went straight to Marietta!"

The lawyer raised a legal eyebrow.

"The ex-agent," Liz said.

"Would she testify on your behalf?"

"She works for him now," Liz said.

"Textbook," said the lawyer.

"Can I at least fuck him up for siccing spies on me?"

"Can you prove it? Anyway, it's perfectly legal to hire private detectives. And to pitch reporters stories. Especially if he made the argument that you might be a threat to his company. He could chalk it up to due diligence."

So, what the fuck was Matt squawking about? Was he just trying to play me, too?

That lawyer lady was super scary. East Coast scary. An Ivy Leaguer who post-divorce moved out here for "more space and for the weather." She drove a Jag, she was Nicole Kidman wrinkle-free, like she bathed in umbilical cord blood, and she had a silver chop cut and cheekbones high as kites on injectables. That day she wore a knee-skimming skirt that showed off her runner's calves, and poking out from her pussy-bow sleeveless blouse were biceps firm as tennis balls—cree-pee!

She said, "I'm okay with you selling your story for real money, like a legitimate book deal. Just so you know, lawyers would have to vet it. But the *Enquirer* is famous for catch and kill."

Which meant they'd buy my story and then they'd own it and then they'd sit on it, she explained, like they did with Karen McDougal. And then I'd never see justice, if and when at some time in the future I joined a class-action suit or other more compelling victims chose to report him to the police.

Who is a more compelling victim than I am?

"Karen McDougal?" I asked.

"The Playboy Playmate who was Trump's mistress," said Liz. She was clearly crazier about the *Enquirer* than I was.

"How much did she get?" I asked.

"One hundred fifty k."

"That's the same as me," I said, glaring point-blank at Liz. "It's all bullshit. She was played and I was played."

"Well, here's some good news," said the lawyer. "Lizzie sent me your settlement, and it is not an NDA, which means it does not include a confidentiality clause. So, you can keep writing. You still own your own life's story."

"Holy shit," I said. "We'd just assumed." Me and Liz high-fived, both of us surprised. "What a shitty lawyer!"

Even Liz had to laugh, which made her look unusually pretty. I wish we could package relief like that into face cream.

I turned to her friend and said, "I'm so glad we hired you!"

According to Google, Madame Legally Gray, heretofore referred to as MLG, was famous for taking on the Man, but earlier in her career she'd cut her teeth defending assholes who were just like him. Bingo, I thought later that night, when I searched for more information. Vampires had sucked out her soul. She'd worked as a strategist for that liver-lipped traitor David Boies.

During our first $900 hour, she sat on the edge of her desk, molded legs crossed in tinted white-girl-with-a-tan hose, like an old-fashioned store mannequin, and told me and Manager Liz that whoever the Rug hired would be playing by her rulebook. She said, "I don't have to read their minds because I'm already inside their heads. First, he'll go about burnishing his own image, and then he'll strive to get back in your good graces. He'll aim to give you something he thinks you need."

Everyone in this town knew what I needed, besides attention. I needed money. The very thing this same attorney was eager to take away from me. That's where Jilly came in. After we left the law offices, Manager Liz called her on my behalf, and Jilly took the call. Liz was prescient: Jilly had indeed found a new producing partner, a private investor, she said, and she was horrified, just horrified, Liz said, to hear about what had happened to me after she'd left that now infamous Telluride hotel suite. She swore up and down she didn't know. (According to TMZ, as soon as I tweeted the room number, it was booked solid for the rest of ski season, which is pretty fucked up, but then people still slow down when they drive by 875 South Bundy. I myself did so the first time I was in the neighborhood, even though Nicole Brown Simpson was murdered before I was born. I know this because my mother wanted to name me after her, Nicole-Brown, with Brown part of my first name, like Mary-Anne, but my daddy said, "No fucking way." If that wasn't a red neon sign that she was bonkers, I don't really know what was.) Jilly told Liz she didn't want me to think for one moment that she had anything to do with his "premeditated sexual assault." (The quotations are mine; I mean, I'm quoting myself. I'm sure she said something like "disgusting rapey stuff." She was like that.) She'd read about Jeffrey Epstein. She was no groomer. No what's-her-face, Maxwell.

Ghislaine—it sounds like French for Vaseline.

Just thinking about it, Jilly said, made her want to take a shower.

Liz said Jilly said the minute she'd heard the rumors she'd picked up the phone and called the Rug herself (later, I found out that part was true) and chewed the fucking shit out of him (true again). And when he put the project into turnaround, she got him to give it back to her, even though it was unclear if he was still committed to financing it. (In this business it's called "fake it till you make it" and "if you build it, it will come"). She wanted me for the second lead, which was another term for the "girl part," supporting actor. A victory for me, even if it was small potatoes financially. You have to remember: at that moment I was totally radioactive. The job was a charity fuck, even though I was, as you will recall one mo' time from our meeting in Colorado, in Jilly's words, "absolutely perfect for this picture."

Well, did Liz and I listen to the high-priced, scarifying MLG? No fucking way. We jumped when Jilly said jump, and we leaped when Jilly said leap. She quickly had me to her bungalow on the Paramount lot for a table read. Me and the next Ben Affleck, then me and the next Mahershala Ali.

They couldn't decide if they wanted the couple—young married professionals who'd just moved into a new house in a new neighborhood and knew no one—to be mixed race or not. The husband seemed like a total suit (you think), and the wife, sweet, pure, but dogged by some kind of dirty past that she'd done her best to hide from him. (How many times have you seen that shit on Netflix?)

She had an ex, and her ex was in jail, but in the prologue, he gets out of the slammer on some technicality without her even knowing it. He goes on to smooth-talk her mom for information. (Maybe there was a part in it for Busy? I thought, ego-stroked enough myself in the moment to feel generous to someone who'd been kind to me.) He then sets about trying to get her/me back through inherent sexiness and a signature seductive man-child brand of intimidation.

The ex was to be played by the next Billy Bob Thornton. Except maybe she still loved him, so it should have been Richard Gere's son if he has one (gotta look that up) or grandson—that dude is old now—but I'd settle for anyone with his genes. Or the actual

Ryan Gosling? Someone hotter than Billy Bob? Chris Pine, Chris Hemsworth, Bradley Cooper when he was young? I could play against his hologram! But then the second husband turns out to be the real criminal, as if you couldn't see that coming, and I end up mowing down a field of bad guys with an AK-47 (that was the feminist part, me committing mass murder) and then running off with the ex, who perpetrated his delinquencies, it turns out, to fund an operation for the child we gave up for adoption back in high school. Cleft palate or club foot? Kidney transplant? A new lung? Gender-affirmation surgery? The whole project had a do-goody feel, enough so that Manager Liz thought it would be a redemptive next step for all of us.

"Kumbaya," we cried in unison. "We're going to make this movie!"

After our latest phone meeting, I was so happy I called Matt to tell him I was back in business. He sounded a little befuddled, but he graciously congratulated me. As soon as those pleasantries were over, I said, "Matt, I've been thinking. You know how to get a hold of Nina. I want to talk to her. Just to straighten things out between us. We were friends once. So, you wanna give me her number?"

Actually, I wanted to brag to her about my new potential gig. Maybe it would remind her of my star power and why she'd liked me in the first place. See what she was missing out on by betraying me.

"Um, no, Meredith," Matt said. "Number one, I can't reveal a source."

"But she's not a source," I said.

"I can't discuss this with you, Meredith."

"Why not?" I said.

"As your friend," he said, "off the record, leave it alone. You don't understand what you're dealing with. She knows your vulnerabilities. She's not afraid to break you."

"I'm not your friend," I said. And I hung up the phone.

I called him back an hour later, but he didn't pick up. I left a message:

"Sorry about earlier. I'm on the rag."

I had other friends. Manager Liz, MLG, Jilly. I thought the backstory alone would get us ink. Jilly and me, wrestling the movie from the Rug, speaking truth to power. Now *that* might impress Nina, I thought. Who'd said, "Living well is the best revenge"? Mae West? Soon I'd be walking the red carpet again, Nina diving into her stale popcorn, fired from spy academy, watching from her home screen on some borrowed nubbly couch in the shittiest neighborhood in Tel Aviv.

I was excited. Both Jilly and the director asked me to let my hair grow, they wanted something "softer and sexier, more feminine, less gamine," which Manager Liz said meant "scrub the butchiness out of your self-presentation." They also requested that I put on a few pounds, so I reupped drinking milkshakes. The next few weeks, as I waited for my next movie-related phone call, I got a little restless. I'd stay up late writing my book and tweet all night, vodka with soda chasers keeping me well hydrated, but when my authorial chops gave out and I started seeing double, I'd try stalking Nina, Jean-Pierre, the Rug, Dark Star, fucking dead Omar—any one of that coterie of miscreants I could dredge up. And just like that I was back on the cyber-perseverating hamster wheel, drinking and doping until I passed out on the couch or on the floor, crawling up the stairs, hoisting myself onto my bed, waking in the afternoons, totally skipping mornings, taking myself nowhere.

So, I decided to go outside for a walk and purchase my daily milkshake. Everything was pretty cool then, as I wandered down Abbot Kinney Boulevard window-shopping the pretty boutiques while sipping away at my frozen concoction, until I sensed I was being followed.

I don't know if you've ever felt animal eyes suddenly boring between your shoulder blades. But if you're like me, you can feel when you're being hunted. As a result, you might whoosh around impulsively to confront your predator, resulting in a face-losing form of whiplash, or perform an impulsive roundhouse kick and fall and break your psychic tailbone. I whirled around and did both and still saw no one. But then a red SUV drove past me blasting the Beatles: Was it Nina sending me a sign?

All I want is you.

When I heard our song, an acute teeth-and-jaw-itching hum began in my mouth and followed the river of my tongue, flooding down my throat, twisting throughout my arms and lashing about my torso, before branching out into my legs and splintering into thousands of tiny little pinpoint pricks that stung the soles of my feet. As if in place of blood, a million hornets were buzzing.

Anxiety is a motherfucker.

This was not just paranoia talking. I'd already been hunted by Dark Star's goons while they were on safari in Europe. There was no reason, as various people had recently pointed out to me, to believe that they had ceased operations just because the quarry in question had hightailed it to California. According to Matt, the Rug was likely paying them upwards of hundreds of thousands of dollars to keep me in their crosshairs (how flattering!), and by then I knew Nina was visiting the ole US of A, undoubtedly with the aim of completely fucking me over.

LA is a car culture city, you've heard that before, I bet one too many times, but I realized just then that there had been all these red SUVs with maybe the same license plate number slowing down to a snail's pace that week and tailing me, and now one had just blared a track from *Let It Be.* Or maybe the streets were full of cheapskates looking for unmetered parking? And then there was this one skate-rat girl, white with blond dreads, who seemed to love to longboard back and forth on my flat strip up on Strongs. I mean, why the fuck would anyone want to do that?

I called Liz and told her all about this, and during our convo I had the distinct feeling we were being recorded. There were little hiccups in Liz's sentences, like there had been in my conversation with Matt, but now there were even more of them. When I got home, I called Matt using my landline, figuring he knew more about this stuff than I did. Matt said that he had felt it, too, that ghostly presence of a spook's ear. "Vintage Dark Star," he said. "I'm such an idiot. It should have occurred to me the last time, I just thought it was static on the line." He said he had a burner phone he'd use with me from then on in, and he suggested I procure one.

I texted Branimir, and he brought me a burner the next morning. There was some guy knocking on my canal-side door while I waited for B, which creeped me out, since no one ever came over anymore except Liz, and she entered like a delivery boy. So, I was standing out on Strongs when Brani drove up and yelled out the window, "Why last time you give me the finger?" But he was laughing when I handed him the dough, so I guess there were no hard feelings. When I went back inside, I saw that a manila envelope had been slipped under my front door. It was from the county courthouse. I shoved it under the couch along with my flips. Then I took a job-well-done-you-deserve-it kind of nap.

Later, I got some good news: Liz had secured me a brand-spanking-new book agent. A Dean Bagley, from Brooklyn, New York, who had an office in a WeWork in Manhattan. He'd started off at a company called Inkwell but was now going out on his own, and he was even younger than I was. Dean called me on my cell, waking me up, a pool of drool on one of the couch cushions crusting white as we talked. I rubbed at it nervously with my finger until it turned to some type of forensic dust. While we gabbed, there was the now familiar hiccuping on the wire.

"It's a funny connection," he said. "Should I try your home line?"

I said, "All my phones are tapped." Then I screamed into the receiver: "Motherfuckers, I'm fucking onto you!" And slammed that sucker down. I reached under the couch and found Brani's burner, and I called Dean right back.

"Wow," he said. "You almost blasted out my eardrum. This feels like out of a movie!"

"Yup," I said smugly. "Welcome to my life." There was a pause. All that high-level espionage caused us to lose the thread of our conversation. "Now, what comes next?" I asked. "I'm writing like a madwoman. Do you want me to just keep going?"

"No," he said. "I think you're at the point where you'd be best served working with an editor. I'm confident we can sell this on a partial."

A partial!

"You're all over Twitter, I want to take advantage of the moment. Although, I might first leak a chapter or two to the scouts, see if it'll play as well with foreign as I think it will, but I already have an editor list and I'm ready to send it out."

"Full disclosure," I said, left-hand fingers crossed for good luck. "What about you-know-who? Did Liz tell you he paid some international spies for an early look at my manuscript? Doesn't that scare you?"

"*Au contraire*," said Dean, "it puts heat on the book and guarantees publicity. And yes indeedy, Liz told me. Nobody wants to play games over things like this."

That was a relief.

Immediately after we bade adieu, I called Manager Liz.

"Manager Liz," I said, "I love you!" I was dancing around my kitchen.

"Great news," said Liz. "The best." Then, "Meredith, don't screw it up."

But I called Matt anyway on the burner and left him a message.

"Hey, Matt," I said, getting his voicemail. "It's me. Don't take any wooden nickels." That was my code for *Please give me a buzz*. My daddy was always saying that. "Don't take any wooden nickels." He said his grandpa used to say it to him, and he had no fucking clue what it meant—were nickels ever wooden anyway?—except he figured after a while it was the same as *Use the head the good Lord gave you* and *Don't be a goddamned fool*.

Matt returned my call as I lay on my hammock on my upper deck that night. I was drinking Laphroaig, the good stuff, and writing like a maniac, even though Dean told me I should stop. As I said, "Hello?" I closed my laptop so I could see the stars.

"Congratulations, Meredith," said Matt, when I told him my good news. "That's tremendous!"

"Thanks, dude," I said, and meant it.

It was an uncharacteristically clear night, considering the red embers on the cliffs of Malibu. Lying on my back that way, I could make out the Big Dipper and what I always thought of as the Westinghouse *W*, but was maybe just Orion's Belt? The ocean wind chased the smoke, skirts hiked, up into the hills.

"I heard from Nina today," Matt said.

"Did she ask about me?"

Me and Matt, it was like we were two teenage girls gabbing. I was swishing the ice cubes in my scotch and instantly regretted the words leaking out of my mouth.

"In a roundabout way. She wants to get together again. She says she has news-breaking info on your tormentor. When you came up in the conversation, she also asked me to arrange a meeting . . ."

"Shut up! You know I wanna see her! Does she have an explanation?"

". . . a meeting of introduction."

"Whaaat? She's met me already."

"Nina Willis met you. Andrea hasn't. It's a ploy to see if you and I are in contact. Of course, I didn't tell her anything. But if I can get some good quotes, maybe some of this will finally see daylight."

I hummed the James Bond theme. "She's a pro," I said.

"Maybe," said Matt. "But I like to think I'm one, too."

After we hung up, I poured some more scotch, smoked some weed, and tweeted up a shitstorm, reaming the the Rug out, because why not? I was a soon-to-be published author! I could go on the *Today* show or be a special guest star on *The View*. I guess as tweets go, I was getting more and more reckless: *Men of Holly-wood save your women! There's a freak on the loose in this town and if you don't stop him, he'll come after your costar, your fiancée, your mother or your daughter and leave her in his filth crying on the floor #believemeIoughtaknow*

I thought, Girls from all over will thank me for my courage. We'll dance on top of tables! They'll buy me drinks in bars.

When I wasn't tweeting, my fingers were tip-tapping across my keyboard, checking out possible future venues for flogging my book. I don't know why exactly, but in the midst of all this search-ing, I guess I got really cocky. It was the imp of the perverse. Why not tempt fate when things were finally going good?

I typed my full name into Google and pressed return. This, when I had been search-engine sober re: myself for a gold star couple of months.

What I saw there wasn't pretty. Actually, it was eviscerating. Counter-ops. Nina was behind them, I was sure of it. First, sec-ond, and millionth results to turn up were both old and new arti-cles claiming I was crazy—exactly what she'd pitched to Matt, the birthing of fresh-off-the-grill pieces on me and some cyber she-nanigans resuscitating the old ones. Thank God he hadn't bitten, although his restraint didn't seem to matter much. Others had!

The cyberspace verdict was unequivocal: I was a deviant. A liar. A two-bit, no-account slut. Then there were the tidbits from my book that I'd never seen in print before. Like my girlfriend from Colorado. Someone procured an old redneck picture of us kissing over the bar. What loser freak from high school had sold that photo to this website? She was taller than I was, and when I leaned over on tippy-toes, my Daisy Dukes rode so high they were halfway up my ass. Plus, more previously unknown fodder: a blind spot about our threesomes with the bartender. My so-called affair with the director who'd raped me, who now no longer wasted time denying it. Instead, he was quoted as saying the sex had been extramarital but "took place between two consenting adults." I was fifteen! Fuck him. He finally had a new film out and I guess was trawling the sewers for publicity.

This shit was all over the internet: blogs, celeb sites, Hollywood rags, Page Six, even a piece in *The Washington Post* that said there was a warrant for my arrest in LA County on drug charges. Lies, I thought. Fake news!

I drank some more and clicked on Google Images. Me again, at the Oscar party, wearing that gossamer golden jumpsuit, with close-ups of my cute little blond mink merkin coiled like a sleeping mouse in front of the roaring fireplace of my privates. There were other more recent candids, shot on purpose to make me look fat. With a muffin top. I have no muffin top! Plus, bat wings. A poochy, roly-poly belly. Ride-'em-cowboy saddlebags. Some neo-Nazi circled what was supposed to be cellulite with a red Sharpie bull's-eye. They'd put my head on top of a body double. That was not my cottage cheese. Damn you, Photoshop!

Worse, if anything could be worse, were the celebrity snaps of me and the Rug, in LA at an industry party, arm in arm at an opening in New York, and videos of me stepping off his yacht onto the gangplank in some port in the South of France: I trip, and the Rug steadies me. I kiss his droopy cheek to thank him, and my lips shine from all that oil. His pores are gushers. We were also all over YouTube. Fuck. The red carpet in Cannes for the film festival, light bulbs flashing like fireflies. (We've killed them off in Washington State, so ask yourself: Are there any of those sparklers left to brighten the sky where you are?) Me laughing hysterically into the loose skin on his neck, as if he'd made some funny joke. (The Rug is completely unfunny. The women who have been photographed smiling by his side are all actresses!) A slide show of us together, his bony claw fanning out across my booty—my black patent leather pants were painted on so tight they'd split—he was shielding me from the shutterbugs. And watching the video now on repeat, I cringed every time I giggled and fessed up. A major wardrobe malfunction on prime time—yeesh. Why was I such a dope? All while the Rug gallantly stood by, masquerading as a gentleman.

What no one on the web seemed to care about was that before that night's festivities I had stood with eighty-one other famous and fearless women to protest the fact that only eighty-two films with female directors had *ever* been nominated for major prizes. I was parked between a César-winning French actress with a perfectly sculptured jaw and a new Tinseltown darling toward the left end of that long line, when the great Agnès Varda took the mike: "Women are not a minority in the world, and yet our industry says the opposite!" Do you think that picture of female solidarity showed up when I needed something to keep from drinking Drano? I searched and searched and searched and also got distracted, so I couldn't find it for the longest time, but when I did, it was sailing in another sea of pics of the Frenchette and the Hollywood hottie sharing knowing glances behind my back. Fuck both of them! I def take Madame Poodle in the looks department even pre-scalpel, and Tinker Bell, she wishes.

There was more. Endless more. More from here to infinity and beyond. An article on a major Hollywood gossip site that I won't dignify with calling "clickbait" said I was transitioning, and all my "hate tweeting" came from OD'ing on testosterone. "'Rone rage," they called it. Buried beneath that bullshit was a copy of a purloined email from the Rug to one of his lawyers posted by a fellow traveler, an "MM" supporter, supposedly from #deepwithintheenemycamp: *Meredith needs to die.*

The heat started at my shoulders and flamed up through my neck. Then the top of my skull flew off, as if it were a manhole cover and there was a gas explosion. After an initial wave of cool air revived me for a moment, my brains *roared* up into the sky like a human blowtorch from all the oxygen.

It's an accelerant.

Oxygen.

(What was in that manila envelope?)

I went into the bathroom and drank a glass of water. Then I pressed my head against the cool marble of the sink and sobbed. A few minutes later, after pickling in my own salt water, I crawled out of my clothing and into the shower, turned it on, and lay in a heap while the near scalding spray washed away my miseries. I was so tired; I couldn't even reach up for the bar soap. Instead, I curved into child's pose and let the H_2O do the healing. It sluiced down my sides and streamed down the dividing line of my bottom. If you can believe it, I actually fell asleep like that. In the morning it was still raining inside when I woke up. I finally managed to turn the damn thing off and air-dried, pulling the bath mat into the stall and using it as a blanket. Matt was going to see Nina, maybe he'd even met with her already East Coast time, and while I hoped he'd fucking stab her, all I could really do was think about how unforgivably shitty I freaking felt. I mean, I'd done this to myself. My bad.

I spent most of the next twenty-four hours sniveling around without the energy to get dressed. It took another twelve or so to finally right myself, and by then, once again, it was goddamned dark out. I walked downstairs to hunt for something to eat. Since I hadn't bothered to call Mercedes back to the house, Manager Liz's welcome basket had been sitting out untouched for about a month and was covered with flies and filled with collapsed and rotting fruit. I got an extra-large Hefty bag from the pantry and threw the entire disaster in there, wicker and all. I opened the fridge and saw that those little sand paintings of jarred food had turned into piles of melting sludge. I threw them in the garbage, too. The moldering juices, the now fuzzy vegetable bowls—I systematically purged all of them. Soon the fridge was empty, and I wiped it clean with bleach. Then I knotted up that putrid mess, and without bothering to put my clothes on, I slipped out the back of the house to put it in the trash bin. It was so late, there was no traffic, and the lights were off up and down my block. But would you believe that skater girl with the blond dreads was still out there practicing her jumps? Our eyes met in a moment of pure blistering communication, just like with my favorite flight attendant and that asshole pilot on my voyage home from France. We took a visual tour of each other's minds.

She backed away then and hopped on her board and headed to town. I wouldn't see her again. Her cover was shot.

Naked, I went back inside my house.

While I was hitting rock bottom, Manager Liz was at her desk, taking me and my career seriously. She called a pal who used to work for the LAPD and told him that I thought I was being followed. This guy told her it wasn't a matter of *if* the Rug would send out more private investigators or *when*, but that he already *had been doing so for quite some time*. This scared the living shit out of Liz, who was hiccuping when she told me the dude suggested I get a handgun. That afternoon we were back in MLG's offices for another $900 hour. MLG said, "Sure, it could be Dark Star operatives in the States, or Meredith could be making things up in that wild imagination of hers." She added, "I'd put money on Dark Star, eighty-twenty," which made me feel the littlest bit believed. I told her about the email I found online, and she said there was nothing we could do about that right now. It couldn't yet be construed as a real threat.

I said, " 'Meredith needs to die' sounded pretty fucking threatening to me."

"It's not a good look," she said, "I agree. And if we're ever in the driver's seat I'll use it. Currently, there's nothing I can do about a rude private email. What does it prove? He's pissed. Big deal. Right now, I'm here to protect you and get you back on your feet. But if you saw it, he's already seen that it's leaked, and he might try to find some way to get back in your good graces or use an emissary, so be wary."

"Driver's seat? You mean when I file charges against him for attacking me?"

"It's a he said, she said. We've been over this before." She sighed rather loudly to make her point: I irritated everybody. "Don't be your own worst enemy. Stop googling and stop tweeting. Dress like a lady. Be a fucking grown-up."

That one really hurt. I stuck out my tongue.

"Meredith!" said Liz. "She's on our side. She only took you on as a favor." And then to MLG, "I apologize, she's not in her right mind."

"Sorry," I said, like the spoiled little brat I was.

With a can't-be-bothered wave of her hand, MLG let it go.

Turns out she had been in a sorority with Manager Liz at Duke. So, I guess there was some sense of sisterhood still alive in the United States of Fucking Over Women. For one hot second, I wished I, too, had gone to college. I needed a sister. A sister could have saved me.

MLG also said, "N-O," to me packing heat. "A gun in Meredith's hand would be like something out of Chekhov, it would have to go off, and then story over. An American tragedy." She pointed her finger in my face: "Just go about your business, Meredith, act in your movie—you've got a part, right? Write your book, you've got an agent. Continue growing your hair. Keep your nose clean."

That "keep your nose clean" remark made me go back and

look at my Instagram DMs when I got home, but I couldn't find the picture of that little pyramid of white powder. Whoever had sent it clearly had decided to unsend it. I thought about retrieving that manila envelope from under the couch, but then I thought, Shush, don't think about it.

I texted Matt: *so? what did she say?*

Finally, I was ready to hear about his date.

Lying in bed, waiting for Matt, I channel surfed, and who of all people was on a talk show? His Disgustingness, unfortunately wearing a tight black sweater, which highlighted both his domed stomach and the slack skin of his turkey neck. The Rug, while promoting a new film, was taking the opportunity before a live studio audience to be cajoled by his butt-licking host (a fellow perv, the whole world found out later) into announcing a $5 million donation to Smith College and another $5 million for a new program for female filmmakers at Columbia. MLG had said he would probably do something high profile to buff his tarnished record, and I'll give him this much; even before he'd messed with me, he'd been all in for women's causes. "Ally as alibi," MLG called it.

I texted: *earth to matt i need to vent*

He texted back: *what's up?*

I texted: *turn on abc*

Then I waited.

we're not in the same time zone, Meredith

so what are you doing up so late?

can't sleep what's on abc?

him

oh yeah, I knew about that he also gave money for a women's stud-
ies program at a center for gender studies in jerusalem

The program broke to commercials.

I picked up my burner.

"I have to tell you something," Matt said when he answered.

"Another source told me he's taking this charm campaign a mile further. He's planning on releasing a statement saying he was sexually molested by a coach in high school."

"Waaay too ugly," I said.

"I know, an all-time low," Matt said.

"No, I mean he is. Nobody would have wanted him. Oh, forget it, what do we do to stop him now? And how do I get my revenge on *her*? I went online and she's done all the shit you said she would."

"Revenge on Nina? She's a temporary employee. He's the nucleus, the power source. He pays her bills. He's the bank."

There was a pause.

I wanted to see her dead.

"I'll go on the record," I said.

"What?" said Matt. "Now?"

As eager as if I'd promised him anal.

"No, I'm too upset now. Tomorrow."

He paused again. "Okay, Meredith, your call."

"I mean it. And then I'll want you to put the tapes away in a vault in case something happens to me."

A small beat. "That's not a bad idea. Plus, all my notes. You, too, my friend."

That time, Matt got in the last word.

The next day I printed out a hard copy of what I had written so far and bought myself a security-deposit box. There were two copies of the key. I kept one under the keys cactus and the other I mailed in a gift-wrapped box to my mother, which also included a printout of the pages and my notes. I enclosed a card: *Do not open until Xmas*. As far as I knew, she still kept that little fake white Christmas tree up all year long in a corner of her apartment by the TV stand (she was the only middle-aged lady in all of America without a flat screen)—it cheered her up, she said. I was betting she'd put my present under that sucker, even though the holidays were a ways off. She was a rule follower, my mother. I get my independent streak from my daddy.

. . .

Okay, so cut to the chase, you say; well, fuck off, you're not the only one getting tired of this roller-coaster ride. Imagine being me! A warrant *really* was out for my arrest on drug charges. This info got back to MLG, and she instantly put me and Manager Liz on a three-way Zoom call: "Why didn't you fucking tell me?"

I said, "My wallet isn't lost."

She said, "They picked up a red leather billfold."

Fuck, I thought. I fucking forgot about that thing.

"I left it in my backpack on my airplane seat when I got up to pee."

"The drugs, Meredith?"

"I dunno," I said, as if thinking out loud. "I went to the bathroom. I left that billfold in my backpack at my seat. The pilot and the flight attendant had some freakazoid eye communication . . . I swear on a stack of Bibles. Not mine."

I crossed myself as I said this. Why not? Both of them could see me. I was on my computer's camera. I had myself an audience.

MLG arranged for me to turn myself in the next day and met me at the courthouse. Branimir drove and escorted yours truly to the entrance. It *was* too bad, I thought, that I actually didn't have drugs on me at that moment; Brani looked like he could have used some. A couple of reporters were waiting there, but we breezed by them. (Manager Liz stayed home, she was having trouble breathing. She said, "It's all this damned heat," although it was fall by then and no longer hot out.) MLG asked that the charges be dismissed. "Depending on where and when the billfold was lost and found, hours had gone by since it was in my client's possession. It is impossible to know who may have handled it in the interim. My client submits that the drugs must have been placed after her property was either lost or stolen. She categorically denies using them."

They were planted. I swore it. Not me.

MLG said, "There is also the question of lack of jurisdiction. On technical grounds, drug crimes taking place on an aircraft in international commerce should be handled in federal, not state, court."

I was released on a $10,000 personal recognizance bond.

This time there really were paparazzi out on Strongs when Branimir brought me home. Photogs and TV reporters.

I got out of the limo and took off my shades. I was wearing that pretty sundress that I wore in the poster framed inside my living room, I'd dug it out of the back of my closet. My hair was long enough now to curl, and I'd tied it up with a scarf-like headband to make me look more girlish.

"You all know who planted the drugs in my billfold," I said. "He's trying to ruin my career, just like how he's ruined my life. But he and his spies and his lies can't stop me." Then I walked inside my house.

By the evening, I was on *Access Hollywood*. They got a counterstatement from one of the Rug's lawyers, a woman natch. That traitor said, "Meredith Montgomery is nothing more than a publicity seeker looking for a payday." Then she showed them an email from ex-agent Marietta the Traitor to the Rug:

> *MM told me she entered your suite consensually, and at some point, you said you wanted to take a shower, so she followed you into the bathroom. She came straight to my hotel room as soon as your breakfast date was over. She said she realizes now that she should not have decided to stay. I'm not a lawyer, but bad decisions are just that, bad decisions.*

Manager Liz FaceTimed me: "Will you please shut the fuck up? You are only making matters worse. My blood pressure is through the roof, Meredith. Jilly's talking about rescinding her offer."

"What the fuck?"

"Turns out Marietta is her new partner. Of the silent sort. Which means we're probably talking about his money."

"How can that be? Jilly hates his fucking guts."

"Jilly says she didn't know exactly where the funding came from, but what do I know. She said Marietta felt guilty and was just trying to help out, but she's in the middle of some kind of nervous breakdown . . ."

"*She's* in the middle of a nervous breakdown? I'll show her a nervous breakdown! She's got kids, a husband, a job! I don't have anything."

"I told you Marietta was a nutcase. You knew who she was. Anyway, Jilly says she'll hunt for new revenue sources. I think she believes herself. But I wasn't born yesterday. Now if I don't meditate and eat some gummies, I'm going to have a stroke. Let's continue on another day, okay?"

"Okay, Lizzard," I said. "Feel better."

Matt texted me: *Are you ready to talk now?*

I ignored him.

Dean Bagley called on the burner. "This is not good, Meredith. You're running the risk of not only looking like a drug user, and therefore unreliable, but you're so out there already, editors are going to want to know what's left to surprise anyone on the page."

I said, "You mean you haven't sent it out yet?"

"One of the scouts I slipped it to said, 'I feel like I've dated her already.'"

"Gross," I said. "You let him say that?"

He paused. "I got a call from Marietta Durand a couple of weeks ago. Nice lady. Someone showed her an earlier version of the manuscript."

Nina! Fuck you, Nina! Jean-Pierre, you motherfucking asshole! I hate your shitty traitor guts!

"She's represented clients published by my old boss and he

really respects her. Apparently, everybody does. Honestly, it wasn't good. She said that you're 'a very sick young woman, poor thing,' and I should be careful about working with you or stressing you out. She said, 'It's not that Meredith lies per se, but that she's prone to magical thinking.' She sounded fond of you. Like she was worried about your well-being."

"Hello?" I said. "That fucking bitch. What a turncoat! She's the liar. She used to call me 'baby girl,' she said he took advantage of my innocence. 'Poor thing,' my ass. I bet she got that language from motherfucking Nina!"

Silence on the line.

"Do not quit on me, Dean. You and I both know who she works for! You know which slimy fucking hairy turd is behind this. He'll do anything to stop me from telling my story. And apparently she'll do anything to be inside his orbit."

"I haven't been in this business a long time," said Dean. "I'm not sure I'm up for this."

"He's a rapist madman. Are you really going to let him get away with it?"

"You know what, Meredith, let's both of us have a think, take a few days, and revisit it next week."

"Have a think? *You* have a think. *You* revisit your asshole!" I said, and I hung up on him.

Now all roads were leading to Marietta. Mother Marietta, my ex-agent. I whipped out my smartphone and began to type: *What do you call a woman who sets another woman up for sexual assault— a groomer or a pimp? #mariettatheexagent*

Then I called Matt. "I'm as ready as I'll ever be," I said.

"Great," he said. "I'm taping the call for accuracy."

We talked for about an hour. I mean, I talked, and Matt listened. Once in a while he'd ask a question, but even then, I was like the Métro in Paris, in and out of stations so fast, there I was and then—*whoosh!*—I was gone again.

After our call was over, I tweeted: *she cut me up in little pieces*

and fed me to my rapist, was that after or before he hired her?
COCONSPIRATOR #mariettatheexagent

I got 3k likes on that one, but then some cretin tweeted back:
you're blaming this innocent, nice lady for getting yourself in trouble?
she's the kindest, sweetest person in the business and you're an insane
bitch!

In my mind it was as if Marietta herself were the one to post it!
Is that what she meant by "magical thinking"?

i came to you brokenhearted with his cum running down my leg
and you said you would help me #mariettatheexagent

I was going crazy.

what about your own little girl? is that how you'll treat her later,
putting her up for sale? #mariettatheexagent

I was worse than Trumpy, all thumbs, typing up a blue streak.

After Matt and I got off the phone the night of our interview, my
doorbell rang. I was still on my balcony, and I chose to ignore it.
It was nighttime and I wasn't expecting anyone. Then I heard the
burner and picked it up.

"Matt?" I said.

It wasn't Matt.

There was silence on the line.

"Nina?" I asked.

"Meredith," *he* said. "It's me."

Instantly there was that familiar anxious feeling, like hornets
buzzing through my veins.

"We used to be friends," said the Rug. "What happened to that
friendship?"

But now it was worse. I was being stung from the inside out.
His venom, like his semen, in my body, in my bloodstream.

"Meredith?"

"How did you get this number?" I stammered, like in a made-
for-TV movie. "Did *she* give it to you?"

It was all I could think to do or say. There wasn't any more.

He said, "That doesn't matter. I'm downstairs now. It's time that we just talked. The two of us. A chat. Like we used to."

A chat?

"What?" I said. "I'm not home. Go away."

"Meredith, I know we can put all of this behind us. This is just a terrible misunderstanding. I thought you felt the same way about me as I feel about you. Let me come inside. I'll explain it to you."

"I'm not home. I'm calling the police. I'll tell them you're a stalker."

As I talked, I hurried back into my bedroom and started to throw stuff into my backpack. Wallet, passport, cell phone, clothes. Credit card case! I hurried downstairs.

"Open the door," he said. "Please. Please open the door, Meredith. We can work this out. You're a beautiful girl. A beautiful person. Inside and out. I always knew that about you. You get a little crazy sometimes, but that's just part of your charm."

"I said I'm not fucking home," I said. "I'm at my boyfriend's place. I'm hanging up and I'm calling the cops." I was on my hands and knees, searching for my flip-flops under the couch.

"A boyfriend? I'm sorry to hear that. Don't hang up, hear me out . . ." he said, as I put down the phone. I left it on the kitchen counter so he could continue talking, and then I ran out my front door, shutting it softly behind me, and stumbled across my patio. It was dark out. I had to feel my way, chalk that up to muscle memory. You can addle the mind, but the body forgets nothing.

It was so late, there were no house lights on across the way, and the canal itself was inky black. My patio was slippery with dew, I guess, and I twisted my ankle when my right foot slid off the rubber of my flips, but I kept going. I could hear the Rug calling from out on Strongs: "I know you're in there. I brought you flowers, Meredith. Peonies. They're impossible to get this time of year. Please let me in."

I hoped he'd wake the neighbors and one of them would call the police. I looked up and down the sidewalk. The sky was pure murk and the area so fecund it felt like I was inside a terrarium. The Rug was just one foul alley away. My eye caught on my red canoe. The only means of escape. I stepped around that silly fence. I climbed aboard, put down my backpack, and sunk down lower than the seat to try to hide myself. The interior was wet and swiftly soaked through my shorts, but I didn't care. I untied it from the dock and grabbed a paddle from the bottom.

I rowed as fast as I could downstream. The channel was still low and pungent from the summer, it smelled moldy and green like guppy water. A few of the houses had low lights on—I wondered if inside couples were staying up late talking, or if on the lower floors they were drinking tea, maybe they were fighting or making love. I wondered if some of those soft globes of light were night-lights—and if I wasn't the only grown-up in Venice who was still terrified of the dark.

I landed just off Dell Avenue. There I called an Uber, and then I hid out in the bottom of that damp boat, just praying, praying, praying, for what I don't exactly know, it was just me and my private mysterious God that night, until the driver texted that he'd arrived. I put on my backpack, and I stepped out into the cool, shallow water and pulled my boat up to someone's dock. I kissed the hull before I left her, beached up against the wood. It's something I used to do when I was a little kid when my mother took me school-shoe shopping. If I picked one pair over another at the store, I'd kiss the set we'd left behind goodbye, sensitive as I was to abandonment. Then I ran down the street in my squishy flips until I spotted the car, a blue Honda Acura. My wet butt stuck to the leather seat, but the driver took me to LAX anyway. As I said, it was late and dark, and I guess there was no way for him to know that I was soaked.

There was a 1:20 a.m. flight to Orlando on American that got in at 10:49 in the morning. I booked it on my phone. There was a Starbucks in Terminal 4, but it was closed by then, so I took a seat at the gate, even though I was chilled and shivering, the AC was blasting, and I was dying for black coffee. There were only about four or five people hanging out in the waiting area, all looking equally exhausted. A fat man was actively snoring, like in those old cartoons, his mouth wide open with a fly circling above him. My hands were shaking, but I didn't know who to call for help. Was anybody left? Plus, if Nina had my cell bugged, couldn't the Rug track me down wherever I was? When I thought that last thought, I turned off my phone. There was nothing to do then but wait. I stood up. I sat down. I stood up again. I went into the ladies' room.

Peering into the mirror above the sink, I saw there was sediment from the canal water on my arms and my face was really dirty. I looked down at my legs. Green and brown muck all the way up to the bottoms of my black shorts, and a long red scratch on my left calf that bubbled with blood berries. I looked like a drowning victim from a zombie apocalypse. But I knew what to do, I'd taken sponge baths in rest stops my whole life. My daddy had me freshen myself up in roadside bars and cruddy restaurants. The LAX restroom was squeaky clean; I assumed the custodial staff had just come through, the day was over and a new one was beginning. I pulled a loaf of brown paper hand towels out of a silver dispenser, turned on the hot water, soaped myself up and down my arms and legs, using the towels to dry off. Then I went to work on my face. As the layers of dirt peeled away, so did the years. I even washed the curly fluff on my head and inside and around my armpits. Then I cleaned up the mess I'd made with additional paper towels and threw the whole pile into the garbage. I went back to the dispenser and got more to mop up the floor. I opened my backpack and took out my cutoff sweatshirt and put it on and pulled the hood over my head and tied it tight.

My shades were in a side pocket along with a red lipstick, and I donned them both like armor. When I stared in the mirror, I saw a fifteen-year-old punk trying to look older, or at least that's how it felt. So, I stopped looking at myself.

Back in the terminal, there was now a couple with a baby at my gate, and the dad dude was diapering the kid straight on the floor, no towel or baby blanket, only that filthy industrial carpeting. There ought to be a license required to become a parent, and first you should have to pass a test. I turned and walked the other way, but since most of the airport was empty or closed for the night, there was nothing else to see or do. I walked back to my original seat and sat down again. After a while, a gate attendant arrived and turned her lights on at the desk and made her first announcement. We would begin boarding on time, in fifteen minutes. I approached her as soon as she gave me a nod.

"I'm wondering if you can upgrade me to business?" I said. "I'm AAdvantage Platinum and I'm happy to pay the difference."

She looked at her keyboard and began to type. There was something about her that seemed familiar.

"Tessa?" I said, pulling the name out of some miscellaneous file in my brain.

She looked up and smiled. "Tessa's my twin sister. I'm Ella," she said. "Do you know her? It looks like I can give you seat 2B for fifty thousand miles and a fee of $350."

I passed her my ticket, my frequent-flier card, and my American Airlines Mastercard.

She looked up at me with a start. "Oh my God! I love your work. I think you're absolutely amazing."

"Thanks," I said. "I know Nina. I'm a friend—I mean, I used to be one."

"Nina?" she said. "I don't know a Nina."

"Samara," I said. "In real life her name is Samara."

Ella looked puzzled.

"Smadar. I mean in Israel she went by Smadar. Samara? Where did I come up with that one?" I made the cuckoo sign near my temple and smiled in a way I hoped was charismatic.

"Yes, I know Smadar," she said. "And you're right. For a while she changed her name on Facebook. When she was in London and doing all that work for women's rights, I think she was afraid of being trolled. I knew her from a student trip when I was a kid. She was an Israeli soldier assigned to accompany our group. We were good friends for a while." She looked at me. "You know, they were hoping we'd all fall in love and propagate the species. It didn't happen for me, but I became friends with this guy on the trip who is now going to be my brother-in-law."

"What?" I said. "Tessa's getting married?"

"So you do know Tessa?" Ella asked.

"Don't tell me she's marrying Joshua."

"She sure is," Ella said. "I introduced them." Now she was staring at me like I had two heads. "Oh, I get it, you're friends with Smadar, so you know the whole saga. All for the best, I say. He and Tessa are perfect for each other."

"He's a great guy," I said. "Congrats!"

I could see I was beginning to unnerve her. But I couldn't stop myself. "You and your sister always look so close online. I envy you that."

"This is why I don't like Facebook." Ella laughed. "We've never met, and you think you know all about me. To be honest, it kind of creeps me out."

"Apparently you know a lot about me, too," I said.

"That's true. I didn't mean to offend. Seriously. You're a great actress. The price of stardom. I really do admire you."

The machine spat out my boarding pass.

"Here's your ticket and seat number. Now if you'll excuse me . . ." She leaned over and pulled out one of those airport microphones: "Ladies and gentlemen, in a few moments we will commence boarding flight AA 702 to Orlando with one stop in

Dallas–Fort Worth. Those who need assistance or are traveling with small children should come to gate fifty-six for preboarding.

"Since you're flying business, you can go on now as well," she said.

I handed her back the ticket, and she ripped off her part and gave me back the receipt.

"Tessa's a doctor, right?" I said.

"Yep," said Ella. "I'm the black sheep. A screenwriter/director who in times of drought sometimes works the night shift. I couldn't wait to get out of Jersey. Enjoy your flight." She now waved me along. "Oh, wait, maybe someday I can show you a script I wrote?"

"What's it about?" I said, stuffing the receipt into my wallet.

"Adult identical twins. One gay, one straight, but because of some crazy circumstances they have to change places."

"Sure," I said. "Send it to my manager, Elizabeth Egan. Her email is Liz@EganCando.com."

"Oh, wow, that's so cool," she said, scribbling hastily. "Thank you. My name is Ella Rosenberg. If you want to reach me, it's Ella Rosenberg, all one word, at wgtv.com."

"Great," I said, and I walked down that jet bridge out of the twilight zone and onto the plane.

It wasn't until I was snuggled up in my business-class seat, buried under an airplane-issued duvet, that I realized I was jeopardizing my $10k bond by leaving the state, but it was too late to worry about that one, and anyhow, I was fleeing for my life. Who couldn't understand that? No jury would convict.

By the time I landed in Florida, the news about Marietta was all over the internet. I'd recharged my phone while we were in the air and turned it on for the teensiest restless peek when I was standing in line at Alamo. I texted Branimir, *you're going to have to Fedex me another burner*. Then I checked my Twitter feed. The first tweets suggested that Marietta had fainted during a breakfast meeting at Chateau Marmont. But then very quickly it became clear that she'd actually had a massive coronary! The EMTs resuscitated her right in the middle of the dining room in front of all those industry people. The humiliation alone could have killed her! Then they took her by ambulance to Cedars-Sinai, where her PR person wrote she was "resting comfortably."

What? What?

Marietta? My Marietta.

My *ex*-Marietta.

I thought, Oh my God, I loved her.

So far the family had no comment. But the internet was abuzz. *Such a tender, kind, gentle person! Get well soon, sweet Marietta!* And: *Beautiful soul! Thank God they got to you in time.* The ubiquitous: *We love you, Marietta. You'll get through this!* Also, industry fans, rivals, know-nothings, people with a lot of fucking time on their hands: *she was so busy giving to everyone else, she didn't make time for self-care,* and then they'd run off at the mouth about diet, meditation, and exercise, as if Marietta wasn't the original spa queen! A bunch of loudmouths sounded off about the Rug and me, especially me! Me and my tweets! They blamed me for the stress all that media attention had caused her. So, it was *our* fault that Marietta had a heart attack. Me and the Rug, now a "we" in the land of infamy.

I felt so guilty, I was ready to off myself. It's not like I meant to physically harm her!

I turned off the phone. I didn't know what to do. Should I call the hospital and say that I was sorry? Should I put a mea culpa up online? Was any of this really my fault anyway? I had nothing to do with her coronary arteries. I didn't want Marietta to die! I loved her, at least I did once upon a time.

Where does dead love go?

Into your bones like the calcium from extinguished stars?

I loved her before she *abandoned* me.

I got out of the Alamo line and went outside and hailed a taxi.

"To the Ocean Winds," I said, when I hopped gratefully inside. Florida was hotter than hell *and* California.

"The Ocean Winds are huge, ma'am," said my cabdriver, a nice middle-aged Cuban with a mustache and goatee speckled with silver. "It's going to take about an hour, an hour and a half with traffic, and it'll cost you around a hundred dollars. You might prefer the shuttle bus. I think it's only thirty-three."

"Thank you," I said, eyes already leaking. "But I just got some really bad news and I think I'd rather stick with you."

He looked at me in the rearview mirror. There was a picture of three young kids in baby suits and party dresses at some girl's confirmation hanging off it, along with rosary beads and a small silver cross. He bent over and then sat back up again and handed me a box of tissues.

"I'm so appreciative of your kindness," I said. And I was. I'd never been more thankful. "The Atlantic Breeze Lofts, please."

I cried quietly for a while. I guess to drown me out, he turned to Florida Man talk radio, "Unfiltered, unafraid, 660 on your AM dial." As I listened, I thought, If this nice guy knew who I was, what I accept as true, and what I think on a good day, he'd probably throw me out of his frigging car.

The highway went on and on and on and on like that old song "Don't Stop Believin'." It was one of my daddy's favorites. I kept singing it in my head to drown out the hate speech and fixed my eyes through the looking glass of the window. Inland Florida could be almost Anywhere, USA, on both sides of the highway, except for a certain breed of billboard. YOUR WIFE IS HOT. BETTER GET YOUR A/C FIXED. SHOOT REAL MACHINE GUNS, with a pic of a gal in a leather bustier taking aim, a faux price tag hanging over her head: STARTING AT $24.99 PER PERSON. Every ten miles or so there was a different variation of the "evidence of God" motif, with photographs of white and brown babies and phone numbers telling you where you could drop them off, I guess, instead of choosing to abort them. My favorite was PRAY & SPRAY, an advertisement for a chapel and shooting range. If the country was in the midst of a civil war, like the man on the radio was saying, I'd just landed unarmed and flat-footed in its epicenter.

Finally, after my eight thousandth round of that Journey song, there was a traffic jam where we weren't *goin' anywhere* and a brick bridge up ahead of us that spanned all four lanes with a yellow-and-brown logo that read THE OCEAN WINDS. Stuck, I got a good long look at the sign, which showed traces of rust and peeling paint. We were entering a down-at-the-heels version of Oz, the ocean itself nowhere in sight. This was completely inland.

"What's with the gridlock?" I asked.

"There's over fifty thousand homes here."

"Seriously?" I said. So, the sprawl had continued to spread like spilled milk.

"They keep building," he said. "It adds up."

"I've always wondered, what's the draw?" I asked, trying to make conversation. I knew what the draw was. Affordability. But I was lonely.

"You've got your tennis, your golf, your clubs, your pools, your pickleball," he said, by way of explanation. "They bring in all kinds of shows, national and local. When you're ready to stop working, with Social Security and a little change, you can live on a government pension, you know, cops, teachers, firefighters, nurses, postal workers."

"Would you want to retire here?" I asked.

"Me?" He laughed. "The Ocean Winds are for white people."

We made a right, sidled up to a lane of golf carts.

"That guy," I said, pointing to a pair of long tawny legs in the cart ahead of us. "He's a person of color."

"Lady," he said, shaking his head, "that's just a spray tan."

He pulled up alongside the dude's vehicle, just to prove his point. He was right.

When we got to the complex, four or five three-story rental

apartment buildings, he pulled into the parking lot. I gave him a great big tip. Like $100.

He said, "Miss, that's not necessary."

I said, "Please, sir, I think it is. I'm sorry for blubbering all over your car. Thank you for being so nice to me," and then I hurriedly opened the door and got out.

"Wait," he said, as I stumbled to my feet (they tend to fall asleep during long car rides, and my ankle was still sore from the great escape of the previous night).

He reached over to the passenger's side and opened the window.

"Here's my card," he said, arm outstretched. "If you ever need me."

I nodded and thanked him again and shut the door.

I need you now, I thought.

As he drove away, I looked at the card: JULIO ALVAREZ, it read. Plus, the name of the company he drove for, his email, and his cell phone number.

If I whipped out my phone and called him to return and fetch me, would Julio Alvarez, with his big heart and God's ear, be able to magically whisk me back in time? He was a nice man, talk radio or no talk radio. Might he have been able to convince my parents into giving me up for adoption? He appeared to be religious. Maybe he'd let me stay with him and his family for a while, in exchange for what—doing the household chores or babysitting? The kids in the confirmation pic were cuties, and at least one of them must have belonged to him. But by the time that fantasy took some form of idiotic shape, he and his car were heading to the highway, a contemporary Moses-type deity parting the waves of the traffic to help him make his safe escape from the likes of me.

I walked awkwardly toward the side entrance of the building, my legs still stiff, and I tripped over the edge of the curb, with my foot slipping out of my flip-flop again, fuck me, and now stubbing my toe on the cement. I kneeled and massaged it with my fingers. With this wheelchair and cane crowd, that rut in the road was a freaking liability. I hoped my toe wasn't broken. I turned around and a man in a MAGA hat was holding open the front door for me. He was wearing a bathing suit and a T-shirt and was carrying a towel.

"Nice day for the pool," he said, waiting patiently. I guess he hadn't seen my fall.

I bit my lip to keep from crying again. I had no idea what to say to him. You've got manners, but you're probably a racist?

"I'm sorry," I said. "I think I just broke my toe."

He said, "Do you want me to take you to the Atlantic Breeze Care Center? My golf cart is in the lot."

"I'm okay," I said. "No problem."

"Suit yourself," he said.

I hobbled past him, as the door swished closed behind me.

The hall was long and narrow, but I knew where I was going. Two ladies walked toward me, and as I flattened myself against the wall with my backpack to make room for them, I noticed that one was the skinny kind of old and the other the pudgy type. They both had on white Bermuda shorts and cardigan sweaters, and after thirty seconds I could tell why. The AC was on full meat locker. The owners of the building probably saw it as a preservative. The elevator was right there, and as soon as the first two residents lumbered by me, the door opened, and another woman got off. This one was wearing a blue-striped T-shirt and white Bermuda shorts, so I figured it was a look. I'd always heard the Ocean Winds was a geriatric sex club. Already it appeared that the men were in the catbird seat.

She said, "Someone has a visitor," and gave me a big smile.

I tried to smile back, but my facial muscles wouldn't cooperate. I gimped down the hall, which was two different shades of beige, carpeting and walls, that didn't match. I guess the design motif was "institutional." The whole place was flipping me out,

and by then I was practically running, running if you count hopping, because that left toe really hurt. You could say I skipped, I
skipped as fast as I could.

You know that feeling you get when you're on a long, long drive
and you need to go to the bathroom, but the closer you're getting
to home, the more impossible it is to hold it? In fact, just as you
turn the key in the lock, sometimes you maybe can't help but pee
a little bit in your pants?

That's how I felt right then. The last thirty-six hours had been
so relentlessly horrible. I couldn't get there fast enough.

When I finally arrived at what the rental agent had referred
to as "the loft," I knocked a couple of times, out of I don't know
what—habit? Politeness? A warning? No answer. I tried the knob.
Yep, it was open, so I walked inside. Never in my entire lifetime
had that woman locked her front door.

And there she was! Just as I'd left her two or three years ago.
Nothing, it appeared, had changed or moved since. She was sitting in the dark with the TV on. Still smoking, smoking inside,
which at the Atlantic Breeze Lofts was enough to get her kicked
out of even the concept of the complex. The fake white tree was up
in the corner, from last Christmas and the Christmas before that
one. It was all just like I'd pictured it. Like a neutron bomb had
hit, but miraculously she'd survived. Outside the sun was bright
and strong. Inside there wasn't a single fucking light on. The
contrast made it hard for my eyes to focus. But even so, I thought
I could see a couple of bald patches on the back side of her head.
She was right-handed, so she liked to pull the hair out behind
that ear first.

"Who's that?" she said, turning around and gazing blankly up
at me.

"Meredith," I said. "Meredith Marie."

"Meredith Marie?" she said. "Really? You've come all this way
to see me?"

I don't know what came over me then, but I speed-hobbled

across the living room carpeting, dropping my backpack along the way, and got down on my knees and flung myself across her lap. Like a child would. A child with a hurt foot. A little girl.

"Why?" she asked, my head buried in her knees.

"The monster has been inside me," I said.

"You, too?" she asked eagerly. In this alone, she was glad for company. "He's been inside me all my life."

"Put your hand on my head, Mama," I said, sobbing. "Pat me, Mama, please."

"Okay," she said, "I will."

My mother did as she was told.

She was nothing like her daughter.

Part
Four

Part
Four

Even though the Hotel Leonardo was on the beach and had a sexy swimming pool–roof bar combo with spectacular views of Tel Aviv, the meeting room the girls were assigned to was on the bottom level, practically a bomb shelter, the industrial brown carpeting patterned with looping white lines that for some reason made Smadar feel both anxious and nauseated. Vertigo. As she helped rearrange furniture, she kept closing her eyes so she wouldn't have to look at it.

On the one hand, Smadar was pissed that after finally completing her training in the Combat Intelligence Collection Corps ("No small feat, brains plus beauty," said her proud mother, cupping her beloved daughter's chin in her plump and clammy hand. "That Roman nose!" Ugh, bad enough to have a big schnoz, but did she have to also wetly kiss it? Why did Mama always go on a beat too long?), Smadar now had to move tables and chairs out of the way for the spoiled American brats she and Tali were supposed to hang with, as equals, while they all toured the country. They had been told to look at the trip as a holiday, but the hotel staff hadn't set up properly, so at the last minute they were called in to help out.

On the other hand, the girls *were* being put up at a seaside hotel at no cost . . . Smadar was crazy about the Mediterranean; never again would she be a sitting duck in a valley surrounded by mountains. Another benefit of this assignment: she and Tali had a minifridge in their shared room that they quickly stocked; already they had a fairly good buzz going.

"I mean, hello," Smadar had said to Tali, hanging up the hotel phone after being asked to come early to the "Welcome to Israel" info session. "Aren't they spoiled enough? A free trip where they can drink legally and don't have to do anything but take pictures and send postcards home about how wasted they got?"

Now Tali motioned toward yet another table that needed lifting and laughed. "The Masa Kumta really prepared us for all this highly skilled labor."

The Masa Kumta was the beret march. Everyone in their squad had to hike forty miles overnight fully armed, wearing their vests (six magazines, two canteens) and carrying stretchers. It would have been great for contestants on that reality show, *The Biggest Loser,* but weight was not Smadar's problem. Her problem, as she saw it, was endless obligation. She was a restless creature, ready to eat the earth! She wanted to be a model or an actress. Definitely her next step was to go to theater school. Fingers crossed, the Asher Adamsky Acting Studio. It was a two-year program, very prestigious, and all the graduates participated in one-on-one training and full-length productions, plus film work, which was the area of "the business" Smadar was determined to break into. But she was stuck in the army for another year and a half and would continue to work her butt off for her country. At the end of that most recent endurance test, there had been a ceremony where all the soldiers received their berets, the ones the girls were wearing right now, to symbolize their achievement and love of the Jewish state. Their families had of course been there to applaud them; Smadar's mother cried so much, it was ridiculous.

The girls lifted the table, side-walked it across the room, and tried to squeeze it between two others in the back. Tali said sarcastically, "My cousin David works for a moving company called Schleppers in Brooklyn. Maybe when we're done with the army, he can get us both jobs?" The blue paint was chipping. Smadar shoved the laminated corner of her end into the wall—another scratch for spite.

"I thought we were just supposed to hang out and seduce them," Smadar said. "Not be the maintenance staff."

"Seduce who?" Ehud asked, setting down a stack of chairs. He and another soldier boy on leave were joining the group. He was a good-looking kid, brown eyes, brown hair, dark skin. A real Sabra, Smadar thought.

"The Birthrighters," she said. "Isn't that the whole point? To get them to fall in love with other Jews and make aliyah?"

"Make Jewish babies, you mean," Tali said.

Ehud gave Smadar a frank, assessing look; she knew he could tell she had a great body even under her uniform.

"I'd be glad to help further the cause," he said, and winked.

"Please," said Smadar. "Don't make me gag."

"You don't look so Jewish to me," he said. "You don't even sound like one of us."

"She's Jewish. She and her mother converted. They even changed their names," said Tali, who knew the whole sad story.

Tali's looks were totally Ashkenazi. Her great-grandfather had come to Palestine at the age of fifteen, before the Nazis marched through Austria. First thing he did was join the Irgun. Then he'd helped found one of the earliest kibbutzim. They made pork sausage and were staunchly secular and didn't get married back then. Their kids didn't even live with them but in dormitories— Smadar liked the sound of that. She vowed that the only way she'd ever squeeze spawn out from between her legs was if she could park the kid elsewhere—that, or she'd need enough wealth to get a nanny to raise it for her. She wished she had Tali's life story to tell and her curly dark hair, big brown eyes, and ginormous boobs.

Tali always said, "Who are you kidding?" when Smadar said stuff like that. "You're a stone-cold fox and you know it; you could be a model."

"What about this?" Smadar pointed toward her nose. "I look like a man."

"No way," said Tali. "You have a strong face. Those cheekbones. The camera will love them. And besides, everyone everywhere prefers blondes anyway, even though we're not supposed to say so," which made Smadar feel better. She knew Tali was right. Men seemed magically drawn to her, and whenever they went out, she got the looks first. Tali's hips were a little too wide, she had some wiggly stuff on her upper thighs, while Smadar's figure eight was perfect; and Smadar could go strapless, she didn't need to wear a bra.

She liked Tali. She was glad they were able to get on the same trip before they started different assignments in the IDF.

"Oh yeah?" said Ehud. "Where were you from and what were you called?"

"Bosnia," said Smadar. "I was Samara, and my mom was Lejla. We were Muslim. She wanted us to get new names when we became *giyorets*. Now she goes by Carmel."

"Like Carmela Soprano?" said Ehud.

"You're not very smart, are you?" said Smadar, and she and Tali laughed. A lot of girls in Israel were named Carmel. He was just showing off his "American" chops.

"What's so funny?" he said. "I loved that show," and they laughed harder just to confuse him.

Then the Birthright kids started walking in, led by their guides. Half the girls were wearing those fringe-layered black boots—like tall suede moccasins—with denim miniskirts.

Smadar pointed at the chairs. "They're still going to need something to sit on."

It was a test of how much ribbing he would take, and Ehud passed. He smiled a quirky smile and hit his forehead adorably.

"Come on," she said to Tali, "let's take pity on him."

They helped bring the chairs out into the middle of the conference room and started setting them up in a circle just as Ari, the fourth soldier, came in, still buttoning his uniform.

"Shit," he said. "I fell asleep." He ran a hand through his short cowlicked hair.

"*Achi*," said Ehud. "You need some gel. You've got bed head."

Ari spit on his hand and tried again to tame the cowlicks in his close-cropped hair. The girls smiled.

"What did I miss?" Ari said.

"Only setup," said Tali. "We did your part for you."

He had the surprised expression of a puppy who'd just woken up. He looked around. "Whoa," he said. "We're supposed to do stuff? I thought we were on vacation."

"Technically, no. In reality, ha!" said Smadar.

"You owe us one," said Tali.

"Wow. Okay. Thanks a lot."

Too bad the army wouldn't let him grow a beard, Smadar thought. Ari could have used a little extra firmness around the jawline, but he had a certain soft-boy charm. She'd take the cuter one. Maybe Tali would end up liking Ari, and the four of them could have some fun. Fun had been harder to come by since she'd joined the army.

More American kids shuffled in, some sleepy from the time change. The girls scoped the party in squads and tossed their hair, already looking for boyfriends. A few of them wore layered T-shirts and thick leather cummerbund-like bands cinched around their waists; some were looser and had tassels. Smadar felt a small sting of jealousy eyeing the belts, which she'd only read about in fashion blogs. It occurred to her they used them as camouflage, because their bellies stuck out, while hers was wash-board flat. But she was sick of wearing a uniform and annoyed that when it came to fashion, Israel was always one step behind the States—people just didn't care as much. She read *Vogue*, *Allure*, and *InStyle* with lust in her heart; her favorite was *Lucky* magazine because then she could theoretically buy the shit, although shipping costs to the Middle East were obscene and there wasn't much disposable income on a soldier's salary.

Identical twin brothers had entered the room; one wore a Yankees hat, and they both had floppy hair like Zac Efron's. A couple of kids wore University of Michigan T-shirts. Most seemed to already know someone else, but they could have just latched on to each other from the airplane ride over or their room assignments. Why did people think there was safety in numbers when solo, a person could move much more nimbly, threading herself around the legs and minds of other people and emerge from a crowd untouched and unscathed as a cat? Humanity was full of freaks who chose to attach themselves to almost anyone or anything, anxious for association. Smadar was anything but desperate.

"A cool customer," her training group leader had said admiringly.

She searched for lone wolves. There was a curly-sandy-haired cutie hanging back, shy or nonchalant or both; the inevitable couple of lonely losers; and an attractive girl in long boy shorts with a short bob who was probably an athlete or gay, leaning against a wall, like she couldn't care less. Smadar liked her look.

"I already count three Nikon Coolpix cameras," Tali whispered in her ear. "Two purple and one baby blue."

Noah, the security guard, came in next—just a couple of years out of the army, he was the only one on the trip who was carrying a handgun—with the tour organizer, Ofer, and they immediately went over to talk to the two guides, Sam and Rachel. Ofer was redheaded and burly. He must have been around forty. Sam and Rachel were both Americans now living in Israel, and they seemed to be in their late twenties or early thirties. They motioned the kids toward a small table set up in a corner with Cokes and water bottles.

"Grab a drink and a chair, we'll sit in a circle," Rachel said.

When everyone settled down, Ofer welcomed the whole group to Israel and to Birthright. He introduced himself, Rachel and Sam, and the four soldiers, making sure to explain they were not there as guardians but as fellow participants, that the parent organization wanted them to enjoy the trip and partake of some well-earned R&R. At that, Ehud gave a thumbs-up and people laughed. Noah, Ofer explained, was there to watch over them, but again, he assured the kids, Birthright had never had a single violent incident in all its many years, they were careful to take their charges only to the safest spots, and this most definitely was going to be the trip of a lifetime. They'd climb up to Masada, go to the Western Wall, Yad Vashem, David Ben-Gurion's house ("Sexy," Tali hissed in Smadar's ear oh so dryly); they'd float in the Dead Sea ("Gross," said Smadar, because when you got out you were covered in salt like a potato chip, but in truth she thought it was worth it for the sensation of weightlessness; it was nice to feel like you didn't exist sometimes) and get to ride camels ("Between the humps," Ofer answered, when one girl asked, "and yes, they stink to high heaven") and rappel down some wadi or another.

Rachel piped up: "The Dead Sea is a great place to buy beauty products, ladies. The minerals are awesome for your skin, and they make for good gifts to bring home to Mom, just saying."

"Thanks for that little infomercial, Rachel. Her family runs one of the cosmetic companies," Ofer said. Then, "Only kidding," when one of the girls looked excited. "Our objective, as you can tell," he went on, "is for you to have a great time in our beautiful country."

There was more, but Smadar took out her BlackBerry. Mama had promised her an iPhone but so far had not yet delivered. Now Ofer was talking about food—"We put French fries in our falafel sandwiches," he said with pride. "Trust me, you'll never go back. I was visiting family in California, and what they call shawarma, well, you've got to be kidding me"—and then he gave them ground rules on decorum: "No drugs, no disorderly behavior, we expect you to be reasonable in terms of alcohol consumption. Boys, please keep a kippah in your pocket at all times; girls, a shawl, a sweater, something to cover up when we visit religious sites." For the next few nights, they were all expected to eat dinner collectively, for bonding purposes—after the meeting was over, they'd break bread en masse in the hotel restaurant. The city itself was only blocks away, and Rachel passed out a handout of "family-friendly" restaurants downtown and at the beach for lunch and snack times.

"It's always the girl who does the secretarial stuff," Smadar muttered to Tali, who nodded and rolled her eyes.

Also on that handout were phone numbers and emergency services numbers, key phrases in transliterated Hebrew, "although everyone speaks English," Ofer went on and on. Finally, he said, "You folks have come from all over: two of you are from the UK, two from Colombia, we've got Paris as well as the United States and Canada; besides our soldiers, there are several other Israeli participants on our trip. Please raise your hands, guys."

The two girls and two boys did as they were told.

"I know they will be happy to help show the rest of you around, so be friendly, ask questions! Noah and I are also always available to help with any difficulties or requests you might have. The objective of Birthright is to strengthen Jewish identity, connections between communities and love of Israel. Together we can create a vibrant and robust future for the Jewish people."

He paused. "Now, indulge me, please, for a second. I'm taking a little private poll, to gauge how Jewish youth feel about the problems we face here as a nation. How many of you have heard of the two-state solution?" A few hands went up. "One state?" A few other hands went up. "Okay, before we split for dinner, can everyone who believes in the two-state solution go to the left side of the room? Those of you who believe in the one-state solution go to the right. And if you're unsure, or don't know what I'm talking about, please just gather here in the middle. We'll do an in-depth dive into Jewish political history in the days ahead."

This piqued Smadar's interest. She and her mother talked about this stuff sometimes. No one believed in Israel more fervently than Mama. Their little family would have perished in Bosnia without the generosity and sanctuary provided by the Jewish state.

Mama believed in the two-state solution. An Israel and a Palestine.

"That's what *saved* Bosnia," Mama said. "The Americans finally stepping in and cutting up the pie. They left a mess, but it stopped all that senseless killing." She sighed loudly. "Once we all lived so happily together in our precious Saraje—"

"That's why they called it the Jerusalem of Europe," Smadar cut in, mocking and supportive at the same time, finishing her mother's well-trodden line.

But apparently Mama heard only love coming out of her Smadarala's mouth; she nodded in fulsome agreement, wiping away a tear.

Smadar didn't like to think about her country of origin. She didn't consider herself a Bosniak anymore. She doubted she ever had; she was too little when they left. Although odd memories could be triggered—like from the vile rug on the floor in this very room, the pattern reminding her of something from the old country, after a bombing maybe. She and her mother running beneath a sheet that looked just like it, or maybe Mama had tied the fabric around her neck as a cape? There was some superhero angle to the story. She hated the way these images crept up on her and tried hard to blow them aside. It was all so confusing: What were her own memories, and what were the tales her mother told her? How much did Mama invent? Sometimes they still spoke Bosnian at home, alone together; Hebrew was fine for Mama, but English made her tired.

Smadar found learning languages easy; she was now working on Italian and French. She was a proud soldier and a proud Israeli. Whatever was best for Israel was best for her.

Now, she watched the kids form their own posses. About five or six of them were for the two-state solution, including one of the locals, the lesbian, the French girl, and the cute boy with the curly hair. About seven kids were in the one-state group, including two of the Israeli students. A boy had disappeared. Maybe to go to the bathroom? The rest of them gathered in the middle like shy sheep.

Tali spoke softly in her ear: "They probably have never heard of any of this before. They don't even realize we risk our lives every day for them."

Ofer said, "We come here together as Jews to talk about our future as Jews. Anyone care to explain the thoughts behind their position?"

A girl from the two-state group raised her hand and said, "My mother shared a bedroom with her grandma growing up. My great-grandma lost four siblings in the Holocaust. I don't think it's right to put different values on human life or to deny anybody full citizenship anywhere. Isn't that what they did to us? The Palestinians live under occupation, and they can't even vote in their own country."

One of the Israeli girls from the one-state camp faced her friends and hissed loudly: "They don't need to vote on issues about our protection. She doesn't live here. She's comparing us to Nazis? My cousin was blown up by a suicide bomber while sitting in a café with her boyfriend right in Tel Aviv." She turned to face the group. "The ZAKA volunteers—the Orthodox emergency medics—they believe it's a mitzvah to collect all the body parts and give them a proper Jewish burial. They found one of Dafna's eyeballs hanging from a streetlight."

One girl gasped.

"The terrorists won't rest until they kill us all. They don't even recognize our right to exist."

There was a hushed silence following her outburst. The girl's cheeks were flushed, but no way was she going to back down.

The Americans don't realize how blunt we are, Smadar thought. They also don't know what it is like for us to go on this way, year after bloody year. She admired this one for speaking up, even though she didn't totally agree with her. And from the displeasure on Ofer's face, she could tell he wasn't happy.

Then a guy from the squishy middle said, "I just came here to meet pretty girls and party!"

A couple of people laughed.

"Okay, that's enough," said Ofer. "This is a discussion, not a joke. We are all guests in the same house. These are thorny subjects, but we are always respectful of each other when we talk."

A few people buzzed uncomfortably, but Smadar noted that the boy with the curly hair had put his hand on the shoulder of the girl who had spoken out in favor of Palestinian rights. She looked like she was crying. Most guys that handsome were total assholes. Maybe he just might give Ehud a run for his money.

"I, for one, am hungry," Ofer said, pointedly changing the subject. "Let's go upstairs and enjoy a lovely dinner together as a program and get to know one another. We'll discuss many things as we learn more about the complexities of the political history of Israel and review some of the trip logistics. Speaking of which, for any of you sleepyheads going straight to bed: tomorrow breakfast at seven, on the bus by eight. No exceptions."

"Hear that?" Ehud called out, as if he'd sensed Smadar's wandering attentions. "No exceptions, Ari!"

Ari turned pink with embarrassment, but others laughed. Ehud had broken the tension bubble. A check mark in his box, Smadar thought.

Later a group ended up at the Hookah Place by the beach. Americans always wanted to smoke *shisha*, so the bars were usually filled with tourists and Russians. Arabs and Israelis favored apple and watermelon flavors, cheap and simple, but HP had a big menu with more than 150 varieties, and the prices were higher than at the local dives because it purported their tobacco was superior. Smadar thought hookah smoking was disgusting; some of the water pipes had four hoses, and although everyone was given their own mouthpiece, the drunker they got the sooner they'd forget and spread their nasty germs. She preferred cigarettes. The place was a goof, when you walked in even on hot summer nights a flat screen played the image of a roaring fire. There were broken-down couches to sit on and games you could borrow to play. Downstairs there were even a few PlayStations. It was like paying money to sit in someone else's comfy, old, moldy basement. She and Ehud stayed upstairs, where there was soft music, and joined a group of Birthrighters, most of whom were drinking fruit beer, pomegranate ale, and iced coffees. She ordered a Fanta, and Ehud had a strawberry banana juice. The girl from Paris was there; Smadar sat down next to her. Smadar offered her hand to shake.

"Smadar," she said. She pointed at Ehud, who had placed himself at the other side of the table. "He's Ehud."

"Amélie," said Amélie, giving Smadar's hand an eager pump. She turned to Ehud, *"Enchanté,"* she said.

"Enchanté," said Ehud. "I like that. *Enchanté* back to you."

Amélie blushed prettily. She was wearing a tank top, but her upper arms were as dimpled as an old lady's.

Smadar rolled her eyes at Ehud. Then she turned again to Amélie.

"Maybe sometime on the trip you and I can practice my French?" Smadar asked. She was trying to up her game—if acting didn't work out, God forbid, she could go into foreign affairs and please her mother.

"*Mais oui,*" said Amélie, obviously flattered. "Whenever you like." She took another hit and coughed, patting her chest. "It reminds me of, how you say? To get high? We say 'bang.' "

"Bong," the nice American boy said, and passed her a glass of water.

She took a sip, then waved her hand in front of her face. "They said this would relax me," she said, "but ouuuf. It just making me feel so dizzy."

"NFM," said Smadar. When Amélie looked at her quizzically, Smadar explained: "Not for me." She was proud of her English, which she was told was flawless. She tried to keep up with all the American slang.

"What are your guys' names?" Ehud asked the rest of the group sitting in the circle.

"Joshua," said the nice one.

"Ella," said the one with the boyish haircut.

"Jordana," said the girl the Israeli had made cry.

So already Ofer's little icebreaker had divided the kids up by political factions. Way to go in encouraging international conversations, Smadar thought. Hearts and minds.

"It's nice how you stood up for your friend," Smadar said to Joshua, as she lit a cigarette. She inclined her head toward Jordana.

"It was really sweet," said Jordana. "Although I'm still not quite sure why I lost it like that."

"You must be tired," Smadar said. She exhaled. "Jet lag."

"That girl was harsh," Ella said. "She also broke my heart.

That story about her cousin. Wow. And Jordana's story about her mother's family, just horrible. I definitely saw your point," Ella said to Jordana. "It's like that Faulkner line: 'The past is never dead. It's not even past.'"

"My mom says her grandma cried herself to sleep all the time," Jordana said. "My mom says every innocent person is an innocent person, period." She made air quotes: "'Of equal weight in the eyes of God.' She told us forgetting that, it's like poisoning your own drinking water. 'It will make you grow up stunted,' she said."

"I've read most Israelis continue to believe the safest way forward is with two states. So, I'm wondering why Ofer opened the trip that way," Joshua said. "To take our temperature as the next generation of Israel's most important ally? Still, he must have realized it was a provocative way to begin . . ."

"Probably to see where we all land at the end of it," said Ella. "I mean, isn't this all about winning us over?"

I like her, Smadar thought. Smart. Straight shooter. A lesbian.

"What do you guys think?" Joshua asked, looking first to Smadar, right into her eyes—his were a disarming blue—and then to Ehud.

Ehud shrugged. "I just want a safe country. We deserve homeland security. It's not healthy to live like this, always on alert, always tense, always in mourning. Otherwise, Israel is a wonderful place to be. It's beautiful, great for sports—I'm a climber myself. Lots of opportunity, business, science, medicine. Go into tech. Make some money. Lie in a hammock and look at the stars."

Smadar said, "If we are picking endless war or peace, I choose peace."

"She's originally from Bosnia," Ehud said.

For a moment all were silent.

"There was a civil war there in the nineties," Joshua said, like he was trying to be helpful.

Maybe these American idiots had never heard of it?

"The crimes were similar to those committed in the Holocaust," he continued, a little too lecturely, she thought. "Obviously, the scope was different, Bosnia is so small . . . But the atrocities . . ."

"You like your history," Smadar said, blowing out her smoke. Then to Ella: "You like your quotes. Where I come from, the past isn't dead, but people wish it was. They are dying to move on. That's what my mother tells me, anyhow. I haven't been back. She went to a cousin's funeral a couple years ago, and when she came home, she stayed in bed for two weeks curled up in a tiny little ball. She said it all seemed the same as if it had happened yesterday, the Sarajevo roses, so many buildings still in ruins, even now very much a war-torn country."

"Roses?" asked Joshua.

"When the mortar shells exploded on the sidewalks, they left these giant ruts in the cement that have been filled with red paint as memorials. If you're morbid, they look like flower petals of blood. The authorities have repaired nothing. Your president Clinton carved it up into three different states with three different presidents, governments, currencies, languages; everyone is corrupt, and no one can agree on anything. My mother says her family and friends that survived and stayed put, they want to go back to the way it was. They dream of Tito and Yugoslavia. Imagine that."

"You mean they are willing to move beyond genocide?" Joshua asked incredulously.

He actually seemed to care about what they'd gone through. A rarity. But Smadar stayed neutral. "What other choice is there but survival? The war lasted only four years. Before that, they say we lived together fine."

Ehud: "Here in Israel, since the moment of our birth we've been fighting for the right to exist."

Smadar took a sip of her soda. "So, what are you guys most excited to see?" She was sick of all the gloom and doom.

"Masada," said Joshua.

"I'm looking forward to the smelly camels," Ella said. When people smiled, she said, "Really. Perversely, I like stuff that stinks. Like skunks."

Ehud snorted. "We don't have skunks in Israel," he said. "We just have 'skunk,' a chemical sprayed from water cannons on our armored vehicles. We use it for crowd control. It's the worst smell ever. Even Ella with the twisty nose wouldn't like it."

"It smells like rotten meat, stinky socks, a public toilet," said Smadar. "It lasts for days, although some people say you can get it out with ketchup. And there's a special soap. Only for officers." She turned to Jordana. "Still, it's better than rubber bullets, which can actually kill people."

"Mmm, skunk, ketchup. I'm going to get us some snacks." Ehud stood up. "Anybody want anything?"

"Get a lot of whatever, I'm starving," said Smadar.

"What are our options?" asked Ella.

"Get them Bamba and Bissli," said Smadar. She ground out her cigarette in an ashtray.

"Bamba are like those healthy Cheez Doodle-y things?" Joshua asked.

"The man did his homework," Ehud said. "I'll be right back."

"Bissli, it looks like fried pasta," Smadar said.

"What do you think we should see?" asked Amélie. "I mean, when we escape the tour guides?"

Smadar thought for a moment. "Well, if you like music, we should definitely go clubbing."

"I love to dance," said Amélie. She did a little wiggle in her seat. The pudge on her arms wobbled.

"Do you guys have karaoke?" asked Ella.

"There's this basement place on Ben Yehuda Street in Jerusalem," said Ehud, arriving back with snack bags. "I forget the name." He tossed the junk food around the table. "It's definitely the best one in Israel. Not my thing." He looked meaningfully at Smadar. "I'm getting tired. Want to head back to the hotel?"

"Sure," she said with a nod, grabbing two bags of Bamba, one for her and one for him. "See you guys tomorrow. Remember, breakfast at seven, bus by eight."

"No exceptions, Ari," said Ella.

This time, everybody laughed.

Back at the hotel, there was a sock on the doorknob of Smadar's room. She looked at it and back at Ehud. She said, "I guess I have no choice," smiled, and took his hand. They walked down the hall to where the boys were staying, and that's how they became a couple. Just add water. Like in summer camp. They hung out the rest of the week together, as if it were a given. Tali and Ari, too. But it was Ella who Smadar really liked. They chatted all the way up to Masada and all the way back down again. In the desert, Ella rode the camel ahead of Smadar's, and Smadar had to watch the poop coming out of its butthole, which both girls found hilarious. "There goes another one," she shouted out to her American friend. "Pee-ew."

"If only we could change places," said Ella. "I could get off on it."

One night in Jerusalem, the two girls snuck away from the group and went to an outdoor café for cocktails. Smadar ordered for them in Hebrew, two sparkling *limonanas* with gin.

"It's like a Southside, except with lemon instead of lime," said Ella.

The waiter, an Israeli Arab, brought out the platters of kibbe and *jachnun* that Smadar had pointed to on the menu.

"What's that?" Ella asked, arching her eyebrows at the *jachnun*, while nibbling on a kibbe. "This tastes like a falafel meatball. That one looks like an eggroll."

"It's Yemenite, usually for Saturday morning. It's rolled and buttered bread. They bake it on a Shabbat hot plate for like ten hours, so it comes out warm and done without anyone having to technically turn on or off an oven. Me, I like to eat, but I hate to cook, so I never plug in anything." She picked up a piece and demonstrated: "You dip it in this crushed tomato thing," she said, which sat in a little saucer, "and also in the *s'hug*." She pointed to an oily herbal condiment. "That's spicy if you want. Then you can put the *beitza* on top like this." Smadar picked up some hard-boiled egg slices and placed them on the red sauce and dotted them with the emerald *s'hug*. She ate her wobbly sandwich in two bites.

"You *do* like to eat," said Ella. "I'm going to try it, too, but without the egg. Not an egg girl."

"Suit yourself," said Smadar, as Ella assembled and bit.

"Mmm," said Ella, "I don't know what this tastes like . . . brioche? Monkey bread. The tomato cuts the grease. It's good together."

"Told you so," said Smadar, lighting up a cigarette. "If I don't smoke, I'll eat the whole thing right away. My mother says it's because we were starving all the time in Bosnia. I am always hungry."

"Well, you're basically a twig," said Ella. "You must have good genes."

"You should see my mother," said Smadar. "She's big, zaftig. And she eats like a little bird."

"Maybe she sneaks food," said Ella. "My sister used to. Now she just runs a lot and probably barfs."

"I never thought of that," Smadar lied. She'd wondered about what her mother did when she'd heard her wandering around the apartment late at night. "Food sneaking." And then, "I didn't know you had a sister."

"Worse," said Ella. "We're identical twins, although we look nothing alike."

"Huh?" said Smadar, reaching for a kibbe. "How can that be?"

"Well, she's super girlie, and I'm butch. It's the same face, but we wear it differently."

Smadar lifted her eyebrows and Ella followed suit, and they both laughed.

"I figured as much," said Smadar. "Although you spend a lot of time with Joshua."

"I like him," said Ella. "He gives straight white men a good name."

"Tell me about your college," said Smadar. "I'm planning on skipping that phase and going straight to conservatory."

"I go to USC, it's in Los Angeles. I wanted to get as far away from Jersey and Tessa as I could."

"Tessa's the sister?" Smadar asked.

"Don't get me wrong, I love her, we're twins, when she gets menstrual cramps, I hurt. But she's bouncy and sexy and premed. I'm a dyke, I write poetry, and I like to hike and go to the movies. I went to USC because of the weather, ha, ha, but now I'm thinking about going on to grad school in cinema studies. Maybe I'd like to write books about film, although that's so 'this week.' The trip was supposed to help me 'find myself.'" She used bunny ears as quotes, one after the other, hopping across the air like musical notes. "I think my mom is hoping I come home 'not gay.'" She paused. She was being funny, but Smadar could tell it was mostly not so funny.

"Do you know what you want to do?" Ella asked.

"I want to be an actor," Smadar said. She'd finished her cock-tail and motioned to the waiter to bring another. "Want one?"

"Naw, I'm good," Ella said. "Theater? Film? Stay in Israel? Go to the States?"

No one had ever asked Smadar these questions quite this directly before. Smadar was so good at languages, her mother told her, "Be a diplomat. We need those." She'd even sometimes whispered, "Aman," into Smadar's ear, which meant military intelligence, and "Shin Bet," which was internal security. "You're so smart," said Mama, patting her daughter's long forehead. "A *yiddishe kop*," which meant "Jewish brains."

Ironic, because there was no Jewish blood in Smadar's body, so how could it affect her brains, which her mother knew well enough, unless she wasn't telling Smadar something—which Smadar highly doubted. In all the years since her father disappeared, Mama hadn't gone out on a single date. She was done with men, Mama. From what Smadar remembered from Bosnia, she couldn't blame her. Whatever it was that had happened that crazy day when they were forced to leave their apartment, it was too awful and blurry now to discuss or even think about. Mama had some male colleagues from work she liked, and her girlfriends' husbands, but mostly she seemed afraid of men. Smadar wasn't afraid of boys at all, even when she hated them. She thought they were entertaining, like windup toys you could play with. She loved it when they stared at her like they would die if she wouldn't fuck them. Ehud looked at her like that now every night. Soon he would be telling her he was in love with her. She liked when boys told her that. There was something "enigmatic" about her, Tali said, even though she was willing to put out. Guys often seemed mystified by her; she was so aloof, it made them want to try harder. Then whenever she seemed even remotely pleased, it invariably drove them wild.

Sometimes Smadar wondered what it might be like to feel that way about someone else, to become undone, tear her hair out; but she doubted that roadblock lay anywhere ahead on her emotional horizon. She wanted too much for herself right now.

Tali told Smadar her grandmother used to say, "It's best to have a *yiddishe kop* and a *goyishe punim*," which meant think like a Jew and look like a gentile, as if anybody had control over any of that anyway.

Now Ella was looking at Smadar with big brown eyes, soft and warm. She was kind but straightforward. She cut through the bullshit. She seemed truly interested in what Smadar had to say. So Smadar dug a bit further than usual. What the hell? she thought. This girl will be history in three more days.

"I still have a slight Bosnian accent," Smadar confessed. "My voice is so deep. I'm told I sound like a guy. I'm worried that my look is too hard for American TV and movies."

"Believe me, you are dramatically beautiful," said Ella. "Like a Lauren Bacall or a Marlene Dietrich. You have a memorable face and voice."

Smadar savored the compliment for a moment. She was hoping it was true.

"Not that I'm coming on to you or anything," said Ella. "I don't like straight girls. It's a terrific defense mechanism. Thank God I was born that way."

"It's just that Israeli performers don't usually make it outside of Israel," said Smadar, fishing for more reassurance.

"Natalie Portman," said Ella.

"Everyone always says Natalie Portman, but she grew up in Washington, D.C., and she looks like Audrey Hepburn. Bar Refaeli could play volleyball at your school, USC. So all-American. Can you name one Bosnian actor?"

"Touché," said Ella. "So, you'll make your name locally and be like that *Fast and Furious* girl!"

"Gal Gadot? I'll drink to that," said Smadar. "Besides, my mother is here. I could never leave my mother."

"I'd like to meet her," said Ella. "I have a few days after the trip is officially over."

"Great idea," said Smadar. "You'll come to dinner. Mama will love you. And you can see what I have to deal with for yourself."

The trip ended just as Ella predicted. They were in another hotel, this time in Jerusalem. By then there had been multiple hookups and breakups, email sharing, a couple of nudes making the rounds for those with iPhones—also, promises of future spring break reunions. At the closing meeting, even before the banquet, half the girls were in tears. Ehud had his arm louchely resting on Smadar's shoulders.

"Poor slobs," he said. "They think they are so close now, but most will never see each other again."

Smadar thought, You're a little smug, aren't you? It's not like we're getting married.

As Ofer finished with a slideshow presentation of all their adventures—their Bedouin guides in the desert, snorkeling and rafting, the Temple Mount, tahini making—he said, "One last thing, guys, before we head upstairs for dinner. Remember what I asked you the first night?"

"If we were still virgins?" The boy who had called out from the squishy middle last time was at it again. "The answer, my friends, is now a resounding no!"

Everybody hooted and hollered, some of the guys slapping him on the back. One of the girls screamed out: "Max, you are so fucking gross!" Another one said, "It doesn't count if it's your own left hand!"

Ofer rolled his eyes and waited for the commotion to settle down. He said, "Still so disrespectful. Have we taught you nothing?"

Max held his fists up in victory.

"One-staters move to the right, two-staters to the left, people who still aren't sure, sexually active or not, can stick in the middle with Max."

The kids migrated around the room. There were definitely fewer in the center than before. Max himself had swung to the one-state side, which had swelled into a majority, although quite a few more Birthrighters joined Ella and Joshua on the left.

"So interesting," said Ofer. "Right now, the majority of Israelis are for the two-state solution," unknowingly echoing Joshua's point, Smadar noted. What else was Joshua right about?

"But there is active growing disillusionment," Ofer went on. "We'll see if you all are predicters of what is next to come. So, thank you for playing my little game with me, I always wonder how the trip changes things for our participants. Okay, it's time for fun. Let's head upstairs and chow down. We have the whole dining room tonight, plus a DJ." He swung his hips and began to sing that new Madonna song. *"I'm gonna party / It's a celebration!"*

Somebody started to clap, Smadar guessed as a thank-you, or maybe just to shut him up. Then there was a round of applause.

Ehud whispered in her ear: "Let's go upstairs, it's our last night together for at least a week."

"Okay," said Smadar, "but I want to eat first."

He kissed her forehead. "You," he said.

They followed the other kids upstairs.

They were in scene study. All the "citizen artists," as the kids were referred to by their instructors, wore black, only black. Every day Smadar wore a black T-shirt or turtleneck, black leggings, black socks with her black Keds (even though there was obviously cooler footwear to be had, like Chanel knockoffs, but she couldn't count on them staying on her feet, and because they reminded her of jazz shoes but were measurably less dopey). Some girls pranced around in actual ballet slippers, not her thing. Adon Elbaz, the director of the program, liked a clean, professional mien, nothing that interfered with "the instrument," aka their bodies, those empty vessels that required an infusion of another person's soul to be of any use at all. The studio itself didn't subscribe to a particular school of thought, but it all seemed to stem from Stanislavski, as there was plenty of method acting being taught, but also the saving influence of Stella Adler—"We don't want any heart attacks or psychotic breaks," Elbaz said at orientation with a laugh. "Think targeted empathy, but you don't have to relive your father's suicide every time you need to cry onstage."

In dance class they went barefoot on Marley vinyl flooring, which the professionals practiced on, so they wouldn't slip but could still slide. There were individual mats for yoga and folding massage tables in the bodywork room—they were all taught to practice physiotherapy on each other. There were communal dressing areas divided by gender; still, some girls were so shy, they changed in the toilet stalls, which was hyper-annoying when you needed to pee. If you can't put yourself out there in the school's ladies' locker room, Smadar thought, how are you going to get up in front of an audience and do a naked love scene? But today, they were in the black box theater, which required footwear.

Elbaz had partnered them up boy-girl, boy-girl, boy-girl.

you'd think queer characters don't exist, she texted her old friend Ella in the United States, *half of the boys here are gay*

beloved do-do bird, Ella wrote back. *he's showing 'em how to act hetero so they don't get pegged*

That afternoon's training session was in stage-kissing. Elbaz was teaching the module himself, which was a big deal. He was like the studio's guru. He had a distinguished, active career in Israeli theater, but in between shows he returned to the institute because, as he said, "I was born here." A lot of what he did was swashbuckle in and out of the place, raising money, being the "face," which was a good thing—he was ridiculously handsome, even now with his pepper-and-salt beard and thick wavy hair, his obsidian eyes—ordering the faculty and staff around, but every once in a while, he would guest coach a workshop. He always wore a suit, like a jazz singer, and a T-shirt and a kippah, God knows why; he was secular, a wild man, they had all heard the rumors. One of Smadar's classmates, Gideon Cohen, said Elbaz told him the yarmulke was to remind the entire planet that he was proud to be a Jew.

"Anything to stand out," Smadar whispered back, because the daily donning of skullcaps belonged to the Orthodox, not theatrical renegades and self-proclaimed creative geniuses like Elbaz.

"Does he wear his lid when he performs in Paris?" she asked. "Now *that* would take chutzpah."

Most of the students worshipped at Elbaz's feet, and the teachers and staff scurried around him like panicky servants. Not only did he act and teach, he also directed—the hero worship was earned, for sure, but these strivers also knew proximity to greatness could lead to something tangible. Some of the cool kids, of which Smadar considered herself a member, were the tiniest bit snarky behind his back, but that took work. Elbaz was truly stunning. Only a few of the students actually trash-talked him: those guys were either so cocky and talented nothing could stop them or so out of favor they weren't long for the program anyway. There was a hefty "cut" policy semester to semester, and Elbaz wasn't above playing with the weaker ones like cat toys. Sometimes this worked to great effect; she'd seen him make total mush out of an ex-soldier boy with a weakened arm and limp who'd been maimed by an IED—Elbaz was always telling him to drop and give him thirty, shouting epithets while the poor kid struggled one-armed to pump them out in front of the entire class. But then when Elbaz gave the guy the opening monologue from *Richard III*, he totally crushed it:

I, that am curtail'd of this fair proportion,
Cheated of feature by dissembling nature,
Deformed, unfinish'd, sent before my time
Into this breathing world, scarce half made up.

After that, Elbaz got him a spot on a Milky commercial, hanging out with some other soldiers in uniform, while a sexy girl *so* not in uniform (*Some of us fight, too!*) spoon-fed him some whipped cream off the top of chocolate pudding. Smadar begrudgingly admired the method behind the master's madness because it worked.

Luckily for her, today she was paired with the class star and heartthrob, Aaron. For yesterday's massage class she'd been assigned to a fellow actor named Shumlik, who had a pimply face and back, she unfortunately discovered when she was instructed to release his shoulders. Shumlik was nice enough and really, really funny, hysterical even, destined to do comedy or stand-up. He had a nerdy charisma. But rubbing his exposed carbuncles with well-oiled hands hadn't been her idea of a good time. When it was his turn to touch her, she had to astral project herself onto the ceiling and watch what was happening to her on the floor from above, or she probably would have puked her guts up.

"Controlling your emotions is what it's all about," Tamar, the bodywork instructor, told them. "What you feel is useless. It's what the character experiences that matters."

Smadar got that. She wasn't a "feelings" person anyway. This is what she told her on-again, off-again boyfriend, Ehud. He was a reliable booty call, someone to buy her dinner, fawn over her on her birthday, bring her a heating pad when she had cramps. But whenever she broke things off with him—which was like every three or four months, there was a cycle to it, something to do with boredom, Ehud bored her, or perhaps hormones? that's what *he'd* said—he'd call and make her a mixtape, begging for more punishment. She had another boy on the side who was better in bed; neither knew about the other. Smadar firmly had her eye on one prize: her theatrical training.

Now Elbaz had her classmates Sarah and Oren center stage. "Kiss her like you hate her," Elbaz said.

"What?" said Oren.

"You hate her fucking guts," said Elbaz.

"Then why would I want to kiss her?"

"Is he kidding me?" Elbaz asked the class. "Someone, anyone, make up a character for this idiot."

"She broke his heart, so he wants to get her back," Shumlik said.

"Ehh," said Elbaz. "If he wanted to get her back, he'd try to be sexy, no? Or tender? Show her the inside of his wallet?"

"No, I mean he wants to get back at her," Shumlik said.

"Okay, so how does that manifest?"

"Maybe he's violent or rough, you know, like Stanley Kowalski with Blanche?" Smadar spoke up.

"That's interesting," said Elbaz. "Go on."

"I think Kowalski was attracted to her," Smadar said.

"Who's your partner again?" asked Elbaz. He never bothered to learn anyone's name.

"Me," said Aaron.

"So, what do you think about what your costar is saying?"

Aaron looked at Smadar. There was confusion in his eyes, but then they made a connection—Smadar could feel it in the backs of her knees—and he toughened.

"Stanley was definitely attracted to Blanche. He could smell the abuse on her. The fact that men and boys had been there before him."

Elbaz pointed at Smadar and Aaron. "You two come up here." He turned to the couple onstage with him. "You guys sit down."

Smadar and Aaron stood up.

"Now you, Miss DuBois, what do you feel when Stanley looks at you like that?"

"Like he wants to control me," said Smadar. "A little scared, maybe."

"Okay, but that's not enough." He turned to Aaron: "Stanley, turn it up. You've got a hard-on for her. Get a fucking hard-on."

Aaron looked at Smadar, up and down, his gaze going from breast to crotch.

"Now you, Blanche, you're fearful, maybe even alarmed, but you 'have always depended on the kindness of strangers,' no? Your sexuality, your looks, are your only defense. What else do you feel?"

"Intimidated, frightened, but turned on, I don't know, confused. Like he knows I'll do whatever he wants. Like he knows I have no idea how to stop him. I can't talk my way out of this one."

"Think about your pussy," Elbaz said.

Smadar swallowed and thought about her pussy. She could feel it get hot down there.

"Stanley?"

"I want to fuck her."

"Okay. Good. What else do you feel about her, besides wanting to fuck her?"

Aaron's face tightened with fury. "I hate her for getting in between me and Stella. She looks down on me. She and her snooty ways. She came penniless to my doorstep, and then she acts like I'm the one from the gutter. We were happy until she showed up!"

"That's right," said Elbaz. "You want to ruin her, to demean her, to use her and throw her away, get her the hell out of your lives." He turned to the class again. "Stanley raped Blanche. But he did that offstage, right? So, the kiss here and now has to stand for all the violence to come. It has to burn through the audience's skin like napalm."

He turned back to Aaron. "Kiss her like you hate her."

Aaron traced one finger down her breastbone, then he lunged forward, and Smadar instinctively moved to strike him. He grabbed her by the arms and held them down by her sides and kissed her so hard, her instinct was to kick him in the nuts. But as Blanche, she was powerless to defend herself. You're Blanche, you're Blanche, you're Blanche, she said to herself. Her body now belonged to Blanche. It was Blanche's problem. Smadar could train herself to kiss anyone.

Someone in the audience gasped.

"And that, my friends, is how it is done," said Elbaz.

Aaron let go of Smadar. His eyes filled with tears. "I'm so sorry," he whispered.

"Don't apologize. You have to leave some skin in the game, that's the work," said Elbaz.

Then he pointed to Sarah and Oren. "Try it again. This time no foreplay. You now know the steps to take. I'm not going to say a word."

Oren and Sarah stood up.

Aaron walked off to the bleachers on the left. Smadar pulled herself together and sat down on the other side of the stage.

She wished she had a knife; she would have stabbed him if she had one. Then she'd pull the blade out of his gut and cut his penis off.

The days at school were long and she'd received a military schol-arship, so Smadar decided to stay at home in Tel Aviv to save money while she studied—she had zero desire to bartend or be a barista—why not let Mama baby her a little longer? There was dinner on the table when she deigned to come home, and her laundry was washed and folded neatly on the bed. Her mother didn't ask her too much about her comings and goings, she was good that way—just grateful, she said, for Smadar's company. Every once in a while, Ehud would stop by for a meal, and they'd all watch TV together. He was now at Kellogg-Recanati, getting his MBA, which kept him busy. He'd taken to calling her Sammi, the way her mother still did sometimes at home.

"Such a nice boy," Mama said. She liked him.

"Too nice," Smadar replied with a sigh.

She met her other lover, Rafi, at his place. Ehud lived in a three-bedroom with a couple of buddies, finance bros just like him. His parents paid the rent while he got his degree. Rafi was more her type, artistic, a grown-up with his own studio apart-ment. He shot rock videos. She was always pressing him to get her a gig—he'd picked her up at an audition—but as he said, he was still a cameraman, not the director, so his input didn't count much. Lately, she'd been going out on casting calls and was getting frustrated. After that last workshop, before he flew to London to stage a new play, Elbaz had found Aaron an agent. Already, Aaron was assigned a part in some experimental something in Haifa and had been screen-tested for a movie. Smadar wasn't one to be left behind.

"It's really goddamned frustrating," she said to Rafi one night in bed. "Why Aaron and not me?" She was still talking about this months later. Rafi seemed mildly irritated.

"I told you, baby, make an appointment with Elbaz and ask him." When she gave him the death stare, he said, "You're so fucking luscious when you're pissed off. Walk in steaming like that into his office and you'll get what you want, I promise you. The way you're looking at me right now, I'd give you fucking anything."

"Oh, shut up," said Smadar. She kicked off the covers and started putting on her clothes, underwear and then bra; they were sitting on top of the pile by his bed.

"You're leaving now?" Rafi said. "We were just getting started."

Just then her phone vibrated in the pocket of her jeans. She tugged it out as she pulled the pants over her hips. A text from Ella.

Smadar looked up from the screen. "I promised my mother I'd be home for dinner and now she's worried about me." Such a reliable skill, lying.

"It's nine o'clock," said Rafi. "I thought we could order in. I'm feeling burgers. You?"

Smadar texted furiously. Then she pulled her T-shirt over her head. "I'm late and she's already set the table. Another time, I'll stay over."

"You promise?" said Rafi. Surprisingly, he looked hurt.

She leaned over and gave him a kiss. "I promise," she said. Then she picked up her shoulder bag and left the apartment.

I'm never going back there again, she thought, as she hit the stairs taking two at a time. What a loser. Too old for me, besides. He's already halfway bald.

Outside the evening was cool and pure. A perfect June night. She was glad to be out of that claustrophobic apartment. As she headed toward the bus stop, she looked down at Ella's response.

great i'll give him your number oy misken! the kid sounds lonely

why? Smadar texted back. *he's been here before it's basically summer camp with terrorism*

he's surrounded by budding bankers venture vultures

that's what Birthright Excel's for, right? a shidduch for capitalist youth across the oceans between future American and Israeli moguls

I dunno let him explain it always thought he had a crush on you anyway but everyone did except me tee hee

well i'm on the market for a new boyfriend, just ended things again

ehud? when are you going to stop torturing him he's so nice and pretty

boring no with Rafi tho i haven't told him yet let him figure it out

e's always been boring joshua not boring

he was hot too right? i can barely remember

now you're lying he's super-hot and you know it love you soul sistah give my best to your mom!

she likes you more than me

not true! you've got the world's most devoted mama! love you

you too ella-boo love you too

It was Smadar's idea to meet for brunch on Sunday. This way the date could easily end as soon as the meal was over. If not, they could walk around. She remembered Joshua was curious about a lot of things, so maybe they'd wander over to the Tel Aviv Museum of Art; a guy like him probably had seen all the old stuff—the expressionists, impressionists, postimpressionists—but most Americans knew shit about the history of Israeli art, so maybe he'd like that? The more modern ones? Yael Bartana? A feminist provocateur, right up Joshua's politically correct alley . . . So, she texted him to meet her at Cafe Sheleg, which was one of her favorites and a hop, skip, and a jump from the museum complex; even if she chose later to dump him, she could point him in the right direction as she sailed away. They could utilize the bike share Tel-O-Fun, which hadn't been in business when he was here the last time but was easy and cheap and the best way to get around town now, she wrote to him in their chat.

awesome, Joshua texted back. *they told us about it at orientation i've wanted to check it out.* Then a few minutes later: *sheleg? doesn't that mean snow? snow in tel aviv?*

it's ironic anyhow we get snow in Israel i mean you can go skiing if you want me i don't like the cold. She paused. Then: *since when do you know hebrew?*

since you last saw me

what else has changed?

Might as well get the flirting started, Smadar thought. Although he was on Facebook, his page was out of date.

Hmm, well i like to think i kind of grew up

Promising, Smadar thought.

She loved riding a bike; she preferred most things outdoors—hiking, biking, scuba diving, and sailing. Inside often drove her crazy. As she pedaled, she went over Sheleg's menu in her head. It was one of her favorite places in the city: mostly locals, old-fashioned building, but hipstery at the same time. Should they have the *shakshuka* or the meze platter? The salads were so fresh, beets, bulgur and dates, artichokes and tahini; the café was tiny and the menu small, but it was located just by the market, so the produce, oh my God! She loved the open-faced sandwich with radishes and tomatoes on dense dark bread, the good salt and the bitter/fruity green Syrian olive oil they drizzled on top of the sparkling vegetables. Since Joshua had reached out to her, instead of vice versa, she figured he was paying. Americans like to take the check, she thought, while we Israelis do all the work. She learned this in the army.

Crossing the street midblock on a diagonal, she spotted him right away. Joshua, who had been attractive a few years ago, was now strikingly good-looking. Smadar was the first to admit to being shallow (that's why she'd kept Ehud on her yo-yo string, she liked looking up into his chocolatey eyes while they were fucking; "I love you so much, Sammi," he would say. "You're my cinnamon girl," from the old Neil Young song, a favorite of his father's). But now, just three years later, Joshua was in a new category. He had filled out, his shoulders broader, more man, less boy. From this angle, his face looked finely chiseled. He must have arrived early—eager to make a good impression, no doubt—because she was right on time, and he'd already snagged one of the few coveted outside tables, a round one—most were square and smaller, with poet types pecking away at their laptops, girlfriends sitting side by side people watching, gossiping, and typing on their phones while drinking their iced coffees. Multitasking jugglers, all of them.

Joshua was perusing the menu as she approached. His hair was shorter, but still sandy and curly, and when she sat down across from him and he looked up, his eyes were two startlingly bright blue beams of piercing light.

For a minute, she wished she'd put on a dress, instead of these old jean shorts and a white cotton belly shirt tied at the waist.

"Shalom, dude," said Smadar.

"Smadar," he said. "It is so good to see you." He said it like he meant it.

She smiled. "Do you like this place?"

"Do I like it? I love it," said Joshua. "It's perfect."

"It's one of my favorites," she said. "Locals come here, not tourists, unless they are crazed foodies who stalk the internet. It's still a little off the beaten track, which is getting rarer and rarer these days." She nodded at the menu in his hand. "Do you see anything you like?"

"That's the problem," said Joshua. "I like it all. I want to try everything."

"The *shakshuka* is very nice," said Smadar. She tapped out a cigarette and lit up. Then she offered the pack to him, but he politely declined.

"You look wonderful," said Joshua. "How have you been? Ella tells me you are studying to be an actor?"

A pretty waitress with purple-streaked hair in a messy bun came over. She had a sleeve of tattoos up one arm, red, orange, purple, an explosion of riotous color. Smadar had thought about getting one just like it—it was so distinctive and said a great big *fuck you* to the universe—but the pragmatist in her worried it would hurt her at go-sees for modeling and acting assignments.

"Are you ready to order?"

"Yes," said Joshua. Then he stared at Smadar. "No," he said. "You just sat down." He turned to the waitress again. "We'll have everything," he said.

"Everything?" the waitress said.

"Even I can't eat everything," said Smadar. "And I'm always hungry."

He grinned at her. "How about one of the five best things and the *shakshuka*—that's the eggs baked in tomato sauce, right? I want that, too. I remember it from Birthright," Joshua said to the waitress. "I'm pretty ravenous myself."

"I like that," said Smadar. Now she was smiling back.

"Okay," said the waitress. "The customer is always right."

As she walked away, Smadar called out, "And please, a lemonade."

"Make that two," Joshua said.

The waitress gave them a thumbs-up.

"It will be like a tasting menu in Paris," he said. "This café, it reminds me of Paris."

"Except the portions will be three times the size." Smadar laughed. "At least that's what I've been told. I haven't been anywhere yet."

"I don't care," said Joshua. "I'm just so happy to be back here."

"Really?" said Smadar, inhaling. "Ella told me you were so lonely and it was my duty to cheer you up." She blew out the smoke through her nose, so it curled. It was something she'd practiced in the mirror at home, for a scene study. She knew exactly how good it made her look.

"You already have," he said. "No, not lonely per se. I mean, they keep us pretty busy. We're each assigned an 'Israeli peer,' someone who they think is like your identical twin. Instead of brother from another mother, brother from another country. I mean, he's not—Guy—but he's close, we like all the same music, jazz and Dylan and new wave and stuff, and he plays chess, reads a lot. He's political like me, too, so that's pretty great. My internship is in venture capital. Green start-ups, which makes me feel less guilty. We attend a lot of lectures, there are many social events, you know, networking things, parties. We visited a watermelon patch." He shrugged. "The kids are nice."

"Kids? I thought you were a little old for Excel myself."

"I took a couple of years off after Birthright," said Joshua. "It inspired me. I WWOOFed in Europe and then I did a year of AmeriCorps at home."

"I don't know what that is," said Smadar.

"AmeriCorps? It's like the Peace Corps."

"I know what *that* is. You run around other countries doing good, right? That sounds like you."

"I was assigned to a school in Buffalo. That's in upstate New York, pretty damned chilly, but I loved the kids."

"You taught?"

"I tutored. I coached. I fed them. I led an after-school history elective."

"Of course you did," cooed Smadar. "Ooh, look, here come our first three courses!"

The waitress brought out the radish toast, the bulgur and dates, and the *shakshuka,* plus two plates and a basket of Druze pita, thin as linen and just as pliable.

"Your favorites," said the waitress, smiling at Smadar.

"You two know each other?" asked Joshua.

"I come here all the time," said Smadar. "Thank you, Irit."

"My pleash," said Irit. She looked at Joshua. "This one's gorgeous."

He blushed.

"I'll be back in a little while with the rest," Irit said.

"So why Buffalo?" Smadar continued the conversation. "From what I've heard it's all blizzards and chicken wings."

"So, you know already," he said.

"You're not the only one who is curious," said Smadar. She spooned half the *shakshuka* on her plate and half on his, careful to keep the egg yolks intact. She passed him the pita, then took one for herself, ripping off a cocktail-napkin-sized portion and dipping it in the sauce. "I'm dying to travel someday.

"Ah," she said. "Delicious. Try some."

He dipped his bread, broke the egg, and shoveled it into his mouth. "Man," he said, "that's amazing." His eyes rolled.

I wonder if he does that when he's coming, Smadar thought.

"So, Buffalo? America's armpit?"

"The other possibility was Boston."

"You picked the armpit over Boston? Where Harvard is?" She reached over for the bulgur salad. "Do you want me to put some of this on your plate, too?"

"No," he said. "Let's just share. You eat from your side, and I'll eat from mine, and we'll meet in the middle." He picked up his fork and scooped up some of the grains and a date. "This tastes amazing."

She took a bite. "I like it, too." She served herself some of the mezes in little puddles on her plate.

"My dad's from the Bronx. He's a Yankees fan."

"I don't understand," Smadar said, her mouth full. A bit of hummus fell out. She laughed, pushed the food back in with her fingers, and then covered the lower side of her face with her hand. "How embarrassing," she said.

"Mashed chickpeas look good on you." He took his napkin and reached out and wiped off her chin. "Boston is the Red Sox. Baseball. Archenemies."

"Here we have baseball, but only for little kids. Here we also have real enemies."

"I liked Buffalo. Then I went back to school."

"Which was where?"

"The University of Pennsylvania."

"So, why Excel?"

"I'm going to the London School of Economics next year. For my M.Phil. Economics and world history. My father said he'd pay for it only if I did something practical over the summer. That's why I'm here," he said. "It makes him happy."

"That's why you're here," she said.

"That, and to see you," he said.

Suddenly her whole body felt like one long vibrating, buzzing muscle. She quickly glanced away. Smadar had never felt this shy before.

When she looked up again, Joshua had a serious expression on his beautiful face.

"I had such a crush on you that summer. Only it lasted. I could never get you out of my mind. It's like old songs say, first thing in the morning, last thing at night, I think about you all the time."

"Me?" she said. "Why?"

"You were so much smarter than the others. Intense but aloof, you know. Almost frosty but composed. Totally, amazingly beautiful. But you were hanging out with that doofus from the start. I had no chance." He shook his head.

That was a long time for a crush, Smadar thought. Three years. She liked that.

"I was too intimidated, but I promised myself, if I ever got another chance . . . So here I am. And here you are."

"Here I am," said Smadar.

"Come," he said. "Let's take a selfie together."

"A selfie?"

Why was she repeating every fucking thing he said?

"We're going to want it someday."

She liked how confidant he was.

He took his phone out of his pocket and moved his chair closer to hers.

"Wait," she said. "Do I still have food on my face?"

He put his arm around her shoulders, posed his phone in front of them, and said, "Even better, you have some in your hair. Now smile for the camera."

And she did.

By the fall, Joshua was in London and Smadar was back in school. Her final term. She'd been auditioning like crazy but not getting a whole lot of bites. Her mother had a friend who owned a store that sold party dresses, so she festooned Smadar in tulle, like a giant pink meringue, and took pictures and put her portrait in the display case. Rafi, in a wild attempt to get her back, got her a small part in a cheesy rock video where she played an evil temptress and wore very little clothing. It was a piece of garbage, but at least she now had a credit for her reel, which was good.

Her mother cried when she saw it.

"She's not anything like you," said Mama. "So common. It will give people the wrong impression."

"I know," said Smadar. "That's the point. I'm an actress. In the video, I'm acting!"

"Maybe you should stick with modeling," said Mama. "You look like an angel in Selma's storefront. I'm so proud every time I pass by it, I go all the way around the block just to see you again in the window."

Mama paused. She took a deep breath.

Sometimes Smadar thought her mother was afraid of her.

"Aman?" suggested Mama gently. "Shin Bet?"

That same old service-to-our-country routine.

"With your brains and gift for languages . . ."

"This is what I want, Mama," said Smadar. "And guess what? I got paid for it. A lot," she lied. She wasn't paid hardly anything.

"Then this is what you shall have," said her mother. "And I will get used to it. Like Gal Gadot's mother did." She kissed Smadar on the forehead.

But that night she googled the Mossad's website and looked up its application for employment. There was a questionnaire. "Select the three qualities that describe you best," it said.

She picked "highly self-confident," "sensible," and "independent."

Question two: "Why are you considering joining the Mossad? Choose two main reasons."

Smadar checked off "I would like a stable job with benefits" and "I am interested in varied work in Israel and abroad."

The last one she bothered answering was "What is your dream job?"

That one was easy. "7. Theater actor/actress."

Then she put aside her laptop.

· · ·

Smadar thanked Rafi politely when he called her after the shoot, asking her out for coffee. But when he boasted that he was the one who had gotten her foot in the proverbial door, not that fancy drama school, she shut him down for good: "I've got a real boy-friend now and we're exclusive."

Ehud asked to meet "the motherfucker" himself, but Smadar said forget about it. She didn't want him to know that he'd already encountered her new boyfriend. It was kind of embarrassing to have met both of them on Birthright anyway; and none of it was his business. She just said, "You and me, we had our fun, but it was never like we were going to get married."

"You're a heartless bitch, you know that, Sammi?" Ehud said.

"Then why do you care if you go out with me or not?" Smadar said.

"I'm going to take that job in Florida," he said, as if daring her.

"Florida? That's where old Jews go to die," she said.

She liked to get in the last word.

Joshua was very supportive of her career. Over the phone, he said, "If it doesn't work out in Israel, you'll come and live with me here, which is all I think about anyway. Hell of a lot more the-ater in London. And if not London, we'll move to New York or LA. Whatever is best for you."

Each of these options held some appeal, England first, at least for a next chapter; it was easiest. Joshua was there already! Num-ber two: the flight was shorter, although Smadar didn't know how she would tell her mother. Maybe when Mama was old enough to retire, they could all live in the UK or in the States—Joshua said his degree might land him a job at the World Bank or at the IMF, and her mother could be the babysitter for whatever rug rats they might produce in the years to come. Joshua was always talking about the future. But that was too far away for her to think about right now. Smadar had her own trajectory to focus on.

In October, Elbaz came back to the studio to lead a lesson on screen-testing. Smadar had never forgotten what Rafi had said about confronting him, but there had yet to be a time or place for it. It's not like Elbaz hung out with the students or anything. For this workshop, he put them through the wringer by having everyone filmed for a mouthwash commercial reading the exact same lines. Then they all sat in the auditorium and watched themselves up on the big screen. The results were as hilarious as they were mortifying. Some of the kids had crooked or even yellow teeth. Blackheads on their noses. Others looked plain ugly. A fat girl's body jiggled while she swished the liquid in her mouth. Smadar jutted her chin out too far—"Too haughty," said Elbaz. "You've got to know your audience. They want you to look 'typical' but attractive. You look like you think you're better than they are."

I *am* better than they are, Smadar thought.

"The rest of you, act like you're enjoying yourselves—minty freshness, all that rot. Don't you guys ever watch television?"

Shumlik was the star of today's performances. He kind of grinned with his mouth closed as he sloshed the liquid around and then began to wiggle his hips to the background music, like he seemingly found the process of teeth cleansing invigorating.

He's got zits under his T-shirt, Smadar thought.

Even Aaron scored low on the exercise.

"You're listing to one side," said Elbaz. "Posture is everything. More barre class for you, young man. Ludmilla [the new Russian ballet mistress] will shove a ramrod up your butt."

When the laughter and the misery died down, Elbaz asked them what they'd learned from the endeavor.

"That I'm fat and ugly," said the girl who jiggled.

"There is room for all body types in the theater," Elbaz said.

"That makeup, lighting, and hairstyling are your friends," said Smadar.

"Yes," said Elbaz. "You have to be prepared. Unfortunately, you can't control who your cameraperson is, at least at first, but it is definitely part of their job to make you look good. What else?"

"Posture counts," Aaron groaned.

A couple of kids laughed.

"What is the point of this kind of commercial?" asked Elbaz.

"To sell mouthwash," said Shumlik.

Elbaz rolled his eyes. "To whom?"

"To normal people," said Shumlik.

"Good," said Elbaz. "That's the takeaway and why you did so well," he cracked.

More laughter.

"Normal people who want to feel better about who they are," said Elbaz. "That's why this guy nailed it." He pointed to Shumlik. "Because as he used the product, he felt happier and more optimistic about himself. The other stuff is cosmetic, that part is acting."

Is it because I am a woman? Smadar wondered. He only praises men.

"I fucking hate his guts," Smadar said. Joshua had flown in from school for the weekend, and his parents had given him money for one of the nicest hotels in town. The Norman. They'd just finished having sex. She'd arrived early, hit the minibar, showered, and arranged herself on the bed with rose petals tactically placed all over her naked body. When he opened the door and saw Smadar offering herself up like that—a strategically wrapped gift!—Joshua dove for her so fast, he hadn't even bothered to fully take his clothes off. When she came, he gently unwrapped her arms and went down on her, swampy as she was. Smadar came again and again in waves that seemed almost endless, until finally with a shudder, and some relief, they ended. It was almost too much for her to bear, being that out of control. As soon as it was over, she pushed him off her, she was sopping wet between her legs. How could he lap up all that she and he had produced together? She rubbed herself clean with the top sheet as he undressed himself and then spooned her from behind.

"I'm crazy about you," he said. And when he got hard again against her butt: "Look what you do to me, Smadar."

"Put it away," she said. "I'm exhausted."

He laughed with what sounded like pure distilled joy.

Why don't I ever feel that way? Smadar wondered. I love him, I know I love him. I mean, I say it all the time.

He got up and went to the minibar and pulled out a champagne split. There were water glasses on a side table, and he popped the cork and handed her one filled halfway up.

"To when you get your second wind," he toasted.

"Your parents will cover the champagne?" she asked.

"Cheerfully," he said. "They are so into you. They'll pay for all of it."

"They've never met me," she said. With the duvet wrapped around her, she sat up against the headboard to take a sip. The bubbly was French, the good stuff, effervescent liquid gold.

"They've never seen me this happy before," Joshua said. "They think you are a positive influence. And you're Jewish."

"I'm a convert," Smadar said.

"They don't have to know that," said Joshua. "Anyway, they won't care. You're Jewish enough. C'mon, you fought in the army. You enlisted. For Israel. What more could any nice Zionist couple from New Jersey claim to want?"

It seemed his dad was a successful businessman—very successful, real estate—and his mother was a doctor, and since he and Smadar started dating, Joshua told her they thought he'd "woken up a bit, in a good way," and "started thinking about my prospects."

"They're great, my parents," said Joshua. "I mean, they really love me a lot."

Smadar knew a little bit about that.

"Both sets of my grandparents were survivors, so they have inherited survivor mentality. They think I'm too idealistic for real life, but they support me anyway. The World Bank was my dad's idea, that and the IMF. He says you can do good and still make tons of money."

"What about your mom?" said Smadar. "She's a doctor, she makes money."

"She's a doctor, she does good. She's a pediatrician, she doesn't make that much money."

"How much money does your dad want you to earn?" Now she was curious.

"Probably a fortune, but he has a fortune, so if I do well enough, he'll help me out. I'm an only child," he said. "He just thinks it's important for everyone to be able to support themselves."

She knew what that felt like, the only child part.

"So, when are we meeting your mom for dinner?" he asked, glancing at his watch. He liked her mother. He always told her that. He thought she was a fountain of nurture, warmth, and benevolence.

"I didn't tell her you were coming in this time," she said. When he looked quizzical, she added, "I wanted you all for myself," eliciting a great big smile.

That wasn't it. Her mother liked Joshua well enough. What was not to like? Polite, good-looking, rich, crazy about her daughter. But he was *galut* from the diaspora, a foreigner. It was as if Mama sensed he was planning to take her kid away from her, and as Mama nervously noted, Smadar had never seemed that smitten with anyone else before. Her mother worried too much. Better off leaving her a little in the dark.

Puppyish, he threw his body across her lap. It was almost too easy.

"So, tell me again about Elbaz. Why do you hate him this week?" Joshua asked. He rolled over and looked up at her—those blue eyes again, the high beams!—head resting on the cool linen.

"He doesn't take me seriously. Nobody does. I'm fucking sick of it. Six more months of this and it's official, I'm a failure."

"No callbacks?" he asked gently.

She nodded, tears slipping out from behind her eyelashes.

"Sweetheart," he said, "it's probably just the wrong playing field. Israel is so Israeli. Your look is more exotic. It will be better for you in London, I promise, you'll see."

She nodded. It was a nice dream. But Smadar wasn't a dreamer.

"Besides, it would be safer for you living there."

"You're going to start in on that, too?"

"There were 320 terrorist attacks this past year. That's what happens when people are imprisoned by occupation."

"I'm hungry," she said.

"What else is new?" Joshua laughed.

"Where do you want to eat?" she said.

"Right here," he said. "I read the website. There's a great restaurant in this very hotel. One reason that I picked it."

She started to get up.

"Where are you going?" he asked, lunging for her legs and pulling her back down again.

"To the shower. To get dressed," she said, laughing now. "So, we can go downstairs and get some dinner."

"Room service," said Joshua. "Naked dinner. An adolescent fantasy of mine."

"Really?" said Smadar. She turned to look at him. She'd never had room service before.

"Tomorrow we'll get dressed and go outside," he said. He picked up the phone. "I'll order for us, okay?"

"Okay," she said. "But I still want to take a shower." She stood up.

"As long as you don't put on any clothes," he said, "I guess that'll be fine."

"Are you the boss of me?" asked Smadar.

"Yes," he said. "I am the boss of you. You can wear a bathrobe. But no streetwear until morning."

"Streetwear? You make me sound like a hooker."

"You're no hooker. You're the love of my life."

As she walked toward the bathroom, she clicked on the television. It was an American show with American actors and actresses.

"My parents are right," Joshua called out. "I didn't know I could be this happy." Then he spoke into the phone: "Yes, room 710. Send us up your two best entrées—yep, sirloin and seabass sound good—a couple of salads, definitely French fries, and at least three desserts . . ."

Smadar didn't hear the rest because she'd stepped into the shower and turned the water on superhot and superstrong, she was dying to get his slime off her. Those Americans on the screen, they all had button noses, and not a single one had an indiscernible accent like hers, they all sounded alike. Is that what it took to break into this business? She soaped up hard between her legs and down the groove between her buttocks from her sacrum to her perineum, and let the shower pelt her lower back first and then her face, hard as gravel.

The last module before graduation was on typecasting. The first year and a half, the curriculum had been all technique and practice oriented. That final semester was predominately centered on the marketplace.

"Now that you are all finely tuned instruments," Elbaz said, "we want you to be able to get jobs and eat. Here at the studio, we pride ourselves on producing working artists."

They were back in the auditorium. The forty graduates-to-be each had a headshot up on-screen and a tagline beneath their picture. Aaron was "The Heartthrob"; Shumlik, "The Lovable Loser"; some of the other guys were designated "The Politician's Son," "The Boss," "The Creeper," and "The Athlete." Plus, "The Hero" and "The Bad Boy." In female world, the fat girl was labeled "The Fat Girl." Other lady roles were "The Cheerleader," "The

Housewife," "The Victim," "The Sociopath," "The Movie Star" (sadly, not Smadar). What, no heroines? Sexism in the theater is just more of the same, Smadar thought. We are treated like dirt everywhere.

Her eyes scanned the giant chart. Her own photo was captioned: "The Femme Fatale." Now, her eyes were swimming. Was this good news or bad? As in, what did it mean for her? Work or no work? She wasn't sure.

More categories listed beneath her female brethren: "The Other Woman," "The Vixen," "The Minx," and "The Manic Pixie Dream Girl." Her fellow students looked stunned, except for the ones who were grinning broadly.

"Okay," said Elbaz, "why do you think I called you all here today?"

"To reduce us to psychological ashes?" asked Shumlik.

"To show you how brutal typecasting can be," said Elbaz, "depending on who you are. I mean, some of you must feel like you're sitting pretty," he said, looking pointedly at Aaron.

"Hey, that's not fair," said Aaron. "I want to be an actor, not a heartthrob."

"Not fair?" said Elbaz. "Not fair? What made you think any of this was fair? Do you really believe that what you want has anything to do with what you'll get? This particular theater is called life, my friend. Nothing fair about any of it."

"What if I refuse to always be the lovable loser," said Shumlik.

"Then you've got to work like hell to get cast against stereotype," said Elbaz. "Or you could go into your father's business." He pointed at Aaron. "You, you need to play the Elephant Man. Remember Daniel Day-Lewis in *My Left Foot*?" He pointed at Shumlik: "You, you need to lift weights, run from the easy jokes, and find an edge. Think Steve Buscemi, scrawny but scary. Or cash in on what you've got—there will always be space for someone like you, at least while you're young.

"That goes for most of you—the youth part," said Elbaz. He

turned to the fat girl: "Now you, you've got something you can ride into old age. Melissa McCarthy. Rebel Wilson. Shelley Winters."

She burst into tears.

"Don't cry," he said. "Sometimes typecasting saves our lives and buys us luxury real estate and expensive cars. I predict when you're my age you'll be sitting pretty."

He looked at their fallen faces. Startled, as if he'd just been rudely awakened, he said, "Why are any of you listening? Don't you know me by now? I'll say anything to get a rise out of you." He shook his leonine head. "I'm not God. The only one you should listen to is yourselves. This is a tough business, and if you can quit, you should."

"Now come on, there's cookies and stuff out in the hall. Iced tea, I think. Go eat and lighten up."

Even as they were pigging out on lemon wafers and some pre-packaged *alfajores*—a transplant from the supermarket, beloved by the many Argentines who'd made aliyah—a bunch of the kids still seemed shaken. Shumlik looked especially doleful. When he bit into the sandwich cookies stuffed with caramel, coconut flakes snowed like dandruff down his black T-shirt. But Smadar felt only determination. She followed Elbaz as he walked down the hall and into his office, catching him by surprise as he was sitting down at his desk. She closed the door behind her.

"Yes," said Elbaz, looking up.

"You said I am a femme fatale," said Smadar. "I want to try the role on for size and see if it fits."

His dark eyes glittered.

She walked around to the back of his desk and fell to her knees.

After she finished sucking him off, he kissed her on the top of her head and groaned, "That was fucking amazing. You definitely get the part."

Smadar stood as he zipped and sat down in the chair across from him. "Okay if I smoke?" she asked.

"Of course," he said, "please," and he pulled an ashtray out of his top drawer. "I think I will join you."

She offered him a cigarette and he took one. Then he removed a lighter from the same drawer, lit hers first and then his own.

Smadar exhaled through her nostrils.

"What about me?" she asked.

"You?" said Elbaz, still somewhat dazed. "Yes, of course you. Why don't we get some dinner and then go back to my place?"

"Sure," said Smadar. "But that's not what I meant."

"Oh," said Elbaz. "What did you mean?"

"I want to be an actor. That's all I've ever wanted. Is it good or bad, the femme fatale stuff?"

Elbaz smiled. The ball was back in his court. "It's neither. There's nothing else you can do," he said. "You'll play soulless, manipulative women because you are soulless and manipulative. You'd be a great spy. A temptress. A traitor. When I look in your eyes, I see endless nothing but some strange tensile strength . . . and wicked intelligence. You're definitely sexy. You've got that going for you. And you're drop-dead gorgeous. There's a weird masculinity to your beauty even though your vibe is totally het-erosexual. You could even make that voice work if you had some-thing inside you to project. But you don't. You're a seducer, not an emoter. My two cents."

She chewed this over.

"Dinner?" he said.

"Sure," she said.

"Then my place?" he said.

She shrugged and nodded yes. "You owe me."

"I'm a man who never welches on my debts," said Elbaz.

She went back to his apartment that night and slept with him on and off until the end of the semester.

. . .

Months later, while Smadar was sitting at Cafe Sheleg, idling away another afternoon reading the StarNow website, hunting for open casting calls and texting with her boyfriend, a woman sat down directly across from her.

"What?" Smadar said, looking up.

Joshua had been going on excitedly about his studies and, more wearyingly, about his job search. His father had gotten him an interview at Barclays Bank.

where would you prefer to live, new york or london or california?
honey just do what's in your own best interest

It was the right thing to say, it's not like they were engaged or anything, but also, she knew that it would drive him crazy. Joshua's favorite word was "us." He hated it whenever she talked about her life in an independent way. On his last visit, after sex, when they were lying together in bed, he said, "How did I get so lucky?"

Smadar kissed him on the nose: "Boy, is your next girlfriend going to hate me." She laughed and watched as he deflated onto her chest.

"No next," Joshua whispered softly into her neck.

She enjoyed keeping him attentive and unbalanced.

Now, her new companion was making herself at home, leaning back in her chair and eyeing the menu that Smadar had clumsily tossed over to that side of the table, having long ago memorized its contents.

"I think I'll have a coffee," the woman said.

She was beautiful, in her late thirties with dark blond hair pulled up into a French twist; it shined like a bronze goblet in the last afternoon light. Dressed smartly in navy pants and a matching blazer, with a rather lovely yellow silk scarf tied around her neck, she had a serious jaw and a certain European élan. Very thin and elegant.

"I come from the prime minister's office," the woman said. She had a hint of a German accent.

Mossad.

Smadar wasn't born yesterday. There was a premium on foreign-born agents; the Hebrew accent was such a giveaway. And she'd heard talk of this greeting before, too, of course, although she'd always thought it to be an urban legend. She'd certainly never expected to hear the words out loud in real life, so they took her by surprise. Had she ever finished filling in that online application? No, she thought, she decidedly had not.

Now, she wondered if she'd actually been spied upon that night. Just googling alone had probably sent a whole bunch of spybots wriggling through her laptop. What else did they know about her? Her thoughts turned to Elbaz. Was he also a recruiter? She wouldn't put it past him. Although their affair had ended when she left school, and they hadn't kept in touch, she knew that he was fond of her. Maybe that was the wrong word. He admired her, she thought. Her steely qualities.

"Why me?" asked Smadar. She inhaled her cigarette and then performed her signature dragon-smoke exhale, keeping her cool.

"You have skills that are right for the job."

"What skills?" said Smadar. "I am an unemployed actor."

"We have been told that your theatrical talents are exceptionally well suited for our purposes."

Elbaz! Or Aaron? Shumlik? It could be anyone from the studio. Or maybe it was Rafi, trying to get back inside her pants.

"You speak English, Hebrew, Bosnian, French, and Italian fluently. *Gutes Deutsch*. Also, a little Spanish I've been told."

"Un poquito," Smadar said. "Not hard between the Italian and the French."

"May I have a cigarette?" the woman asked.

"Of course." Smadar passed the pack and lighter across the table, but not before snagging herself another. She lit it with the still red burning embers of the first one. "How do I know you are who you say you are?" asked Smadar. She inhaled again.

"I haven't said I'm anyone," said the woman.

Smadar looked into her eyes and saw nothing. This woman was infinitely cooler than she was. She didn't like that at all, but she respected it. Still, she shivered.

"Are you cold?" the woman said. "It's a nice day for March. 17.8 Celsius. Not bad."

"A goose walked over my grave," said Smadar. "My boyfriend says that a lot."

"The American. The American living in England. The phrase itself is, I think, British in origin. He must have picked it up there."

"Whatever," said Smadar, thinking: so you've really done your research. "I'm fine."

Slowly assessing her, the woman said, "You *are* beautiful. And you do keep calm and steady, everyone says that about you. We need someone like that, that men will want."

"A femme fatale," Smadar said a bit smugly.

The woman laughed.

Smadar didn't like that, either.

"I'm not sure that would be my word choice," the woman said, apparently reading her mind. "But all right. Women are gifted with tools men don't have at their disposal. As long as you are not afraid to employ them. Especially when it is for the good of the country."

Smadar considered this. "Think about your pussy," Elbaz had said. The power between her legs. She wasn't above this, obviously, as long as it remained her choice when she wanted to use it.

"Is that what you do?"

The woman laughed again. "What I do is talk to people like you."

Smadar frowned. She did not enjoy being played with.

"Don't make a face. You've no idea what it is I'm offering you.

The sky's the limit for a girl like you." She stubbed her cigarette out in the ashtray and put the butt inside her purse.

Smadar liked the sound of that.

Her companion took a folded-up piece of paper out of her inner jacket pocket. She handed it to Smadar. In typescript it read: "Your imagination is my reality. Join us to see the invisible and do the impossible." Beneath the quote was a list of phone numbers and websites.

"A moment ago, you asked why you? You were a soldier. You bike and hike and dive. You are an actress. Would you like to travel?"

"Since my mother and I first arrived, aside from London, I have never been outside this country."

"I know that," the woman said.

You seem to think you know everything, Smadar thought.

"Can you keep a secret?" the woman continued.

"Of course."

"If you join us you will travel. You will see all there is to see. But no one can know what you do, not this current boyfriend and not your beloved mama. If they knew, it would only endanger them both and you most of all, not to mention our other colleagues."

"I'd never tell."

"If you join us, your loyalty is only to Israel and the Israeli people."

"I understand," said Smadar. "No one loves Israel more than me and my mother." She inhaled one last time and ground out her cigarette on the sidewalk with her foot.

"We leave no trace," said the German lady. "It's not nice to litter."

So Smadar picked up the remains of her leisurely afternoon and put them in her napkin.

But by then the German lady was gone.

. . .

The main headquarters of the training academy were right out-side of Tel Aviv, at the midrasha, close enough to home that she could still bunk with her oblivious, trusting mother.

At the beginning, she went through a period of rigorous examinations—physical, psychological, and intellectual—passing them all with flying colors. Mama had indeed been right, her *shana madela* truly had a *yiddishe kop*!

Imagine, a convert scoring at the top of her class, Smadar thought. She'd racked up more points than the Jews by birth!

Plus, her love of sports gave her an innate advantage in the freshman class. The gym and coaches at the institute were the world's best. Several had already served their home countries by participating in the Olympics.

As the weeks and then months passed, Smadar was taught how to spot, engage, and cultivate future agents, so that one day she, too, could be as successful and beguiling as that striking Teutonic serpent from Cafe Sheleg. Wouldn't it be great to beat that lady at her own dangerous game? Smadar always had one eye out for her in her rounds throughout the agency, but she never saw that glamour-puss again.

This was a good time in her life! Many of the skills Smadar was learning were fun, and almost all were useful, she liked to think, for whatever she decided to do next. How to avoid being a target, for one, which required the utmost care regarding safety in her car and on foot, and how to smoke out counterintelligence, so she wouldn't get fooled into being picked up by enemy agents, like the clueless Mordechai Vanunu, the peace activist who gave Israeli nuclear secrets to the British papers and spent eighteen years in solitary for his troubles. Often her instructors used scene stud-ies as preparation, just like in theater school: "You're sitting in a chair at a café, and you need to draw your weapon." This was a skill she learned to perform gracefully and without calling atten-tion to herself, practice making perfect as she translated it into muscle memory.

Bang bang! You're dead.

No one suspects the hot girl in the miniskirt, who is seemingly so stunned by the violence erupting before her, she continues sipping her orange soda.

She learned how to memorize names and faces by envisioning dropping photos into a mental file. New practical skills were added daily to her arsenal: the subtle arts of lock picking, phone hacking, lamp bugging, and photographing documents on the sly.

Once, when she thought she was on a Sunday afternoon outing with some other trainees at the Carmel Market, senior spies threw firecrackers to simulate a terrorist attack. One minute, Smadar was perusing the outdoor spice bins, taking in the strong scents and the rich hues of the open baskets of cumin, cinnamon, and paprika in the afternoon sunlight and questioning whether the line was too long for her to pick some up for her mother. The next minute, feeling too lazy to wait, she'd moved on to a vegetable stand, where the fat red radishes clustered in bouquets were so pretty Mama always said you could carry them like roses at a wedding. She was asking herself why her mother's comment had always irked her, when suddenly: *Smash! Boom! Crash!* There was smoke and explosions and flashing lights everywhere. Babies cried, and people were screaming. Smadar didn't bat an eye. She was raised on this shit.

After the fact, when teachers and pupils all gathered back at the institute and learned that the "attack" was just a training game, one of her superiors screened a video he'd taken on his phone at the "crime scene" in one of the smaller auditoriums. There in living color, surrounded by mayhem, Smadar was a portrait of composure. She hadn't even flinched, while several of her compatriots freaked out and ran away. One of her tallest classmates, six-foot-three and buff, actually got down on his knees and wept. Smadar had helped an elderly woman to her feet, checked to see if the lady was all right, and walked her calmly out of the square, without bothering to turn around and gawk at the chaos shaking loose behind her.

Ha, ha, I've been here before, Smadar thought, when she watched her performance up on-screen. The spy stuff, it's just like in drama school. Although this time, I'm the star performer!

In the Negev desert, she learned how to drive a motorcycle on an operational course and rode faster and scored higher than all the men in the trial. In the ocean, she water-skied from one boat to another, climbed her way on board without alerting the crew or captain. Not all the recruits could hack it; some quit and some were informed that their services were no longer required, but Smadar performed steadily. After months of preparation, she was put through a full-scale interrogation to see if they could break her. They tied her to a chair. No food, no water, no bathroom. She calmly peed inside her pants. Twelve hours of flashing lights and superloud music. They tickled her with feathers with her hands tied behind her back. Again and again, they asked her name. Again and again, she gave them her alias, the Canadian Miriam Schecter. She cried on cue at all the moments a blameless tourist would—thank you, Adon Elbaz!—feverishly proclaiming her innocence. That brutal session ended with an "attagirl" and a round of smattering applause.

Each time she was praised by her superiors, Smadar thought, Validation!

By then, Smadar was living in a small apartment by herself in Jerusalem. She'd told her mother and Joshua she'd taken a job at the Ministry of Foreign Affairs, hoping to be transferred to the Israeli embassy in London. "I'm not getting anywhere with the acting," she said, "so I'm doing what my mother always wanted me to do and joining the foreign service."

"What a good girl," Mama said. "Aman!"

Ha, ha, thought Smadar, Mama's proud now. She would die if she only knew!

Her mother was thrilled, but Joshua was impatient.

"I love you, but I don't get you," he said, one night when they were talking on the phone.

Smadar was sitting on the edge of her bed, doing her nails on her nightstand, painting them a translucent pearly white. They looked very professional, appropriate for an office, she thought. Her mobile was on speakerphone.

"You were supposed to move in with me a year ago."

"I like it here," said Smadar. "Come to Israel. There are plenty of banks. Guy or one of your other Excel bros could set you up. Or you could just stick with 'Golden Slacks.' You could join their offices on Berkowitz Street, near the art museum. I'd move back to Tel Aviv for that. I like it better there anyway."

There was a moment's silence, as if he were gathering courage.

"Even John Kerry says that if Israel doesn't make peace soon, it could end up being an apartheid state," Joshua said.

"What?" said Smadar. "Where did that come from?"

He was so exasperating. He'd made her smudge the polish. She used her right thumb to edge out a barrier between the nail and cuticle on her left pointer finger.

"I don't want to raise kids in the next South Africa," Joshua went on.

Smadar hung up.

She couldn't stand the sound of his voice. Spoiled little American banker boy. What did he know about living in a war zone?

When he called back, she turned off her ringer.

When he texted, she blocked his number.

She blew on her nails.

Holier than thou *and* a total sellout.

It was a week before they made up.

"Look," he said, "I don't think we fundamentally disagree. I think if we sit down and talk rationally, we'll realize we're on the same page. I just miss you. We don't see each other enough. We need time together. I'm tired of postponing."

"I'm sick of flying to London," she said. "Dreary, dreary London. Every time I cross the street, I think a bus is going to take my head off. I can't get used to them driving on the wrong side."

"Let's spend a week in New York together, then," said Joshua. "Maybe that's the place for us anyway. My parents are there, you can be Jewish without compromise . . ."

"Now I'm the one who's compromising?"

"No. No, I'm sorry. I didn't mean that. Sweetheart!" He sounded both consoling and exasperated. "Just put in for a little vacation. Maybe you can visit the Israeli embassy in Manhattan. Charm them there. See if they have an opening."

The line went quiet.

"So?" he said.

"So, I'm thinking it over," she said.

"Smadar," he said.

"Joshie-bear."

"Oh my God," he groaned. "Just say you'll come!"

"I'll come," she said. It was a childhood dream. New York City.

"I just love you so much, Smadar," Joshua said. "If you knew how much I loved you, you'd never let me go."

The trip to the Big Apple should have been amazing. They went to Jing Fong in Chinatown for dim sum, which Smadar found interesting but greasy, and the Village Vanguard to hear jazz. Joshua's favorite. It was located in a basement, a little too airless and claustrophobic for her—she hated going underground—so she left early. But it was close to their Airbnb in the West Village, which was cute enough, and an easy stumble home. The next night they were invited to a rave in Bushwick, not her scene. And after to Veselka in the East Village to eat kasha and eggs at four o'clock in the morning, which was fine, but it wasn't like she craved an eastern European experience. She reminded him that she'd been looking forward to shopping in SoHo and Nolita, which made him roll his eyes. But even when hanging out with his friends from college, on rooftop bars in Brooklyn and the Red Rooster up in Harlem—his jam, not hers—Joshua seemed uncharacteristically sullen. "You don't pay enough attention to me," he said. "You seem more interested in anybody else." It wasn't like him to be so grouchy. He was such a downer, she posted pictures of him pouting on her Facebook page, to needle him and to prove her point. He was cranky and he aggravated her. She thought she was being a good sport. Did he not want her to pay attention to all his cute friends? She knew him already.

Toward the end of the week, they went out to New Jersey to see his parents. The older couple had visited in Israel, but she'd never been on their home turf before.

"Smadar, you keep getting more and more beautiful," the father said, when they sat down in the living room with drinks.

The mother glanced at him and then back at Smadar, as if she didn't see what he saw in their son's girlfriend, or maybe she didn't like the way he was saying it.

"We're so glad you came with Joshua this visit. What were your first impressions of the city?" Marilyn seemed overeager, somewhat strained. "We're hoping you two will move home, so we can see more of both of you." She made a show of crossing her fingers. Bands of ice and platinum twinkled on her left hand, and one J.Lo-worthy solitaire.

Smadar smiled through her teeth. This was not her home. And clearly, this woman did not like her.

"We are actively thinking about it, right, sweetie?" Smadar said. She leaned over and placed a hand on Joshua's thigh as she kissed him on the cheek.

For the first time all week, Joshua perked up. "I'd love to live in Williamsburg with you," he said. He looked at her questioningly.

"In one of the new buildings?" asked Smadar. "With a view of the skyline?"

"Sounds fantastic!" said Joshua, his face lighting up.

"Oh, this is so exciting," Marilyn said. "Progress." She sat back and smiled for real.

Saul, the father, put a restraining hand on the wife's shoulder.

Smadar looked from one family member to the other. Joshua had the mother's coloring, and her hair was curly, too. The blue eyes and strong jawline were from the father, now a silver fox. Their living room was opulent, overstuffed, with Oriental rugs, a Siamese cat, a grand piano, built-in bookshelves. A huge ornate crystal chandelier.

"My grandmother smuggled that one from Prague," Marilyn said, following Smadar's eyes.

"How on earth?" asked Smadar.

"She put it in a trunk and covered it with her fur coat," said Marilyn.

"Smart," said Smadar admiringly.

She looked at the pearls around Marilyn's neck. I wonder if she smuggled those out in her vagina, she thought.

The chandelier was probably worth a small fortune. Not at all her style.

For a moment Smadar considered the proposition of making the big move, as if she were free to do whatever she wanted. She probably *could* get a job at the Israeli embassy here and not give up being undercover. She was so proficient now at her double, triple life, sometimes she lost track of which character she was playing. Was it *beshert*, foreordained, the way things were now unfolding? God rolling out the red carpet to help her become a working actor or even an actual movie star? During prep at the agency, she had been instructed in the rules of cloak-and-dagger; how to build a cover story, a new identity; how to change her appearance with hair and makeup, dress young or old, male or female—far more utilitarian skill sets than all the theoretical nonsense theater school had peddled. In her covert training, it was determined that she major in psychological operations. Every new mission began with professionals working as a team to build in-depth profiles, so Smadar would know exactly how to manipulate and control her marks. What kind of a dossier would they have presented her with if Joshua and co. were officially her quarry?

Joshua's dad was the type of guy who always needed his dick sucked, preferably in front of an audience. Saul seemingly had to be the smartest, most powerful person in the room, even when he wasn't. With his money, he'd been able to make things easy for his kid, but now Smadar bet he wondered if perhaps he'd made it a bit too easy and the kid was spoiled rotten.

She thought Joshua was. Everything had been handed to him.

Maybe, Smadar thought, Dad was a secret prick. Maybe, with the way he was looking at her, he was fantasizing about having sex with her right now. She'd been around enough men, including his own son, to register the heat of his stare. Even that bitch, his wife, seemed to have caught a whiff of him. His vulnerability to Smadar was potentially quite useful, and she added it to her how-to-manipulate-Saul file. Although she'd have to be on her toes, because she sensed he was sharp enough to see through her.

Marilyn was trickier. The doctor, the Jewish mother. Ultra-competent, attractive enough, but controlling and high-strung. Smadar could smell the distrust on her breath. Marilyn would have been happier if her son had hooked up with a local girl, a professional, someone who would cheer him on as he found his way. She couldn't understand why Smadar wasn't going for that gold. A nice, rich, handsome Jewish boy, when what Smadar wanted, now that she thought about it, was a man.

And then there was Joshua himself: smart, kind, loving, super-cute Joshua, full of myriad ideas but also kind of spineless, cossetted, lacking a clear vision for his life.

"I love this idea," said Smadar.

Joshua grabbed her hand.

Smadar looked his father directly in the eye. "Saul," she said, "with your connections, before we leave, would it be possible to hook us up with some real estate brokers?"

"Of course he can," said Marilyn. "You can right away, can't you, Sauly?" And when he nodded yes, Sauly's bright blues still locked on Smadar's green irises, the mom said, "Maybe we can all go apartment hunting? A family outing. That way we can spend more time with the two of you and get to know Smadar a little better."

"Thanks, Mom," said Joshua. He looked happy and relieved.

Smadar and Saul continued conversing with their eyes.

The Ministry of Foreign Affairs was a half-hour walk and fifteen-minute bus ride from the Jerusalem Institute for Israel Studies. Since Mama had such a long commute from Tel Aviv, Smadar would meet her near her offices for lunch. There was a little place, Hachapuria, that served those Georgian pastries, basically bread boats filled with molten cheese. Sometimes you could add spinach with an egg poached on top. Both Smadar and her mother were crazy about them—they were cheap and filling and could be spiced up with house-made s'hug and tomato sauce that accompanied them in little plastic cups. Sometimes they sat at the wooden counters when they weren't lucky enough to get a table. Mama always wanted to split a salad, so they did, but no one, not even her precious mother, could get close to sharing Smadar's "usual," the classic, with acharuli cheese and butter, especially on days she had a hangover. That, she ate by herself, although inevitably, Smadar's fork would wander over to her mother's plate after she scarfed down her own meal, but Mama never seemed to mind.

"So, I am thinking of moving to Jerusalem," said Mama. "I'm not getting any younger, and the commute is getting to me. And you, my precious girl, are here, of course. At least you are for the near future?" Her mother's eyes were question marks.

"You're not so old," said Smadar. "You can handle it. Besides, I'm not planning on staying here much longer. I like Tel Aviv. It's far more entertaining and contemporary. I want to start auditioning again anyway."

"Really?" asked Mama.

"Yes, really," said Smadar. "Theater's in my blood."

"Then you should," said Mama, patting Smadar's hand. "You are a born actress. And I'd love having you close to me."

"Thanks, Mama," said Smadar.

"But what about that poor boy? His parents bought him an apartment . . ." her mother said.

"Poor boy?" said Smadar, moving her fork to her mother's plate. "He could have afforded his own apartment if he had any kind of backbone, he makes enough money to make his own decisions. Anyway, I liked it there, but it's not here."

It was true, New York was okay enough. After an operation was completed, it had been fun to dip a toe into the big city, although she found it too large, frenzied, and messy for her tastes, and she missed the sea. With each passing trip, Joshua felt less and less like a lover and more and more like some weird roommate or a wet blanket draped across her shoulders. She found him suffocating.

"Where is the boy who wanted to order everything on the menu?" she'd asked him during their last fight. They'd just had breakfast—that is, she'd eaten a muffin. He was so ascetic by then, vegan, sober, a Brooklynite; he wouldn't even drink a regular cup of coffee, just some gross mushroom concoction called MUD\WTR. The smell of it made her nauseated.

"Where is the girl who used to be so nice to me?" he countered.

"I am nice to you. I'm always nice to you," said Smadar.

"No, no, you're not," he said. "In the beginning, you shined your light on me, but as soon as you got under my skin you started taking me for granted. Everything is at your convenience. You come and go when you want. You do what's best for you. You don't care about me. Honestly," he said, as if the concept was just this second dawning on him, "you're the most selfish person I've ever met."

"That's not true," Smadar said. "I've done nothing wrong."

"And according to you, you're never wrong," he said. "If anyone challenges you on your bad behavior, you ignore them. And if anyone is better than you at anything, you set out to eviscerate them."

"What are you talking about? You're crazy," said Smadar.

"Oh, come on. If a woman is prettier or smarter or thinner or sexier, you immediately cut her out. You can't stand the competition. The only reason you stayed friends with Ella as long as you did was because she's gay and that doesn't threaten you. But then you cast even her aside."

"I did not cast her aside. I outgrew her!"

(Ella had become such a pain, hounding Smadar to be more honest with Joshua, even suggesting that she break up with him. "He's a great guy," Ella had said over the phone. "And you don't really love him. Set him free, why don't you, babe! Let him find somebody new."

"That's none of your business," Smadar retorted. "Stay out of it, Ella-boo. I'm warning you.")

"Ella! Who is more loyal than Ella? Even your mother loves Ella, and your mother only loves you!" Joshua said in his apartment in Williamsburg. "I remember you picking apart all the other actresses when you were in theater school—the fat girl, the skinny one. Your latest friends, Noa and Sarah, you talk about one's hips and the other's ass. Neither is smart enough. Even my mother, according to you, needs a neck lift!"

"Well, she does," Smadar said, laughing. "You know it's true. And she can afford it."

She reached out her hand to cover his, but he moved it away.

"Come on, stop being such a grump. Besides, no one is prettier or smarter or sexier than I am," she said, again trying for a laugh.

"I'll give you a massage, would that cheer you up? Would you like that?"

"I don't want a massage," Joshua said.

"You don't?" Smadar said. "But you love massages."

"I don't like being bought off."

"Fine," said Smadar. "I have to visit the embassy." She looked at her watch. "Maybe the real Joshua will be here when I come back."

"This is the real Joshua," he said. "And I don't believe you are going to the embassy. I think you lie. I think you lie all the time. That's what my dad says about you, and he should know. He's a consummate liar himself."

"He's a businessperson," said Smadar. "That's what he's trained to do."

His father was the one she was going to meet. Why was Saul talking about her behind her back? This was interesting. To take Joshua off the scent of their affair, or because of his own possessiveness and sense of competition? Did he now want her wholly for himself?

"You're never going to move here, are you?" said Joshua.

Smadar thought for a moment. She searched her heart and her mind and throughout her body. She felt nothing.

"No, I'm never going to move here," Smadar said dully. She lit a cigarette.

They sat in silence while she smoked.

"You are unreliable and inauthentic," he said.

"You're unreliable and inauthentic," she said back to him.

"Your breath smells bad. Your teeth are yellow," said Joshua.

"Go to hell," said Smadar.

"My mother said you were cold. That you're missing something. She said you have no center of self."

"You can go fuck yourself," said Smadar. "Mama's baby boy."

Then she got up and packed her bag and went to see his father.

. . .

Saul had booked a room at the Lowell Hotel in the East Sixties off Madison Avenue. Luxurious and discreet, the way she liked it.

"Food first," she said. "Sex second."

But he'd already ordered up room service, anticipating her requirements. *Omelette aux fines herbes,* toast and apricot jam, a large milky latte, and raspberries and cream for her; for him, scrambled egg whites, orange juice, and coffee. When they had sex, she looked up at his icy blue eyes and crinkled papery lids, the large mole on his left temple, and thought, This is what being married to Joshua would look like.

After, while lying in bed in Saul's arms, she said, "Why did you tell Joshua that I'm a liar?"

He stiffened, then stroked her hair. "He's my son, I'm his father, I have to look out for what's best for him."

"You once offered me money to break up with him," Smadar said, slowly sitting up. "Now the time has come." She reached over for a plush white robe and slipped it on. "I need to take a shower, and then I'm going to catch the next flight home."

He looked surprised but not unhappy. "I'll write you a check. Can you cash it in Israel?"

"Yes," she said. She now knew how to cash a check almost anywhere.

"Can we still see each other?" Saul asked, as he reached for his wallet and picked up a pen from the end table on his side of the bed. "I've grown quite fond of you, Smadar."

She walked to the marble bathroom, past the orchids and the lilies he always had sent up to please her, and said over her shoulder, "Maybe, maybe not." Then she closed the door.

"I'll book your flight for you," he said, his voice muffled. "Business class."

After that, all she could hear was the shower running.

From there, with a payday in her pocket, she went to the airport and flew back to Israel.

She'd been a little surprised that Joshua hadn't called her since. They'd fought before, and he'd always come running back in the past. Fuck him. He was a weakling anyway.

Smadar kept eating from her mother's plate.

"Relax, Mama, fear no more. I broke up with him," said Smadar in between bites.

"You did?" said Mama.

Smadar nodded.

Her mother grabbed her arm and pressed. "He's a nice boy, but I never thought he was right for you. You need a man who takes your breath away. You need a real Israeli."

It wasn't long before Smadar moved back to Tel Aviv, booked an agent, and began auditioning again, for TV, theater, and the movies, a full-court press! She started training at Liky's gym. Gal Gadot had gone there, and the Hadids' third sister, the fashion designer, was a regular—sometimes she and Smadar chatted in the changing room. There were two teachers per class, and Smadar took HIIT six times a week. Already she could see the results even on top of her agency training.

For visibility, she hung out at the restaurant Mr. & Mrs. Lee, where she'd heard Mick Jagger met up with Bar Refaeli. And now she got her nails done regularly at Yullia, no more doing them herself, where the technicians regaled her with tales of the niceness of Natalie Portman. Might as well hang out where the stars did. Smadar even touched base rather coyly with Elbaz— she emailed; he was touring. He'd written that he was glad she was back in business, and he would keep an eye out for her when he knew of appropriate upcoming roles—had she heard he was married with a baby? That last line made her laugh out loud. She noticed he hadn't asked her what she'd been up to lately, but she figured he already knew.

On Sunday nights, she performed as a backup vocalist with a band at the underground bar Pasáž, on Allenby Street, although singing was not her forte. But at least, she thought, she was getting herself out there. All she needed now was a little luck.

Her plan was to tell her superiors when she got a real gig—but not before her next assignment in Tunisia, in a port town on the Mediterranean. Sfax was built on top of Roman ruins, with a beautiful walled old city, made up of tight cobblestoned alleyways and clandestine homes and shops. Smadar was set up in an apartment along the perimeter of the medina, where Sfax turned modern and the stucco edifices were painted such a blinding white that in the heat of the day under the desertlike sun, she had to wear dark glasses while sitting on her small third-floor terrace. This time she went undercover as a visual artist. It was an easy assignment. Her job was to paint, or pretend to paint, at an easel on that same balcony, which was both boring and kind of pleasurable. Her old love of makeup and nail art had her fooling around with mock advertisements, which she modeled on her own face and hands, as she had no audience, so no one to poke fun at her. In this manner, she'd drink iced tea and smoke the afternoons away. Some days she walked up and down her block and sat in a tiny park or even ventured behind the ancient walls, where there was a wonderful fish market and loads of vegetable stands and dark, hidden cafés. She quickly grew fond of the traditional coffee, *qahwa arbi*, which was a lot like the Turkish type she was brought up on, finely ground beans boiled with sugar in a pot called a *zizwa* and topped with a little float of rose water. Every once in a while she drove the little Peugeot she kept parked on the street to the Gulf of Gabès. Thank God the madness of the world ended at the sea. Only in water was there true escape.

Smadar lived on the same block as a Hamas operative on the

down low, who was a rocket mastermind back in Israel. For a couple of weeks, while she painted, she observed his comings and goings. He drove past her place in his convertible on the other side of the boulevard in the mornings and directly below her apartment on his way back home at lunch or at the end of the day. When it became clear that there was no real predictability to his schedule, she had her backup team members intervene. (They were staying in a hotel across town.) Two men posed as Al Jazeera reporters, asking to set up an interview.

"Any ego can be stroked," said Smadar, when they came up with the plan, and it worked, as he met the men at a borrowed office on the specified afternoon, all according to plan.

After their meeting was over, one of her comrades called to tell her their mark was on his way back home. "In the next half hour, I suppose," he said. "Nice guy, for a terrorist."

Around 3:30 p.m., she put down her brushes and picked up what looked like a TV clicker, pointing it at her car, which was sitting in her usual spot on the street. When the engineer drove by in his convertible, she pressed the detonation button. The blast sent his car flying into the air, where it exploded, too, shooting flames and body parts as high up as she was.

I changed your channel, Smadar thought, as she moved inside to get away from the heat and the fumes and the noise. She needed to vacate the premises and fast, but when she passed the mirror on her way to the front door, she noticed some of his bloody flesh had landed in her hair.

She remembered the Israeli girl from Birthright telling the story of her cousin Dafna's eye. Stupid. With that information, she should have taken an apartment on a higher floor.

"Yuck," said Smadar as she rushed to the kitchen sink. It took a wad of paper towels and a lot of dish soap to get the water to run clear.

I need a better job, Smadar thought, as she combed her hair

into a ponytail in front of the hallway mirror and picked up her bag. That had been really disgusting.

Then she left the apartment, taking the stairs and using the rear exit, where a member of her team was waiting in his rental car to drive her to the airport.

Something more glamorous, she thought. Also, a lot more money.

Like a living ghost, Smadar vanished from Tunisia.

Part
Five

Who's spying now?

That kind of sounds like a line from an old song, doesn't it? More than a smoking-hot intro for the last chapter of a hopefully (God willing) soon-to-be-published (knock on wood), take-the-top-of-your-head-off manuscript—just attempting the world's teensiest, most tentative, humble bow here, as it has been almost two years since that bastard raped me, and I'm this close to finis, but I don't aim to effing curse myself by getting ahead of my skis.

What I'm saying is, I want you all to read on to the end. I mean, I need you to. Please read on to the end. Pretty please. Please, just do it for me.

Maybe then you'll publish my story or buy it or write about it or do a segment on it or turn it into a series, or maybe a documentary, or a real live action-packed movie. What an original idea, huh? I have an auto-umbilical connection to a "star on hiatus" who would be perfect for this picture.

Which of these exciting platforms ultimately gets the brass ring—think synergies! franchises!—is dependent on who *you* are and how brave and courageous *your* outlook is. My executive assistant, Branimir Novak, is available to answer all your questions about my memoir (aka call to arms) regardless of whether you are an editor, an agent, a member of the press, an internet site, a TV showrunner, a producer, a DA, or a lawyer. (You get right of first refusal, MLG! I'm not one to forget a friend.) He can be reached at Novak@wgtvl.com. Just put my name in the subject line. *Meredith Montgomery!*

I'm grabbing the bull by the balls now. I've got to. As you are all well aware, if you've hung in this far, I've risked my stupid life to write this thing, and baby needs bank.

You may ask yourself, how did Nina and I both get so fucked?

You may ask yourself, why this motley pair?

You may ask yourself, does God (that asshole on a good day) have it in for *all* his favorite puppets of the female persuasion?

You may ask yourself, when did a couple of warring, living large queen bitches join the roiling underground universe of mole people?

Hiding out. On the lam.

Two hearts, born to run. Who'll be the lonely one?

Those last lyrics are from Journey, my daddy's numero uno band. The others I made up. These days I can't get all his faves out of my head. They braid and tangle into word clusters. Musical larva. Earworm candy.

My point: after barely escaping the Rug's clutches, I spent the next six months—that means Thanksgiving, Christmas, *and* Easter—living incognito in the Ocean Winds in East Jesus, Sumter County, Florida, with my certifiably insane mother.

(Yes, she'd parked the "present" that I'd sent to her for safekeeping, these very pages, by her perennial fake white fir tree; that crap was never coming down, just as I'd predicted, and I had to sneak in bath salts and soaps wrapped up in a similar gift box with the same cheesy Santa paper just to get the book back.)

My mother's mother, Stephanie, christened her Lorelei, which means "alluring," according to nameberry.com, and is kind of white trash if you ask me. My mother told me I was named after her.

Stephanie? Meredith? What?

"It's the same name," my mother said.

Go figure.

Their family surname was Lee. My daddy stuck her with the Monroe moniker. That's why I changed mine to Montgomery. Meredith Monroe? Why not simply call me Marilyn? This from the woman who'd wanted to inscribe Nicole-Brown on my birth certificate. I may be repeating myself, but that bit of family lore tells the entire story. Instead of this extended hard slog, I could have just written it down on a slip of fortune cookie paper and handed it to you—*My mother wanted to give me the name Nicole-Brown, like Mary-Ann*—and saved the time and effort of writing this book. But that's not my jam. Blame it on genetics. We're both over-the-toppers, my mother and me! We do everything the hard way. And no matter how much we tried to escape our roots, Madonna and child ended up with the autographs of aspiring porn stars.

I stayed below the radar in Florida with her for so long because I was terrified in unequal proportions by the aforementioned vile and sickening brute the Rug, the press, the law, and the malicious and cruel social media world—the "nasty-verse," I call it. I needed to heal myself.

Nobody else was going to do that for me.

Hot tip: If you ever want to get lost, like nowhere-to-be-found lost, the Sunshine State is the place for it. Everyone's faces are literally covered with shades and hats, and no one seems to show any interest in where you came from or what you did *before*. It feels like the state's residents are addicted to revision and reinvention. Plus, there are no taxes. And there is the homestead exemption. If you become insolvent, you can keep yourself comfy, it's not like going bankrupt at all.

Still, we were thrifty. My mother's apartment was a one-bedroom ground-floor unit. The "lanai" (brochure-speak translation: tiny cement patio) faced the parking lot and a couple of wobbly palms. That sorry excuse for a lawn looked like some of the younger inmates' thinning domes (male and sadly female), piecemeal and scrubby. The mornings I convinced my mother to have our coffee outside—perched on a couple of beach chairs I'd picked up at Target—spinning tires spit gravel whenever anyone pulled their car out of park. Every so often, those pebbles stung one of us in the shins.

"Ouch," my mother would say, newly startled whenever a rock hit her. That was the problem in a nutshell: no matter how regularly life pummeled that lady, it always came as a surprise.

Mostly, I grinned and bore it. After all the wellness embracing I'd done in LA, I wanted a little break from the cigarette smog inside her palace. Call me the "Fresh Air Fund" for our tiny, low-rent clan.

When I first dumped her here a few years before, my aim was to buy her an actual house, a small one, which was not, I repeat not, a shit ton of money back then or now. The Ocean Winds is a retirement community for formerly working-class, conservative white people and a must stop for Republican candidates. It's filled with folks who've toiled for what they have and believe that at this point in their lives they deserve a little fun and rest and relaxation before they croak. What I'm saying is that I was self-lessly thinking ahead. I wanted my mother to be able to manage on her disability checks in case something should ever happen to me. But wouldn't you know it, that lady was scared to death of *sinkholes,* even more so than she was of the devil, hallucinations, and her own skinny shadow. She put a kibosh on the whole homeownership thing from the start.

"Florida is built on a swamp," my mother said. "And I don't know how to swim."

She seemed to possess some strange faith that sinkholes were only dangerous to houses and couldn't slurp her down in a low-rise rental.

That's how I ended up on a foldout couch at the Atlantic Breeze Lofts over an hour away from the ocean, letting the woman who gave birth to me take the bedroom, like any good daughter might. In the beginning, I believe she was glad for the company, inasmuch as she could follow my train of thought when I talked, at times incessantly, when I wasn't also crying.

"Baby, who's Marietta again?" she'd say, when I babbled on about my guilt (I'd quit googling again, afraid of any more bad news about my ex-agent, afraid of any more bad news about almost anything). But mostly she would just space out smoking or pluck strands of her hair one at a time, dreamily.

God knows what planet gave her a visitor's pass most days, but at least with me in the house there were groceries—besides Lean Cuisine, dry cereal, and diet soda. I mean, I made her drink her juice, the way Manager Liz had made me drink mine. She didn't know it then, but she was modeling behavior, Liz. The women in my family had to be taught *not* to starve each other to death. We weren't trying to. It's just that we didn't often think about anyone else. We barely knew enough to feed ourselves when we were hungry.

I should rot in hell for all the worry I caused Manager Liz back then. She was the only one on this whirling globe who'd expressed any legit affection for me, even if she was kind of channeling her own dead kid, and when I reflect upon it now, I cringe and bang my head on any available wall or table in an act of penance. I'm a hard person to love. But when I first left Venice, I left completely.

No one knew where I was but Branimir. It was too dangerous to reach out to Manager Liz or MLG or any of my erstwhile friends. I needed a break from Matt, too, and it would have been suicidal to go back on Twitter. Brani was my only contact, my source for burner phones and new credit cards and fake IDs and other stuff I shouldn't write about out loud here. I was too frightened to let anyone else know my whereabouts in case they wanted to stalk me again or even kill me. Plus, I was frigging exhausted. I went cold turkey off the internet, just like that.

While we were roomies, my mother liked to stay up late watching TV, smoking like a chimney, so sometimes when I got tired and my eyes burned from all those airborne carcinogens, I took my bedding and slept in the tub. I kind of liked sleeping that way, the cool white enamel, the air filtered by the fan, the sloping sides and bottom impenetrable as a clam shell.

My real problem was how much she hogged the bathroom, because eventually she came in and kicked me out. I don't know what all she did in there, day and night. Stare through the mirror into her past? Sometimes when I couldn't hold it in anymore, I just went outside on the lanai and opened the door and did my business behind a golf cart or bush—I didn't have it in me to run to the public restrooms in the clubhouse several blocks away. There was usually no one in the parking lot at night, so I had few worries, but people did get up early for tennis and golf. Ergo, mornings were tougher. My mother rose at 5:30 a.m. religiously. She had an old-fashioned alarm clock, her phone, and a timer on her wristwatch, and all three would go off in an arpeggio around the room like church bells; she was ever anxious about getting ready for her day.

Why?

She used to work as a teller in a bank. It took all her resources to get there on time and do her job and find her way home and clean her house and defrost her dinner and fall asleep on the couch in front of the TV by 7:30 with a ratty old afghan swaddling her like

a baby. Now, she didn't have anything to do. More, she didn't like
to do much. No weekly card game for my mother; while all those
other striped busy bees ran from one standing date to another—
Monday tennis, Tuesday pickleball, Wednesday golf—she stayed
home. They joined clubs: knitting and line dancing and investing
and toy painting (where they actually decorated the wooden play-
things themselves and did not render portraits of dolls or trains
or marionettes in oils or watercolors, just to be clear; for grandchildren, I suppose, or orphans, or their siblings and friends
with Alzheimer's). But my mother couldn't shake her routine.
She continued to spend hours getting up and getting ready, only
to then spend more hours on the sofa or in her chair. Sometimes
she went to bed, but mostly she didn't. There was one club called
"Scrapbooks for Night Owls," which you might think would have
been right up her alley, but there was nothing much in her life she
wanted to remember, she said. She didn't hold on to keepsakes or
photos or souvenirs of anything.

Not even articles and reviews about me.

I became determined to find her something to do, just for
the physical exercise of escorting her somewhere. And because
there's a specific pain in watching someone else's brain atrophy.
Once a week I'd read her the latest edition of the *Ocean Winds
News,* me sitting at the little round faux-wooden table between
the living room and the open kitchen, drinking her instant coffee; she, as per usual, glued to the telly. That local rag included
a schedule of all the various club meetings, performances, and
events, and it went on for pages. I reminded myself of asshole
Amber from Washington State, still in her wet raincoat, home
from work, dog-tired, holding up a can of Campbell's Chunky
Soup, saying, "Guess what's for dinner, fellas?" like a real live
mom from a soup commercial. It was her last-ditch effort to light
a spark, before interring herself in a brewski-induced bubble of
solipsism and despair.

"Look, Mama," I said, as brightly as I could manage, reading the listings one night over the noise of her *Friends* rerun. "They even have a club for Dirty Uno."

"Lorelei," she said.

"Sorry?" I said.

"No 'Mama.' You can be a sister or a cousin."

She was under fifty in a fifty-five-plus lifestyle community, but she didn't want anyone to think she was old enough to be my mother, even though I was famous and paid her way, and she didn't have any friends. Zero. Plus, she almost never left the house, so who gave a shit anyhow?

She'd gotten knocked up and popped me out, I'll give her that much. I got my Elizabeth Taylor irises from her, which bought me my career. Once in a blue moon, when I was a kid, she'd give me something to eat while she was already nibbling on something, when I reminded her I was also in the room. And then after a couple of years of the two of us on our own, she'd handed me over to my daddy, no backsies. So, she was right, sort of. "No 'Mama,'" indeed.

Poor Lorelei. A living shell with a pretty-girl ego buried deep inside her along with her multiple mental illnesses, like intestinal parasites or the tongues of sea urchins, the whole tangle of her maladies creepy crawly and hard to fathom, impossible to excise. Eerily, she seemed not to have a care in the world; she was anesthetized by a cocktail of drugs and anxieties to the point of utter fossilization, but she also still possessed signature vanities and concerns.

Later, when I was cooling my heels in prison (yep, that tawdry tale is coming up in this exciting chapter!), the shrink there said that I was a physical manifestation of all my mother would rather sooner forget: encroaching age, an unlived life, lack of agency. The same old, same old.

(They called them "correctional psychologists" in the big house, as if they could tweak us into better behavior. I ask you, why are we taxpayers paying for this shit? I bet I could have gotten more insight from a Moodfit app.)

"No worries. I don't want anybody to know I'm your daughter, either," I said, swallowing the hurt and lashing out at the same time. My default mode. "But it's exclusively you and me in the apartment right now. No one else can hear me speak. Just us and the gang at Central Perk."

I nodded toward the episode of *Friends,* even though she was gazing at the screen and couldn't catch my eye roll. A wasted visual tic from when I used to fraternize with people who actually looked at each other when we conversed.

"Did you go there when you were in New York City?" my mother asked, surprising me by swiveling her head around and fixing me with an imploring look. Her neck, it actually seemed to work.

"Central Perk?" I said.

"Yes," she said.

"It's a TV show," I said.

"Well, you were on a TV show," she said. "Don't they have buses that go between them?"

It was time to change the subject.

"Lorelei," I said slowly, demonstrating, I think, the patience of a saint. She'd disowned me several times before, and besides Uncle Sam, I was the sole contributor to her bank account. "I thought you liked Uno."

It was the one game she'd play with me when I was a child. I mean *Uno* Uno, rated-G Uno, clean Uno, but as I learned the next day at the public access computer at the Ocean Winds Library, this naughty offshoot came complete with shot glasses embellished with cartoon figures doing it doggy style and all sorts of other acrobatic fornication. Apparently, this was only news to me.

"No way, José," she said. "Not the dirty kind. There are bad people who play that game. The men here, they're all dying to transmit their diseases. They're randy *and* they're grandpas. Some of them are penniless and are looking for a meal ticket. Like my pal, Mac."

She had a pal? A pal named Mac?

"There's a dozen hungry girls for every single one of those losers, and the divorced guys are even worse. It's a horny widowers' paradise, if you ask me. They're always strutting around like peacocks, like they're the hot stuff smoking out the window in the back of the church camp bus."

This was the most strung-together set of words I'd heard come out of my mother's mouth in years. That savvy soliloquy kind of freaked me out. But it also made me feel sort of nice inside to think maybe my companionship had done her a bit of good.

If you water it, it grows.

My daddy used to say that when pissing on a tree.

"I'm not joining that stupid club," Lorelei said, continuing to sound oddly rational. "There's nothing in it for me."

"Now you're talking," I said.

Because the last thing my mother needed was herpes or anal warts to add to her list of woes. Besides, she'd told me a long time ago my daddy and his selfishness and cheating had beaten the lust right out of her, which was too bad because she'd gone on so long without love, maybe her whole entire life, and that's Just. Plain. Wrong. Everyone deserves love, not only perfect people, and even though she did her best to hide it, she was still a beautiful woman, so she could have had many opportunities if she wanted them. I mean, appearances shouldn't matter, but they do. I'm very clear on this.

Once I started taking her out on little jaunts, I noticed that the old guys in town and driving by in their golf carts gave her the looks, and the old biddies, drinking their smoothies, gave her the glares. Early on, when we were sitting outside Dunkin' on the covered porch some afternoon or morning or evening—time stood still in the Ocean Winds; even as it marched on, it marched on in place—innocently drinking our iced coffees (no milk, no sugar for either of us), I heard one Spandexed bleached blonde stage-whisper to another: "The boys all say 'That Lorelei is so cute.'" She was wiggling her hips when she said it and staring at my mother, assessing her in that classic mean-girl way.

Those two were members of another subculture—not the long-white-shorts-and-cardigan type like my old lady, who wore that uniform I guessed to disappear, but the tight-pink-pants-and-sparkly-top strain of retiree on the make. The kind to spend their Social Security checks on bottomless margarita brunches and getting their hair done. They were the twenty-first century's brand of village hotties and harlots, divorcées going after the rare dudes with money. Another time, another place, I could have easily grown up to be one of them.

This gal's companion was her exact replica—gaunt enough that they both still evidently shopped in the juniors department—but older, so tan and leathery that when she whispered back her face cracked like the seat of a timeworn club chair.

"That Lorelei *thinks* she's so cute," she said, and the two of them cackled in unison.

But that catty assessment was total bullshit. My mother assumed she was invisible. She lived in a cloud of not-thereness. Although she was inherently proud of her good looks, in actuality they'd bought her nothing but trouble—her marriage to my daddy, for one, and various other husbands too short term and feckless to mention—so she erased herself from any picture she was drawn in. That day at Dunkin', she was off in la-la land, sipping her cold brew through a straw, probably still moonwalking with Michael Jackson in tweenage romantic dreams that no amount of elec-troshock therapy could dislodge, while those two blond bitches snorted along in chorus. The loose skin of their twin cleavages wrinkled accordion-like as their fake boobies shook with their idiot laughter. My mother was seemingly deaf, thank goodness, to the malice. But I lowered my sunglasses and shot them a look of total unadulterated evil, which shut those cows up for good.

Soon we were in a rhythm, Lorelei and me. Most afternoons I walked her like some of the other residents walked their pups. That's when I found out that, among the infinite amenities in the various communities, there was even a club for canines. Dynamic Dogs, they called it. Doting owners could deposit their furry friends at special doggy day cares while their pet parents went off to shop, or play mah-jongg, or meet with their kidney cancer support groups. And for those into flirting with other Lassie lovers, there were dog runs and dog parks and dog shows with prizes. By this point, I was getting poorer and poorer and more and more restless. At first boredom felt like relief from my endless series of damaging days, like soaking my feet in Epsom salts and hot water after tending bar back in Colorado; and then boredom was just plain boring, like soaking my feet in Epsom salts and hot water in a trailer bathroom without space for a radio or TV.

Our "piazza" in the gigantic Ocean Winds complex was called the Atlantic Breeze's Ranch, a Disneyfied version of a nineteenth-century Floridian cattle town, and every night it had some kind of live entertainment on an outdoor stage with aluminum bleachers for seating. A lot of country-western cover bands played there, but hillbilly just wasn't my scene, and even when I tried to tap my foot to it, my restless mind wandered.

For our entertainment and viewing pleasure, Atlantic Breezes also had a movie house called the Cattle Ranch Theater, three projection rooms in one big old barn. Maybe you'll understand why I wasn't hungry back then for the silver screen. Almost every movie that came through our town square advertised a star or starlet or producer or assistant or hair or makeup person I knew who had been royally fucked over by a filthy man, physically, emotionally, sexually, economically. If you could think of it, it had already been done to someone by somebody else. Or maybe there was a cast member or executive or writer associated with the film I simply hated and/or was jealous of. I didn't know the full scope of the Rug's criminality back then, but I do know it now and so do you, so don't pretend like you're all innocent and pure, like a bottle of Smartwater, and that your dollars haven't padded his sweaty fur-lined pockets. I find it breathtaking the number of women this one asshole fuck abused and how long he got away with it, almost twice my lifetime. Not to mention all the other victims of all the other predators who got smoked out of the woodwork along with that rat bastard: Spacey and Cosby and Lauer and R. Kelly and Larry Nassar and that TV chef, Mario Batali, with his "rape room" above his friend's restaurant and his sickening oily red pigtail at the base of his balding, spotted head.

Of course, ordinary cocksuckers abound, too, they are every-where like cockroaches, but no one cares about them. Think about all the waitresses and nurses and hotel room clean-ers and shopworkers and wives and girlfriends and nieces and daughters—*your* daughters, too—who get manhandled and worse every fricking day.

The movies playing in our town square reminded me of all that collective agony. They took me back to my own private hell. And they reinforced the painful fact that I wasn't a cast member in any of those pictures. I wasn't taking meetings or auditioning or getting a part or in preproduction or out shooting anything at that very moment. I was just hiding out with my mentally ill not-Mom, my loony "auntie" or whacko "cousin." Even Lorelei's TV shows gave me the heebie-jeebies, thinking about all I was miss-ing out on. At heart, I'm a delicate flower.

Still, there were things about our tidy life that I liked, like the farmers markets on Saturday mornings and the Beer Universe, a tavern chain, on Saturday nights, where I would belly up to the bar when I couldn't stand hanging out at home. (Fun fact: I've since read that the Ocean Winds had "the highest consumption of draft beer in the state of Florida"—an explanation for all that venereal disease and the hot black market on Viagra.) I went to McGuire's Deli for sandwiches I didn't eat and pickles and chips that I did. By this point my hair was longer and dyed white blond—by me! Nice'n Easy. I stuffed it all up into an Ocean Winds baseball cap. The color alone made me fit right in. I wore my mother's clothes: the shorts, the striped shirts, that hat, my sunnies. So far no one had figured out who I was. Maybe they thought I was Lorelei's paid companion? The cleaning lady? Or maybe nobody gave a fuck. Here's a test-taking tip: In the game of life, check that last box. It's usually the right answer.

My favorite place in Atlantic Breezes was the Fluffy Puppy Paw-tisserie, a full-on bake shop for animals. I loved to stare in the window at the birthday cakes, bone- and shoe-shaped cookies, and cannoli for pets, made with rye and pumpernickel flour, a ton of molasses, sugar and oil, peanut butter filling and red, yellow, and blue food coloring. The treats looked so real, I wanted to eat them all, but since they were for cats and dogs I couldn't. That's the perfect combo for an ani like me, fixation and deprivation. Sometimes I bought actual popcorn there! Doggy popcorn is truly just like *popcorn* popcorn (unless you buy the kind with meat or chicken spray on it).

Before I arrived, my mother didn't have a car or even a golf cart, and the Ocean Winds was golf cart city, so I leased us one, blue with a white awning with blue-and-white-striped fringe. She also hung an American flag off the back, but I wasn't going to raise a stink over it. This was MAGA country. For a lefty outlaw, it was a perfect hideout. There were specific authorized golf cart parking lots and spaces and golf cart bridges and tunnels, and in the neighborhoods with houses, there were separate golf cart mini-garages, often next to the regular-sized ones for cars. Once we had ours all kitted out to Lorelei's liking, she would agree to accompany me on our errands. We'd exit straight from her lanai to the parking lot to avoid the possibility of being forced to socialize in the building's hallway, then take the designated golf cart underpass into town.

There we'd pick up groceries. Sometimes I'd force Lorelei to go to the dentist—her mouth was a mess from all those years of club drugs and methamphetamine—or we'd buy more bug spray at the Publix. On special occasions, we'd stop to get our skin checked at the Skin Cancer Center. When I couldn't fucking stand it any longer, I'd sometimes drive her home so she could sit in front of the TV and rot, and then I'd go back out to pet the puppies. I'd stand outside the bakery, which also sold pet products and had a grooming service, watching the shaggy ones go in and the newly shorn ones come out. That's how I got into the dog-walking business. One lady let me play catch with her mutt, half shepherd, half poodle, and after the two of us ended up chasing each other around the trees, she asked if I'd run him again for money.

"Cuddles has got way too much energy for me," she said. "I'm an old lady."

I wasn't one. And this place was full of them. There was my light bulb moment! Soon I had four different furry friends I'd walk three times a day: Butch, Cyclone, Cuddles, and Fifi. Fifi was a Great Dane and Butch was a Chihuahua mix. It was hilarious that they came in reverse size order than what their names suggested.

"At last," my mother said, when I told her I'd found work and that I might not be around as much. "You really get on my nerves."

She patted my hand before pointing the clicker and changing the channel.

So fine. The affection may have been one-sided, but she was a scab I needed to pick. She was my mother. I had some kind of emotional disorder: separation anxiety, fear of abandonment, I think, depression, trauma—my lawyer used language like that in her opening arguments to swing the judge my way. Yes, I did go out during the day to walk the dogs—it was my job!—but in between rounds I scurried back to Lorelei like an imprinted lit-

tle duckling. Project Mother was on the top of my agenda, then.
I was haunted by Marietta and how close her kids had gotten to
losing her. To absolve my sins in that department, I wanted my
own old lady in some semblance of working order, to stretch and
fortify her, in case I ever had to leave the nest again or, God forbid, something happened to me. I was thinking about cashing out
on my place in Venice and, once more, about buying us a house
in the Ocean Winds, but because of her sinkhole phobia, Lorelei
repeatedly explained that she couldn't move into a house because
she didn't know how to swim. None of that made any sense, obviously. Apartment buildings aren't immune from sinkholes, and
no one can swim their way out of a sinkhole, anyway. But these
were concepts she could not, would not, grasp, and I was not buying a house she refused to live in.

I became determined to help her conquer her greatest fear.

It took almost a month of wheedling to get my mother to even
approach the pool, she was so afraid of the water. If you lived in
the Lofts, there was one you could use for free—no way was Lorelei ever going to pony up the $950 a year for basic minimum spa,
pool, and golf privileges, which even the rank and file did so auto-
matically because those activities were the whole reason anyone
moved there in the first place—but it was part of the clubhouse
complex, four buildings away from ours, which she said was too
far away for her without using the golf cart, and she demurred.

I'd wanted her to get some exercise. "It's good for you to walk,"
I said, grasping for something I thought might finally convince
her. "It'll keep your breasts from sagging."

Didn't her violet eyes go wide!

(For the record, hers and mine both still point up to the sky.)

So that very day, between my noon and five p.m. rounds with
the pups, she and I left the apartment in our white shorts, no
bathing suits—I think she was afraid if she was properly attired,
I might just throw her in, sink or swim—and slowly traversed the
quarter mile to the pool. As we trudged along the asphalt road in

the heat—there was no designated sidewalk; Ocean Winders in general aren't big on walking—I could feel it melting the bottoms of my flips.

The Leaping Dolphin Rec Center was a nice enough place to hang, with billiards and table shuffleboard inside, an open-air kitchen and fireplace outside. On that day, the pool looked pretty inviting, the bottom painted a Caribbean turquoise, a design trick that made the water shimmer Kool-Aid blue—even though the shape of the structure itself was a little odd, like a pudgy dick with two Mickey Mouse ears for testicles. In one of those round circles, we saw some ladies in big floppy hats, each a color plucked from a handful of rainbow sprinkles, jogging in place in the water with aquatic weights held high above their heads. An aqua aerobics class. It was led by a cute Cubana in a short light green terry romper, who demonstrated the moves on land while shouting out instructions over the sound of her boom box. "Happy" by Pharrell Williams. I always hated that song. Honestly, I found it demented. But now I was practicing affirmation therapy, so I hummed a few bars.

Clap along if you feel like a room without a roof.

Maybe that cheerful cluster of bobbing AARP confetti might provide my mother with some inspiration.

"Come," I said, "let's sit over there in the shade and watch those gals have fun."

I pointed to two chaises under a beach umbrella. I picked up a couple of the gratis towels from their stack on another plastic chair and laid them out on the vinyl webbing for each of us. Then we sat down, leaned back, and drank the now lukewarm iced tea—water I'd picked up at Dunkin' earlier. I'd also bought my mother some sudoku books and grabbed a bunch of free periodicals on the trip into town as an anticipatory reward for good behavior. While we lounged, she obediently put *Ocean Winds Magazine* on her lap, but with her sunglasses on I couldn't tell if she was reading or just spacing out like usual. It didn't matter. There were a couple of wayward grandkids splashing around in the pool's other ball—I could tell they belonged to one of the aerobicizers, that lady kept turning around to wave them toward the shallow end. Sometimes she yelled and sometimes she shushed so loudly, worrying that they would bother the other swimmers, she became more of a bother herself, but my mother sat there sucking on her straw in a state of contentment. It occurred to me then that it was no picnic being retired with kids you were suddenly responsible for, like it was no picnic being retired with a retired mother. And that all family sucked, of course, but I was glad I was finally tethered to someone, someone I was related to, someone I daresay I actually truly *loved*.

This epiphany was interrupted when an older gentleman who had been doing laps came up for air at the northern tip of the pool. Taking five, he looked around, and when he and Lorelei saw each other, they saluted. I mean, he started it.

Aye aye, Captain, he motioned to her.

She did an obedient monkey see, monkey do.

"Who is that?" I asked.

"You don't know Mac?" my mother asked, in a state of genuine astonishment, as if he were the most famous man on Earth—Kanye or Brad Pitt or Jesus Christ himself—and she couldn't help but wonder what was wrong with me, her one and only pitiful excuse for offspring.

"No, I don't know Mac," I said, trying not to sound too peeved.

"He's my pal, Meredith," she said.

Then she slapped my hand gently, sending my iced tea–water overboard.

"You goose," she said.

The old guy turned around and started breaststroking to the other end.

"Okay," I said, licking the spilled liquid off my wrist. I didn't like being treated like an imbecile. But I sensed an opportunity. "Lorelei, why don't we go over and say hello?"

"Oh no," she said. "I couldn't do that."

"Sure, you could," I said. "Say 'yes, I can.'"

"But I can't," she said.

"But you can," I said. "Mac is your pal. You said so yourself."

I picked up my towel, and I took her hand and helped her to her feet. Then I grabbed hers, too, and the rest of our stuff, and I walked us over to the shallow end, where I kicked off my flips and sat down on the pool's concrete lip. When I tugged her gently, her legs bent then folded, and she dropped softly next to me, the way a fig might fall from a tree. A gentle plop. She must have created a little breeze because my hat fell from my head, but I didn't care, it didn't go in the water. I laid it across the sudoku and the magazines. And then I shook out my hair. The hat had made my head hot.

"I'll take off your shoes for you," I said, and like a child, she let me. Then I immersed my feet in the water. It was cool but warm enough. Honestly, it was sort of amazingly perfect.

"It feels so good," I said. "Why don't you try it?"

My mother contracted like a cat when it's scared, her back rounded, and she pulled her knees up into her chest and held them in place with her palms. We sat side by side for a while, until I could sense her slowly begin to relax a bit again. When she settled down, I put one hand in the pool and then lightly placed it on her right arch, so she could get used to the feeling of the water. She didn't squirm, but she also didn't breathe much. I thought, If she doesn't pass out, we can officially call this progress.

Mac was back at the other end by then, taking a rest, and he saluted us once more. This time she and I individually saluted back.

A whole decade probably went by while he made his slow bubbling strokes downstream, head rising as his hands pushed through the water in prayer. Was he erasing the pain between my mother and me through his moving meditation? Could be, because by the time he reached our end, somehow, we both were dangling our feet in the pool.

When you think about it, miracles happen all the time. The world would feel weird without them. But that was the last miracle I can remember from this life, my mother and me resting our feet together in that soothing water. She had a pal. He was wending his way home to her. She wasn't scared. And for one hot second, I wasn't totally exasperating.

A couple of yards away from us, Mac stopped swimming and stood. He was a thin man around seventy, with a silvery-white hairy chest, who must have been taller before he got older.

He said, "Hey there, Lorrie."

Lorrie.

She blushed.

"This must be your sister," he said.

Are you fucking kidding me? I thought.

"Yes," said my mother.

"You two have to be twins," Mac said.

"Everyone says that," she said.

No one ever had, but who cared? She was beaming.

He waded through the water to shake my hand.

"I'm Meredith," I said, reaching out to squeeze the pruned fingers that he offered me.

"Mac," said Mac. And then to my mother, "I thought you were afraid of the water."

"That's all in the past," I said.

"In the past," she echoed.

"That's good info," said Mac. "Maybe soon I can get you swimming laps?"

She shook her head no with a twisted smile. She was out of practice, but I guessed it was an attempt at flirting.

"How do you guys know each other?" I asked.

"Lorrie was kind enough to let me stay with her for a while when things got a little iffy."

"What do you mean?" I asked.

"I live with my brother and his wife," Mac said. "Over by Lake Timucuan. My brother likes to fish."

"That's nice," I said.

"I've tricked out their garage just fine, and for the most part we get along real good. I keep to myself, you see. But his wife, she's a drinker. And when she's drinking, well, sometimes she throws me out. I've got a car I share with my brother, and every once in a while I take off in that until she cools down and dries up. But then there's nights I need a solid roof over my head. Other times I might stay with a lady friend, but when your sister took me in, I was what you call between them. Lady friends, I mean."

"Mac's a gigolo," said my mother, her hand now over her lips to keep from laughing.

"Now don't give it all away, dear, please," said Mac. He looked over his shoulder to see if anyone was near enough to hear us.

"What's she talking about?" I asked.

"Well, she's not lying, but I would never presume to take advantage of her," he said. He walked over to the stairs and climbed up out of the water. "Would you be kind enough to hand me a towel?"

I turned to my mother. "Remember what you told me about the men around here?"

"Guess who's the one who taught me that?" my mother said. This time she actually giggled.

I was holding on to my towel then.

"I said can I get that towel?" he repeated himself.

It looks like a demand when I type Mac's words down like this, but they didn't sound that way coming out of his mouth. He said them firmly but sweetly.

I slowly handed it to him, and he wrapped it around his waist, tucking one end under the other near a rib. A practiced old-guy move.

Then he sat down next to her.

"I told Lorrie to stay away from those types. They're after one thing and one thing only. They'll tell you they love you and maybe they'll even marry you, but what they really want is money."

"Also, they'll give you diseases," said my mother, looking at Mac for confirmation.

"Some of 'em," he said with a wink.

"Did you take advantage of her?" I asked, sounding like a father, a father on TV.

"No, never," said Mac. "I protect her from the likes of me. Lorrie's special. Fragile. She's a little darling."

"We met at Dunkin'," said my mother. "He asked me to buy him a soda."

"I was low on cash," said Mac. He shrugged: *What can you do?* "Your sister here"—he pointed to my mother—"let me stay with her during Hurricane Irma. My brother's wife was on a real bender, and their kids were doing an intervention-type thing on the phone. It was tense over there, and I don't like tension. I didn't have cash for a hotel, so I slept on Lorrie's couch and I cooked us supper. I stayed about three weeks, and then we became pals, isn't that right, dear?"

She nodded yes. "He sandbagged the lanai for me," she said.

I didn't know how to respond. Was Mac a good egg? A bad one? He seemed harmless enough the way the two of them told it, but still a little creepy. He lived in his brother's garage.

My daddy and I used to live in a truck.

It takes all kinds.

Who was I to judge?

Then he took a good look at me.

"You, young lady, seem mighty familiar."

Uh-oh. Stomach drop. Panic button. Shit!

"I think I just read something about you in the newspaper," he said.

"Say what?" I said.

"You know how *The New York Times* has been going after that movie producer?"

"I don't read the papers," I said.

"Really?" he said. "Not even on your phone?"

"Nope," I said. "I learned the hard way that the internet and me are a lethal combination."

Mac nodded slowly. "Well, someone put some pictures of him up on *USA Today,* and I think you're in one of them."

"How do you like that, honey?" my mother said. "You're finally famous!"

"Finally?"

I'd never been so insulted in all my life.

"Are you completely insane?" I said to her, standing up. And then to him, "You must be mistaken."

"Now, now, don't you worry, you showed me yours, and I showed you mine. We're practicing mutually assured destruction. Your secret's safe with me."

Talk about power plays!

"We're pals," my mother said.

"I need to go home," I said.

"No," said Lorelei. "It's more fun here."

"Now," I said.

"Why don't you just calm yourself down a little, missy," said Mac. "I'll get her back to the loft safe and sound. After all, I know the way."

I'm ashamed to say it, but given the choice—my mother or my sanity—in the heat of the moment, I left her alone, poolside, with her pal, Gigolo Mac, and hightailed it out of there.

There was a picture of me and the Rug in *USA Today*! I'd been recognized by a thousand-year-old man! God alone knew what might happen next.

Back at my mother's place, I lit one of her cigarettes and called Matt Anastos from a phone Branimir had sent me, on the last burner number of his that I had—it was dead, of course—then

I tried him on his landline. My heart was beating in my throat, I was so nervous. Even though it was hot as balls outside, I was shivering in the apartment.

When he heard my voice, he said, "Meredith? Is it really you?"

"It's m-me," I said, teeth chattering.

"Where the fuck have you been?" said Matt.

"Off-f-f the grid?" I said, more a question than a statement. I walked over to the thermostat and turned down the AC. My words were coming out syncopated because my body was still quaking.

"Well, I've been trying to reach you for months now," he said. "It's like you just upped and disappeared."

"G-good," I said. "That's called stra-strategy, Matt."

"I even reached out to your manager," he said.

"Liz? You spoke to Ma-Ma-Manager Lizzzzz?"

Just saying her name made me sob.

"Don't cry," he said. "She's okay. I mean, she's fine, except for being worried sick about you."

"Oh boy," I said. I inhaled sharply. Smoking is sometimes like a deep breathing exercise. Plus, it spreads heat throughout the body.

"She made me promise that if I heard from you, I'd let her know right away."

"Okay," I said. "That's n-nice."

Manager Liz truly cared about me. Wow.

"The police are looking for you."

"Is it because I left the state?"

"I didn't know you left the state. No one has a clue where you went. If you were dead or alive, even."

That was good news. Maybe even the ex-Mossad agents had lost track!

"You didn't show up for your own hearing. For a while there, they were breathing down Liz and your lawyer's neck, but then the story kind of disappeared, until the Toupee Guy made the news again."

I inhaled deeply and started coughing. Fucking menthols.

"You mean for stalking me at my house in Venice?" I rasped. "How did they find out about that? Unless the neighbors actually reported him?"

I was hopeful in that moment. I actually thought, People are good. People are good!

"He stalked you? Wait a sec, is this on the record? Can I take notes? Do you have any documentation? Surveillance footage?"

"No!" I shrieked into the phone. "He'll kill me. He'll literally kill me this time." And I meant it. Who the hell knows what would have happened to me if he'd gotten inside my house that night. My hands resumed shaking.

I walked over to the sink and doused my cigarette in a coffee cup. Then I pulled out a glass from the draining board and filled it with whiskey. We kept a bottle on the counter for the rough days. I bolted some. And I poured another couple of fingers. Then the more rational side of me prevailed and I went to the fridge to get an ice cube and plunked it in. It was when the first giant shot hit my bloodstream that I remembered that Manager Liz had made me install SimpliSafe when I moved to Venice. I wondered if the cameras that night had picked up anything.

"I might have footage, now that I think about it. I could call the security company, but he'll kill me, Matt!"

"Relax, Meredith. He's not killing you. He's not killing anyone. He's too busy lawyering up, bullying people, and getting his PR team to try and defuse the situation. We should take a look at those tapes. Put in the call! His business is in jeopardy. It's possible his board is turning against him . . . The DA announced an investigation."

"So, you're saying he's now even more of a wounded animal? That's *not* supposed to scare me?" I finished my drink. "Manager Liz taught me that!"

"I'm saying he's got bigger fish to fry."

That's when I took the bottle and glass and sat down at my

mother's round faux-wooden table with the rest of her pack of Newports and the table's resident ashtray, while Matt filled me in on the whole story. Here's the hook I told you about earlier: Matt wasn't the one to break the Rug story. Matt's turf was Dark Star. It was two daring, brilliant woman journos at *The New York Times,* two smart-ass vaginas with pens, who landed this one (*Viva la femme!*), and according to Matt, they found out not only that the Rug had violently attacked more important people than yours truly, but they'd also gotten those VIPs to go officially on the record. There were two A-listers and a whole bunch of B-teamers. Dead girls talking. None remotely hirable after the Rug was finished fucking her over. All, I'm guessing, with lawyers who said it was too late to press charges, like mine had. That's what I call corroboration. The Rug had honed his attacks down to a science. Some female employee would prep the victim, arrange or escort her to a meeting, and then leave the "poor thing" alone with him. The rest is history. Some journo got an unnamed source from the inner circle to quote him, I guess as a kind of mitigation. He said, "I never had to pull a Cosby."

He was revolting.

This is what passed for Rug pride: he never dosed our drinks. He simply violated us by intimidation and brute force! The big lie: all the sex he'd had took place via mutual agreement.

But the *Times* reporters had his whole MO. Once lured into his hotel room with promises of fame or fortune, or having wheedled or pushed himself into a woman's apartment, the Rug would then rip the clothes off the back of said actress, or model, or secretary, or producer, or director, or waitress, or maid, or delivery girl, or anyone else with a pussy, and fuck her against her will, in the cunt or in the mouth or both. Then, like he did with me, he'd flip her legs over her head and force her to endure oral sex from him. *This* was his version of reciprocity.

"*I* could have told them all that, why didn't they interview me?" I said.

"You still figure in," he said. "But you're kind of a tainted witness, Meredith, because you're, you know, you."

I didn't even have to ask. He answered.

"The tweetstorms, Marietta, the drug charge—"

"He planted that shit on me, it was a setup! You know that, Matt!" I interrupted. "And don't talk to me about Marietta. That's unfair! I didn't put crazy inside her brain!"

"Sorry," he said.

"How is she, anyway?" I asked. I held my breath.

"Better," he said. "She's doing better. She had a bypass and she recuperated at home. I think the whole fam went vegan? Not sure what her next steps are workwise."

"Thank God," I said. "But why didn't you tell me? I've been frantic, I—"

"I'm truly sorry. I knew that you'd be worried. But then again, you disappeared, you know," he said.

"I know," I said. "It's my fault. But someone should have interviewed me *before*. When I was still around. When I hadn't hurt anybody yet."

"I believe someone did interview you, Meredith. And you're talking to him."

Why was he right? Why was I wrong?

"Matt," I said. "I'm a jerk. And a moron and an asshole. I should be apologizing to you. I am apologizing to you . . ."

"Some of these women are squeaky clean," he said. "Don't get me wrong, I do not agree with that assessment. But they're more sympathetic to the public, ergo they are easier to rally the troops around. And again, you went AWOL, and the *Times* couldn't even reach you."

As if I hadn't been trying my hardest to get their attention all my livelong days!

"I wasn't clean enough to be a good sexual assault victim, you're saying," I said.

He paused. Meaningfully. "*I* couldn't reach you," he said.

Like now, I'd hurt his feelings.

Or maybe that was just me projecting.

"So how did I end up in *USA Today*?" I said.

"Is that why you called?" he said.

I nodded, but of course he couldn't see me.

"Did you read the article?" he asked.

"No," I said. "I've been on the wagon. No World Wide Web. No nothing."

He exhaled loudly. "You're going to hate this, but it's only fair to warn you. That Bosnian Mossad agent, Andrea? I mean, Smadar?"

"Nina," I said. I said it like the air being let out of a tire. Of course. Of course it was Nina.

My Nina.

"Well, she's going by her original name again, Samara. Except now, suddenly, she's married. So, she goes by Samara Mizrahi."

"Married?" I said. "Hoo-boy! To a woman or to a man?"

Over the phone, I thought I could sense his eyebrow arch.

"A man. Mr. Mizrahi. I don't know. She gave another interview to *The Daily Beast*. They tracked her down. The writer's an old buddy of mine, he told me this part on the down low: she's living in this country. Boca Raton. She's working in real estate."

"She's in Florida?"

She's in Florida. *I'm* in Florida. Coincidence? I thought not!

Did she come all this way just to find me? To torture me? Did she want to smoke me out? Or maybe she came to her senses and wanted to apologize? She wanted to explain herself! Was she trying to fuck me up, or wasn't she?

A laundry machine was whirring inside my brain. Water and suds and soap and really dirty clothing, stains so deep nothing could get them out.

He said, "Again, this part is off the record. She desperately wants a fresh start here in the States."

Why? I wondered. How many new beginnings could one girl get?

"All I know is it was time to leave the Holy Land," Matt said.

"Israel?" I said. "Why?"

"God, you really have been on the wagon," said Matt. "How much don't you know?"

Isn't that always the million-dollar question. *How much don't you know?*

"How can I possibly know what I don't know, Matt?" I was borderline hysterical.

"I blew her cover," Matt said. "I broke the story on Dark Star in *The Atlantic*."

"What happened to *Esquire*?"

They were too chickenshit, he said, afraid of the Rug's lawyers. So, he took his story to an independent magazine where "they still believe in journalism."

"Good for you!" I said, and meant it.

Matt continued: "I started publishing pieces a few weeks after you disappeared. And as the truth came out about the slime bucket, more and more attention became focused on everyone around him. Too many enemies. Or, to be exact, too many high-octane cronies and sleazeball associates. The sheer reach of this guy's connections across different power industries—entertainment, legal, political, and, yes, international spy agencies—was breathtaking! Closer to a head of state than what you might expect from a schlump from the Bronx who grew up to make movies."

He took a sip of water, beer, wine, something. I could hear the liquid go down his throat, which grossed me out.

"When Samara's cover was blown, again by me," Matt preened—Matt fucking Anastos, Mr. Humble Professional, cool as a cucumber Matt, actually fucking preened—"that meant her spying days were over. When that happened," he said, "she became an unsavory character not only in the eyes of the world but also in her home country. So she very quickly got married to this guy who lives in Boca and left. Remember, she'd been a heroine before, she'd been a member of Aman and then a Mossad agent. Dark Star is another story. Israel has been backpedaling, rapidly, ever since all this leaked, trying to divorce itself from Toupee Guy and his money. Ironic, ha? First, he was a Jewish American savior. Now, justifiably, a pariah!"

For six months I'd been living incognito but also out in the open. No one in Podunk, Florida, but Gigolo Mac had burned a calorie bothering to recognize me. But now Nina was so famous, she had to leave her own country. I was the unknown, and she was the celebrity! It was a role reversal made for Hollywood.

"*The Daily Beast* did a follow-up on her when the newest round of reporting broke. There was so much shade being cast her way, she was eager to tell more of her side. And this is the part you're going to hate. She blames a lot of it on you."

"Me?" I said.

"Yes," he said. "She said when they did background checks, you presented as a legitimate danger to Toupee Guy's business. She's held tight to that line of defense. They had no reason to suspect his interest as degenerate. According to her, you checked all the boxes for a reasonable and appropriate investigation, even in retrospect."

"The Rug," I corrected him. "Not Toupee Guy."

"Whatever, Meredith," he said.

He paused again. Why? To let these fun details sink through all three layers of my very thin epidermis? Or to look at or send a text message? About me, maybe? I was feeling a little paranoid. I couldn't see his face.

"When that story came out, your hairless friend, *the Rug*, got his people fanning the flames about your missed court date, and that's when a warrant was issued for your arrest. That's how you ended up all over the news again. Some of it trickled down to *USA Today*. My bet is this info came from *her*. There's something about her fixation on you that's weird. I know I said she was a contract worker before, but this all goes well beyond her expiration date at Dark Star. It's borderline obsessive. She's so vindictive when it comes to you."

He used the word "obsessive"! As in Nina was obsessed with me. She couldn't get me out of her mind! My feelings *were* reciprocated. I'd hoped! Now I knew it was true.

"But you just said she's working as a real estate agent. No more Bond girl. So why would anybody pay attention to her now?"

"Think about all the books people are writing about him! She's a player in his story."

"Book? I wrote a book," I said. "At least I'm almost finished writing one. I'm 'a player in his story.' Anyway, fuck his story! What about *my* story? Why can't I get arrested?"

"That's what I'm telling you, Meredith. You *can* get arrested. I repeat, there is a warrant out for your arrest."

"Oh," I said.

That's when Mac and Lorelei entered the apartment and I hung up on him. Honestly, I'm not even sure I said goodbye, which would have been super-shitty, considering how good an ally he'd been to me. There was nothing wrong with Matt, except he was a member of the press.

Mac and Lorelei were carrying groceries. Uh-oh. It was later than I thought. I was supposed to have walked the dogs.

"Gotta bounce," I said.

I went to the fridge and grabbed a Corona, then opened the hall closet and put it in my backpack. Then I ran out the front door quickly, leaving those two crazy kids to have their playdate happily unsupervised.

I should have been suspicious then, I mean, what? Had Mac really gotten my mother to walk all the way to the store and back again? God bless him if he had. But I had other things on my mind at the moment. I ran, ran, ran from building to building picking up my furry charges. "Sorry, I'm so late," I said as I rang doorbell after doorbell. And then instead of taking the pups for a nice long walk, like I usually did, I went to the dog run, let them off their leashes, sat on a bench, and pulled out my beer.

Mea culpa. I'm always knocking Florida. But it was nice out there that evening. Me and my canine crew were alone, they were fighting and frisking about, the temperature was falling, and I had a choice—again, my fault, totally—and I made the absolute wrong decision. For the first time in months I backslid. I took out my old iPhone, slipped in my burner's SIM card, relapsed, and googled. *USA Today* and *moi*. I found said photo right away. It was the one I had shown to Nina and Jean-Pierre at the dinner at Jean-Pierre's place: me practically sitting in the Rug's lap, his mouth open in a giant guffaw. I mean, it was *exactly* the same photo! It was taken on my cell, and I'd never shared it with anyone. How did she get up inside my phone? They must have taught her at Spy Academy.

The caption read: "Anyone laughing now?"

My eyes burned. My hair had been bleached white in that pic, too, so no wonder Mac had recognized me. It was the same color and just a bit shorter these days than it was on that website, and it curled similarly as soon as I'd taken my hat off at the pool. A rookie mistake, when I prided myself on being such an expert. I'd forgotten about that phase. Instinctively, I reached into my backpack and pulled out a spare baseball hat and put it on, even though it was too little too late. What a fucking moron.

Then I swallowed the red pill and went down a long, dark cyberhole, uncovering what had been going on these past weeks and months without my knowledge, while my pups sniffed around untended, peeing and pooing at random, definitely a dog run no-no. History was being made out there, in the world, on TV, and in cyberspace, but even after all my efforts, it was leaving me behind. So many other female victims were coming out of the woodwork, it was like worms on the sidewalk after a rainstorm. I was proud of them and cheered the growing groundswell of information and outrage, but you must know me by now. You've met me before. This was *my* revolution! I felt so totally left out.

Finally, I looked up and read the *Daily Beast* interview with Nina. There was an accompanying photo of her, now with auburn locks, beauteous and enigmatic as ever. They gave her name as Smadar Marantz. So, I'll quote "Smadar Marantz": "I'm an investigator. That's my job. Not so different from yours," she said to the reporter. "Our former president made the introductions, how were we to know this man was a bad actor? We had a whole team working on it. If what you say is true, Dark Star of course will make a donation to women's causes."

The article also said the Rug paid the agency $2 million for its services.

All I got was a measly $150k.

What was that nasty girl really up to?

I googled Ella. Ella Rosenberg. And then I stopped googling, because I suddenly remembered her shouting out, "Ella Rosenberg, all one word, on wgtv.com," as I walked down the Jetway. Instead, I sent her an encrypted message from one of the untraceable email addresses Branimir had set up for me, just in case.

Ella! Meredith Montgomery here. My manager was just talking to me about a project written for identical adult twins!!! Except it sucks. Wanna send me yours? PS I just heard through the grapevine that Smadar got married to an old boyfriend. Not your sister's present one, right?

After that, I returned the dogs to their various owners and retrieved my SIM card and then trashed that burner in one of the other building's dumpsters, and when I got home, I picked up another one from my stash under the couch. Lorelei and Mac were puttering around in the kitchen. I went out and sat on the lanai. There was an old blue Caddie parked in the lot. I didn't think much of it then except to note it. It wasn't one of the usual vehicles that made up the daily landscape, and who drives a Cadillac anymore? I was too wrapped up in my own fear and loathing then to realize that Mac had taken the first baby steps of moving back in again. He'd driven her to the store and then parked on our proverbial front lawn. I later learned he always stowed a pillow and a sleeping bag in the trunk. Just in case.

I thought about using the phone to call someone, but I couldn't think of who to call.

"Meredith," my mother beckoned. "Come on in for dinner."

In my entire lifetime, had she ever done that before?

As I reentered the living room, she was pouring the wine, red, in glasses on the already set wooden table. She must have bought the bottle under Mac's guidance, with my credit card, while she was gallivanting around with him. Now he was chopping and stirring. As they worked, I studied this new phone. I liked Matt, but I had faith in no one. Then I extracted yet another burner from my hiding space, just to be on the safe side, and slid both into my backpack, which I shoved into the hall closet. Then I went to the bathroom to wash my hands. When I reemerged, the grown-ups were sitting down to full plates. Someone, maybe Lorelei, had already loaded one up for me, and they were waiting for me to join them.

Mac made his famous spaghetti sauce that night. Dressed-up Ragú, it tasted pretty damn good, considering it came out of a jar. I ate about a third of mine, which was a lot for me in those days. Lorelei chowed down. Apparently it was her favorite. He said the taste had something to do with the heavily salted water he used for the pasta and the onions he'd caramelized in oil. Plus, there was his secret spices recipe that his mother had passed down, but when I cleaned up the kitchen later, I saw the Hidden Valley Garden Italian mix in the garbage. We each also ate a wedge salad. For that they'd procured a bottle of your typical orange faux French vinaigrette. I scraped mine off with a fork.

Later that night, after pointedly walking Mac back to his car, I unearthed the business card of the cabbie who drove me from the airport when I'd first arrived, out of that same handy-dandy get-away backpack I'd rammed into the mess in the hall closet. Julio Alvarez. I texted him: *I don't know if you remember, but you took me from Orlando to the Atlantic Breeze Lofts about six months ago. You were very kind, and I gave you a $100 tip because I was so grateful. I'm looking for someone to drive me down the coast tomorrow and back. It'll be a long day. I'll pay you whatever you think is fair, on or off the meter.*

As those little texting bubbles began to appear, I started typing faster. I wanted to cut him off at the pass. I couldn't have stood it if he'd said no. I'd started thinking of him as a good luck charm.

Mr. Alvarez, I wrote, *I trust no one, but I instantly trusted you. You appear to be a good, religious man.*

I'll be there at 9, he wrote, *$500 for the day plus gas. No tip necessary.*

Then for the first time in months, one of my phones registered an email from EllaRosenberg@wgtv.com.

Dear Ms. Montgomery:

I am so excited to hear from you. My agent has been trying to reach your manager, since we so comically and fortuitously ran into each other, but alas to no avail. Enclosed is a copy of "Double Trouble." It's registered with the WGA West. I can't wait to hear your thoughts!

Sincerely,
Ella Rosenberg

P.S. Thank God, no, Smadar did NOT get back with Joshua. (In fact, Tessa just got engaged to him!!!) This is so weird, Smadar married a guy she went out with on our Birthright trip. (Her mother wrote me!!!)

I emailed her back:

Who's the dude? And Ms. Montgomery? Whaaat? Merry, please!

Half a minute later she returned:

Merry! Happily! He's nice, cute, a little dull. I never thought she liked him that much . . . He's always been crazy about her! He works for Enterprise Florida handling Israeli imports—medical devices—so she and her mother (who's thrilled, by the way, he's a real Sabra) moved to Boca and are now in real estate. I guess he'd been pining after her all those years. Typical Smadar!!!

You could say that again, Ella Rosenberg!!!
I deleted the emails and texted Branimir to trash the domain.

The next morning when I left, I handed over both my dog-walking route and my mother to Gigolo Mac. I guess he'd slept in our parking lot and then drove to Dunkin' when the sun came up to bring us all our morning coffee and doughnuts. He seemed a little rumpled, but it was clear that he'd refreshed himself somewhere because his hair was combed and his breath was fresh. I wrote out the sked, complete with pets' names, habits, and addresses, and figured they could walk the pups together, a little aerobic exercise. He smiled when I told him he could collect and keep my pay.

"Sounds like a way to make some nice pocket change," Mac said. "What do you think, Lorrie?"

"It's all she talks about," my mother said. "Those dumb dogs."

"I'll be home tonight," I assured them both. "But don't wait up. Feel free to eat dinner without me."

Lorelei and Mac smiled and waved from the lanai. They looked a lot like a nice grandad and his daughter.

As the cab pulled out of the parking lot, I thought about a part in a picture I'd been up for a couple of years back, one of the many that never got made. That film was supposed to be built off a story about some spoiled radicals in the '6os—you know, wealthy kids who assembled bombs in the basement of their parents' West Village town house and maybe blew it up by mistake. Only it wasn't about those exact privileged dimwits but two others, a girl and a guy, comrades in love; they even had a baby. Those geniuses were going to rob a bank or a Brink's truck or something, to end the war in Vietnam?—I dunno, it's been a while since I read the script, but maybe it never made sense to begin with. I mean, with a lot of this shit, it's like you can't make it up, the true-life accounts are much more inexplicable than the garbage they feed us on a screen, even when you pay close attention and try your hardest to parse it out.

So, this couple hired a babysitter for a few hours to watch the kid, while they went to get the job done, figuring they'd be home to put the baby to bed. The girl ended up driving a getaway car, and the guy was part of a trio of dudes with guns. When things went wrong, one of them ended up shooting a bank teller and a security guard, or maybe a cop and a mother with a toddler in a stroller? Matters. Doesn't matter. This was a movie. They were killers. Although the male lead def didn't pull the trigger. (The producers were between drafts, so I think I read a couple of different iterations.) Anyway, they were both charged with murder "in concert," but the girl, being the rich kid in the duo—to be played by yours truly, of course, someday—got out on bail and went on the run for the next forty years before turning herself in. (I guess they would have finessed the aging part with hair, prosthetics, and makeup.) The guy it was based on is still in jail IRL and, as of the last time I read it, also in the script. I always wondered what happened to the babysitter when they didn't show up that afternoon like they said they would. Not that evening. Not that night. Not ever. And the baby. Who fed him? Bathed him?

Put him to bed? For the rest of his life, I mean. Since they'd lived in the suburbs, he couldn't have crawled into the woods to let the wolves take care of him or move to Hollywood like I did.

That day, I was leaving Lorelei with Mac for, at the most, twelve hours. As Mr. Alvarez pulled out of the parking lot and drove us south via the turnpike, I reassured myself I would be home that very evening. She and I would go back to being the way we were, finally, now after all our years of estrangement. Mother. Aunt? Sister? Daughter. Twins? Mac could find another lot to park in, another pal to live off of. The world as I knew it would keep on spinning under that brilliant Florida sun, a continuous explosion in the sky, shedding light everywhere, even when I was too blind to see it. Like a lucky rescue pet, I'd thought I'd finally found my forever home.

Mr. Alvarez listened to his old friend Ed Tyll on Florida Man talk radio for most of the next three hours and forty-five minutes it took us to drive down the coast. The man said a few things I didn't like, and I kind of chatted myself up, saying, "Jesus fucking Christ," out loud by accident.

"Excuse me?" said Mr. Alvarez.

"I'm so sorry, I just bit the inside of my mouth," I said, pressing my fingertips against my cheek to illustrate my pain, when he swiveled his head to look at me.

"I thought you said you were religious," he said.

"I said *you* were religious," I said. "I was raised in a barn. Please excuse me. That's the way my daddy talked. I'm trying to unlearn it and how to control myself. But sometimes I slip up."

He nodded solemnly, and then he switched to a Spanish-speaking network. "Okay?" he said.

"Fine," I said. "Perfect. Thank you for asking." It was easier to listen to that bullshit in another language.

Meanwhile, I worked on my game plan. Nina was easy to find. That is, Mrs. Ehud Mizrahi was easy to find. That's how she was listed on the Temple Beth El donors page: *Mr. & Mrs. Ehud Miz-*

rahi. She and her husband lived in Boca Raton Estates, a private residential country club, with four designer golf courses and three thousand families. They rented in a neighborhood called the Villas Encantadas, a development of 108 attached townhomes near a community pool. Her mother, Carmel Marantz, also lived in Boca Raton Estates, in an area called Fragrant Gardens, in a garden apartment. The owner of that particular property was her son-in-law, Ehud. On a rather barebones website page, both Carmel Marantz and Samara Mizrahi were listed as coagents in the M&M real estate corporation, describing themselves as specialists in Boca Raton Estates home rentals and purchases, which included fifty-five neighborhoods, single-family houses to luxury condominiums. I made an appointment online, using my mother's email address—I was the one who set it up for her—as Lorelei Monroe, to meet Mrs. Ehud Mizrahi at one o'clock for a tour of the place, starting at the country club, which would give us entry to the wellness and fitness center, dining facilities, aquatics complex, and private spa. From there, we would explore the different neighborhoods. I expressed special interest in a place called "The Private Isle," which appeared to whet her appetite. The return email was positively gushing. It was par for the course for the seductive Nina I had known in Paris. The love bomber:

> *How exciting! It's the jewel of Boca Raton Estates. There are twelve distinctive and exquisite homes there, perfect for the most discerning customer. And right now, two are up for resale! That's quite unusual for these spectacular, rare, and prized properties.*

This was the closest contact I'd had with her since I'd left Paris. A small victory.

After that thrilling high, I wrote to SimpliSafe and asked for the footage from my last night in Venice. Why not take advantage of five seconds of good fortune?

How I wanted to stick it to the both of them. The Rug and Nina, agents of my destruction. Protagonists of other people's books. Wait until they read mine!

The Private Isle was a private gated community *within* a private gated community. According to the internet, after you were granted access to all of Boca Raton Estates, you could then drive onward to another staffed checkpoint, and once awarded permission there, too, you could enter this most exclusive of all the enclaves by passing over a little moat. The Private Isle was super-restricted, completely surrounded by water, hence the name, so of course that's why I glommed on to it. It sounded totally safe and cloistered, and a girl's gotta dream big, even when phonying it up, right? Also, I figured Nina would jump at the chance of meeting with a high roller.

"Mr. Alvarez," I said, "how far is Boca Raton Estates from the ocean?"

The entire six months I'd been in Florida, I had yet to glimpse the Atlantic.

"Twenty minutes," he said. "Not far."

"Can we go after my appointment is over?"

Nina had moved here for the sea. All this time, I'd been stuck inland with my loony mother. Now I wanted my day at the beach!

"Sure," he said. "When do you think that will be?"

The information online said the tour would take an hour and a half, and for a second, I almost said that, when it dawned on me that I wasn't really coming to see the country club, to assess its pools and tennis courts and golf courses; that I wasn't sincerely comparison shopping, for me or my mother, for a higher-class, more polished version of the Ocean Winds. Instead, I had to remind myself, I was doing what I was born to do. I was acting. I wasn't going second-home shopping or even window-shopping. I was going to see Nina. To confront her, to beat the shit out of her, to beg her to take me back.

I mean, I think that's what I thought. Truth be told, I had no idea why I was actually going to see her. Was it for closure? Retribution? To make her feel the way she'd made me feel?

It was hazardous at that point for me to be seen out in public. I should have thought about that danger more deeply. At least I should have donned a different disguise. I also might have called Manager Liz and MLG, or even Matt again, to help me figure out, I don't know what, something? Next steps. A rational course of action. The best way to turn myself in for a crime I swore I hadn't committed. But I was in that cab, on that day, risking a lot, almost everything, including my heart, because I needed to see Nina one last time.

Period. Exclamation point.

"I think I'll be done in less than an hour," I said. "It's hard to know. Perhaps while I'm there you can go get a bite? You must be tired, and I won't mind waiting . . . I'll text you when I'm done."

Maybe when Nina and I saw each other, she'd take me in her arms? Maybe for the second time, she'd kiss me?

Or maybe I'd rapturously kick her in the teeth?

"Okay, miss," he said. "But can you pay me now? At least half up front?"

"You know what?" I said. "Silly me. I forgot to pick up cash. First things first, when you come back and fetch me, we'll do a drive-by through a cash machine. Right now I'm late for my appointment."

I took my mirror out of my backpack. My hair was a blond curly cloud, long enough to tuck behind my ears. I put on my shades. They hid half my face. I rummaged around for some lipstick, which when applied—it was bright red—seemed to up the sophistication factor. Although I was still wearing my mother's signature outfit: white shorts and a white cardigan and a blue-striped top. I hardly looked the part of a big spender.

Nina would have to take me as I was.

I met my first obstacle when we drove up to the entrance gate.

Either Nina had forgotten to give the security guard my name, which I had typed in as "Lorelei Monroe" on the online form I had to fill out to start up our client-realtor correspondence, or it was "just protocol," as the dude at the gate said, for me to sign in at the Welcome to Boca Raton Estates office. Mr. Alvarez, looking only slightly unhappy, was then sent on his way in his cab to town. I told him he should eat and relax, to get the receipt and I'd pay him back for his food and buy him an ice cream cone at the beach before we headed north again.

"First we go to the bank," he said.

"Of course," I said, and waved as I got out of the car.

The security guard pointed at a bungalow near the gate, so I walked over and went inside. Please note: I signed my own John Hancock. There was nothing I could do about it when I realized my mistake, while in the midst of looping the *n* in Montgomery, I mean, I couldn't exactly cross it out and start over. Then I was handed a whole stack of PR materials by a lady in a colorful silk blouse, white bell-bottoms, and a ton of golden bangles. The brochures covered info I had pretty much memorized on the drive down, so I handed them back politely. That lady looked annoyed, but she fake-smiled and picked up a phone and asked for a driver to take me to the clubhouse. I wondered if part of her job was to get rid of inventory—it had been part of mine when I handed out restaurant menus at beach parking lots when I'd first arrived in Venice. Sometimes at the end of the day I just dumped the remainder of my pile in the trash cans by the boardwalk.

The cab had been cool, and the real estate office had been frigid, but it was hot and humid when I exited the building to wait for my ride. I'd been so excited and nervous, I hadn't noticed the weather. I had just taken a seat on a little wooden bench when a kid drove up in a Boca Raton Estates golf cart and waved for me to join him. I hopped on in and asked him the time. He displayed his phone; this little side trip had cost me at least fifteen minutes.

I explained that I was running behind for an appointment with a realtor.

"She won't mind my tardiness?" I asked him, hoping for reassurance.

"We're used to it here," he said. "Traffic. It's the only fly in the ointment."

He was right. Boca Raton Estates was paradise. The website had not done the resort justice. The grounds were lush, hyper-green, with palm trees like giant beach umbrellas wavering in the endless blue sky. Everywhere I looked there were flowers and bushes and velvety lawns, the road itself was surrounded by lakes and ponds, and golfers. Golfers as far as the eyes could see.

"We pride ourselves on our courses," he said. "There are four of them. This one was designed by Arnold Palmer."

I was pretty sure I'd heard of him. I knew I liked the beverage!

Next, the kid pointed out the dog park on the right, and the sports complex on the left, and the pickleball and tennis courts up ahead. He trained my attention to a short game practice area and then a driving range, a golf and activities center that con-nected to the country club itself. It looked like an elongated mod-ern plantation, four large glassy attached buildings. Each more swellegant than the last.

"This place has it all," he said proudly. "Everything you could ever want, and if you don't see it, we'll bring it in for you. Want a steak cooked rare at four o'clock in the morning? Just call the resto and it's done. You name it, you've got it. There's free break-fast every day in the clubhouse. Bagels, smoked salmon, cream cheese, yogurt parfait, and fruit salad. Once you move in, you never have to leave. I'm saving up to buy my own apartment. A lot of people who work here also live on the property."

I nodded in a way I hoped he would find encouraging, but my heart was racing, and my eyes felt like they were bulging out of their sockets.

"I'm studying at the Real Estate Initiative at Florida Atlantic University."

Who cares? I thought. Can't you drive any faster?

In front of the stairs that led up to the main entrance of the central clubhouse was a tall dark blond woman, no longer the faux auburn that Matt had promised, waiting by a golf cart, wearing a sleeveless navy shift, a yellow scarf, and ultra-white tennis shoes. Her hair was wrapped up in a French twist.

She looked oddly Germanic.

It was Nina.

Nina.

I suddenly forgot how to breathe.

"Thank you," I said to my driver. "I can take it from here," and I gave him a little Mac-like sailor salute, trying to calm myself enough to keep from leaping from the golf cart and running over and tackling her to the ground. But the driver cheerfully saluted back. No one was onto me yet.

I walked over to her. Same green eyes, same everything, save for the hair. She was still amazing looking.

"Nina," I said. I took off my sunglasses. "It's me. It's Merry."

She squinted for a moment, like she was trying to focus. Then she spoke in a higher register: "I'm sorry, you must be mistaking me for someone else."

I stared at her. "You don't sound like you."

"I'm waiting for a client," she said, still in falsetto. She glanced at her big gold watch. "Perhaps she is looking inside for me?" Nina asked charmingly. Flashing a gigantic smile, she turned on her heel to leave. Her teeth were notably straighter. Was she wearing Invisalign?

"Okay, I am your client," I said. Two could play that game. "I'm touring a couple of houses on the Island. Meet Lorelei Monroe." I held out my hand to shake.

She took out her phone. Pretending to check out something on it, she left my hand like a fish on a hook, flapping in the air.

"No, sorry. Your appointment must be with someone else."

A trim middle-aged couple in tennis outfits approached and walked up the stairs behind us.

"I'm so hungry," he said, "I'm ready to eat the entire buffet."

"I just want a salad," she said, as he put his hand on the small of her back, guiding her. Then he opened the door and allowed her to enter first. Nina looked like she wanted to run in after them.

"My appointment is with you," I said, "unless you're not Sammi, Smadar, Nina, Andrea, or Samara Marjanovic, Marantz, or Mirzrahi?"

Nina's jaw muscle tightened, just like a man's. Remember James Dean's, that little throbbing electrical bolt under the skin in *Rebel Without a Cause* that, male or female, made your knees go weak?

"I don't know who you are," Nina said coolly.

"It sounds like you don't know who *you* are!" I jabbed back.

"Madame, you are mistaking me for someone else."

This was ridiculous and nonsensical. Really, she couldn't have been cuntier, except we both knew she was playing a losing hand, and I was beginning to sense the flop sweat.

Did she really believe a person could just do that? Change history by pretending it never happened? I'd read about narcissistic amnesia when I was preparing for a part once, but this truly took the cake.

"Excuse me."

She started to walk up the steps, so I grabbed her by the arm.

"Let go of me," said Nina, as she tried to wriggle her way free. "Or I will call security."

"Nina," I said. "This is completely ludicrous. You know who I am. You were paid to spy on me. You took advantage of my innocence *and* my affection. You totally fucking betrayed me."

"Take your hands off of me," she said. "I've never seen you before in my life."

"AND," I said in big block letters, "you confessed all of this to *The Daily Beast*."

She lifted her phone to her ear. "Ehud," she said, "there is trouble here. A crazy person thinks I'm someone else."

"I am not crazy," I said. "You're the one who's crazy."

"I don't care if you're at work," she hissed into her palm. "Do you think I would bother calling you if I could 'handle it myself'?" She paused. "I am not a drama queen!" She shook her head in disbelief. "Asshole," she spat, and hung up on him.

That's when I jumped in. I reached out and grabbed it away from her.

"My phone!" she said.

"You're trying to gaslight me, you lying bitch," I said. "What's to keep *me* from talking to *The Daily Beast,* too? Or *The New York Times*? Or the *National Enquirer!*"

"You're an absurd, preposterous person," she scoffed. "No one wants to talk to you!"

I started waving her phone in the air like a cheerleader. "NOW, I've got the goods on you." (Same big block letters!) "Imagine all the secrets that are locked up in this thing. They'll definitely believe me with evidence. You're a shitty actress and an even shittier double agent!"

That last one seemed to land. Her face turned bright red.

"The guards will be here any minute!" she said.

"You're lying," I said. "But what else is new? You're a compulsive, reflexive liar. You're pathological! Ehud is no guard, he's your husband. And from what I just heard from that phone call, he's not coming. He's probably as sick of your bullshit as I am. Honeymoon over already, Nina? How did you dig him up so fast? Some kid you blew in the army? What a fool! I bet he's just a way for you and your mother to set up camp in the States."

"How do you know anything about me and my mother?" she said angrily.

"You're not the only one who does her research," I said.

In an instant her entire demeanor changed. Her eyes narrowed into slits. Her voice deepened to its natural octave.

"You're wanted by the police, you know," she said.

"I know," I said.

"And now you're making a scene," she said.

"You're making a scene," I said. "You have as much to lose as I have. You're probably here illegally. Do you want your new clients and neighbors to know about that? Or about your former scumbag employer? He's all over the news now. And you're his sleazeball accomplice. Do you even have a real estate license? You've been in this country like half an hour. Did Dark Star teach you how to get over on immigration? Or is your entire persona as shoddily built as your bullshit website?"

"Give me back my phone," she said. She looked me straight in the irises.

When that death ray didn't get her anywhere, she abruptly changed the channel.

"Please," she said, all liquid-eyed. Almost like she was begging me.

There were golfers in the distance. Also, tennis players. You could hear the thwack of a ball. The gentle swish of the lawn sprinklers. Maybe there were more couples and different friend groups inside eating lunch, or in shouting distance by the pool or in the spa? But there was no one else in the immediate vicinity, no audience, although I'm sure Nina could have made more of a commotion if she'd wanted to. But why would she? She had a nice life at Boca Raton Estates, it seemed, living under the radar. Why would anyone fuck with that?

She set her jaw, and her lips formed a thin, straight line. Then she crossed her arms. "Okay, Merry, what is it that you want?" That same funny eastern European accent.

"How could one woman do this to another woman?" I asked.

I stood trembling before her. I really wanted to know.

"Oh my God, Merry," she said, avoiding my eyes. "You are so annoying."

I said, "I trusted you. Answer my fucking question."

"Woman, shmoman," said Nina. "I was just doing my job. You Americans. You're all such whiners. Who set you up, Merry? Other women. *American* women. I read your book. Your agent. Your producer. Those skinny little girls who answered his phones."

"Some tried to help me. I thought you were trying to help me."

"Seriously? You didn't need any help."

"I needed help!" I said. I always needed help.

"You were in it for the fame. You were in it for the money. And who could blame you?" Her face shrunk into a fist. "I'd like fame, too. I'd like to make real money. You with your little white upturned nose. You and your *indiscernible accent*." She said this last bit in a mocking tone. "Your perfect tits, your bunny rabbit tail. Everything comes so easily to you, Merry."

"Are you kidding?" I said.

"You flutter your lashes and you get on TV. You were on a series! You were in the movies! So you got fucked by an ugly rich disgusting man, a powerful ugly rich disgusting man—wouldn't I have done that in a heartbeat? He would have paid you off for it. Look at how much he paid us!"

"I'm not a hooker!"

"Really? That's not what I read in your manuscript!"

"Fuck you," I said.

"Fuck you!" she said. "You've had it so easy. Try my life on for size! How dare you criticize me?"

"You're just jealous," I screamed.

That's when an old lady came racing up in a golf cart.

"That's her," Nina called out, face beet-colored now and the tower of her hair askew, pointing her long red manicured fingernail at me.

The old lady got out and trotted over the best she could. She was pudgy, puffing loudly in acid-washed pedal pushers and a purple cotton blouse with a three-quarter-length sleeve. Her long gray hair was tied back in a braid. She was dripping in sweat.

"Sammi," she cried, as she ran toward Nina. "Ehud called me. He said you might be in trouble."

"Mama!" Nina said. "This woman is completely crazy!"

I started to laugh. "He called your mother?"

Nina turned to me. "*My* mother always comes for me."

She was the meanest girl in the world.

"What's going on here?" Nina's mother had to stop, bend over, and place her hands on her knees. She couldn't catch her breath. The old lady stared up at me.

"Do you know what your daughter did?" I said. "Do you know what she did to me?"

"I'll kill you!" Nina shouted.

"She delivered me to my rapist!" I said.

"Rapist?" said her mother.

"Your daughter works for rapists. She takes money from them to hurt other women! Innocent girls like me! But you know that already, don't you? It's all over the news. Here and in Israel!"

Nina's mother's face went white.

Come to think of it, so did Nina's.

"Oh, Mama," she said. "Don't listen. She's obviously psycho-logically disturbed."

"He raped me on the floor of a bathroom. My head kept hitting the toilet. I tried to get out from under him. There was nothing I could do to get him off me!" I started to sob then, just thinking about it. "His pubes got in my mouth. I felt that hair on my tongue for like the next six weeks. Your daughter knows that. She knows all of it. And she knew, *she knew,* I'd been raped before!" I was really crying then. "The first time I was just a kid . . ."

They both watched me in silence. Nina's mother's hands were pressing against her cheeks. Her eyes were telegraphing pain. Did I have her attention? Her pity?

"Nina was hired to destroy me! Your daughter took money from a rapist pig to destroy me!"

"Nina?" asked Nina's mother. "Smadar, do you also call yourself by this name?"

Nina looked at her nails.

"Smadar," said her mother, "I'm talking to you."

That's when Nina's husband came racing up in *his* golf cart, followed by the police and Mr. Alvarez in his cab.

"Police?" I said to Nina. "Are you kidding me? When did you have time to call them?"

"I didn't," said Nina. She was shaking her head violently. "What a schmuck. Why did *he* do that? All this fuss is the last thing that we need."

"Ehud," screamed the mother. "Thank God you came to your senses!"

A great big hulking handsome Israeli in a suit came running over. *"Neshama sheli,"* he called out. "Are you okay?"

"I'm fine, you idiot," Nina hissed. "Stop drawing so much attention."

The cop car pulled up, the driver got out, and his partner, a woman, exited out of the passenger side. From the back seat came the lady I'd met in reception, the one with the silky colorful top.

Mr. Alvarez stayed inside his cab.

"Are you Meredith Montgomery?" asked the police officer, his hand on the gun on his waistband.

"Are you fucking kidding me?" I repeated myself.

"That's her name," Mr. Alvarez yelled through his window. "That's the one she gave me!"

"That's what she signed in as," added the reception lady, calling from the vicinity of the cop car. "She was supposed to be Lorelei something!"

"I can explain," I said. "Lorelei is my moth—"

At that moment Nina reached out for her phone and tried to

wrestle it away from me. No way was I going to give it up without a fight.

She kicked me in the shins, and I elbowed her in the gut.

"Sammi!" her husband screamed. He was scared for her safety. He grabbed me from behind. Now, I was really kicking and screaming. That's when Nina took the phone away from me.

"Samarala!" screamed her mother.

"Sammi," Ehud said. "Your mother's talking to you." He kept swinging his neck so I wouldn't headbutt him. "Are you okay? Did she hurt you, baby?"

Nina stepped back, running a hand through her hair, setting it loose in long goblet-colored waves. Like a supervillain.

She appeared to be examining the screen of her phone for damages.

She looked up at her husband and rolled her empty eyes. Then she looked at her mother, and then back at the phone, and then she blankly looked at me.

Nina was bombed out, a vacant building. There was nothing inside. Had there ever been, really? It was *as if* Nina was a person who could attach and love and feel the pain of someone else, but in her core, she was empty. So she mined the world for tactics on how to dupe those of us who felt things.

"Why, oh why, did we ever move here?" her mother asked.

"For the goddamn fucking ocean," said Nina.

Mr. Alvarez got out of his cab, and he, too, pointed his finger at me. Everyone was pointing fingers. "That woman, I don't know what she's done to you, but she owes me a lot of money."

So, all right, here's a bit of true-life comedy. It was Alvarez who called the cops. I mean, Ehud called them, too, after he sent his mother-in-law to do his dirty work, but before guilt took hold and he put his own pedal to the metal on *his* golf cart. But it was Alvarez who gave them my name; we learned all of this in discovery. He said I "pretended" to believe in Christ, which I never said, and he was afraid I would cheat him out of his money. The cops called it in, and the warrant for my arrest popped up. When they arrived at Boca Raton Estates, the woman from reception showed them my signature. That's how I, Meredith Montgomery—the victim here!—got wrestled to the ground, when the police took over from Ehud.

First I came down superhard on his instep, and then I kicked him in the groin, but by that time the police were all over me, and Ehud was rolling around on the grass, grabbing his crotch and moaning. My hands were cuffed behind my back, and I was forced facedown onto the hood of their vehicle. It was still a month prior to the Rug's indictment. It was before I got the SimpliSafe reel and sold it to *Entertainment Tonight*. (Yay, me!) Conviction for him, back then, was still only a survivor's dream. I was the perp in the moment. The criminal. I was the one going to jail. Not him. Me.

Let that marinate a little.

They held me for fourteen days, and then MLG got me extradited back to LA, where I rotted in prison for another week until my hearing, when she finally had me sprung.

Manager Liz arranged for a monthlong stay in a fancy bughouse up in Malibu, where the doctors played around with my meds so I could cool my jets. Calmed me down some, but never enough. Tranquility and I don't tango.

(For the record, it was *crystal meth*. The anonymous moron who had DM'd me the coke reference really messed me up. I'd never even *tried* blow before, and I'd forgotten all about the crank in my card case by the time I was flying back to the good old US of A. At that point I truly thought it was all just a frigging hoax. When I was confronted by MLG and Manager Liz about the warrant and realized what had happened, I was so embarrassed I'd lied to everybody. I mean, someone Dark Star–ish was low enough to steal my stuff off the plane in the first place, so the fuckers could have planted something if the billfold had been empty. I'd scored the actual shit at Place de la République in Paris earlier in the summer; I'd planned on giving it to Brani as a coming home gift. He has phantom limb disorder, which at times can be excruciating. His arm's gone but the pain remains. Americans beware. Civil war completely and totally sucks. We should try our best to avoid it.)

By the time I got back in touch with Lorelei, pal Mac had already put a ring on it, so there was nothing I could do about that horny deadbeat. He'd simply walked off with my pups and added six more furry critters to my roster. Can you imagine the wrinkles on that old man's ball sack? Lorelei made her own bed, and now she's forced to lie in it.

I didn't know any of that, yet. That's what I like about book writing, you can play around with time, find its most meaningful iteration. That day, however, I was as present in the moment as I'd ever been. I was all pure animal extinct. I knew I had to fight like hell if I ever hoped to get free. Nina allowed her husband to hug her after he stumbled to his feet, as some of the golfers finally wandered over to take in the scene. I looked up as a crowd started to gather.

Nina's mother was still staring at me. Her braid was long, and her eyes were sad. "It will get better over time," she said.

She looked so totally defeated.

Even now, the thought of her makes me cry.

At that moment, the man who had walked his wife up the steps twenty minutes before came running out of the clubhouse with a napkin stuffed into his collar and a chicken leg in his hand, while his wife tried to pull him back. "Jesus, Ted," she yelled. "Let the police handle it. Go back inside and eat your lunch."

As everyone turned to watch them, I used the interruption to bite the arresting officer's hand, and he stepped back, howling and bleeding. I suppose that's exactly when Nina took the picture with her iPhone.

Matt told me later she sold it to the tabloids for a pretty penny, which she probably ended up needing, as they had to leave Boca Raton Estates after that messy scene. I don't know where they all went next or what has happened to any of them since. But guess what? This is the best part! The spell was broken. I honestly couldn't have cared less.

In the moment, however, I was too busy raging and struggling, spitting and baring my bloody teeth to notice or pose or anything. *That's* the image Nina caught on her camera. Me in my mother's clothing, hands cuffed behind my back, legs treading the air as the female cop tightened her grip. My fangs were out, my mouth was wide open in a silent scream. I was a 100 percent bleached-blond wolverine!

I love that shot.

As a teenager in the 1970s, growing up during the height of second-wave feminism, I truly thought things were only going to get better for women. (Just as, running around barefoot on the first Earth Day, I considered myself lucky to have been born in an era when we committed to protecting the environment.) Well, we know how that worked out. Five decades later, I am furious on the best of days, and like a lot of women, I still often feel demeaned, underpaid, overworked, overburdened, and hypersexualized. When all the #MeToo stories broke—Weinstein, Cosby, Lauer, ad infinitum—I was so angry, I thought my head might explode. And yet I was not entirely surprised. Sadly, such abhorrent behavior is disgustingly familiar. But what was so shocking about this breakthrough round of reporting was the sheer scale of the crimes and the insidious web of those who enabled the people who committed them: that is, these entitled and protected *mass* rapists had been supported by other rich, powerful men and institutions as they committed one sexual assault after another. In some cases, they were also abetted by women in their employ or in their spheres of influence.

The galvanizing idea for *Lucky Dogs* came when I read a Ronan

Farrow piece in *The New Yorker* about Black Cube, the private Israeli spy agency that Harvey Weinstein hired to intimidate and prevent the actress Rose McGowan from publishing her memoir, *Brave,* which included McGowan's account of being raped by Weinstein. One of the two undercover agents assigned to McGowan was a woman named Stella Penn Pechanac, who befriended McGowan under false pretenses and betrayed her trust. As a child, Pechanac had been a refugee of the Bosnian War, escaping with her parents to Israel—yet another country caught in a perpetual, ruinous civil war. Reading more on Pechanac in *The Guardian* and *The Jerusalem Post,* among other sources, I felt as if a story had fallen out of the sky. I was reminded of that famous quote attributed to Michelangelo: "I saw the angel in the marble and carved until I set him free." Here was a narrative to which I could harness the inchoate, helpless fury I was feeling. My first question when I read about Pechanac was simply: How could one woman do this to another woman? This novel, the fictionalization of these characters and events, is an attempt to answer that question.

Let me repeat: *Lucky Dogs* is a work of fiction. I am not pretending to represent Pechanac, McGowan, or anyone else, either directly or by inference. But in my efforts to understand the actual history, I read all of Farrow's game-changing work on the subject, as well as that of the remarkable Megan Twohey and Jodi Kantor, who first broke the story of Weinstein's abuses in *The New York Times.* Jelani Cobb, another *New Yorker* correspondent, was a thoughtful resource. Ken Auletta and Ben Wallace nobly shared their own impressive research to help make the story available to the public. These brave and intrepid journalists, among others, are all heroes to my mind, as are the women who supported other women and those who spoke out against their abusers, many at great personal cost.

ACKNOWLEDGMENTS

I am so fortunate that every year, through my job at The New School, I am granted a graduate research assistant to work with, each a talented and dazzling writer in their own right. Thank you, Yasmin Zaher, Avinash Rajendran, Evangeline Riddiford Graham, Nicole D'Alessio, and Ruth Weissmann, for investigating anything I asked for, tirelessly delivering books, articles, and documentary films on the Bosnian War, #MeToo, the Mossad, and the texture of life in Israel, Venice Beach, and Florida, so that I could bluff my way toward fluency on these subjects. You are human treasures.

A special thanks to *Travel + Leisure*'s editor in chief, Jacqueline Gifford, for sending me to Bosnia to write an article on travel in that country and to Hannah Walhout for editing it. That boots-on-the-ground reporting made all the difference. A big shout-out to my guides on the trip, Branimir Belinić (whom I adored so much I gave his first name to one of my favorite characters—who is nothing like him!), Džana Branković, and Zijad Jusufović, all of whom generously shared their painful experiences of the war, while making me feel at home in their beautiful country. Janine

Acknowledgments

di Giovanni's journalism and *Zlata's Diary* by Zlata Filipović were also immensely helpful resources.

People often say the writer's life is a lonely one, but I was never alone. Endless gratitude to the Guggenheim Foundation for giving me a fellowship in 2019 and to The New School and my dean, Mary Watson, for meeting that fellowship and allowing me time and space to write this book. Many thanks to the Betsy Hotel and its Writer's Room residency for providing a blissful week in which to complete this project. My sister-in-law and brother-in-law, Susan Handy and Matt Richter, twice offered the use of their lovely home to hole up in and write. I can't thank you two enough. Ditto old friend Dan Boeckman for graciously providing me a retreat in New Mexico.

The past few years have been hard on all of us, but I have been buoyed by the tenacity, hard work, and literary love of my splendid students at The New School and the friendship and support of the faculty and staff, especially Director Luis Jaramillo, Lori Lynn Turner, Laura Cronk, and John Reed, who kept us all afloat from Zoom to masks and back again. WriteOnNYC.com is an organization I started with my graduate students that brings creative writing and literature classes to middle and high school kids. Thank you from the bottom of my heart to my partner in this project, Phineas Lambert; to Catherine Bloomer, Kelly Lindell, A. E. Osworth, and our founding donors, the Gottlieb family: David, Vicky, Kay, and Ben; plus all our generous patrons, the talented fellows, and *their* amazing students. Your passion and commitment got me up and out of bed during the dark times throughout the years it took to write this book. Always you were a source of courage and hope.

Steve Lipman—research assistant, hotelier, chef, chauffer, BFF—thank you for shlepping me endlessly across Florida and not throwing me out of the car for talking too much. Harvey and Adrienne Berkman, you were wonderful hospitable tour guides, as was Sam Winberg. Thank you to Rebecca Sacks for leading me to Benjamin Balint, who became a crucial set of eyes regarding all things Israeli, as I could not make the trip because of COVID restrictions. Ronen Bergman's book *Rise and Kill First* was a useful gateway into the world of the Mossad. My son, Isaac Handy, was my major resource about Birthright Israel, and his sense of detail and the complexity of his thoughts were inspiring and enlightening.

Finally, I am so grateful to the people who have literally been in the trenches with me throughout the writing and designing of this book. Denise Bosco, beloved friend and gifted photographer, has been making me look better for more years than I care to count. We've known each other since we were fourteen! The wonderful team at Knopf, Janet Hansen, Nancy Tan, Nicole Pedersen, Pei Loi Koay, and Romeo Enriquez, made this book the beautiful, precise, and hopefully readable object it is today. I'm so thankful for their talents and patience. My editor, Jennifer Barth, is a marvel; brilliant, persistent, funny, careful, kind, she tirelessly went over every single word in this manuscript and then some. The book is wildly better for her intelligence and capacious grace. Sloan Harris is not only my longtime agent but also my dear friend and most cherished reader—I'm out of words about how much you mean to me, Sloan. My darling husband and in-house editor, Bruce Handy, held my hand every step of the way through writing this, as he does every day in the endlessly interesting ongoing project of our life together. Lastly but firstly, my adult children, Zoë and Isaac Handy—what can I say? I'm just crazy about you both.

A NOTE ABOUT THE AUTHOR

Helen Schulman is the *New York Times* best-selling author
of six novels, including *Come with Me* and *This Beautiful
Life*. She is the fiction chair at the Writing Program of
The New School and executive director of WriteOnNYC.com,
a program that trains MFA candidates to teach creative
writing and literature to middle and high school students.
Schulman has received fellowships from the Guggenheim
Foundation, the New York Foundation for the Arts,
Sundance, Aspen Words, and Columbia University. She
lives in New York City.

A NOTE ON THE TYPE

The text of this book was set in Filosofia, a typeface
designed by Zuzana Licko in 1996 as a revival of the
typefaces of Giambattista Bodoni (1740–1813). Licko
designed Filosofia Regular as a rugged face with reduced
contrast to withstand the reduction to text sizes. Born in
Bratislava, Czechoslovakia, in 1961, she is the cofounder
of Emigre, a digital type foundry and publisher of *Emigre*
magazine, based in Northern California. Founded in 1984,
coinciding with the birth of the Macintosh, Emigre was
one of the first independent type foundries to establish
itself centered around personal computer technology.

Typeset by Scribe,
Philadelphia, Pennsylvania

Printed and bound by Berryville Graphics,
Berryville, Virginia

Designed by Pei Loi Koay